The Tyranny of Friendship

by
John Boman

Grosvenor House
Publishing Limited

IF

If you can keep your head when all about you
Are losing theirs and blaming it on you,
If you can trust yourself when all men doubt you,
But make allowance for their doubting too;
If you can wait and not be tired by waiting,
Or being lied about, don't deal in lies,
Or being hated, don't give way to hating,
And yet don't look too good, nor talk too wise;

If you can dream-and not make dreams your master;
If you can think-and not make thoughts your aim;
If you can meet with triumph and disaster
And treat those two imposters just the same;
If you can bear to hear the truth you've spoken
Twisted by knaves to make a trap for fools,
Or watch the things you gave your life to, broken,
And stoop and build'em up with worn-out tools;

If you can make one heap of all your winnings
And risk it on one turn of pitch-and-toss,
And lose, and start again at your beginnings
And never breathe a word about your loss;
If you can force your heart and nerve and sinew
To serve your turn long after they are gone,
And so hold on when there is nothing in you
Except the will which says to them: 'Hold on!'

If you can talk with crowds and keep your virtue,
Or walk with kings-nor lose the common touch,
If neither foes nor loving friends can hurt you,
If all men count with you, but none too much;
If you can fill the unforgiving minute
With sixty seconds' worth of distance run,
Yours is the Earth and everything that's in it,
And-which is more-you'll be a Man, my son!

Rudyard Kipling.

The right of John Boman to be identified as the author of this
work has been asserted in accordance with Section 78
of the Copyright, Designs and Patents Act 1988

The book cover is copyright to John Boman
Cover image copyright www.istockphoto.com/gb/portfolio/natcha29

This book is published by
Grosvenor House Publishing Ltd
Link House
140 The Broadway, Tolworth, Surrey, KT6 7HT.
www.grosvenorhousepublishing.co.uk

This book is a work of fiction. Any resemblance to
people or events, past or present, is purely coincidental.

A CIP record for this book
is available from the British Library

ISBN 978-1-83975-032-8

DEDICATION

The theme for the novel came from a conversation with Alan Organ in a café in Wimborne, Dorset, UK. Thanks Alan.

ACKNOWLEDGEMENTS

I have had a lot of help to get this novel together.

Lesley Foot cut plenty from it. Ouch! Thanks Lesley.

Vin Miles carefully cut some more but learned how to make tea. Thanks Vin.

Helen Baggott gave it insightful professional editing but cut less. Thanks Helen.

And I still needed Grosvenor House Publishing's help. Thanks Grosvenor.

Chapter One

I stood at the back of the van with Dave Bennett, watching him concentrate as he rolled a cigarette. He licked the edge with care and winked at me as he lit it. Another day, another week of decorating for Dave, me, and our boss, Lisa; today we would be painting the ceiling of the huge lounge in the beautiful bay-side house we had just arrived at. And today my dull life was about to be disturbed.

The house was spectacular, just as Dave had described it. It was ultra-modern, with smooth, cement-rendered walls in gleaming white masonry paint with angles and levels and lots of blue-tinted glass to make for perfect overall symmetry. Glass and stainless-steel balconies overlooked its gardens on three sides; the biggest balcony overlooked the bay at the rear of the house. The view was stunning – 'worth a million pounds'. Estate agents don't always exaggerate. Waves gently lapped at the boathouse and jetty at the bottom of the garden. *Miami in Dorset?*

Lisa came round to the rear of the van already dressed for work.

"Come on, you two... and your filthy habit," she said with a grin that lit up her face. "What are you going to do next to avoid work?"

Dave was searching for somewhere discreet to stub out his cigarette; he took one last drag, defiantly blowing the smoke at Lisa's back.

"Come on then, old man. I suppose we'd better do something." Dave sighed.

I trod my cigarette out, pulled on my not-so-pristine painter's over-trousers and slipped my indoor work-shoes back on my cold feet.

I had been painting and decorating for over forty years and yet another Monday morning had me feeling as gloomy as most working people at the start of a new week; *especially in January*.

As I walked towards the house I couldn't help thinking that back in the sixties, I wouldn't have belie-ved I'd be painting people's houses in *my* sixties. I can even remember thinking at some point then, why would anybody want to live beyond forty? As the Who almost said, we all thought we'd die before we were old. *But we change our minds, I guess, along the way.*

Here we are in a new century with the 1960s long gone and the house I'm working on belonging to a current world star, a young British female singer.

I once thought that I would have a house like this one. It's big. It's beautiful. It overlooks a wonderful Dorset bay. However, I do not have a house like this one with its views, space, comfort and style, a lift, and a swimming pool in the basement. I was working on it for Lisa, my young boss, and her business partner, Emma. I had worked for them for a few years now, almost since they had started up their decorating company. They've done very well too.

"Come on, old man." Dave woke me from my meandering thoughts. He pushed me gently in the small of my back towards the door. He grinned and pushed me harder.

"It's all right for you," I told him.

We went in through a side door and across the gleaming tiles of the hallway into the lounge. The first job was to spread dust sheets, or drop cloths, as some call them, over the floor. I'd asked Dave to put the masking tape on the hardwood skirting boards and architraves to save my old knees on the hard floor. I could get down but getting back up was another matter. We covered the lightwood doors with polythene sheeting and were ready to go. Lisa knelt on the floor stirring white emulsion paint. She looked up as we stood over her.

"You and I will cut in, Tony," she said, "and you can roll, please, Dave."

She poured paint into two kettles – one for me, one for herself – and stood the paint beside Dave's paint tray. Dave was staring out of the huge windows on the other side of the massive room. Looking past him I could see the tired January garden and beyond to a cross-Channel ferry on the dark sea that filled most of the view to the mottled gunmetal sky. Two seagulls skimmed their way across the bay and more followed. He waved to the distant ship and turned to see if we were watching him. Lisa raised her eyebrows at me in mock despair and shook her head. As I watched Dave from across the room I started to wonder if he had dreams… ambitions.

I climbed the platform steps in the farthest corner of the room and began to paint the cornice and ceiling line. It was a lovely squared, stepped cornice in an art deco style that suited the house so well. Dave had begun to roll the bed of the ceiling. We cautiously painted around the many circular downlights inset in the ceiling; there were dozens of the shining eyes.

Lisa painted around the last of them and glanced from Dave to me as she backed down her stepladder.

"That's that, then," she concluded with a sigh, wiping her brush around the edge of her paint kettle. I opened another can of paint, stirred it and topped Dave's tray up.

"I wonder if our client is up yet," Lisa said, looking at her paint-speckled watch. She asked me if I'd heard any movement in the house. I hadn't and neither had Dave. His face was now covered in tiny spots of white emulsion paint; a larger drip in his eyebrow gave him a clown-like look where he had wiped it across his face with the back of his hand. I had called him Adam Ant once before when he had a similar smear across his face but he is too young even to remember Adam Ant and I gave up trying to explain my joke in the end.

Just then a rectangular pool of light appeared halfway down the wall to my left, a figure silhouetted in it. It reminded me of the entrance of a championship boxer to the arena. I half expected a mist of theatrical smoke to be billowing from the doorway light and some loud inspirational music announcing his entrance. The silhouette moved forward into the room. No music or smoke though. No boxer in his gown, beating his gloves together. Instead the tiny figure of our customer appeared. She stepped into the winter gloom of the lounge. It seemed almost magical as she took more small steps on to our dust sheets, the bright light of the room behind her pooling in the doorway around her slender figure. I could see her looking down at her bare feet, slight distaste registering as she acknowledged what she was standing on.

4

"Why is it so dark in here?" Daisy asked. Lisa walked confidently over to our client and greeted her professionally.

"Good morning, Daisy. How are you today? It's hard to paint around downlights with them glaring in your eyes.

"Oh, I see," said Daisy, sounding unconvinced.

"I could smell cigarette smoke when I woke this morning."

Lisa turned to look at me, then at Dave, who was still rolling the ceiling – head back, engrossed.

"I'm so sorry, Daisy. These men still insist on smoking. It isn't completely banned yet though." Lisa swept an outstretched arm meaningfully in our direction.

Daisy Belle Bliss was our new client's stage name. I hadn't heard her music until a few weeks ago when Dave insisted I should know who our latest client was. He seemed to worship her. He had insisted I put the earphones on from his phone and listen. This was difficult, as he would snatch them from my ears every so often to check it was OK or if it was loud enough or what track it was. In truth I still hadn't heard a whole song yet because Dave had the earphones on more than I did. I can't say it sounded much like my sort of music even though I'd always prided myself on liking many different genres. Besides, I was still trying to work out how so much music was on his phone. We didn't even have a phone in the house when I was young.

Of course I'd seen her on television sometimes, on posters, or bus shelters and giant hoardings. She seemed to appear everywhere. Ubiquitous is the word, I believe. The ubiquitous Daisy Belle Bliss. However, I had to agree with everyone: her delicate beauty was real enough. Now

I was in the same room as her I could see that the posters and television didn't do her full justice. She was almost perfectly beautiful. Her skin was so smooth it seemed to glow; I expected to see dew on her face. And this was in the morning, at home, with no make-up, special lighting or airbrushing. Even the memory of Dave's crude and fanciful words of speculation of when he met her on the job, couldn't taint my first impression. Standing uneasily on our dust sheets, in barefooted simplicity, her hair awry, she was exceptionally beautiful. And young enough to be my granddaughter.

Dave had finished his contribution to the job in hand, and now his features took on an expression I find hard to describe as he approached the young singer.

"Good morning, Daisy," he said, as if he knew her. He had laid the roller on the tray and was rubbing his hands together as if rinsing them in mid-air.

"Sorry 'bout the smoke. We didn't think it would matter out by the van."

I wasn't sure, but I think his cheeks might have coloured up. He had this ingratiating grin on his face that was making me angry, or at least making me embarrassed for him. The obsequious David Bennett meets the ubiquitous Daisy Belle Bliss.

Daisy looked at Lisa. "It's my voice. I must take care…" She trailed off as Dave came closer to her, but then continued. "I've campaigned for ages against cigarettes. I had lunch recently with an MP and said to him that they should ban them."

I thought Dave's tongue would hang out as he apologised to Daisy once more. I had to look away.

"They have," Lisa reassured her, "but so far only inside public buildings. It won't be long before they

won't be allowed to indulge their filthy habit at all."
Again she looked from Dave to me and thankfully I
knew her well enough to tell from her intonation that
she was just being playful. She was subtly taking the
mickey out of Daisy's naïve assumption that her
opinions carried enough weight for politicians to make
laws according to her wishes. I don't think Daisy
understood Lisa's true meaning. *Politicians and pretty
women… not unprecedented.* However, Lisa then told
Daisy she'd make sure we smoked further from the
house in future, and she probably meant this. All the
talk of smoking made me want a cigarette badly.

I watched them talking animatedly and my heart
sank. A selfish sentiment, I know, but they were young
women in what I felt was now a woman's world and I
was a man, and an old and remarkably unsuccessful one
at that. Daisy looked my way from time to time as the
two women chatted; I caught her eye on one occasion.
Now she came towards me, presumably to point out the
error of my smoking ways. The humiliation I was about
to endure made my forehead prickle as I prepared
myself and my self-control. Some disturbing thoughts
raced through my mind. I felt foolish and even a little
angry.

She looked me in the eye. "My granddad knows
you."

I must have looked surprised or something, because
she said it again as if I hadn't heard her the first time. I
was confused, I admit.

"My granddad knows you. You were both at the
same school a long time ago. Your name is Tony Smith."

I knew she was right because that *is* my name, but I
didn't know how she knew. I confess my thoughts were

befuddled. I felt stupid. From the corner of my eye I saw Dave stiffen and he and Lisa exchanged a look. Daisy smiled then and I felt myself relax. How ridiculous, I thought to myself, that I should feel any sort of confusion or awe in the girl's presence. She may have been famous to most people in the country, if not the world, if Dave was to be believed, but she wasn't to me. She was just a young woman who was standing in front of me telling me her grandfather went to school with me, although at that precise moment I could make no connections. I wanted to smoke a cigarette even more now.

Daisy twirled a tail of hair between her fingers silently looking at me till I began to feel self-conscious. "Oh," was all I managed to say at first, but she remained silent. There was warmth and something else I couldn't quite fathom in her eyes as she continued to look at me. I'm not sure what I mean – empathy, maybe? I knew it was something positive but I couldn't read the look. I saw Lisa and Dave watching me. Lisa looked baffled and inquisitive but Dave still had the same silly grin on his face and was probably finding it very difficult to remain quiet. The moment stretched as I sought for some clarity in my head.

"Who is your grandfather?" I finally asked.

A warm light seemed to come on in her eyes. "Nigel Glover." She watched my reaction, then she added, "But he doesn't know you are here in my house... yet."

There was also some amusement in her expression. Maybe at my unease – I couldn't say for sure. As Daisy waited for my response, something like an electric shock was running through me. I was remembering a boy at school with eyes just like the eyes looking at me right at that moment. That boy with the unusual, dark-flecked amber eyes had been a friend of mine and we shared a secret that had cast a shadow over most of my life. The mention of his name brought to my nostrils a damp, earthy smell and one of death.

Chapter Two

Throughout my life I had always marvelled at people who could recall things from when they were very young – perhaps a seaside holiday when they were only four or five, or Christmases when they were just eight years old. It didn't bother me so much these days; I just accepted that I had a bad memory. There were times in the past when I sought some understanding of myself but it just led me to feelings of sadness rather than clear answers. Now when I start wondering if the glass is half full or half empty I have a cup of tea. I had spent enough time during my thirties and forties tossing and turning in sleeplessness trying to remember my childhood, usually triggered by something as simple as bumping into old friends. Nigel was one of these old friends but one with whom I did share a disturbing memory. It was well over thirty years since I'd last seen Nigel Glover and – poor memory or not – I would not forget our last meeting. My head swam. It was a shock to be reminded now.

Over the years, I'd spent many hours thinking about schooldays, and the time I shared with Nigel Glover. What did it matter now? I didn't know. But it had often troubled me, not least because my wife had left with my heart and my children because I 'showed no ambition' at around the same time Nigel left my life. Somehow in my twenties my ambitions had left with Nigel Glover. I could see now that I began to change when he left for

America; disillusion crept in, uninvited, when he went. I thought he was going to help me. I thought we would be friends forever. I felt betrayed. I could see now how I became negative in my ways, and that Jenny left because I had changed. I remember we would argue about almost anything. I then lost all motivation when she left. In the past I had punished myself endlessly, wondering where I went wrong. I still had twinges of disappointment in myself but it no longer overwhelmed me. It was too late now, anyway. It's my guess that most people go through some of this in middle age for one reason or another. For me now, I suppose, that is why it had become easier in recent years, because there was no time left to change anything. Resignation, I suppose. I had once been ambitious and full of ideas. When I was young nothing was insurmountable. Everything was exciting in the sixties and seventies. I had so much energy then – always trying something new.

I searched my dusty memories. I was in my twenties when I had last seen Nigel Glover. We would make time for each other whenever we could, even as life after school gradually took us in very different directions. We quoted Rudyard Kipling's poem 'If' to each other many times without any self-consciousness. The sentiments of the poem had carried us through schooldays when needed and memories danced in my head now, memories sparked by the young woman in front of me. Tears began to fill my eyes, unheralded and unwanted. She put a small hand on my arm. It was as though she could read my thoughts; I wondered how someone so young understood.

"I am a Glover," she said in a whisper. "Bliss is a stage name I gave myself. Daisy Belle Bliss is a name

I dreamed up." Our eye contact had the effect of disclosure and of a very personal confidence she was sharing only with me. I sensed Dave and Lisa, motionless, hanging on every word and movement, but Daisy was unaware of them. I was assimilating this news, this introduction, and my mind was tripping over itself with different reactions as thoughts and memories churned.

"Daisy Joan Glover doesn't have the same appeal," she continued. "I changed my name just before my first hit." Her next comment had me reeling.

"My first recording was titled 'If'."

She could read my mind! How could she know? I had just remembered Nigel Glover and Rudyard Kipling's poem and how we used to quote it to each other. The fact that she'd entitled her first hit 'If' maybe wasn't so strange, it could simply hark back to her granddad's liking for the poem. But her mentioning that to me now, having just that second had the memory, well that was just weird.

I often reread the poem, for no particular reason. I still couldn't remember all the words and lines, and couldn't quote the whole as Nigel always could, even though it was me who introduced it to him. How old were we then, was I twelve, thirteen? I was in the year above him. It was inspirational then and it still was now. Though nowadays when I did read it I would mourn for the boy I was and once again wonder where Nigel was. Did he ever think about me? How could this young woman possibly know it held any significance for me?

I asked Daisy if her CD was a recording of Kipling's poem.

"Oh no, not exactly, but the album was completely inspired by it. I took lines from it or themes from it for each song," she told me. What she said next stunned me.

"It was because of it – the enjoyment I got from it as a little girl when my granddad would recite it to me. He told me how another boy had introduced it to him and how they would recite it or parts of it to help them through tough times at their boarding school. That boy meant a lot to him. And now I have met you."

Her eyes were sparkling as she once more put a small, soft hand on my arm and one tear escaped down her cheek. She made no attempt to disguise it.

"He let you down, didn't he?"

I was struggling to absorb all this. Dave and Lisa had begun going through the motions of working but they were still listening and watching, I could tell, confused though I was by the whole situation. I put my hand over hers and met her eyes. The significance was seeping slowly into my brain, though I couldn't yet make sense of it. Daisy broke my stumbling thoughts by removing her hand from beneath mine, taking a step backwards and clapping her hands together. I jumped back to reality at the sound and was now left feeling awkward.

"Shall I put the kettle on? I'm sure you could all do with a cup of tea or coffee. I'm certain you all deserve a break." As she backed towards the lighted doorway she gave me a smile that seemed to acknowledge that something had changed.

Lisa and Dave immediately put their brushes down and stopped pretending to work.

"Yes, please," Lisa agreed.

I wanted that cigarette more desperately than ever and I could see Dave fingering the tobacco pouch in his pocket. He was trying to catch my attention by holding up his lighter and clicking it on and off, hiding it quickly when Lisa glared at him. He made his affected 'naughty boy' look with his bottom lip and Lisa raised her eyebrows and rolled her eyes in equally mock resignation.

"Go on to the driveway away from the house if you want to smoke your cigarettes," Daisy said with a knowing smile. Lisa looked at her. Dave grinned at Lisa.

"I'll give you a hand with the tea," Lisa offered and followed Daisy through to the kitchen.

Questions flooded my head as Dave beckoned to me from the side door in the hallway, again clicking his lighter on and off and still grinning stupidly as he opened the door. I could hear his questions queuing up.

"What was that all about?" he said, standing too close to me. He was rolling his handmade cigarette with fingers and thumbs without taking his eyes off me. He watched me intently, looking away briefly to lick the edge of his creation. He lit it, inhaling deeply; he repeated his question with smoke pouring from his nostrils.

"Come on, tell... tell your friend Dave." He then came closer still.

It was dry and cold as we stood facing each other; the sky was leaden grey and streaked with low, darker smudges that threatened rain. I shrugged off a shiver as I blew smoke at the clouds.

"Come on," he prompted, "you must know. What did she mean about her granddad?"

I'd worked with Dave for some time now. As a person, he was harmless; what you saw was what you got. He questioned little as far as I could tell; a likeable young bloke. His conversation revolved around limited subjects – often women – with crude comments, mostly. Television was also a favourite topic: what was coming or what he had seen, but the most important thing in his life was Arsenal Football Club and its past, present and future. I don't dislike football at all and I understand loyalty and following but not obsession with anything, including a football club. Dave could name teams from every year since he was born and knew plenty before those. He knew home and away results, goal differences, scorers, future fixtures, even youth players, names to 'look out for' as he put it. I marvelled at his memory for facts and figures. He told me unashamedly that he had cried when Thierry Henry left his club. I swear his eyes filled as he confessed this to me one lunch break, sitting on paint cans eating sandwiches. I think I nodded sympathetically at the time. What was impressive, though, was that he had gone to evening classes to learn Spanish. His hero then was Cesc Fàbregas, as Dave had told me many times, but to have tried to learn his hero's native language 'in case I ever meet him' shows what motivation can do. The chance of that meeting happening seemed slim to me.

He would look puzzled if I mentioned a tsunami or famine as topics. The only reason he knew the names of some African countries was because Arsenal had signed a few African players. I asked him once why he didn't learn French to discuss football with Arsène Wenger, or because it was the first language of some of the black African players. He told me Arsène spoke very good English, but he simply would not believe that some Africans spoke French.

He was also not the person to confess to, what Nigel and I had done in 1975.

Lisa came out to where we were standing and handed us each a mug of tea. She fanned a hand in front of her face in an exaggerated way.

"What did she mean, 'he let you down'?" Dave persisted. This was his third time of asking. Daisy had said this in a whisper; I don't know how he even heard that. Luckily for me Lisa distracted him.

"We still have work to do... despite everything," Lisa added as she looked back at me. She was obviously as curious as Dave was. Not nearly as puzzled as Daisy had left me however, with so many questions of my own to ask.

We had a sandwich for lunch then we started the ceiling all over again for its second coat and that saw the rest of the day off. I didn't see Daisy again that day. I didn't answer Dave. It would be impossible to explain to him. He persisted and I deflected and ignored, hoping he would soon give up. How could I tell him that I'd known this famous singer's once-up-on-a-time equally famous grandfather, and that many years before, we had concealed a murder? A murder committed by her grandmother.

Chapter Three

Lisa dropped me off at the corner near my cottage, and I plodded wearily to my front door. The house was cold. I turned the thermostat up and heard the boiler growl and rumble into action. I clicked the kettle on, then lit a cigarette just outside the back door. I began thinking about Nigel Glover and Daisy Glover. I hadn't had another chance all that day to quiz Daisy but had spent the afternoon with a mixture of memories and questions. I finished smoking and was cold again. Back indoors, I switched on the radio.

I was still stirring my tea when the announcer on the radio got my attention. "Daisy Belle Bliss, the recording artist and actress, is on the telephone now to answer the question so many of you have been asking. Are you there, Daisy?" he said.

I could detect the fawning tone to his voice over the radio and sneered to myself.

The questions I needed to ask crowded into my thoughts, but I pushed them aside and listened closely.

"Hello, John, I'm here," she said.

She sounded somehow older on the phone – on the radio – more mature.

"Is it true you're leaving these shores to live in California?" John asked.

"John, you naughty man, you shouldn't believe everything you read in the newspapers," the newly recognisable voice cooed over the airwaves.

"My grandfather lives there as you probably know and though I intend to visit him more often, I live here. I'm staying here. I bought another house here in beautiful Dorset... what more can I say to convince you?"

I was beginning to understand why she was so well liked; I could hear the smile in her voice and a natural charm.

"So you won't be leaving us despite your huge success in the States?"

What success? Indeed, what newspaper report?

"It's my grandfather's success I would sooner talk about," Daisy came back with.

I was listening hard now. *'Granddad?' 'Success?'* John didn't help my curiosity. He continued with a trill. "It's you we all want to know about... we don't want you to leave us."

I could hear Daisy sigh, despite the phone and my ancient radio.

"I won't be leaving, I assure you."

John told her that he was as happy as everyone in the United Kingdom must be with that assurance and he wished her well and a safe trip.

I leant back in my chair. It creaked and I sipped tea.

Living in California? Nigel Glover? Success? What's all that about? I couldn't wait for tomorrow to ask... if I got a chance.

The house was beginning to warm up and I enjoyed a supermarket pop-in-the-oven ready-meal and wondered about Daisy and Nigel and their successes, and this only led me, yet again, to think about where I had gone wrong. I wondered where my ex-wife was now and how my daughters were doing. One daughter was in London, the other in Sydney. I glanced at the clock on the wall, and knew at least what one of the three was doing; it would still be night-time in Australia. Jaime had emigrated after 'travelling' there in the nineties and meeting her Aussie partner. They had all left me by 1978. They had grown up mostly without me and they certainly didn't need me now. I had seen my 'London daughter' a few times; Julia even came down to visit me once just a couple of years or so ago. Not a memorable visit. It transpired she had been 'doing some business nearby' and had been staying at a 'decent' hotel in town. It is not a nice thing to say about your own daughter but I felt that she wished she hadn't called on me. She had seemed distracted for the hour or so she was here and the only time she'd looked anywhere near relaxed was as she was leaving. As I leant forward to kiss her goodbye she had given me a double 'air-kiss' and climbed into the pre-arranged taxi without looking back.

I sat in the kitchen and listened to the clock, trying not to brood. I did think of them; Jaime was born in 1976, Julia in 1977; my daughters, my flesh and blood. I remember being so excited when each was born, Jaime in that hot summer; it was so hot at night that year their mother occasionally even slept in the garden. I tried to think back to when exactly Jenny had decided I was not good enough for her. Was it after a year or two? Before the girls were born? After? Was it weeks – or months – after her affair with her boss? I still don't know. For a long, long time I wondered when I had stopped being 'good enough'. I couldn't understand why she kept saying that I had changed.

I picked at paint splashes on my hands and turned the volume back up on the radio in an attempt to fill the room. I had been down this route too many times before. I didn't fight her; I hardly argued or protested. It was as though I heard her and simply believed her: I was not good enough. I stopped working hard and I stopped working for myself. It *was* my fault: I *had* changed.

Now I think I know why; it was what happened in 1975. It was when Nigel left. It was what I had agreed to do before he left. I recalled the fear in his eyes as we shook hands at Heathrow for what proved to be the last time I would see him. I reassured him as I had always done. He went to America and had never returned to England as far as I knew. For a long time I expected to hear something from him – for years in fact, but I never did.

That last time we met might have bound us together but it also kept us apart. We wouldn't have much in common now anyway, I thought, as I slumped into my armchair in my little lounge and turned the television on. A film was part-way through; I had no idea what the film was or what was happening so I turned it off and sat there for a while listening to the thoughts in my head. I could *hear* Nigel pleading for my help that night in September 1975. "Please, Tony – I really need your help. Yes, he's dead."

On the way to the job the next morning Lisa and Dave quizzed me about Nigel Glover, as I guessed they would. I didn't know what to say. I told them that I could remember him and they both seemed impressed that I knew him. I explained that it was many years since I had seen him. I told them that we were friends at school and how we had seen each other through our teens and early twenties till his band took off.

"Was he always good at music?" Lisa asked.

"Always, from the time I knew him at eleven years old but maybe before that even. I googled him last night."

Dave started laughing, and Lisa joined in.

"What's up with you two?" I said. "What's so bloody funny about that, then?"

"Don't you remember telling us how you tried to chat up the tutor when you first got your computer?" Lisa reminded me. "She was married and you were too embarrassed to go back and finish the course."

"Yeah, well it wasn't *that* funny. I just said I googled Nigel Glover. I hadn't ever done that till now. That's not funny."

"It was," said Dave. "I offered to give you lessons on how to chat women up and Lisa offered to help you with the computer."

Lisa nodded. "That's right, Tony, I did... if you promised not to chat *me* up."

"Anyway, do you want to know or not?" I said. They calmed down and listened with interest as I told them what I'd found out about Nigel, or 'Smudger Smiff' as he liked to be known professionally.

"I came come across a *Guardian* interview in which he'd been asked why he'd adopted that stage name. 'In honour of a very good friend of mine, who I wanted to be like,' he had replied. I'd always just thought it was his shyness that caused him to hide behind the alias. Then again, Nigel was not exactly a 'hip' name even in those days. I found pages and pages about The Strikes, his band that began life in Bournemouth. I could see the massive proportion of The Strikes' music catalogue for which Nigel was credited – most of it, it seemed!

I couldn't resist trying to imagine the royalties, just comparing other big stars of music and their ways of life that the media reported all the time like Elton John or Paul McCartney."

"And Daisy," added Dave.

I had once seen Nigel on a Times Rich List in the late eighties when I happened to be leafing through the magazine in my dentist's waiting room. I had even decorated for a few successful musicians, and, I'm ashamed to admit, nearly always with some envy. From what I could work out Nigel would have more than most. His band's music had been around since the seventies, they'd had hit albums, as well as singles, and most had been written by Nigel. There were several awards mentioned across the years, one as recently as 2002. I couldn't even begin to estimate his net worth, but it must be a staggering amount.

"How come he was friends with you, then?" Dave asked, and I could see Lisa paying keen attention.

"I wasn't always an old painter, I'll have you know. And Nigel wasn't always rich and famous," I told him.

"Yeah, but—" Dave had begun when Lisa interrupted him.

"Perhaps you'll tell us one day, please, Tony – I'm fascinated."

It was very apparent she was distracting Dave for my benefit. I was relieved when we arrived at the job.

I spent most of the day thinking about my past. Nigel Glover had been one of those kids at school who other boys had decided they didn't like. They set out to make his life a misery. I never did understand why.

His main antagonists were mostly from nice middle-class homes. They would creep over to his bed after 'lights out' in the dormitory and tip him out of bed, or just bundle him and the mattress onto the floor and spit all over him or punch and kick him. He never fought back; he would just remake his bed and appear to go back to sleep; but he would sob quietly sometimes. It was a punishable offence to even talk after 'lights out'.

I recall one occasion in particular when Hobbs, a prefect, caught him remaking his bed.

"What are you doing, boy?" Hobbs shouted. "You disgusting little creep. See me tomorrow outside the prefects' study at six o'clock precisely," he bellowed, making sure we'd all heard him. "Now, silence, all of you!"

Nigel took a beating from that prefect the following day rather than report what had really happened. That was the day I decided to help him; I had, on more than one occasion, felt the shame of looking the other way out of fear of them turning their attentions to me. I admired his stoic ways but I couldn't stand by any longer. I caught up with him after breakfast. I'd written out Rudyard Kipling's poem 'If', and before we set off for our classes I thrust it into his hand and told him to read it, without further explanation. We met up after school; he was waiting for me as I crossed the quadrangle heading to the boarders' locker room.

Back in the 1950s, life at this very minor boarding school was harsh; I had had my share of beatings and occasional bullying but I fought my corner or talked my way out of trouble more often than not. This boy didn't seem capable of any defence, and I had seen enough.

Some of his tormentors were in my own year, the second, or maybe the year above – but all were old enough to know better.

From the masters we had the cane or steel ruler on a hand – but usually a cane on the backside – and the prefects would use a gym shoe. When you are eleven or twelve years old, a prefect of seventeen or eighteen may seem to you to be a 'near-man'. It hurts, I assure you, when bent over a chair in pyjamas and a prefect runs across a room to get more power into a whack on the buttocks from a gym shoe. It hurts a lot. On more than one occasion I had blood drawn on my backside and welts that lasted for more than a week inflicted by a cane from a master. That hurts even more. You had twenty-four hours a day in which to upset people.

Nigel came right up to me and said hello.

"Thanks for this. Why did you give me it, though?"

"I thought it might give you some inspiration when things were going badly," I told him.

He just listened in a quiet, shy way. I told him too that I admired his way of dealing with his tormentors. I noticed his back stiffen. However, a tear did then roll down his cheek and I handed him my handkerchief. He dabbed his eyes without taking them off me. "Thank you," he whispered.

From that day I did try to help him, and my intervention saved him sometimes, but on more than one occasion we were both subjected to a beating or some other punishment. One Sunday, for example, not long after, I walked in on an exceptionally brutal attack. I heard noises coming from the rear of a waste-bins area and went to see. Six boys were trying to strip Nigel of his clothes; they were cackling and screeching like a pack of hyenas ripping flesh from a dying antelope. There was terror in Nigel's eyes as he kicked and writhed. I waded in with feet and fists without thinking.

Bullivant, an overweight boy from the third year, seemed to be the leader of this little bunch of cowards so I aimed my first and hardest punch at him. His nose burst, and his hands went to his face as he staggered backwards in disbelief. Deeney, a skinny, pale boy from my own year, looked at me and ran. I would get to him later, I promised myself, and I did. Bullivant began screaming at the others to get me. I kicked one hard on the shin and back-elbowed another, splitting the skin above his eye. Nigel struggled to his feet and watched silently. Owen-Davies, whose eye I had split, began to pull the others off me but not before Rickard punched me hard in the stomach. As I got my breath back from the punch the 'red mist' completely descended and the others ran for it.

All of us, except Branson, were called to the headmaster's study later that day after chapel and to my amazement none of us were further punished by him. Robert Bullivant glared at me through swollen eyes, Owen-Davies had had a few stitches in his gash at the local hospital and Steven Branson, the boy whose shin I had kicked, was still at the hospital waiting for a plaster-cast to be put on the broken bone. The others hung their heads as we were lectured about the wrongs of physical violence. This seemed somewhat disingenuous from a man who seemed to gain pleasure from caning boys.

Then the following day the headmaster and the house master, Mr Gillingham, held the whole school back after assembly for more lectures and warnings about bullying. It was my subsequent belief that Mr Davies, our headmaster, who lived on the school premises, had known exactly what had happened. I thought he could probably see that bin area from his house.

The school had boarders and day students, all boys from surrounding towns and villages. My mother could not cope with life or one small boy. Schizophrenia was a new word to both me and my dad. So, having managed to get a grant, I was shipped off as a boarder.

Nigel was there as his stepmother 'thought it was a good idea'. His mother had died in childbirth, and his father didn't object to his second wife's decision. He was as indifferent towards them as they clearly were about him.

Some of the boarders seemed 'posh' to me; those whose parents lived abroad. For example, one boy lived in Kenya and could speak Swahili, or so he said. Who could tell? Another boy had a sister who was an actress and he assured us she was in 'lots of films'. I found out some years later that he was telling the truth – she was in many Hammer House of Horror films; usually the beautiful victim of a vampire or a mad scientist. I wonder what became of him – was he now also an actor?

Like me, most from our school were destined for much less; they became minor scientists, estate agents, worked in their parents' businesses, were dentists, civil servants... not many house painters, though, or rock stars, like Nigel.

It takes something for most boys and men to cry, or at least it did in the past; I still recall how Nigel cried, not when he was beaten or bullied but whenever

I voiced my admiration for his restraint. I would praise it, but was puzzled by his lack of fight-back and anger. He would just say, "You give me strength."

These memories and more distracted me throughout that day at work.

Chapter Four

We'd passed through the gates, Lisa had parked the van and Dave was already lighting a lumpy roll-up so I joined him. As Daisy was in London for an appearance on breakfast television that morning I was not going to find out any more that day.

Lisa set out what our plans for the day were; I had already asked if she had seen the paper I had to hang on a feature-wall. She'd said that she thought it was a stripe of some sort and that it was to be hung horizontally.

I tried to think if Daisy looked like Nigel; I could remember that his eyes were a similar colour, though I wasn't sure they were as attractive as Daisy's. Hers had soft, mid-brown rims and small flecks of amber; they were beguiling.

Joanne, the housekeeper, let us in and offered us a choice of tea or coffee. Lisa wandered around the huge lounge adjusting things and checking that the dust sheets were in place and tidy. Dave was chatting to the housekeeper, a smiley and pleasant woman in her mid-forties. She seemed very efficient, with the relaxed manner of someone comfortable with herself. She was almost plain, but not unattractive, and had a neat, blonde crop that Lisa had commented was 'not a cheap cut'. Her pale, grey eyes and slim figure made me wonder: was she married? She didn't wear a wedding ring. Long-term partner but not married, perhaps?

We finished our drinks and got some paint out and set to work on the walls, although Dave was only able to start after he'd finished complimenting Joanne. She seemed to appreciate his compliments but they were embarrassing and corny; Lisa tutted and sighed as we listened. Dave pestered Joanne about whether she knew Daisy's grandfather. She told him that she didn't know him, though when I asked her later she said she'd heard plenty about him. She too was intrigued that I had known him. She said that Daisy was clearly very fond of him and that there was a strong bond between them even though he lived in California. My curiosity was once more aroused. I knew Lisa was listening and Dave was so close to me whilst she was talking I found myself shifting sideways, slightly off balance. When she added that her partner loved The Strikes' music she must have wondered why Dave thought that was so funny.

"Tomorrow we'll start another room, Dave, while Tony papers the lounge feature-wall," Lisa was saying as we pulled away in the van at the end of our day. I reminded her that I might need a hand to hang the paper – an eight-metre length of pasted and folded wallpaper is awkward to handle horizontally on your own. We chatted about the jobs for the following day till Dave jumped out. He'd told us he'd recorded breakfast TV to see Daisy's interview that morning, and Lisa and I laughed as he trotted away from the van.

"Silly bloke," she said as she watched him go. "Men are pathetic," she added with a chuckle. Finally she dropped me on the corner of my road. *Another day in paradise!* I said goodbye and made my way to my front door.

To my surprise Daisy Bliss was talking on my radio again as I switched it on. I stopped in the middle of getting out a teabag and mug and paid attention to the radio instead; I hadn't even taken my jacket off. I turned up the volume. Daisy was saying that she was off to America to see her grandfather. I realised it would now be some time before I could ask her about him. Why and how did she know that he knows me? How come? I was left to ponder. I made my tea and wondered as she said goodbye and thanked the interviewer for wishing her a safe trip.

Some things cannot be forgotten, however bad one's memory is or however hard one would wish to forget. I wondered what he might have told his granddaughter about our past. Clearly he and Daisy had talked about me; she must have known who I was before we started working on her house. Was it more than a coincidence that Lisa and Emma got this job? How much of our past – mine and Nigel's – had they discussed? The poem, of course; our schooldays too, it seemed. They had certainly discussed our friendship; our close friendship. But had they talked of what happened in 1975? Did this young woman know what her grandfather and I had done then? Did she know we had hidden a crime? Hidden a body? Did she know the circumstances of what we did in the New Forest? Her own grandmother's shocking part? Of why Nigel's successful band finished so abruptly? Of the singer vanishing? Of our part in his disappearance?

That whispered statement – "He let you down, didn't he?" What did she know of this? Why? What conversation had led to that opinion? The questions were flooding my brain. Dark thoughts of my part in helping to hide a murder all those years ago came back to me and with them the memory of how overwhelming my feelings had been when my friend abandoned me.

I lit a cigarette. I had disciplined myself to always smoke outside the house, but this was forgotten. My heart was thumping in my chest. My breathing had shortened. I could smell the body in the back of my van in 1975. I could see Nigel's strained face semi-lit beside me in that van. I heard his promises of financial help with my ambitions.

"When the royalties start coming," he said, "I'll finally be able to help you. A retail business... whatever you need help with... it'll be my turn to finally do something for you, my friend."

I found these sorts of promises slightly embarrassing but in truth I had begun to make plans. I was bursting to get going at that time.

I couldn't have dreamt when we met up, that such an event would occur and completely alter our courses. Money was not why I had always championed him and helped him, but I did have ambitions and ideas for myself, and Nigel would be in a financial position to help.

I drifted off into an uneasy and fitful sleep in my armchair only to be awoken by a nightmare: a hand – a skinny, white hand – clawing its way out of the misty mound of an unquiet forest grave... and then eyes, staring accusingly. My body ached, my head felt like it was in a vice, and my forehead was beaded with sweat despite the cold room. The lamp was still on in the corner. At last I stood, and climbed the stairs stiffly and carefully. I relieved myself, splashed water over my stinging eyes, and then fell onto the bed, still dressed, for a few hours' sleep. My head teemed with images of my dream and jumbled thoughts of that autumn night so many years ago.

I would be back at work in a few short hours.

Chapter Five

Daisy settled herself into the comfortable grey leather seat in Virgin Atlantic's Upper Class lounge. She sipped the offered orange juice, having declined the champagne, and she now looked forward to seeing her grandfather very soon at LAX airport. She slept for a lot of the journey but she had also enjoyed chatting to the red-suited flight attendants. The journey passed quickly enough, and it wasn't long before she saw the hazy sprawl of Los Angeles from the window as the Airbus A340 made its approach.

Her granddad – looking slim and tanned, she noted – was waiting for her in the VIP area. He waited as Daisy smiled for some photographers but soon they hugged. More cameras flashed, but they ignored everything, standing back several times to look each other up and down, still holding hands.

"Look at you," she said to him. "Very handsome!"

Nigel's white teeth matched his closely cropped white hair as he looked her up and down.

"One day you'll be as beautiful as your gran was."

"Yeah, I doubt it," Daisy replied with a grin.

After her suitcases had been loaded into his Jeep the journey to his home just south of Agoura didn't take long. They talked and talked right up to the gates of his house. He aimed the remote and smiled as they opened.

"Home. Here we are."

Daisy watched him as he walked around the Jeep to open her door. The English coast on which her new house stood seemed a million miles away as she stepped out and looked skywards to clear blue. She smiled as her only living relative, this man in his crumpled tee shirt and baggy khaki shorts, wrestled her suitcases from the back of his Jeep.

"Give me one of those," she insisted. "I've got to look after you – you're all I've got."

They wheeled the suitcases across the driveway to the front door. Daisy stood for a moment and admired the weatherboard house, the sun glinting from white dormer windows in a pale blue tiled roof, the same blue as the sky on most Californian days. 'A very pretty house, but nothing ostentatious,' she thought. The only things on the outside of the house that were neither blue nor white were the two black letters of its name on the white ceramic plaque beside the front door: 'IF'.

Daisy showered while her grandfather made lunch; they spent the rest of the day sitting on the patio at the rear of the house, talking and laughing till the air chilled.

"How's your new house?" Nigel asked.

"I'm having it redecorated," she told him. "I met a lovely pair of female painters and decorators in a local bar nearby and they've already started the work. They do employ some men and one of the two men at my house is a Tony Smith." She watched his reaction and waited before continuing.

"What about that for a coincidence when you've mentioned his name for so many years? You've talked so much about your schooldays with him. I didn't want to tell you by email or when we spoke on the phone, I wanted to watch your reactions." She sighed, gently touching his hand. "I just knew it was the same man you had told me about – the man who meant so much to you."

Her granddad was quiet for some moments, his gaze towards the distant hills.

"Smiffy," he shrugged. "What's he like?"

Daisy sat back and twirled a length of hair between her fingers as she considered her answer. Nigel watched her.

"He has a quiet, almost sad way about him but seems very nice as far as I can tell. Lisa, his boss, says she thinks the world of him."

"The ladies always did like him," Nigel grinned.

Daisy told him she didn't think Tony was married, but he made no reply. He leant back in his recliner, hands behind his head, and closed his eyes. Daisy watched him as his breathing gradually slowed.

He'd told Daisy many stories about his friend over the years, of his kindnesses, his ambitions, and his steadfast support in the face of bullies at school. He had often thought about seeking him out, but had resisted the urge. It surprised him to hear that Tony was still in the building trade. *He had so much ambition.* He remembered how much he thought of his old friend. He owed him a lot, he knew that, and maybe hoped that one day they would meet again, renew their friendship. This reconnection through Daisy, however, wasn't something he could have anticipated.

They talked till the sun went down, then showered again and changed.

"Come on, I'm going to show you off," he said as they left for dinner. "It's a family run place we're going to, not one of the fancy-priced restaurants you have become accustomed to," he teased her as they left the house.

They had a relaxing meal even though Daisy drew plenty of attention. Lots more people spoke to Nigel than usual, he noted with amusement, though he was very well known there by staff and regulars. Even here in this small Californian city everyone seemed to know who she was, but her looks would probably have attracted just as much attention even if she hadn't been so famous. The level of interest and Daisy's popularity was still somewhat surprising to Nigel.

Over breakfast the following day Nigel quizzed Daisy, wanting her to describe Tony Smith again. She told him that Tony smoked cigarettes and that his hair was mostly mousy – light brown with some grey – but it had a stylish cut. She described him as probably ten or more pounds overweight. Nigel smiled at this; Daisy was so slim and toned that he supposed everyone would seem overweight to her. She repeated what she'd said the previous evening about him seeming to have an almost 'sad way' about him.

"He looks older than you, Granddad," she concluded.

Nigel leant back with his hands entwined behind his head and momentarily closed his eyes. Daisy waited.

"Did I ever tell you he started a business while he was still in his teens? Not too many did something like that in those days. He was so positive – always prepared to try things. He'd organise bookings for bands I was in, all sorts. I thought he'd be a rich man one day; he had so much energy and so many ideas. So many ideas. Even at school he was irrepressible. Always up to something. I've probably told you this before, but the fact that Tony always had time for me helped me get through; he just never realised it. At school he would praise my crude attempts at my music and encourage me when no one else gave a damn. After we left school when we still used to meet, he would ask me to join in some venture or other but I always said no. I would see his disappointment but he would say nothing. Obviously something got in his way. Something sidetracked him… something knocked him off course if he's still a house painter."

"And I didn't come all the way out here to listen to you talk about an old man who's painting my house in England," said Daisy.

Nigel winced almost imperceptibly but stopped anyway.

"Yeah, you're right, my dear." He grinned, and added, "You came out here to do some TV shows."

Daisy slapped his arm playfully. "I'm sorry to stop you talking about your friend, Granddad. I know he meant so much to you, and that whole time, too. And I came to see you first and foremost, never mind any TV shows they arranged for me. So there."

In the days that followed, Daisy's grandfather took her everywhere she had to go; to television studios, parties and receptions. He would find himself a quiet corner in which to wait for her and watch with unabashed pride. Nigel Glover was not an unknown himself at a lot of the places they went to but his granddaughter eclipsed him now; the media wanted her, not him. Everywhere he took Daisy, people said hello or waved, or otherwise acknowledged him, most calling him 'Smudger', a few preferring 'Smiff' or 'Smiffy'.

He was well known in the music business around Los Angeles but it was in the city of Agoura Hills that he chose to live. It reached down almost to Malibu on the coast, the place Nigel had been staying at back in the seventies when he made his first accidental visit to Agoura Hills. He'd got lost while driving away from Malibu on unknown roads, and found himself going through the mountain pass. He had thought there and then that this was somewhere he would like to live. The hilly part just to the south was to become his favourite when he was looking for a house. Most houses were Spanish-style or at least seemed very modern to his English eyes. He was used to red-brick British boxes: all gables and bay windows. The house he lived in now he'd had built to his own specifications on a lovely elevated plot just outside town in the Morrison Ranch district. The city itself was built in a valley – The *Conejos*, or in English, 'Rabbit Valley' – along Highway 101. A city with 'a very low crime rate and good social life', he had read at the time.

Grinnini's Ristorante would guarantee a welcome and good Italian food from part-owner Giuseppe, an ebullient and outgoing personality. Another of Nigel's favourites was the Wood Ranch BBQ, which was great for ribs or steaks, and had a huge, lively bar. Nigel had sat in with some local bands here and jammed on many occasions.

It's the sort of small American city where you would see women out jogging in pairs quite safely. The odd stray coyote was a common sight, too, for in the outer districts of Agoura Hills plenty of wildlife still flourished, and occasionally a deer or a skunk or a raccoon would show itself. It was also rattlesnake country. He had often thought how lucky he was to have stumbled on it and was more than happy to be part of it. He was really enjoying showing Daisy his city and his city was pleased to see her.

His chaperoning, however, was grating on Daisy's manager, Sam Jackson, who had recently arrived in Los Angeles and where most of the parties were taking place. Sam Jackson had grown used to a little limelight himself in her company – there was even talk of him becoming a judge on *America's Got Talent* – and he resented being sidelined. He had spent the last few days trying to divert and discourage Nigel.

"Who the bloody hell looks after her interests – me or that bloody man?" he said to himself as he watched Daisy arrive in Nigel's Jeep at a television studio for an early-evening chat show. He had decided that he would point some of this out to the old man when they all met the next day at the Agoura Hills restaurant. That also annoyed him, that he had to go to Agoura rather than somewhere more upmarket in LA. He would reassert control, he had decided: enough was enough. He secretly wished he had his father's strengths and could use some of his methods.

Chapter Six

Sam's father had been known to Nigel. Izzy Jackson had been a well-known agent and manager in London, and when the 1960s explosion of pop music, singers and bands from all over the UK happened, he was in a position to sign up as many as he could. Many bands desperate for success fell foul of Izzy's business practices; his bully-boy tactics towards band members who challenged him were to become notorious during revelations and court cases in the 1980s and 90s.

Nigel had been well aware of Izzy Jackson's reputation when The Strikes were approached by one of his associates in the early days, and had carefully avoided him. Some very famous bands did huge tours for Izzy's company – mostly in America, but sometimes global tours – only to find that the money they expected to receive did not filter through to them. Others were just so excited to be touring and making music in a whirl of alcohol, drugs and girls, that they didn't even notice – or care. Sam himself had grown up in luxury in Kensington and the south of France on the back of 1950s crooners and big bands and the 1960s beat bonanza that had made his father very, very rich.

One of Izzy's favourite tricks in the sixties was to add his name to a band's songwriting credit; that way, the composers would receive their royalties but so would he. He did this to so many groups and individuals that the money just poured in from every direction for years after. On the other hand, he would soon drop a band if they questioned him or lost popularity; he was ruthless. It was not until the 1980s, and the media exposure of his methods of business, that it was revealed – not only how much money he had scammed from his clients but also how many tragic personal stories of addiction, suicide and despair emanated from connections to him. One of his less savoury methods was to send the heavies round. If a band member had complained about money, or song choices, or volume of bookings – anything – 'the boys' would pay them a visit and ask if they would like to be replaced. Fear usually won.

He was suspected of being instrumental in the breakup of The Dead Legs in 1974. In the August they were on the crest of a wave with a second platinum album and headlining Reading Festival, but, by the turn of the year, Simon Willis, their drummer, and Julian Fitzsimmons, their singer, were dead. Simon had drowned in his swimming pool, reportedly whilst on a bad LSD trip, and Julian had lost control of his E-Type Jaguar at the bottom of the long, straight hill down into Henley-on-Thames in Oxfordshire, near where he lived. These two supposedly unconnected accidents occurred after the *News of the World* had published stories of a row between the band and Ishmael Jackson Associates containing allegations from band members of money vanishing from a tour of America earlier that year. Nothing would ever be proved, but whilst it was the end for The Dead Legs it was the beginning of the end for Izzy and his gang, and as the 1980s progressed, more and more stories came to light.

Mutt Mutley and Freddie McGregor-Paterson, the two remaining members of The Dead Legs, went their separate ways: Mutt with a new, young wife to somewhere in mid-Wales where he took up farming, and Freddie to live the good life in the British Virgin Island of Tortola where he ran a yacht club in a small Cay until his death in 2003.

Yes, Sam did sometimes wish he had the same control as his father had once had; 'these modern stars were too quick to employ lawyers and accountants'. Still, he had the hottest star in Daisy Belle Bliss and he was not about to be messed around by her grandfather – or anybody else, for that matter.

Two weeks had passed quickly for Daisy and Nigel. They had appeared together on a local chat show and followed that with a national show, the ratings for which were staggering. The figures, quoted on most news stations during the following few days, were the highest in the history of this particular national chat show, and the fact was duly reported on breakfast television back in the United Kingdom. "Daisy is ours!" one presenter insisted.

Sam Jackson had tried on quite a few occasions to express the anger that continued to brew in his mind. He was a celebrity in his own right and here was this old man upstaging and overshadowing him. Opportunities had come and gone, and each time nothing seemed to stop him becoming sidelined. It was grating badly. He had expected to be on the national television show with Daisy but he hadn't even been near the studio, he'd been stuck in a hospitality suite with a couple of gay young assistant producers while Nigel Glover was doing the show with her. How was he to know

Nigel-bloody-Glover knew Dotty Duran the TV host? Dotty was the biggest television host in the US. One of her houses was in Malibu just a few miles south of Agoura Hills, and she considered Nigel Glover one of her very few trusted friends.

Nigel was well aware of Sam's resentment towards him, and he chuckled to himself on the journey back to Agoura when Daisy asked how he knew Dotty well enough to get on the show instead of Sam. Daisy already knew her grandfather's opinion of Jackson because Nigel had tried a long time ago, at the beginning of her career, to dissuade her from taking him as her manager. She had needed somebody to arrange things and Sam Jackson, after all, was well connected in most parts of the world, particularly in America and of course the United Kingdom.

He often rued the fact that he had not been in England at important times in Daisy's life, and this was a big regret given his opinion of Jackson's father. She had signed Sam Jackson's contract even though Nigel had beseeched her to seek good legal advice before doing so. He still would love to read that contract himself, if only he dared ask. He had relaxed somewhat after getting assurances from her British lawyers on the telephone before she eventually signed. When Daisy discussed it with him by telephone she proved to be more astute than he thought he could hope for. He knew now not to worry for her.

They were in Nigel's favourite local restaurant, just the two of them – relaxed, enjoying margaritas before dinner – when Sam Jackson arrived, accompanied by two young women. Nigel quietly cursed this arrangement and reluctantly stood as they joined him and Daisy. The man was a prize, gold-plated, smarmy, avaricious parasite, just like his father, Nigel had decided. Daisy, aware of her manager's attempts to undermine and irritate Nigel, was a little uneasy as the three took their seats, but she smiled and did her best to hide her concern. She knew what her grandfather thought of Sam, but also that he would try not to let it show.

The Cantina Rosa in Agora Hills was in the hands of the second generation of the same family. Héctor Díaz, who had started the business many years ago, was still around most evenings. Usually he would sit at the bar sipping a mineral water or a fruit juice that would wet the huge white moustache that adorned his tanned and craggy face. He would join regular customers for a chat at the least encouragement or invitation.

The business was now run by two of his sons, Manny and Joe, or Manuel and José, as they were christened. Rosa, Héctor's wife, still helped in the kitchen even though Manny's and José's wives would be forever telling her that with all the kitchen staff and chefs they employed, they could cope well enough. Nothing could stop Rosa flitting industriously around her kitchen. Always, the next night, despite the daughter-in-law protestations, Rosa would be tying her apron on. "It was Héctor who had the heart attack, not Rosa," she would say.

Héctor waved from his bar stool when he caught Nigel's eye. Nigel waved back then left Daisy, Sam and the two beauties, who he now knew to be Cindy and Ashley, at the table. When Sam had introduced the girls they had been genuinely polite and respectful to Nigel and his granddaughter.

Nigel shook hands with Héctor, who had stood up to greet his old friend and customer. Héctor said what a beautiful young woman Daisy was, but Nigel detected the restaurateur's reluctance to ask about his latest dinner guests. Héctor excused himself to Nigel and beckoned his youngest son José over to admonish him:

"*No los mires fijamente.*" José glanced at Nigel and gave a little bow. "*Señor,*" he said.

Nigel smiled to let him know he was not offended. He was not the only one to stare at the man in the pink jacket, black silk tee shirt, black trousers and white moccasins and his two scantily clad companions. Manny and José had the privilege of serving Daisy Belle Bliss. Manny had been playfully slapped by his wife when he entered the kitchen and talked about their guest and customer a little too enthusiastically. There were often famous faces in the Cantina Rosa but the family and their staff all respected the privacy of the diners. Héctor, however, could not observe his usual discretion on this occasion and asked Nigel if he had two more granddaughters that he had never mentioned before. Nigel noticed the twinkle in Héctor's eyes.

"You bad man, Héctor!" he admonished.

"*Ooh, la, la!*" said Héctor, and chuckled whilst putting a huge meaty hand on Nigel's shoulder. "You must buy a pink jacket, Mr Nigel."

"And a black tee shirt with sequins on, I suppose?" said Nigel. He looked over to his table. "And white shoes with gold buckles too?"

"This is Mr Jackson, your granddaughter's manager, no?" said Héctor.

"Yes – the bloody creep," Nigel confided in a conspiratorial whisper.

"I wonder if you could arrange something for me, Héctor. *Por favor*."

Nigel explained his request to the man at the bar, then had to wait until Héctor Díaz had controlled his laughter, then his breathing, and had slipped back onto his stool, still dabbing at his eyes.

"*Si, si* – of course, Mr Nigel, *mi amigo*. It is you who are bad man, Mr Nigel," said Héctor, his face impassive, but eyes with a glint of approval. He patted Nigel on the shoulder, slipped down off his stool and headed off towards the kitchen.

"How's Héctor?" Daisy asked as her grandfather sat back down at their table.

"Oh, he's bored, as usual. I guess when you've worked hard all your life it's very difficult to do nothing."

Nigel asked the young woman nearest to him her name again. She leaned forward, and he didn't know quite where to look.

"I love your accent," she told him, "and it's Ashley."

Sam leaned back in his chair and waved for attention.

"More drinks, if you don't mind," he snapped to Joe, who nodded with feigned obsequiousness.

"Margaritas, *Señor*."

Joe bowed and shuffled backwards with a discreet glance to first Nigel and then Daisy. Daisy nodded. Nigel asked for a *cerveza*.

"I'm hungry," Cindy drawled, turning to Sam.

Daisy relaxed and watched with amusement as her grandfather chatted with Ashley. When do men eventually grow up? She determined to ask him when she got a chance later. Was he fascinated by the white beads and silver around her neck? Or the many bangles on her smooth, tanned wrist? Or perhaps even the shimmering, silvery-pale-blue sheath of a dress she had poured herself into – were these what interested him? Or was it her conversation?

Sam told Ashley not to hog Nigel to herself.

"She's fine, Sam, really. I'm telling her about England. And where it is," he added with a wink at Daisy. Daisy put the drinking-straw to her lips and disguised a grin. She could see he was enjoying himself.

Joe returned with the drinks. "*Gracias.*"

"I'm hungry." Cindy took a sip of her drink.

Sam caught Joe's arm as he left. "Three more margaritas, *Señor.*"

"I'm hungry too," Daisy added.

"I'll order food when Joe comes back." Nigel turned from Ashley briefly.

"As you're my guests I'd like you all to try my very favourite: Rosa's Special." He looked around the table for agreement or dissent. The three girls all agreed readily, and Sam agreed but asked for ribs as well.

Nigel returned to his eager companion. Sam raised a disapproving eyebrow in Ashley's direction but after a quick glance at Daisy decided not to say anything. He simmered silently, swallowed the remaining drink and looked across the crowded restaurant for Joe. He was already returning to their table with more drinks. Sam smouldered, cursing the fact that her grandfather had already drawn Daisy's attention from himself and was now doing the same with Ashley, one of *his* guests. He was finding it difficult to contain and disguise his annoyance.

"Three more, *por favor.*" Joe hadn't even finished putting drinks down on the table before Sam's new order.

Joe met Nigel's eyes. Nigel raised his eyebrows in resignation.

"May we have five of Rosa's Special chilli dinners, please, Joe? I'd like my guests to try my favourite." Nigel smiled and Joe bowed very slightly again in acknowledgement. "Oh, and one serving of ribs in barbecue sauce, please."

Sam tugged at Joe's arm. "Lots of ribs, and make them your best ones!"

Daisy exchanged a look with her grandfather. Héctor waved from his bar stool and Nigel returned the wave.

"Now, Miss Ashley – what were we talking about?"

It seemed that Nigel and The Strikes had been her mother's favourite band back in the 1970s. "Mom will be soooo jealous when I tell her who I had dinner with! Smudger Smiff of The Strikes," she cooed, wrinkling her nose, shrugging her shoulders, and smiling her beautiful smile at Nigel.

Daisy idly wondered how the painting and decorating of her new house back home was coming along. This led her thoughts to her grandfather's relationship with Tony Smith, the old painter. It was strange how life could lead people to such different destinations from the same starting-point. As her thoughts meandered, she privately renewed some old vows to herself: she would not become demanding or boorish; she would not become a spoilt diva; she would not take unnecessary advantage of money or privilege. This attitude and her naturally uncomplicated personality had endeared her to most she met, from hotel staff and backing musicians to photographers and, of course, the general public. It drew many endorsement contracts too, as she was so easy to deal with for so many, and so many wanted a part of her. Once or twice she had had the headline: 'Blissful to deal with' – the *Daily Mirror* perhaps first with that one. However, if anyone took her niceness for stupidity, they were very much mistaken; she would not be treated badly or taken advantage of, and she did not suffer fools gladly. She feared no one and would quickly correct anyone who tried anything on.

Manny brought two plates of food to the table and placed one in front of Daisy and one in front of Ashley. He quickly returned, with Cindy and Sam next to be served. Finally he placed a Rosa Special in front of Nigel. He then returned once more with a basket of bread, whilst Joe, his brother, put two jugs of iced water on the table, checking if anybody needed anything else. Sam drew breath but Manny was already nearly at the table with a platter bearing a large rack of ribs covered with sticky sauce. Sam asked for more drinks. Nigel tucked the white linen napkin into the collar of his tee shirt and crammed a forkful of Rosa's chilli beef and rice into his mouth appreciatively. Sam emptied his glass again and broke off a rib. Cindy pushed food around her plate putting tiny amounts to her mouth occasionally. She sipped iced water and carefully picked crumbs off a piece of bread and ate them. Nigel watched her.

"This is great," Daisy told the others without looking up. Ashley was also enjoying her food. She too sipped at iced water between mouthfuls of chilli and rice and bread. She exchanged a smile with Nigel. "Mmmmm, honey," she said, and wrinkled her nose again. Sam wiped his hands on his napkin and picked up his fork.

Nigel asked Ashley if she was enjoying her dinner. Ashley screwed her face up in a bunch with obvious pleasure. She made a little moan in Nigel's direction, closing her eyes again in an exaggerated way. Even Cindy was now paying her food more attention. Yes, it was very good and she couldn't resist just a little more. Sam put down his fork without having tried his dinner, and tore off another rib. Nigel watched him.

"Yours will be cold, Sam," prompted Daisy innocently. The three girls agreed it was a delicious dinner. Nigel leaned back in his chair and sipped his beer, all the time watching Sam. Sam picked up his fork looking closely at his Rosa's Special. Nigel returned to his own dinner but watched, leaning forward over his plate. He didn't want to miss the result of his request to Héctor earlier.

Sam Jackson held a forkful up and addressed his fellow diners. "You all keep telling me how good it is, so here goes." As he piled food into his mouth, Nigel held his breath and waited and watched. He saw Sam shovel in a second forkful, quickly followed by another. Sam Jackson coughed quietly, his smooth, Botoxed forehead beginning to glisten with tiny beads of sweat; Nigel disguised a laugh by sipping some mineral water. Sam's hairline was becoming as pink as the jacket he was now taking off. His hair was slicked straight back; he thought it made him look like an Italian movie star, but the effect was more 1950s English footballer. His forehead now shone and the pink began to deepen. Nigel's jaw tightened with control. Sam's upper lip and his eyes now glistened. When he put yet another large, loaded fork to his mouth Nigel very nearly lost control. Sam dabbed his forehead with his napkin and drew the back of his hand across his glowing forehead. The tips of his ears now crimson.

"You OK, darlin'?" Cindy asked. "You're very red in the face."

Daisy looked puzzled. Ashley thought he had had too much to drink… or had taken something else. Cindy carefully nibbled the edge of a piece of bread. Daisy looked across at her grandfather. She didn't know what was happening but she knew he had something to do with it. Nigel, meanwhile, dabbed the corner of his mouth with his napkin and pushed his seat back. He excused himself, saying that he had to go to the bathroom. He touched Daisy on the shoulder and squeezed fleetingly as he passed her. Daisy watched her grandfather cross the restaurant. Sam's face was by now flaming. Tears streamed from bloodshot eyes and he was dribbling from pouring the last of the iced water down his throat too rapidly. He snatched Cindy's margarita from her hand and gulped it down. He tried to speak to ask for more iced water but no sound came out. He waved his arms about in hopes of catching Joe's attention. Joe had seen all right, having just been told by his father of the plot Nigel had hatched with him earlier. Joe approved.

The fiery chillies were grown at Héctor's home but for competition only. They were champions and not usually used in Rosa's Special. Héctor eventually took pity on him and directed Joe to deliver another jug of iced water to the table.

Sam Jackson glared at the waiter as if Joe had caused the fire in his mouth but he was still unable to speak. Joe stifled a grin and placed the water slightly out of Sam's reach. Sam stood and grabbed the jug and quickly poured glass after glass.

Other diners in the restaurant had been taking more than a casual interest in Cindy, Ashley and Daisy. It was not discreet recognition of Daisy and her grandfather; tonight it was different – more blatant. Héctor watched from his stool, a twinkle in his eyes. Joe and Manny were now beside their father, leaning with their backs to the bar and their elbows on the waney-edged hunk of timber. Héctor was whispering something to his sons. When Manny returned to the kitchen his wife soon poked her head out of the door, craning across the restaurant, wiping her hands on her apron as she looked at the table with the three good-looking young ladies and the man who had eaten her father-in-law's champion chillies.

Daisy was still chuckling to herself as she lay in bed. Her grandfather had ordered taxis for Cindy and Ashley and paid the driver enough to take them back down Highway 101 to Los Angeles and their homes. Sam had still been incoherent as he passed the line of three – a father and his two sons – who thanked him for coming and said how they hoped he had enjoyed his visit to their restaurant. He tried to speak; he had waved his arms and some gurgling gasps had escaped but Héctor had just nodded and smiled and given Sam's hotel address to the taxi guy. Joe had bowed as he held the restaurant door open for the man with the red face carrying the pink jacket. Nigel had paid the bill, wincing slightly at the drinks part of the total bill but still adding a hefty tip. They left after the others, Daisy standing by the door waiting for her grandfather to stop laughing and hugging Héctor. The word of what had happened had by now gone right around the remaining late diners. Many knew Nigel and he stopped to elaborate to some.

He would receive many free drinks in the future from those who wished to hear the story once again of Héctor's Champion Chillies.

Daisy and her grandfather spent two quiet days together. They talked endlessly about family, Tony Smith, and England.

"I've finished my recording and I've no more appearances or dates here and I'm going home tomorrow," Daisy said sadly.

A shudder went through him. "I'll miss you."

"Me too," breathed Daisy, "but I hope to see you soon." She squeezed his shoulders.

The next day Nigel put his granddaughter's suitcases on a trolley at the back of his Jeep outside LAX airport.

"By the way," he said, holding her hand, "there is something I'm slightly ashamed to tell you."

Daisy stiffened. She immediately thought he was going to tell her that he had changed his mind about his promise to visit her in England for the first time and to meet up with Tony Smith. She clutched his hand.

"I made a date with Ashley," he said, watching her reaction. "You know, the young woman from Cantina Rosa." Daisy kissed her grandfather and hugged him tightly, then stood on tiptoe to whisper in his ear.

"And why not?" she said.

Then she turned quickly to go through to the VIP departure lounge.

"Bye! I love you, Granddad."

Nigel was glad she went quickly. He sat in the Jeep for a few moments to let his eyes clear, then as he moved off and headed for Highway 101 back to Agoura Hills and an empty house, a tear trickled, unchecked, down his cheek.

Chapter Seven

I was swallowing the last of my second cup of tea when Lisa tooted outside. It didn't raise my mood. The air was cold, the clouds seemed to be only just over rooftop height, and a fine drizzle was falling. I put my paperhanging tools in the back of the van and we muttered our 'good mornings' as Lisa put it into gear. We pulled away and set off to collect Dave, the wiper blades clack-clacking.

"I'm not sure you'll want your paste-table, Tony," said Lisa, turning towards me as we all pulled up at Daisy's gates once more. Dave hopped out and punched in the security number on the panel on the gatepost. They were opening quietly as he jumped back in the van. Lisa switched the engine off up by the house. Dave had already begun to roll a cigarette. I stayed in the van and asked Lisa why she thought I might not need a paste-table. She told me it was a ready-mixed adhesive, and although it was recommended for this particular wall covering to apply paste to the wall I would still need the table to cut the lengths.

Dave and I had our customary last smoke before work; in my case my first of the day too. I knew I should cut down, or give up. The fine rain was soaking us as we stood at the rear of the van. *You have to suffer sometimes for things you want.*

Once we'd finished smoking, we took my tools case and table into the lounge.

Lisa and Dave would be doing the gym in the basement down by the swimming pool. She and Dave were taking equipment and paint down to make a start and Dave picked up a pile of dust sheets from the corner of the lounge making exaggerated grunting noises. I smiled to myself. Couldn't he do anything without mucking about? Was he taking the mickey out of me? Did I grunt when lifting? Probably.

Lisa grabbed a pile too, leaving me the few I needed. I split open one of the boxes that the wall covering had been delivered in, and until this time, concealed in. Another box contained two large oblong tubs of a ready-mixed paste; it was thick and white, a bit like toothpaste. This was my first look at what I was to hang. I like to look over and handle it before I start any wallpapering, normally to see where and how a pattern would match, also to get a general 'feeling' for it and of course to check that all rolls come from the same batch and have no visible faults.

I put my table up and my apron on; I favour a decorator's white apron with a front pouch for tools when I am wallpapering. Dave had helped me arrange a sequence of steps and double-layered scaffolding planks the full length of the wall and at a comfortable height to put the first length at ceiling level.

It wasn't long before I could hear Dave's radio from below, where he and Lisa were working. It was a local station playing a cheery mix of old and new middle-of-the-road music and adverts for local businesses. I shut the lounge door but the muffled music still seeped in.

Dave always liked it when a customer was not at home and he could play his radio loudly. I took my own radio sometimes for Radio Four or a golden oldies music station. Sometimes they even played a Strikes track!

I felt eyes on my back as I finished off the second length. Dave and Lisa were both standing behind me, watching, with steaming mugs in their hands.

"You are a clever ol' bastard," Dave said, grinning.

"It's going to look great," Lisa said.

I got down from the planks and joined them for a mug of tea. I hung a third length before lunch break. The next lengths went fairly easily and then I crawled along the floor putting on the last one. Before we packed up to go home, as I was waiting for Dave and Lisa to come back up, I stepped into the lounge. The room was dark by now, as I had only put a few of the downlighters on in the area I was working in but now I put every single one on and the room was bathed in light. The wall-covering looked spectacular. It was a fabulous effect. The metallic chips and streaks of silver and gold glinted and shimmered and it looked wonderful against the whole room – absolutely perfect. The background matched the other painted walls but sort of glowed and sparkled in shaded stripes. The slip of paper within the rolls had told me it was made in Denmark. I'd wondered all day what it might have cost. I'm very glad I didn't know as I was doing it. Lisa now told me it cost in excess of £3,000 for the wall. That made it over £600 per roll – one of the most expensive I had ever hung. The specks of silver and gold were real. I had already gathered the off-cuts and decided I would take them home and find a small corner in my own house to use them up – maybe an alcove or something like that

– I would find somewhere. I could have my own 'Cloth of Heaven' on my wall – well, a little bit, anyway. I made the mistake of telling the others this. Lisa continued to admire the wall. She said again that she thought it was beautiful. She asked me later in the van after we had dropped Dave off, what I had meant.

"Where did that come from?" was how she put it. "Where did that come from – 'The Cloth of Heaven'?"

I hesitated, and I admit I did wonder if she was sending me up, but I told her that I thought it came from a poem by W. B. Yeats. I burbled on that he wishes for 'Cloth of Heaven', and describes 'heaven's embroidered cloths'. I could see she was genuinely curious by now and not laughing at me. The vague memory of parts of the poem had been triggered by the wallpaper, in a room of light and half-light. Lisa looked at me differently as she sat with the van's engine running just before I got out and went home. She had a softness in her eye that I hadn't seen before; warmth too – it was as though something of her soul was exposed. And I had witnessed it.

She told me some days later that she had found the poem, read it and knew what I meant about the wallpaper. Thank goodness she had the sensitivity to not talk about it in front of Dave. I was glad of that. Lisa looked at me slightly differently though – maybe with a little more respect. I hoped that was what I detected; I wasn't entirely sure. It didn't go unnoticed by Dave, however. It irritated him. "Cloth of effing Heaven," he muttered and clicked his tongue.

That's what happens sometimes – the tiniest changes can cause a problem.

One day during the next week, after we had finished the main bedroom at the top of the house, Lisa asked me to put some dust sheets back up there. It was no hardship to comply; it was the most attractive room in the whole house – the views made it so. It had a huge curved glass window framing the spectacular vista. Lisa had explained that somebody was coming to paint some murals on the walls up here at the top of the house.

As I finished I went onto the balcony. I was gazing across the bay enjoying the view... and a surreptitious smoke. I heard movement behind me and quickly put the cigarette out. I turned to see a young woman standing there inside the room with her hands in the pockets of filthy paint-spattered jeans; a frail figure in an equally paint-splashed and once-upon-a-time-white tee shirt. It was difficult to guess her age; she was pale with dark rings around her eyes and thin, too thin. The eyes were slightly sunken and had a sort of faraway look but they were watching me intently. I sensed the intelligence behind them. I was already thinking that she might have a drug problem or maybe an eating disorder. She had part-bleached hair that stuck out in every direction and it looked to me as though she had probably cut it herself without the benefit of a mirror. There was a wooden box on the floor on each side of her. Each box had a substantial central carrying handle that looked like leather from where I was. I assumed that this was the mural painter and the boxes contained her tools, brushes and perhaps paints as well.

"Morning," she said with a smile. "Lisa said Tony would be up here, so you must be Tony." She held out a slim white hand towards me. We shook hands and chatted for a while about the view and the house in general. I was surprised by her accent from her looks. Terrible of me to prejudge, I know. She chatted intelligently, with humour and enthusiasm, in a lovely cultured accent. She was charm itself, I thought; I liked her already. I didn't want to go back downstairs and help the others, but I did. The girl had told me, when I asked, that her name was Charlotte and that most people called her Charlie. I had told her I would see her later and reluctantly left her to it.

I asked about Charlotte when I found Lisa and Dave painting in another bedroom on the first floor. Apparently Lisa had heard about her from another client and had taken her name and contact details but that it was the first time she and Emma had used her for work. They had both gone to see some of her work and it was very, very good. *I was already sure it would be.* A few evenings before she set off for California, Charlotte had come over to the house to hear what Daisy had in mind and to discuss the possibilities.

Dave had been listening quietly while he rolled the walls in. He turned as he finished into a corner.

"You been chatting up that scarecrow, Tony? You dirty ol' man." He held the pole for the roller over the paint tray and grinned at me. Lisa tutted her disapproval at Dave. He pulled faces behind her back at every opportunity for the rest of that morning like a spoilt child. It was pathetic but I couldn't help laughing.

Charlotte joined us outside at lunchtime, scrounging a roll-up from a begrudging Dave. Her roll-up was lumpier and fatter than the ones Dave made; I could see his critical look as she lit it. We learnt that she had been to school at St Mary's School in Wantage, Oxfordshire, that her father was a lawyer and her mother a journalist, and that both had thoroughly disapproved of her art degree. It soon became apparent she came from a wealthy family. She laughed a lot, as she told us that she was the black sheep of her family and the only rebel from two brothers and one sister. She told us that she lived alone in a 'shack' in the New Forest and how she had come there a few months previously to try to beat her 'interest', as she put it, in drugs and drink. This lively-minded young woman talked and talked throughout our break. Lisa was fascinated; I was too, but Dave made his dislike of her obvious, which I thought was rude. She went on to tell us about the place in the New Forest. It was in the garden of a friend of her grandparents near Ringwood, and was a 'cheap rent'.

It's funny how some strangers will share so much personal information so readily. I learnt as much about her in half an hour as I had in years of knowing some other people.

I couldn't wait to see what she was going to be doing upstairs. The whole top floor was practically one large bedroom, with its spectacular view, a door going through to a huge walk-in shower, an area with double hand basins and mirrors, and another with a bath tub. There were walk-in wardrobes, a dressing room with a single divan bed and more storage cupboards and shelving, and a separate WC room on the landing. *What a space!*

Lisa and I couldn't resist a peek, before leaving for the day.

"How're you getting on, Charlie?" Lisa asked, as we entered the bedroom.

"Fine, fine," was all she said, without stopping. She stood back a little and considered her chalk marks with her head on one side. There was not much to see really, just marks here and there in different colours.

"Just setting-out," she told us, turning her head at a variety of angles without taking her eyes from the marks. She would take half a pace back now and then or step forward and adjust a mark with a touch, or what appeared to me to be just a squiggle of blue or pink chalk. Sometimes she would glance at Lisa or me and give us a diffident, toothy smile. She then explained that it would take a few days, and continued to tickle and touch and stroke chalk marks onto our recently applied emulsion. It actually looked a mess. I couldn't see any pattern or form. Lisa said the same later as she dropped me off at the corner of my road. Dave's petulant mood hadn't changed.

"You two are easily bloody conned," he'd told us as we dropped him off, as requested, at his local pub. We both laughed. Lisa shook her head as she pulled away.

Earlier Charlotte had told us that she would be staying on the job and that she was going to use the single bed up there in the dressing room. She had explained that it was usually one of the conditions she insisted upon in taking on a project. She would only paint in an empty room, and she alone must decide what hours she would work. If a customer or potential client didn't agree she would not do the job.

We found out why when we eventually saw what she was capable of. She would prove to be an extremely talented person, if not uniquely so. And she was in no doubt or confusion about her own skills. Well, I'm using the word 'skills' but I think I should have said 'gift'. That would be why she could dictate her own terms.

She was seriously determined to lose her 'habit' – 'get clean', as she termed it. "I will win," she had told me as we shivered in Daisy's back garden during a smoke break – and I believed her. I said then that if I could help her in any way, I would. She looked genuinely touched when I said it, and thanked me.

She began to seek me out over those first few days – just because she liked my cigarettes, I supposed – but I was also enjoying her company and the conversations I was having with this intriguing young woman.

By the end of the week, her work was blossoming, for what emerged from the chalk marks was just that: blossoms. The room was covered with delicate trails and blossoming flowers that were so subtle, even up close, they seemed to have grown there. The trail had a painted shadow that made the whole look three-dimensional when you stood back. The completed room shimmered with tiny flowers. It was alive. You expected to be able to pick them or to smell their fragrance. The trailing vines seemed to glide or hang near the wall rather than just be paint on painted plaster walls; it was a truly magical effect. I was stunned when I first saw the finished room, and so was Lisa. She had wiped a tear away as she approached the work.

"Wow… wow… wow… how does she do it?" Lisa had breathed. "It's stunning." Lisa stood in awe, shaking her head slowly almost in disbelief.

"It's magical," I had said. "*Trompe l'oeil* of magical quality."

"That is a great description, Tony. Magical, yeah, magical," she repeated to herself. Her eyes glistened and tears welled once more.

Charlotte, we knew, was fast asleep, although it was not quite four in the afternoon. She had worked through the day and night of Thursday until she had finished an hour or so ago, exhausted but satisfied. I peered round the doorway at a spiky head that was just visible protruding from a pastel, cream-coloured duvet which rose and fell to her breathing. I closed the door carefully. Time for us to go home. Dave did not view the room.

Daisy's PA had handed Lisa a cheque earlier in the afternoon for our work. Each week Lisa would present an invoice for the previous week's work. A week in arrears was really good terms for our sort of work. 'As good as it gets'.

Lisa and Emma would find out the hard way one day, I guessed, as I watched Lisa fold the statement of payment made and put it in the back pocket of her jeans. I knew that sooner or later they would come across problems getting paid – it was inevitable, in my experience. Anyway, Daisy Belle Bliss was certainly not one of 'those'; even whilst she was away she had made arrangements to pay Lisa and Emma.

At the end of the following week Lisa mentioned that Daisy would be home soon but that she was not sure which day. We had been painting other bedrooms and we still had more work to do in the house. Next week I would paper just one feature-wall in most of the bedrooms, same pattern but in different colourways. Charlotte hadn't been at the house that week but was due back to continue her theme through the dressing room, bathroom, and shower areas off the main bedroom. I looked forward to seeing her again.

Chapter Eight

It was Friday, the end of yet another week. I wearily closed the front door behind me and looked forward to another quiet weekend. My kitchen always felt extra gloomy on a Friday evening when I came in from work. I vowed so often to make an effort and try to be more sociable over weekends but once again I probably wouldn't. I remembered how Jenny and I were out so much in our early days and even after getting married we saw lots of people and had fun going to gigs or days out. I hadn't been out or even talked to anyone else other than those at work for weeks. I tried to tell myself I liked being on my own.

I would nag myself to at least wander down to the pub on a Saturday night or Sunday lunchtime in hopes of finding someone to have a chat with. The last time I'd gone out on a Saturday night I hadn't known a soul in The Hope and Anchor, my local pub. I had ended up being back home by ten o'clock so I was in bed by ten-fifteen feeling even more hopeless. I would probably do my usual things. I would do a bit of washing, or ironing. I would go to the supermarket. I had recently read or heard somewhere that supermarkets are good places for single older people to meet others.

I stood reflecting; I had filled the kettle and done all the other things I had to do, like turning the thermostat up. I vanished into my thoughts at the back door as I lit a cigarette. I thought about my ex-wife and my absent daughters. I listened to my body, which needed oiling after the week's work. I tried to think of what I needed to buy at the shops tomorrow. I went on to think about that huge bedroom on our latest job and I pictured the young mural painter and what she had achieved. It lifted my spirit just picturing her work. I was planning to walk down the road later to get some fish and chips. I couldn't be bothered to cook myself a meal, and besides, for a change I was hungry. My mouth watered at the thought of crispy battered fish and fat chips with a sprinkle of salt and a good splash of vinegar.

Jenny, my ex-wife, wouldn't eat fish and chips in case she put on weight. She called it 'common' as well, so I rarely had them when we were together. In fact on only the second night after she had gone I went down to Lucky's Fish Bar where I intended going tonight. Because of her past disapproval, even though it was now over thirty years since she had taken my daughters and gone, I still feel an extra tinge of enjoyment every time I had fish and chips.

I called her 'my little Jenny Wren' when we first met. She had fine cheekbones, soft brown eyes that I found very attractive when I looked into them, and lovely, slim, shapely legs. The fine features of her face were framed by a tightly cropped auburn haircut in the sixties 'mod' style that Twiggy made famous. She had the shape of those willowy models like Jean Shrimpton and I thought back then that she should have been a model. She would always say that she wasn't tall enough but I knew she liked me telling her so.

I remember looking at her the day she told me that she was going to leave. She still looked good to me.

Then she dropped the bombshell. As lots of others have said in the past and I guess lots more will in the future, I should have seen it coming. I had a new business idea I was planning to try, and Nigel had promised to invest when his earnings 'came on stream'. I was doing all the extra work I could so that I would be able to put some money up for capital myself. Isn't that what she kept asking for? Her increasing use of 'we haven't got this' or 'we can't do that' was a sign, on reflection. I never felt like a failure until she told me I was one. I had been enjoying the struggle to improve and advance myself and to help Nigel make something of himself in the music business. We do have to choose to be victims, I know now. However, in the months following her departure, her words just floated around and around in my head: 'I want more from life than you are ever going to provide as a painter.' I was puzzled by her vitriolic use of the word 'painter' as if it were an insult; and it hurt.

Still, this was many years ago – I had been on my own for a long time now. These days, I just put one foot in front of the other. I go out in the morning and continue in a small circle that brings me back to my front door. I work, eat and sleep, and each day, week, month, is much the same as the previous one. I gave up trying to start a business and went to work for others.

I nearly jumped out of my skin when there was a knock at my front door. To my complete surprise Charlotte was standing there. I blinked in shock and was a bit lost for words.

"Hi," she said cheerily, as if I was expecting her. She wore a clean tee shirt advertising something or other not quite visible that peered out from a black quilted

Barbour jacket with a corduroy collar. I looked down at paint-free, tight blue jeans with rips at the knees, then stood back from the door and awkwardly asked if she would like to come in. She smiled and stepped in. I beckoned her towards the kitchen.

"Well, well, well, this is nice." *Not exactly an inspired welcome.* "A pleasant surprise." That'll do, I thought – that's friendly.

I pulled out a chair and motioned her to sit down. I didn't quite know what to say or do. The young lady slowly turned in the centre of my kitchen, taking everything in, it seemed. I was wishing it was tidier.

"Tea… would you like a cup of tea? Or coffee? I've got coffee too," I said.

She walked over to my kettle, checked it had water in it and then clicked it on. She asked for tea and told me she liked milk but that she did not take sugar. She sat down on the chair I'd offered some minutes ago, gazing at me intently. I busied myself by getting another mug from the wall cupboard, secretly checking that it was clean. I told her how before we had left Daisy's house I had gone upstairs and seen her fast asleep. She smiled, saying nothing at first. The smile reached her eyes and I noticed a flicker of what I took to be amusement.

"Checking up on me, eh?"

I became self-conscious about answering this perfectly ordinary, rational little question. Luckily the kettle boiled at that moment and I turned to fill both mugs and stir for a short time. I fetched the milk from the fridge and added a little to each, still stirring slowly.

"Yes, I suppose I was," I finally muttered as I put her mug down on my old table in front of her. I asked her if she would like more milk. She declined and appeared in thought, watching the tea in the mug. Then she was looking at me so directly again.

"That was nice of you." She continued to look me straight in the eye. "That was very nice of you to check on me."

I was still standing and I sipped my tea. I wanted a smoke. I proffered the pack and she took one. I then apologetically explained that I made myself smoke outside the back door. She followed me out bringing her tea with her. We lit up. Charlotte gazed up and around.

"This is cute," she said, blowing smoke at the corrugated PVC roof above us. I had built an open lean-to outside my back door – one side was the next-door neighbour's wall and two sides were open. I said that I thought of it as my veranda, then adding by way of explanation that I knew it wasn't really a veranda but that I had once dreamed of having a house with a veranda with a wooden floor, like in cowboy films. I then realised that she might not have ever seen a cowboy film. I kept a few wicker chairs out there and a wicker table that didn't match them; I'd rescued it from a skip. It was dark, so I switched on the outside light I'd rigged up. It was only a low- watt bulb but it seemed bright, and the dangling bulb had a warming effect on the little area, making it seem cosy as we sat there in the pool of light.

"Cute," she said once more as she pulled her coat tighter around herself.

"If it's raining I can have a smoke without getting wet," I explained. As we chatted and finished our cigarettes, I noticed her shiver slightly.

"Come on, let's go indoors – I can see you're getting cold," I said.

Back in the kitchen, she sat down nursing her empty mug. I switched the kettle back on and then pulled up a chair and sat down with her.

"What brought you to my door?" I asked. I immediately thought I had said it a bit too bluntly, as if I was annoyed, whereas I was more than pleased with the interruption to my Friday evening. She leant back on the chair.

"I phoned Lisa when I woke up. I asked where you lived. Perhaps she breached data protection but she told me anyway. I enjoyed chatting to you in our brief conversations at the job... the house. So I thought I would come and talk some more. You don't mind, do you?" she added, in the direct manner I was starting to expect from her.

"Not at all," I heard myself blurt out with rather too obvious enthusiasm. I asked her if she had eaten.

"Not for nearly two days," she informed me. She explained how she became embroiled in painting the bedroom and how she had just kept going and going until it was finished and how sleep then came before eating. While she was telling me this I had been unconsciously shaking my head in disapproval as a parent might to his child. She noticed me doing this and explained how it was when she was working. "Tea and tobacco, sleep, tea and tobacco and sleep." She repeated this several times as she described how she would become engrossed and how these were her only distractions. She giggled that she might use a toilet sometimes though. This, she told me, was why she wouldn't work on an occupied room or place. Complete lack of interruptions for twenty-four-hour periods. She talked and talked. I made more tea and listened. Her customers would mostly go out of their way to comply, and commissions were often organised to be done whilst they were away on holidays or business trips, unless the house was big enough for the occupants not to get in her way. I waited till I was sure she had finished.

"Your work is beautiful. I can understand why you are so in demand. Beautiful."

"Oh, thank you, kind sir," she said, and put a hand over mine.

A jolt of electricity went up my arm and through my whole body. I hoped she hadn't noticed the effect this small gesture had had on me as she took her hand away.

"Would you like to have some fish and chips?" I asked. "I was going to fetch some for my dinner. I'd love it if you would." I don't know what possessed me to add the last sentence. I felt embarrassed as soon as I said it. My stomach rumbled loudly. She laughed and told me that she could tell I was hungry. It glugged and gurgled loudly again and I stood up.

"I would love some – I'm famished," she replied.

"Cod or haddock – which do you prefer?" I asked as I put my coat on. "I won't be long. Make yourself at home."

'Lucky' was really Mr Leong, who had opened for business many years ago after arriving from Hong Kong, and always produced very good fish and chips. Now his son Peter and his wife helped too. I had often dreamed of seeing Hong Kong, with all its skyscrapers that seemed so tightly packed, and I always wanted to ask Lucky if they had fish-and-chip shops there, but never did either.

It was a clear, cold night and the sky sparkled with stars as I walked towards the welcoming glow of Lucky's

Fish Bar. Frost sparkled, too, on the pavement and on the parked cars, and my breath plumed out in front of me. The queue in the shop was long, I could see, before I even entered the welcome warmth of the waiting area. They were very well organised and I knew I wouldn't be waiting very long. I rubbed the tips of my ears, nipped by the cold air, and took my place at the end of the queue.

"Tony," Mr Leong eventually asked. "What you like?"

I ordered two cod and chips. I smiled at his look of surprise, almost querying my order for two. My mouth watered with anticipation and my stomach growled with expectation.

"Night, Tony," he called out.

"Good night, Lucky. Thanks," I answered over my shoulder. "See you." He knew me as a customer only but we would always have a little chat if we saw each other away from his shop. Sometimes we would bump into each other in the supermarket or garden centre. I chuckled to myself as I walked back. I suspected he would quiz me when next we met. He was one of those people who asked lots of questions about you but never answered anything about himself.

I walked back briskly, put the key in the door and called out. I found myself happily remembering the girl in my kitchen with whom I was about to share a meal. It was well past seven-thirty; normally I would have eaten by that time.

Charlotte had laid out two sets of cutlery on the table, and a plate of buttered bread cut into triangular halves was in the centre. Salt and pepper pots stood beside ketchup and HP sauce bottles. She had even found a bottle of malt vinegar in one of my cupboards.

fine dining!" I said, grinning stupidly.

"I'm really looking forward to this," she said.

I forked my battered fish onto the plate with some of the chips, added a little more salt and lots more vinegar and got stuck in. Charlotte, meanwhile, had opened up her parcel on the hot plate and was busy eating straight from the paper with her fingers. She had poured some ketchup on the side of the plate and dipped another chip into the red puddle. She broke off a piece of fish, closed her eyes and gave a little moan of pleasure. I looked up from my plate and smiled at this strange young woman. I wondered at her easy manner, her composure and her confidence. I completely cleared my plate including all the little crispy bits in some bread and butter and leant back contentedly. Charlotte puffed out her cheeks. I started to clear the table and my mind began to spin with what to say or do next.

"More tea? Or I've got a couple of lagers in the fridge," I said as I put the plates in the sink.

"Did you say you had some coffee, earlier?" she replied. I made two cups of coffee and this time she asked for some sugar.

"Sugar spoils tea – makes coffee," she said. That's my opinion."

I asked if she'd like to sit in the lounge where it was more comfortable but she told me she was happy in the kitchen. I was beginning to feel awkward again; conversation had all but ceased while we ate, and I silently scolded myself. I guess I wasn't used to company, let alone the company of this strange but charming young woman. In the end we smoked at my back door and we talked for a while till she went.

I climbed into bed shattered but I couldn't sleep. The night's event and the conversations rolled around my head. It had been nearly eleven o'clock when she had finally stood up to go; she had apologised for keeping me up as she put her coat on. She had placed a hand on my arm, thanked me once more for her dinner and then seemed to lean forward a little towards me as if she might kiss me. I lay there thinking about this moment but dismissed it as my imagination; my own daughter tried *not* to kiss me, after all. She had mentioned how she loved David Hockney's work. I had said she should visit Bradford to see some of it and to try Yorkshire fish and chips too. She hadn't said anything to this. I had found myself telling her things that I now thought I might regret. She had asked about my family and my ex-wife. We had talked about Daisy Belle Bliss and Lisa and Emma and we'd exchanged anecdotes about jobs we'd done and the people we'd done them for.

She'd seemed to avoid my questions about her own family. She had experimented with a few drugs whilst at art college but it was some while after that it had become more serious. She'd been vague about how it had started and I hadn't pushed it, I just let her talk; how much she wanted to tell me was up to her. I had said to her at one point that it was a privilege to be told such personal problems. She had touched my hand again and thanked me for 'listening not judging'. I had watched her drive away in her funny little van. Now I lay awake, curious to know more. I eventually drifted off to sleep still thinking about my fascinating and intelligent young guest.

I woke on Saturday morning with the bedside light still on and with sleet spattering my bedroom window.

I gradually came to and after a while climbed stiffly from my bed and went to the bathroom. I descended the staircase carefully. I pulled my dressing gown tighter whilst the kettle boiled and I looked at two plates on the sink's draining board. I went outside through the back door and coughed my way through a B&H until the kettle boiled. Radio Four talked to itself while I was outside. My chest crackled slightly and again I thought about giving it up or at least smoking less. For some reason the tea tasted extra good this morning. I listened idly to the radio talking about bankers' bonuses, a murder inquiry in Truro, then about a well-known professional footballer's wife divorcing him.

After one more cup of tea with the last drop of milk and two more smokes I went back upstairs and showered. Then I spent the rest of the morning cleaning the house, did two wash loads and ironed the remains of last week's laundry. Saturdays and Sundays were long days for me. I would eat a little, smoke a lot. Today felt different, though. I finished hoovering at about five in the afternoon and was listening to the football results. The philandering footballer's team had lost by two goals to Tottenham Hotspur. My team had won by three goals to one, a rare away win. I didn't go to matches these days but I still listened out for their results.

I went round every room in the house squirting a spray of air-freshening mist into each corner. I hoped she liked lily-of-the-valley. I was sure it was an improvement on last night's fish and chips. She had asked me if she could come round and watch a film on Saturday evening, saying she didn't have a television and that it was film she had always wanted to see – *Water Lilies*, a French film, I think she had told me

– but I was so tired by that time the previous night I wasn't sure. It would start at nine o'clock. She had also told me that she would bring something for us both to eat. I was hungry now, having only had the couple of slices of toast. I looked at the clock; it was almost six. I would have to go up to the convenience store quickly and get some milk and cigarettes, so I scribbled out a note to stick on my front door – 'BACK IN 5 MINS' – and almost trotted up the road. I couldn't see her van outside my place as I turned the corner clutching the milk and a box of chocolates. I hung my coat up and looked through the house to the front door, then went back upstairs to the bathroom, opened my shirt and sprayed deodorant under my arms. I started downstairs but then remembered there was some aftershave in the cabinet: Calvin Klein's 'Eternity'. Hoping it hadn't gone off, I went back and sniffed it. It smelt OK so I sprayed a bit under my chin and went back downstairs to wait.

I put the television on only to see our client dancing across the screen. Daisy was singing her heart out; caressing her microphone seductively, her skimpy outfit glinting under the television studio lights as she moved. She was more beautiful in real life than she appeared on the screen, I thought. But tinier. I had once seen myself on a TV screen, years ago when I happened to be stopped in the town centre and interviewed about our then local MP and the scandal he was involved in. I hated how I looked and how I sounded. I hated that MP too for siphoning off money from his so-called charity works. I remember it well because I ended up doing some decorating work for the cameraman and we became friends till he and his family moved up to Manchester. We both shared contempt for people like

Jeremy Swann, that disgraced former Member of Parliament.

I had laid the table and was still wondering whether to put sauce bottles out or not. I decided not to. I had no idea what she might bring. Takeaway? She might even bring something to cook. I didn't know; she hadn't said. I then found myself contemplating what Jenny might have been doing that evening. Getting ready to go to a theatre? Or out for dinner at a decent restaurant somewhere in the West End of London, maybe?

I lit a cigarette at the back door and wondered if my daughters had ever described the little house to her as it is now. I recalled the time years ago when Julia had paid me a visit one Saturday and spent most of it describing how wonderful her mother's house in Kensington was before they moved to Islington. The doorbell interrupted my thoughts. Charlotte was standing there holding up a brown paper carrier bag as I opened the door.

"Ta dah! I hope you like Chinese food," she announced, stepping into my little hallway.

Chapter Nine

Nigel buzzed Ashley through the gates and stepped out onto the front porch to watch her walk up the driveway towards him. "I hope you like Chinese food, honey," she said, holding up the box she was carrying. He put his hands on her shoulders and kissed her on both cheeks.

"My favourite!" he said.

"I thought you told me Rosa's was your favourite food, honey." She giggled and waggled a long, slender finger at him. Nigel followed her through the house after giving her directions, privately appreciating the rear view of tight white shorts, bright pink tee shirt and shining blonde hair. He poured two large glasses of a light and local Chardonnay, the wine misting the goblets. Then he busied himself at the kitchen counter with the contents of the box. Ashley sprawled in a corner of the brown leather couch across the other side of the kitchen. Nigel put a glass of wine on the stone table in front of the couch and Ashley thanked him. Her bare, tanned legs squeaked as she moved on the leather to take the drink.

"I love your granddaughter," she drawled.

Nigel selected some food, returned to get his own wine glass then sat down on a wicker chair opposite the young woman. He offered her chopsticks and a fork and she took the fork. He was hungry and he noticed that Ashley had a good appetite too. She would stop only to push a few stray noodles in with her finger or to smile and shrug her shoulders at Nigel to show her appreciation.

"I love your granddaughter Daisy Belle," she said once more after a few minutes and between mouthfuls. "She is so cute. I just love her accent when she talks. I didn't realise she would sound like that – her sweet English accent. She doesn't sound like that when she sings."

"I miss her already," Nigel replied, looking up at his guest. He could see that she was quite sincere. He watched her with pleasure, not just at the sight of her but in the natural happiness she exuded. She would giggle at him, wrinkle her nose or give a little shrug of the shoulders. He was quickly getting to like these little mannerisms. He had fallen for them at Rosa's but could now observe them with none of the distractions. Ashley stopped eating and raised her glass across the table at Nigel.

"Thanks, honey. You're such an English gentleman."

Nigel asked if she would like any more food. She declined, and then settled back into the couch with one toned arm along the back. He picked up his last chicken piece with the chopsticks before standing and putting on a Van Morrison CD at low volume.

'Just like Greta Garbo,' Van sang.

She said, "I thought your name was Smudger but somebody called you Nigel the other night at the restaurant. I have never heard that name before. Is it an English name? My mom loved lots of English bands but especially The Strikes."

"How many Smudgers do you know, then?" said Nigel, laughing.

"You're cute, honey. You're joshing me aren't you?" Her face lit up as she spoke, animated and curious at the same time. Nigel watched her reactions. A pert, freckled nose over smooth, tanned skin; small, pink rosebud mouth, perfect white teeth and soft, expressive grey-green eyes that told of fun and experience, of innocence and knowing; an intoxicating mixture. Maybe not as young as he had thought when they met.

Ashley patted the couch beside her and gazed up at him wide-eyed, beautiful and smiling.

Nigel said, "I enjoyed meeting you the other evening at Rosa's."

Ashley pouted and placed her hands in her lap, fingers clenched together. She hung her head slightly, fidgeting and avoiding eye contact. Nigel watched her from across the table.

"Tell me something about your family. Tell me something about your mom. Talk to me about yourself, your hopes…" Nigel trailed off, unsure.

Slowly, she began to tell Nigel how she came to California from Justin, Texas. Justin was a small place not far from Fort Worth, Dallas, she explained to him. As she continued to talk, she began to relax. She described the cowboys with their 'big pickup trucks and small brains'. She described how they always felt that they were entitled to take anything they wanted and how her high school years had been filled with fear. If she liked a boy he would assume she wanted sex, and if a boy liked her he would assume they would have sex. She talked and talked, and then she looked Nigel in the eye. She patted the couch beside her. Again despite her playful pout of disappointment, he stayed where he was. She told him how she went to Fort Worth Stockyards and the rodeo with some of the cowboys and about Billy Bob's, a big nightclub there.

Nigel didn't interrupt, but he knew Billy Bob's; he had played there a few times, not with The Strikes but back in the late nineties, sitting in with several bands just for fun.

"So I came to LA to seek my fortune. But I'm still looking, honey," she said, a sad and soulful look appearing on her pretty face.

Nigel leaned back, his hands behind his head and watched as she talked. So many came with false hopes and dreams, he thought to himself. She was pretty, he could see, she was very personable, but what, he wondered, had she thought she could offer. Other than what she now offered. She quizzed him again about his name.

"So, it's your turn. Tell me more about you." She smiled.

She listened as he described his wife, Daisy's grandmother. He explained how the band's success was so fast once it took off. How his wife fell for Rudy, The Strikes' singer, or Pete Davis, as his real name was. How quickly Pete's personality changed as drugs took over. He described how Pete aka Rudy became so destructive and how he had corroded most things around him. How he himself had not always remained sober and how memories and pain were sometimes washed away or dulled with alcohol until the band eventually came to its sudden and dramatic ending. He didn't tell her how that came about, though. He told her about the real

Smudger Smiff, the friend he had left behind – the friend to whom he owed so much – and how he had recently agreed with his granddaughter to go back to England for the first time since 1975. Of his trepidation at the thought of seeing his home town again and meeting up with his old friend after so many years. It surprised him, how much he wanted to unburden on this stranger.

Nigel admitted to her that he had painful memories of how Cherry, his own daughter, had grown up with too much privilege and too few rules; she had had plenty of money but no guidance from him. Ashley listened silently, enthralled.

"When news came from England that she had been found dead in a hotel room in London I hid on a ranch for weeks. She was alone and had choked on her own vomit... only just in her thirties. My concern was Daisy. I did think maybe her father would step forward, but he didn't."

"Who was Daisy's father? Where was he?" Ashley asked.

"Nobody knew, least of all Cherry." Nigel sighed.

He then told Ashley of some of the initial happiness of his brief second marriage in Los Angeles to Sarah Holloway, an English actress. Ashley interrupted to say that she hadn't heard of Sarah Holloway. When he told her that Holloway was her real name but her stage name was Sarah Hambledon a flicker of recognition crossed the young woman's face. She was intrigued by his stories and revelations. He would fall silent from time to time as he felt once more the painful memory of Sarah's death. When he revealed what had happened, Ashley cried.

"Sarah had returned to the United Kingdom to promote a film and she committed suicide on that visit. No one had any idea why she did it… Still haven't," he added a few moments later, more to himself.

When he described the abandoning of Tony as 'a crime', she failed to understand how he could call it that. To her mind it was nothing like the lifestyle that led to the three untimely deaths: of a wife, a daughter and an ex-wife.

He never went over his past like this, even to himself, never mind to others. The beautiful stranger across from him, had, for some reason, opened up something in him, made him want to talk.

"I'm sorry. I don't know why I'm telling you these things."

She stood and went around the table and sat on his knee. "Oh, honey, it helps to talk sometimes. My daddy left too, you know."

He could smell her hair and her skin and he kissed her shoulder gently. "My friend," he whispered.

She nuzzled into his neck. "I'm so sorry I misjudged you earlier. I just assume all men only want one thing. I'm not used to decent men."

She stood up again, kissed him on the head, crossed the kitchen and filled the kettle.

"I know what English gentlemen like. Tea!" she exclaimed. "And you are my very own English gentleman friend." She glanced over from the counter. "I could feel your pain," she said more seriously.

They'd been chatting for a while when Nigel asked how she would get home. She stiffened as if in shock when he asked.

"Do you want me to go home now?"

To his amusement and surprise she held his hand and told him in a small, grave voice that her real name was Darlene Richardson. "Darlene died too, honey."

He hugged her. He told her he didn't want her to go. He closed his eyes and smelled her hair again. He let her go and asked her to follow him. The kettle had boiled. She followed him down the corridor. She gazed around in baffled amazement. It was not where she assumed he was leading her; it was his music studio. Panels began to blink with lights as he switched on equipment; a drum kit was in one corner. Guitars hung on the wall or were in stands around the floor. Two keyboards were either side and cables were going in all directions. She touched a console gently and listened attentively as he explained what each thing did. She lingered over a cello and the three violins, two traditional and one sleek skeleton for electric fiddle. The cello was his pride and joy – he had had it shipped from the UK many years ago but hadn't played it much until his recent recordings. He liked to think that Jacqueline du Pré had once played it but there was no provenance to substantiate his hope. He found himself telling the young woman of his love of the beautiful but mournful sounds from a cello. She hadn't heard of Jacqueline du Pré but still her eyes filled as Nigel related the cruelty of the multiple sclerosis that took such a talented musician.

Nigel had always updated equipment if he learned of a newer or more 'state-of-the-art' device than the one he already had. Other professionals were quite happy in Nigel's studio. He had begun to record what he jokingly thought of as his magnum opus; it was to be a life story.

"Are you musical?" he asked.

"Not really, but I used to sing sometimes when I was little, on the back porch, and only when I thought nobody was listening. There isn't much privacy in a trailer park, though, honey," she said.

Nigel's curiosity was aroused and he made a mental note to pick this up in the future, if he got a chance. If she looked this good she might just sound good too, he reasoned.

"I'll have to invite you back again to hear you sing. Would you sing for me?"

"I'd love to come back and I'd love to be your friend but I don't think you'll like my singing, honey," she drawled in a comically exaggerated Texan accent.

Later he dropped her off at her place in LA and they agreed he would ring her soon. When he pulled the Jeep up she leant across and kissed him on the cheek and he smelt the wine on her breath and the flowers of her skin and hair and he almost regretted his chivalry.

"Anytime," she called as he drove away. She stood on the sidewalk and waved to him, a puzzled look still on her pretty face. Nigel glanced at her in the rear-view mirror and wondered at how he had opened up to the stranger on the sidewalk.

Chapter Ten

Daisy Belle Bliss was quiet in the back of the Range Rover as it cruised down the motorway through Surrey, then Hampshire. Saskia, her PA, had almost given up conversation as her fingers tapped at the laptop computer that sat on her knees. Bob the driver whistled tunelessly, peeking at the two young women in the back of the vehicle in his rear-view mirror from time to time. Saskia had met Daisy at Heathrow airport as soon as her flight had landed. Virgin's 'special service' agent had escorted Daisy off the plane and through to immigration fast track to where Saskia had been waiting with Bob.

Daisy watched the leaden sky through tinted windows as they sped towards her new house in Dorset. Seeing her grandfather had stirred questions about her past, and his too. Why had her grandmother taken a fatal overdose? Was it an accident? Whether it was accidental or deliberate was never quite made clear to Daisy. Why had her grandfather not returned to England for her mother's funeral? She was his daughter after all. What had happened to her grandmother even longer ago? Had Peter Davis caused her death and run as most theories supposed? After all, the only known fact was that his passport had never been found. Was he still out there somewhere? Perhaps some of the reports of sightings were for real? Her grandfather had more answers, she felt certain. He could be so evasive, when they were so open about everything else. She vowed to try others who might know something. It was obvious her grandfather had reasons not to talk about some of his past and she wanted to know what they were. She wondered if Tony the painter knew anything. She was quite sure he would. The Range Rover pulled into a services car park and Bob went in and returned with pastries and coffee for Saskia and Daisy. He sat at a picnic bench nearby with his own coffee and a small cigar.

"You have to add some more rehearsal time for your dance routines," Saskia was saying. "Some of the dancers are new for this tour." She checked her laptop. "We might be adding a couple more dates too… how do you fancy Bournemouth?"

"Bournemouth would be good," said Daisy.

Daisy was listening whilst idly watching Bob. Nootropic was the name she had given her spring tour. Saskia brought up some visuals of designs and advertising on the screen for Daisy to see. PR had begun a long time ago for the tour and every venue was sold out: Manchester, Glasgow, Edinburgh, Newcastle, Leeds, Sheffield, Birmingham, Cardiff, Brighton, and now Bournemouth too and the O2 Arena.

Daisy felt her whole being relax as they left the M27 and began to cross the New Forest heading for home. This road, though busy itself, made her feel different; 'peace' was the word Daisy used to describe the feeling. Saskia never quite understood Daisy's enthusiasm, feeling the complete opposite herself: she felt that she had left the real world and arrived in a forgotten place. Her senses were confused when out of a city. Saskia even felt a bit 'lost' in any city other than London.

To catch up with Daisy it was essential to join her but Saskia would normally drive herself to Dorset so that she could return to London on the same day. A form of agoraphobic anxiety began to rise in Saskia at the thought of being trapped in Dorset overnight. She had checked with Bob several times to confirm that he was returning back up the M3 the same day.

Lisa's van was parked in front of the garage as Bob opened the doors for Daisy and then Saskia. Daisy couldn't wait to see how her house had changed.

The white stucco exterior walls appeared grey in the gloomy light. They went through to the kitchen area whilst Bob brought suitcases from the car. Saskia fired up her laptop. She engrossed herself in its contents and busied herself on her iPhone sending or checking messages. Bob asked Daisy where to put bags and he volunteered to put the kettle on. Daisy thanked him and told him which cases were to go upstairs to her bedroom and which would stay to be unpacked in the downstairs utility room for laundry. Bob put the cases by the lift doors. Daisy looked at the clock and asked him to make three more mugs of tea 'for the decorators'. Excitedly she went to the lift, hesitated a second or two by the doors and then turned to run up the helix staircase instead, right to the top. Dave peered out of the room he was painting but Daisy slipped by, heading for her own bedroom first, anxious to see the effect of the mural painting.

"Wow," she muttered to herself as she gazed wide-eyed at the floating blossoms and trails on her bedroom walls. The subtle, delicate trail continued into her dressing area past the hand basins, shower and bath tub. Daisy sighed with delight. It did not look 'over the top' as she had feared. "I love it. Love it, love it," she whispered, hugging herself. She inspected a small trail more closely, marvelling at the skill of the painter. She touched a leaf gently. It was as though each blossom floated in air just off the wall. Daisy raised a hand and touched some petals as if she might be able to feel their soft and silky form. She ran her fingertips gently across a painted twig. It was so much better than she could have imagined.

She used the lift to go back down to see the lounge next. She had seen the wallpaper in a Paris hotel and decided then that it had to go somewhere in her new house. She knew how good the effect was but still gasped with pleasure taking in the whole, newly decorated lounge. *I am so lucky*, she thought. Lisa came up behind her and Daisy half turned.

"Lisa, this is beautiful. Thank you so much – you have done such a lovely job."

"Tony did the papering," Lisa said, then asked Daisy about her trip. They discussed Charlotte's work and agreed it was magical.

"Bob has made you all some tea in the kitchen, if you tell Dave and Tony." Lisa was impressed that Daisy remembered her employees' names.

"Lisa…" Daisy had turned and was standing square in front of her. Lisa momentarily wondered what was coming. Had they done something wrong? Daisy continued: "My bedroom is so, so…" She trailed off. "… Outstanding. It's magical – it's beautiful. I don't know how she does it. It's…" Daisy hesitated once more. "Yes, magical. Is she here? Is Charlotte here? I must thank her. Magical, yes, that's the word."

Lisa explained that Charlotte would be back next week.

I came down in the lift. It amused me to be able to, apart from saving my knees and hips. I could see the two women through the open lounge doorway. I popped my head round and both turned and looked at me.

"Do you like the paper?" Daisy asked.

I went through into the room and stood slightly behind them but facing the wall with its expensive wallpaper gleaming and winking at us. I told her that I loved it. I said, "Cloth of Heaven." I also told her how glad I'd been that I hadn't known how expensive it was as I hung it. They both smiled at me.

"Well, I love it!" Daisy concluded. "Well done, all of you! 'Cloth of Heaven' – I like that description too. I might write a song called that." She chuckled to herself at the thought. I left Lisa and Daisy talking and went to the kitchen to get my tea. Dave tugged me outside and we shared a smoke with Bob beside the black Range Rover with its tinted windows and fancy number plate which no doubt cost more than my van is worth. Dave and Bob soon found that they were both 'Gunners' or 'Gooners' so I left them talking football. Lisa came through the side door and I went with her to the back of the garaging area that we now considered our canteen. We had a garden table and four chairs set up there out of the wind and the rain, and out of the house. Lisa asked me why Charlotte had wanted my address. I was unsure what to tell her. I hesitated, so she asked me again, her head on one side in anticipation. Perhaps she was simply making conversation. I lied though. I don't know why.

"Do you remember that old site hut I scrounged a couple of years ago or whenever it was?" I asked Lisa. She nodded with a mouth full of sandwich.

"I'd told Charlotte about it the other week when we were chatting. She was wondering if she might be able to use it as a studio."

I stole a look at Lisa. She didn't appear to be suspicious or to doubt what I was telling her. She asked me if I would let Charlotte use it. Of course I had no proper truthful answer to this question. It was at this point I thought maybe I should really suggest it to Charlotte the next time I saw her.

Lisa, Dave and I and two other painters had been working on a housing development a couple of years ago. The site agent was a contact of mine but he was happy to deal with Emma and Lisa and they were happy to take the business. The developers had no use for the site hut any more. It had been used as part office, part store, part canteen and it even had plumbed-in toilets at one end. *Plumbed, flushable toilets, a rare luxury indeed on a building site!* It was a good size and was made from substantial timber. The carpenters had dismantled it and it sat in a stack of its components on site. The agent, Ron Gilkes, had told me some weeks before that they had no future use for it and that they just wanted to be rid of it. I feared they would burn it. I asked for it there and then and he had even arranged for his company's truck to take it to my place. I paid the driver and I paid the two carpenters who had dismantled it to come round and help me put it up again at the bottom of my garden. I had spent many happy hours adding improvements to it. It now had electricity and I had painted it inside and out and fixed leaks in the roof, but the main thing was the decking I had added across the front, complete with rails and a roof. I had scrounged what I could of any old timber to save money. I enjoyed messing about down there. An old rocking chair that I'd bought second-hand from the classifieds in our local paper just looked good on the boardwalk but I don't think I'd ever sat in it. It amused me to build the boardwalk across the front of the shed in an attempt to look like something from old cowboy films. When I was down there I always seemed to sit on an old pine captain's chair that I had glued back together after rescuing it from a skip. I had taken the two toilet pans and cisterns from the end section and had kept that sectioned-off end for my garden tools and mower in one 'cubicle' and my work tools, paste-table, etcetera in the other. This left the huge, empty hut sitting in my garden without any real purpose. I had thought of several ideas for it but I never quite got round to following up on any of them. I did have a dartboard I had kept from many years earlier when I worked on lots of pubs. It seemed too good to be thrown out just because the refurbished pub would no longer need a dartboard. I had recently managed to carpet more than half the floor with some very good quality carpet from a private house we had worked on. The only cost was to bribe the carpet fitter who fitted the new stuff to bring the old carpet round in his van which was long enough for the purpose. It was better than any I had in my house.

Lisa and I chatted about our job here at Daisy's, as we often did. There was not much left to do – perhaps a week or so more, we agreed. Charlotte was to come back next week and add some small touches to one or two of the bedrooms, the ones where I had not papered one wall. She would also do something on the walls by the swimming pool, Lisa told me.

I thought of our itinerant way of life, job to job, most of which I had always enjoyed. It certainly was one of the things that appealed to me way back when I had started: never being in the same place for very long... on to the next. I would never have settled in the same office or factory for month after month or worse still, year after year. The same place with the same faces would have driven me nuts. I wondered if Lisa felt the same: is that what she liked about our job? Is that what appealed to her?

Whenever I had asked Lisa if she was seeing anybody, she'd seemed to shrivel a little. We had worked together for some years and we knew some things about each other but conversations about our personal lives were usually very short. The age gap more than opposite sexes, I supposed.

I could hear Dave and Bob cackling with laughter as I went for another cigarette before we went back to work. Bob acknowledged me with a nod and Dave continued with a joke I had heard him tell many times. He winked at me as he reached the punchline and Bob howled with laughter as it was delivered.

"See you again, maybe," Bob said to us both. "I'm off back to London when Saskia is ready. Maybe see you at the Emirates one day?" he added to Dave with a pat on the shoulder.

About a 60,000-to-1 chance.

I found myself thinking about Charlotte and my shed as I pasted wallpaper. I was papering a feature-wall in one of the bedrooms. It went with the pale, neutral shade of emulsion paint we had used on the other walls.

Each of these bedrooms had its own en suite bathroom, the smallest of which was still bigger and better than my own bathroom at home. I nipped this thought 'in the bud'. Back when I still knew Nigel Glover and before I even married Jenny I might have dreamed of a house like Daisy's. As I brushed paste onto the next few lengths of paper, I idly thought that 'en suites' wouldn't have existed in most houses until relatively recent times. Was it during the Thatcher years that most of the *I-must-haves* started? Showers, too, were fairly rare, only found in foreign countries or schools and some sports facilities. Cold and dangerous ones at my school!

Things change.

Chapter Eleven

Once more back home in my own kitchen I turned the oven on and went over the day's events. Daisy had come home. I hadn't seen her again during the afternoon. I was contemplating how I could engineer an opportunity to talk to her in the next few days, to ask about Nigel Glover.

The phone rang and it was my youngest daughter from Australia. She told me how hot it was and I said how cold it was. She said she'd phoned to see how I was; I couldn't help thinking that I might have died since she'd last called. For the sake of something to say, I told her I was working on Daisy Belle Bliss's home. She was very impressed, and for one moment I thought she was going to ask me to get an autograph. She couldn't wait to impress her friends in Coogee Beach with the fact, she told me. When I'd said goodbye and put the phone down I wondered why she'd rung. Our brief conversation had been about nothing. I was waiting throughout the call for news of something from her – maybe a grandchild – but... nothing. She might be my flesh and blood but I thought it weird to ring with nothing to say. I supposed that I was equally lazy about ringing her. I continued to stir the frozen-vegetable mix on the hob. Steak-and-kidney pie, oven chips and frozen mixed vegetables on the Smith menu – and a little bit of gravy, of course.

I showered and changed, made a cup of tea and got out the book I'd recently bought at the supermarket. Lisa and I recommended books to each other sometimes and this was one of hers: *The Girl with the Dragon Tattoo*. I didn't get very far with it that night before putting my bedside light off and entering sweet oblivion.

The next few days at work were busy. We were progressing well towards the end. Daisy came over to me whilst I was on lunch break.

"Hello, Tony. How are you?"

"I'm OK... I think," I said.

"I've been staying with my grandfather, Nigel Glover. I told him you were doing some work here and he asked to be remembered to you." She sat down on one of the 'canteen' chairs in the garage.

"Lisa is making some tea for you in the kitchen. I told her I was coming for a chat with you."

I put my sandwich down and pulled my chair round to face her. *God, she's so pretty*, I thought. *Silly old fool.*

"He told me about you and him when you were at school together." She rolled her eyes playfully as if she knew some secret information. I asked her if Nigel was her grandfather on her maternal or paternal side, though of course I knew that he was her mother's father. Her face clouded as she answered. I was puzzled at that reaction but did not question it.

"He's my only living relative," she continued, "and I love him so much." She looked away briefly. "We had such a lovely time together. He was part of my inspiration to do well in my career, to earn enough money to be able to visit him whenever I wanted. He would always give me money as I grew up but I needed to show him I could make it on my own."

I confess I was confused. Why tell me these personal things?

"I was lucky my first recordings went very well. And that was that." She shrugged her shoulders and chuckled diffidently; a moment of modesty… and understatement. Obviously I showed my confusion. She even commented on it.

"You look puzzled. Grandfather wouldn't come back to the UK. I assumed you knew that." She leant back in the chair and drew a deep breath, then blew it out equally slowly, all the time staring directly at me. She was giving herself time to think how much to tell me.

"Oh, I assumed. I assumed you knew why."

My heart was racing. I wanted a cigarette. Did she really know why he wouldn't return home? Did this young woman know of our last meeting? I wanted that cigarette badly, but I didn't want to stop her talking. I was in shock though. What if she did know? It seemed as if she might. I was feeling sick.

She went on: "My mother – his daughter's death. My grandmother… she took her own life and that was in this area – the New Forest area."

She was speaking quietly. "Fairly near to where we are now, actually, in a house she shared with Pete Davis, or Rudy, The Strikes' singer. Well, up until the day he vanished, that is. I guess she loved him. Couldn't live without him. I still can't understand how Granddad could continue with the band when she left him for the band's own singer. So, so cruel of her! Leaving my mother behind too."

She slowed and drew breath, fixing me eye to eye.

"You might be the only person who can help me."

She was whispering these last thoughts.

I thought about what to tell her. I said, "Your grandfather has an inner strength to overcome most situations – he always did have. The music meant so much to him. He couldn't let his personal feelings get in the way. I don't really know how he coped with that situation either, though."

Tears were in her eyes. She was watching me closely.

"He should have stayed in touch with you."

I didn't know what to say.

"He always leaves me with as many questions as answers. Like what did happen to Rudy? Where did he go? What did he do to Joan? Was it suicide? Did he come back to the house and force her to take an overdose? I understand there were always plenty of LSD and all sorts of legal and illegal pills in that house."

Her eyes almost pleaded. "Did you ever go to that house in the forest?"

She watched me absorb her questions.

"Do you know what happened in 1975 that made my grandmother take an overdose? If that is what happened? Do you know where Rudy might be? Or why my grandfather left the UK and has been so reluctant to visit his home country? Have you both got something to hide?"

As shocked as I was, I wasn't ready for the next question.

"Why did he abandon you, his friend? He has never stopped telling me what a good friend you were." She looked directly at me. "But he left you."

I stayed silent; I didn't know what to say.

"It wouldn't have been difficult for him to find you." I could feel her eyes on me as she spoke.

I was speechless. The blood was thumping in my ears. My heart raced. I think she deliberately let me regain my senses by continuing to talk.

"Grandfather was paying people to look after us, Mother and me, even though Joan had treated him so badly. He always managed to see that I was well looked after." Daisy paused a moment then continued. "Without ever coming back. You see, I completely understand how he just could not bear to be in England where first of all Pete and my grandmother were together. Then the mystery of Pete vanishing off the face of the earth. My grandmother killing herself. It's easy to understand how he wanted a new life in America."

She watched my reactions and I hoped didn't see my relief as I realised she appeared not to know the main reason her grandfather had never returned to England. The things she knew were bad enough but a murder was worse still; a murder her grandmother committed. A murder that I helped conceal.

"He didn't return for the funeral and he hasn't been here since. Not even when Cherry, my own mother, brought him more sadness. Not even years later when the other major catastrophe in his life happened and Sarah, his second wife, also took her own life. They'd only been married a matter of months. I never met Sarah; they had married in California and I was still at school and not allowed to go."

She stopped to draw breath. Most of this I knew, of course. Some I didn't, but there was the one part of her grandmother's history that Nigel and I alone knew. She continued, telling me how Nigel had probably decided to live in California before the band came to an end. She asked me what I remembered of Pete Davis, The Strikes' singer, and the mystery of his disappearance. I shuddered when she asked, but fortunately she didn't notice. She assumed this was after we had gone our separate ways and I suppose it was to a great extent. When The Strikes were on the rise they rarely came back to their home town, and the bigger they became the less I saw of Nigel. Their tours took them away, first from Dorset, then from the United Kingdom. They travelled across the world: to Japan, Australia and New Zealand. They played most of Europe, America and Canada too.

I sneaked a look at my watch.

Daisy continued. "I was a baby when my mother…" She trailed off and looked away. Just then Lisa came in with our tea and the moment was gone.

I quickly told Daisy I would like to continue our conversation. "Soon, if possible," I added.

She whispered, "We will. I have much more I would like to talk to you about." She put her hand on mine. She smiled almost sheepishly and got up as she caught Lisa's eye. Lisa had seen the gesture and I could now see that she was bursting with curiosity and surprise. Daisy returned indoors without a word to Lisa and this probably added to Lisa's intrigue. She sat staring at me. She sipped her tea and pushed a mug nearer me. I could tell she was urging me to begin an explanation. Where would I begin? I remained silent. Lisa spoke first.

"Come on, then. You're a dark horse. Out with it: what's going on between you two?"

I tapped the side of my nose as Del Boy Trotter would do. "We're having a secret affair… please keep it to yourself for now; I don't want Dave to be jealous."

She laughed but wasn't satisfied. She stood, came round to my side of the table and teasingly pretended to shake me.

"Come on," she pleaded.

I then told her enough of the truth. How Daisy's granddad and me had known each other when we were young and that he had asked about me when Daisy visited him at his home in California, all of which Lisa pretty much knew already. It wouldn't quite explain Daisy's hand on mine.

"I guess because I had known her granddad so well once she thinks she knows me better."

Lisa drank some tea and watched me over her mug. We talked some more about Daisy in general. She asked me if I knew about Daisy's forthcoming tour – the 'Nootropic', *whatever that meant*. The older I get, the more I realise how little I know about anything. She told me also that Bournemouth International Centre had been added to Daisy's tour. This was news. I had seen the adverts in the *Mail on Sunday* but it must have been printed before Bournemouth was added. I had the longed-for cigarette before going back to work in the house, and the remainder of the afternoon flew by.

Another weekend in prospect, I wandered up the road after buying a local paper, a can of baked beans, a loaf of bread and a pack of cigarettes. I plodded along the road, said hello to a neighbour and her little boy and sighed with relief as I put the key in the door. I slumped onto a kitchen chair, relieved to be sitting; relieved it was Friday. There was a live FA Cup football game on television Saturday and I looked forward to seeing it. As I sat with my tea I reflected that I now knew a little more about Daisy, Nigel, and that in a way the truth about 1975 may be beginning to surface, if only in my memory.

Chapter Twelve

During the time I knew Nigel, both at school and after, he was a shy person, nervous even, no real confidence in himself – and I had tried to help with this just because I liked him. I tried to involve him in things that I did; anything to get him out of his introverted ways. My dad would take him to football with us sometimes, when he occasionally came home with me during school holidays, though I knew he wasn't particularly interested in sport. He was happier sitting in his bedroom practising on his guitar. His parents didn't encourage visitors. If I ever went round he was always ready to burst out of the front door and lead me away from the house. In fact I'm not sure if I ever saw beyond the hallway of the substantial detached house where Nigel lived. It was over in a better part of town, on a tree-lined road.

I knew something about odd behaviour; my dad and I were always worried if anyone came to our house. We never knew what my mother might do or say next as she deteriorated. If she was calm we would still be anxious in case it didn't last. Even aged eleven I knew how relieved my dad was that I was going away to school, but I also knew that it broke his heart. Mum was in and out of hospital throughout my boarding-school days, and though I would see her sometimes, I don't think she really knew who I was; she was on some powerful medication – 'chemical cosh' is the term nowadays, I believe. Whenever I saw her it would leave me upset. How my dad coped I'll never know but he has my respect and admiration for loving her despite who she became with illness; to this day he is my measure for loyalty. 'In sickness and in health' – he meant it. She developed a wild-eyed look and the sweats, and that is still the image I have of the last time I saw her in hospital a month or so before she died. I wouldn't take Jenny or the girls to see her. She had looked away when I tried to show her photos of our wedding, and of the babies, her grandchildren. She showed no interest at all. When I was seventeen, nearly eighteen, the doctors had told us how well she had responded to some new drugs and they recommended a week at home over Christmas. My dad cooked a Christmas dinner of sorts and we got through the day. She had seemed OK but quiet.

On Boxing Day I was up and in the kitchen making her and myself some tea and I had begun to fry bacon and eggs for all three of us. I asked Mum to go and get Dad up. She went upstairs to where my dad was still sleeping and severed his jugular vein with a kitchen knife. It was on that day all those years ago, trembling, as I waited for help to arrive, that I resolved to hold myself together; I thought life could never test me more. I determined it with the intensity that only a seventeen-year-old can. This resolve would not be tested until the day Jenny told me what a disappointment I was to her, and I failed the test.

I still fought the images of what I encountered when I'd gone upstairs to see what my mother was laughing at on that Boxing Day morning. The amount of blood was astonishing and overwhelming as I took the knife from my mother's hand and led her downstairs. The sheets and bedding were red. I never told anyone this story: I had no wish to relive it. I never told Nigel and I certainly never told Jenny or my daughters how my father died.

The painting and decorating job at Daisy's house was stirring some unpleasant hidden memories for me. I recalled the newspaper headline: 'Smudger Smiff's new wife found dead'. It was 'Smudger Smiff' that first caught my eye: my nickname, but Nigel's adopted name. It was hard to understand how a young woman who had so much to live for had deliberately taken her own life alone in a London hotel; it didn't make any sense. I felt for my old friend when I read it in the newspaper. *Lightning can strike in the same place more than once, it seems.* I did expect him to come over to England for her funeral, despite knowing however firm his resolve was 'never to return' to the United Kingdom. I can clearly remember thinking how I would seek him out.

Somewhere in the house I still had some cardboard boxes with my old vinyl LPs in and amongst these were at least three by The Strikes. I knew for certain I had a copy of *If Only*, their biggest seller. It had been bigger than Mike Oldfield's *Tubular Bells* and Pink Floyd's *Dark Side of the Moon*. I had these two as well. *Doesn't everyone have these three at least?* Samples from *If Only* are still often used over adverts or television documentaries. Some of their other albums would get a mention too from time to time but it was *If Only* that defined The Strikes. I was now off down memory lane thinking of well-known bands and performers I had seen long ago. I had gone up to Hammersmith with Nigel in 1963 to a show starring the Everly Brothers, Little Richard and Bo Diddley, plus a new band on the bottom of the bill called the Rolling Stones. What a line-up! That same year we even went to a gig in thick fog just after Christmas when Bournemouth's very own exotically named Dave La Kaz and the G-Men supported the Rolling Stones at Reading Town Hall. I can also remember the local Reading band Kay and the Coronets on that bill. I thought they were pretty good too. Afterwards, it took us hours to get back to Bournemouth, driving at a snail's pace. I've never seen such a thick fog since – at one point it was so thick we lost the road and drove through a rest area lay-by.

I popped two slices of bread in the toaster and poured baked beans into a saucepan: a royal feast at the end of a week of labour.

I finished my meal and flicked through the local paper. There was a profile of Daisy Belle Bliss, who was 'now a local resident', it reported with unabashed delight. The article even mentioned that her grandfather, 'a local man', had played with the 'once-famous band The Strikes'. They also mentioned singer Pete Davis, another local man, and devoted a few column inches to his 'mysterious disappearance in 1975' and a selection of the conspiracy theories that had tried to explain it.

They were all wrong: he was dead. I knew!

Nigel had written most of The Strikes' music; I learned this from sleeve notes and long-ago conversations. The media had all but forgotten him till Daisy became famous. Nigel had quickly vanished from gossip columns many years ago, appearing briefly as the 'husband of Sarah Hambledon' then fading back into obscurity.

Royalties just quietly flowed in to facilitate his continued comfortable anonymity in California.

The sound of the doorbell interrupted my thoughts, and Charlotte stood at my front door. Her fine cheekbones had some colour to them and her eyes, I swear, were clearer. Her skin looked altogether less sallow. I invited her in as if we were old friends. She asked if she was interrupting me. I assured her my diary for the evening was less than full.

"I would hate to be a pest," she explained, "just turning up at your door like an uninvited orphan."

I again reassured her that she was welcome to knock my door any time she chose to. I could see that she began to relax as she stepped into the kitchen. I put the kettle on and asked if she had eaten. She had not, so I offered toast and the remains of the baked beans. She scolded me for apologising at the lack of 'haute cuisine' and told me that she loved beans on toast. There then followed a few moments of uncomfortable silence between us. Neither of us spoke until the toast popped up. I pulled a chair out for her then put a knife and fork on the table in front of her. She watched me as I buttered the toast, then as I spooned the beans over the toast. I met her eyes a couple of times but neither of us said anything. I made an exaggerated waiter's bow as I put the plate of food down.

"How are you doing?" I asked her. "Where've you been working this week?"

She wiped some bean sauce from the corner of her mouth with a fingertip and said she would tell me all about her week when she had finished eating. I felt a bit clumsy again so I left her to it, switched on my external light and went out of the back door and of course smoked. Thinking mostly of how I must cut down on cigarettes I watched a snail crawling up a flowerpot I'd left on the garden path. I idly compared the creature's life to mine, slithering slowly up a surface with no knowledge of where it might lead. Would he be disappointed when he reached the top and found only a hole to fall into? I jumped when Charlotte opened the back door and came out.

"Sorry," she said. I showed her the snail and told her what I had been thinking. She laughed and touched my sleeve. Now it felt natural and more comfortable. I almost embarrassed myself, or both of us, by telling her this as we stood on my veranda smoking cigarettes on this chilly Friday night.

"How are you getting on at Daisy's house?" she asked. I told her what we'd been doing and that Daisy had returned from America. Then I reminded her that she was going to tell me about her week.

"Shall we go back in the warm and I'll tell you all about it?" she said. Once inside, she told me she had been looking for somewhere to work, and described some of the places she had looked at. She explained how, being busy with her painting and mural commissions, she'd grown to miss, as she put it, 'creative personal painting'. She now badly wanted somewhere to put brushes and paints: a space of her own to work.

"Somewhere that's mine, somewhere to go to when I want to paint for myself." She then gave me news that I was very pleased to hear: she had been off drugs for some weeks now, hadn't touched any alcohol and was really beginning to look forward to better health and a less chaotic life. I wanted to hug her.

She told me some of what she charged for murals and a typical hourly rate if she was charging that way. "And I always make it clear that I will be charging for my sleeping hours on the job too. After all," she added with a smile, "I dream about their jobs: what I will be doing, what I have done, how I'll do it. That's how I work best. They're welcome to tell me roughly what they would like but I insist on my interpretation and I do genuinely dream ideas. I wake knowing exactly what to paint."

Her enthusiasm was obvious as she spoke. I thought of the old adage: 'Find a job you like and you will never work again'. This girl did not work, I thought. The money she earned was fantastic compared with my usual hourly rate, but then I didn't have her talent. I asked her if she had decided on a place out of the ones she had seen. She had liked one, she said, but she hadn't liked the people who were letting it so would probably not consider it.

"I thought of you this week," I said. I noticed the colour in her cheeks rose slightly. I stood. I held out my hand to take hers.

"Come with me," I told her.

She looked puzzled but took my hand. I picked up the torch I kept on a shelf by the back door.

"Follow me, young lady," I commanded. With my torch illuminating our way, we walked to the door of my site hut. I undid the padlock, opened the door, leaned in and switched on the light.

"Have a look in there," I said, stepping back.

She looked at me with a puzzled expression. I motioned her to go in. She stood in the open doorway in the cold night air and peered in as if afraid to cross the threshold. She looked at me. I smiled and said nothing. She stepped in. Charlotte now stood in the middle of the floor and slowly turned through three-hundred-and-sixty degrees. She was taking it in, the cobwebs on the ceiling and the dusty corners. She would stop turning and watch me in the way I had begun to notice she did, very directly. I stood just inside the door clutching the cold metal of the padlock in my fingers. Charlotte walked up to one end, and then back again, occasionally glancing at me but still hadn't said anything.

I finally prompted her. "Well, what do you think? Would this suffice? I don't quite know what you need – what you're looking for. I don't know what you may need." I realised I was burbling and repeating myself. Then I began to explain how I came by it. I told her how I had scrounged the kitchen units that were all along the far end from a kitchen refit I had helped with. I told her it had only cold water, and how the water supply had been rigged up by a plumber mate of mine one Sunday morning. I even suggested that perhaps, since electricity was installed, a small electric water-heater could easily be fitted over the sink. I lit a cigarette to stop myself waffling on. Still she said nothing. She wandered around, stopping now and then to touch a wall or glance at me, but she remained silent. I was beginning to wish I hadn't brought her down here. Had I embarrassed us both by suggesting my shed as a studio? Was she offended? I hoped not. Finally she watched me again in the intense way she had.

"I like it." She spoke so quietly I wasn't sure what she had said. She repeated it, though. "I like it, Tony." I heard her this time and I was sort of excited.

"Do you really?"

She replied then with an enthusiastic 'Yep'. She was grinning and looking around once again. Then she told me that there were a few things she was not sure about and my heart sank. I wanted her to want it by now.

"I'm just wondering how much natural light... I think it faces north."

"Is that bad?" I asked.

"That's good, but I'm still unsure of how much natural light there'll be. The windows are fairly small." I didn't know what to say. She then went on to answer her own concern, saying that if it was a painting where she needed extra daylight then she could easily wait for bright, dry days and work outside. She explained that for most of her work the level of light was not crucial. I think I understood what she was saying. She was watching me again, stroking stray hair from her forehead with her long, elegant fingers.

"Let's go back to the house. It's cold down here, and you can think about it in the warm," I said.

She nodded. I put the lights off and the padlock on and followed her up the path, shining the torch beam just beyond her feet. I shut the back door and shuddered. I hadn't realised how cold I'd become. My new young friend was already sitting at my kitchen table. She told me she would like to come back in daylight the following morning. "If possible?" she added.

"Of course you can," I said. I told her how it had been there almost unused for a couple of years already, how I had hardly ever used it and how I just sort of liked it being there. I sat down at the table, put a mug of coffee in front of her and waited for her thoughts.

"There are a few problems I can see though, Tony," she said, peering over the coffee mug as she spoke. She blew on her drink and tried to sip it as she watched me.

"How much would you like in rent for it, being one, and another being access? It's in your garden, after all."

I had thought of this myself.

"Well, you only need a key to the side gate and a key to my back door for the toilet." Her eyes lit up then narrowed as I spoke.

"I can see you are tired," she said. "I know I've already imposed quite enough. Is ten o'clock in the morning OK with you?"

I agreed that was not too early. I glanced at the clock on the wall; it was gone nine and I hadn't showered. We said our goodnights at the front door. I had a shower and fell into bed. I was soon asleep, despite the evening's events.

Chapter Thirteen

On that Saturday I had been up since about seven-thirty and felt rested for a change. I had a morning shower and shaved and then, I have to confess, sprayed on aftershave. My creased face looked back from the mirror. My hair still had most of its original colour; not too bad for a man over sixty years of age. I had a slice of toast and marmalade and I made coffee instead of my normal tea. The radio was keeping me company and I felt at peace with the world. I made a shopping list of a few things I knew I needed. I had a second cup of coffee with a cigarette outside the back door.

The sky was a dark grey and fine rain filled the air, like a sea mist. The shrubs in my garden border drooped miserably. I stared at the wooden building further down my garden and began to imagine Charlotte working there. The lights might be on at this time of year. The windows and door might be open all day in summer.

And then for some random unknown reason Nigel's and my dark secret crept into my thoughts. I tried to dismiss it.

I considered how Charlotte would not want to be disturbed if she was working on a painting down there. I knew from her methods at Daisy's house how she liked to work; once engrossed she might even work for perhaps twenty-four hours non-stop. I guessed she would work in the same way in the studio. I was wondering about whether she might want any alterations or improvements made to the hut, and the costs involved, but I really couldn't think of any problems. There were benefits, though; not least her being nearby.

The doorbell rang and I rushed to the door but it was somebody trying to get me to change my electricity and gas supplier. I was just back in the kitchen when it rang again and this time it was my new young friend. Before I put my brain in gear I heard myself saying, "My, my, you look good." And she did. Her hair had been cropped very short and it really suited her. The denim jeans were probably brand new and the fresh black tee shirt was visible under the usual Barbour jacket.

"Thank you, kind sir," she said in a strong West Country accent, and she dipped her knees and held her hands out with the palms up.

"Do you like my new hairstyle? I had it done this morning. I was first in the salon – I followed the hairdresser in. I like it. What do you think?"

We hadn't even got out of my hallway.

"It really does suit you. I like it a lot," I said as we got to the kitchen. I wondered if my answer was delivered with too much enthusiasm.

"Thank you, Tony Smith. You're very kind," she said, again using the exaggerated West Country accent and dipping her knees in a mock curtsy. She stood in the centre of my kitchen as if she was already comfortable there, took off her jacket and put it on the back of a chair. I noticed that her breasts were a little fuller than when I had first seen her at Daisy's house. Perhaps I shouldn't have been looking, but 'HELP' was spelt out in silver sequins on the front of her black tee shirt. It was too late.

"You're a Beatles fan, then?" I muttered with a nod to her chest.

"Beatles fan?" she repeated.

I went through to my lounge and as quickly as I could rifled through the pile of vinyl LPs in a corner. I produced a copy of the Beatles album *Help* and held it up in front of me as I returned to the kitchen.

She just chuckled. "I knew what you meant," she said. I felt a bit foolish. She peered down at her chest then told me she didn't think it was supposed to be a Beatles connection, that it was just a word, a word that she liked the irony of on her chest. I wished I hadn't said anything. I was thinking... Help!

"Tea? Coffee?" I asked. I sensed she was amused at my discomfort. She fiddled in the pocket of her coat on the back of the chair, eventually producing a small notebook with a ballpoint pen in the spine.

"Ta dah," she announced. "I made a few notes and questions for you."

I sat down with her. She related some of her notes hesitantly I thought, as though she wasn't sure of herself or of the possible decision. Amongst other things she wanted to know how much rent I had in mind and if I would restrict her hours of coming and going and working in there. She mentioned the cost of electricity and water. I hadn't thought of those – I was just so happy about the prospect of her using the building. When she stopped with a last glance at her notebook she leaned back in the chair.

"Well?" she said.

"I don't want any money from you and you can come and go to suit yourself. But only you."

"I promise it's for me and me alone. I wouldn't want anybody else to use it, or even visit, for that matter. I'd allow only one visitor." She paused for effect. "And that is you, Monsieur."

"That was a worry of mine," I admitted. I went on to prevaricate about certain associates she had told me about before. She smiled at my discomfort.

"Look, Tony, I'm not a kid; all that's behind me now. Your hut, or whatever you call it, is just perfect for me. I wouldn't take advantage of your good nature." She put her hand on my arm. I looked at it there and put my other hand over hers. She watched me do this. I was relieved at what she'd said, not only for the practical reason of not wanting her to share it but also because of this declaration to put her past in the past and to stay clean. I told her so. She was grinning. Our eyes met.

"Deal, then," I said and held my hand out to be shaken. We had a conversation about money for a few minutes, with me assuring her that I did not want rent and her saying she had no wish to take advantage of me. Finally I agreed to some remuneration. My suggestion was for her to pay for a Chinese takeaway for us once a month. She agreed with a chuckle. We talked about her bringing equipment round and went down to the hut when she asked to see it again. I undid the padlock, let her in, then stood at the open door and watched her thinking about where she would put things. She had a way of scratching her head when in thought. It had made her spiky hair even more wayward before but it made no difference to her new tight crop. She looked over to me.

"Would you mind if I had a small bed or couch in here?"

"I assumed you might want that. You must do whatever you want."

I told her that I would insulate it before she began bringing her stuff in and she agreed that this was a good idea and that she would pay for the polystyrene sheets I had in mind to insulate it with. She was planning as we talked. I was giving some thought as to how I might insulate the floor: I wasn't sure. I was to measure it all up for materials and tell her the cost. I would sort this out on the coming Monday.

I left her down there and went back to the kitchen.

She had a studio. I had a friend.

Chapter Fourteen

Dave wasn't at his usual pick-up point on Monday morning. Lisa rang his mobile after we had waited about ten minutes. She repeated "OK, OK" several times, then shut her phone off, put the van into gear and pulled away from the kerb. "No Dave today; he'll be back with us tomorrow. He's been partying all weekend and tells me that he is still wasted. At least he was apologetic," she added. "He's met a new girlfriend and I suspect that's where he was still when I rang him and that the hangover is not altogether the whole story." She grinned, so was not too annoyed with him.

We talked for a while before we started work. Lisa revealed that she and Emma had been invited to a party that was to be held at Daisy's house when the job was finished. No date had been set, but Lisa said Daisy described it as a house-warming. I joked with her about rubbing shoulders with the stars, Daisy's showbiz friends. Lisa added that Charlotte would be getting an invitation too. I have to admit I was surprised to learn that Dave and I were invited too, though Lisa couldn't see why. I knew she was going to mention seeing Daisy's hand over mine again. She did and it started her giggling again. Ever practical, Lisa told me that she and Emma hoped to make more contacts from it. I often wondered about Lisa. I had worked for Emma and her for some years now but I knew very little about their private lives. I liked them both. They treated me well. Lisa was good company at work, and though I rarely saw Emma she was always very pleasant whenever our paths crossed. She liked my help with pricing jobs sometimes and she would always thank me with a pack of cigarettes or some other token. When I think of some of the bosses I have worked for over the years, with bounced pay cheques, no last week's money and impossible low piecework prices, Lisa and Emma were the best I had ever come across.

Dave returned on Tuesday and we had to spend the whole of the rest of the week hearing how wonderful his new girlfriend was. I felt I knew Leanne by Friday. He even ambushed Daisy, thanked her for his invite to her party and asked if he could bring Leanne along. He had no inhibitions; he seemed to sail through life with few hang-ups or complications. I envied him sometimes.

I had ordered the polystyrene sheeting, several rolls of extremely sticky scrim tape, some brackets, and other bits and pieces I thought we might need to insulate the hut, or the studio, as it would soon be. I left work early on Friday to take delivery in the afternoon.

I was still in the bathroom the next day when I heard the doorbell. I threw some work clothes on, went down the stairs as quickly as my legs would allow and there stood the young artist Charlotte smiling all over her face, dressed in a navy-blue boiler suit. I noticed that she was wearing a little more make-up each time I saw her. She had been wearing none at all the first day I saw her in Daisy's top-floor bedroom.

I stepped back and let her in. I told her to go through to the kitchen while I just popped back upstairs. I wanted to make sure I'd left it tidy up there and I still hadn't shaved. I glanced at my watch on the shelf: she was earlier than I expected. I was still at the basin, I could hear movements downstairs: the kettle going on, the toaster, then the chink of mugs and the squeak of my fridge door. I liked her familiarity in my kitchen and I enjoyed the sounds of somebody else in my house. I didn't put on 'Eternity', though I thought about doing so.

We had tea and toast with some marmalade that she'd brought with her; a quality marmalade, not the cheaper supermarket own-brand like I normally buy. We exchanged a few pleasantries. I told her what I had been thinking, about how nice it was to hear her from upstairs. Telling her this made us both a bit self-conscious, but the feeling was dispelled as soon we went to the studio and started work. We took it in turns to go back to the kitchen to make more tea and by four in the afternoon, tired and hungry and with daylight gone, we had finished. The studio walls gleamed white with the polystyrene panels. I had taken an old oil-filled electric radiator down there earlier for some warmth as we worked and I could already tell just from this source of heat that the insulation would help a lot.

I left Charlotte in the 'studio' and went along the road for two fish-and-chips. I blanked Lucky's question about my having a visitor by just smiling. He was too busy to pursue it. When I got back I had to call Charlotte from the studio. She talked endlessly about her plans. She thanked me several more times for letting her use it. We agreed to find an electrician to put some more lighting down there; she knew of some particular strip-lighting tubes that approximated daylight. She asked me if she could start bringing some of her things round the next day; Sunday. At this point I tried to tell her to relax and stop asking questions, and told her she must come and go to suit herself and do exactly what she wished to do, at which she jumped up and kissed me on the cheek.

She left about eight-thirty that evening. I gave her keys to the side gate, and for the padlock to the studio. I also gave her my spare back door key so that she could use the kitchen and loo. As we said goodnight by the front door, again she kissed me gently on the cheek. I watched her drive away, did the washing-up, and then fell asleep in front of the television. The *Match of the Day* theme tune woke me up but I went to bed.

I hardly saw her on Sunday. I took her a hot drink and a cheese sandwich but I left her to it; it was apparent she wished to do things alone. I told her an electrician mate of mine was coming round the following week to fit the lights, and she seemed thrilled with this. She said she would see him in and pay him and tell him where she would like them fixed. She seemed very, very happy. Late in the afternoon I looked down the garden to see the studio in complete darkness. I hadn't noticed her go and I was a little disappointed that she hadn't said goodbye. I had bought two frozen roast-beef dinners and had been hoping for a bit of company. I ate mine early that evening and left the other in my freezer for another time. I watched some uninspiring television and went to bed early.

During the following week I knew she had been coming and going whilst I was at work but it was Thursday evening before I actually saw her again; the lights were on down there when I got in from work. There was a tap at my back door and there she stood. She invited me down to see what she had been doing. She stepped back and watched me with a smile playing on her lips as I went in. It was a totally different place. Not my hut. It was a studio and a cosy space at the same time, and bright from the new strip lighting. There were easels standing to attention, there were tubes and jars of paint, and pots full of brushes covered a table made out of an old door on trestles. There were two large wicker armchairs filled with brightly coloured cushions. Against one wall was a stack of blank canvasses and in another corner a single divan bed with a black-and-white duvet in a bold geometric pattern. I stood just inside the door taking it all in. Then I noticed that the small table between the wicker chairs was laid with knives and forks opposite each other. She indicated that I should sit down, then pointed to the kitchen worktop I had fitted at the other end of the hut but had never used. There stood a kettle and matching toaster, a stainless-steel microwave oven and a small counter-top fridge. She went across and clicked the kettle on, then produced two brand-new mugs from a wall cupboard. "Ta dah!" she said as she put the tea in front of me with a small curtsy. She went back to the kitchen equipment, held up a container in each hand and grinned.

"We missed our Chinese on Saturday so tonight we are dining here. I just have to heat these in the microwave and dinner will be served shortly." A few minutes later she put two plates of steaming food on the little table.

"Do you like what I chose?" she asked as I stared at the plate. I guess I seemed a bit bewildered. I gazed around the former builders' hut and marvelled at the changes she had made to it in a few short days; she had transformed the place, and I suspected she had not finished yet.

This interesting young lady was now part of my life.

Chapter Fifteen

Daisy Glover put her phone down. She had phoned her grandfather a few times since she had returned home from California, but talked to him on Skype mostly. She had sent a few emails too when the time difference precluded phoning. He had finally relented. Daisy was confident that she really had got him to agree to a return visit to England. He had promised her. He would stay with her at her new house in Dorset and would be at the house-warming party that she planned for the springtime. No date was set but she was beginning to plan anyway. Bob, her driver, already knew about picking her grandfather up from Heathrow. She sighed, and hoped Nigel had not humoured her just to stop her pleas. She had come to know that despite his quiet, easy way he could be very stubborn too.

She noticed on the recent visit that he could be found watching the BBC World Service on television, and from this she surmised he still had an interest in his home country. When she confronted him with this when she walked in on him watching the BBC he had tried to dismiss it with a laugh. Yes, he did occasionally get curious as to what the UK was like these days but 'seeing it on television satisfied his curiosity adequately' he told her. On another day when trying to get a decision from him, pressing him why he had been so reluctant, so adamant about not returning, he had seemed to be on the brink of telling her something, but then stopped. This only added to the intrigue. She knew it was serious from his demeanour. There was a tone in his voice that she had never heard before. He almost whispered as he resisted her questions. She saw a distant look in his eye, a look that only a family member might register; it was fleeting, as though he was remembering something disturbing but then regaining control. She had held his hand at this point and she could see him soften and relax. She knew, somehow, that whatever it was, it involved her history too, and that he would tell her once he was in the UK.

The O2 concerts would mark the end of her UK tour. She would then have a week or two without too many commitments to make plans for his visit and her house party. She had made it very clear to Sam Jackson, and he had done the same to her agents: 'no bookings, no commitments'.

Daisy sat at the kitchen island unit and sipped coffee. The cleaners had gone, Saskia, her PA, had a few days off, and Joanne, her housekeeper, had gone home early nursing a cold. The last thing she wanted before a tour was a cold or the flu. She had some dance rehearsals and she was waiting for Bob to take her to the London studio for these. She had decided to stay up in London for a couple of days and then return to Dorset for some rest before the tour.

She was thinking about her mother and her grand-mother in the silence of the house. She wondered what it was she didn't know about her grandmother. What was so difficult for her grandfather to tell her? What was there to hide that could stop him returning to his country of birth? He had almost told her. He had stopped and left her more concerned than ever. Her own mother had been only seventeen years old when she was born. This thought sat in her mind for a while and she concluded that at least she had managed to avoid that family trait of producing a daughter. Her family history was sketchy to her still, but she would learn more during his visit; she was confident this would happen and was determined to get him to tell her as much of it as possible. She needed the truth, even the dark bits, if that was the case.

She knew, of course, that both her grandmother Joan and her own mother Cherry had taken their own lives, unless it really was Peter Davis who had administered the fatal dose to Joan. She had been devastated to learn this in her teens, but she hadn't known either of them. It was at this time that her personality had shown itself to be so much like that of her absent grandfather: she had cried but she had not wallowed in it. Despite his absence her grandfather had been a constant influence on her upbringing. His letters to her had encouraged insights beyond her age, his regular phone calls since she was tiny, his financial and personal organisation from afar had given her as stable a background as anybody could wish for. She hadn't ever considered that her way of life was unusual. She came to realise that other children who did have mums and dads didn't necessarily have idyllic childhoods. Hers may have been unconventional, but it was happy with the foster parents her granddad had found for her. She still loved them, and over the years they became more like friends than parents. She had never been lied to; she knew they looked after her for her grandfather. When her career had become established and his regular payments were no longer needed, he paid them off very generously and the house she had been brought up in had been given to a children's charity as a halfway house for families in crisis. Nigel was still in touch with that charity and made an annual gift for its upkeep and periodic gifts for music teachers to visit and inspire the children. This was all administered by the same lawyers Nigel had entrusted with his granddaughter's needs. Daisy now used them herself in her business dealings.

She had begun to wonder more and more how much Tony Smith knew of her history; she felt sure he probably knew quite a bit. It was funny how often her grandfather talked about him, but never in any real detail. He had told her why he had taken the stage name Smudger Smiff, and he even became sentimental when talking about him. She had noticed this a few times without attaching much significance to it. There was something more to all this than just old friends who had drifted apart.

Now she began wondering why they hadn't remained in contact, notwithstanding the distance and the very different paths in life they had taken. Was it the gulf in wealth? Was it that simple? Something had kept them apart. She had to know. She had to find out. He still talked about Tony Smith with affection. It didn't make sense.

Her grandfather had married her grandmother Joan when they were still both teenagers, she knew that. That was where she got her middle name of Joan from. She knew also that Joan had left Nigel and taken Cherry, her own mother, to live with Pete Davis, the singer of The Strikes. As far as Daisy knew, Cherry was only a toddler when this happened. How Nigel had handled that situation Daisy could not guess; his own wife and daughter living with a fellow band-member. The band had begun its ascendancy worldwide at that time and Daisy thought that maybe they were on tour so much that neither saw Joan and her baby. She had gleaned little bits here and there, as a lot of her family history had become public knowledge over the years. Her grandmother and mother were both often mentioned in documentaries about their different eras. She had seen some black-and-white footage of her grandfather's band on BBC's *The Old Grey Whistle Test*, and the presenter Bob Harris had even mentioned the tension between Rudy and Smudger, saying that it was a wonder they made such great music, given the personal complications. This had triggered her to google her grandparents and subsequently her own mother.

Google and Wikipedia knew so much about her family. Cherry seemed to have a history of appearing in gossip columns, mostly for the wrong reasons. Daisy found some parts very distressing. No mention of Tony Smith, apart from a reference in an early-nineties interview to Nigel Glover's name-change being to honour a friend. That was proof enough to Daisy that there was a strong, if mysterious, bond with Tony Smith. It existed for a specific reason, not just the nostalgic ones her grandfather had palmed her off with to date.

Cherry had repeated Joan's mistake by becoming pregnant in her teens and was, by all accounts, 'incapable of looking after herself, never mind her own child'.

During her short life, Daisy's mother could, at the height of her antics, have filled an entire tabloid newspaper all by herself. She was rarely out of the papers, often photographed drunkenly leaving a club.

The 'wild child' they generally called her. She had known for a long time that it was her father's money and influence that had brought her up.

Cherry Glover had such a peculiar background herself: Nigel and Joan had had Cherry, and Joan had left Nigel to live with Rudy before Cherry was two years old. Joan, known in the press as Jojo, and Rudy, shared a large country house in the New Forest with many others; people who called themselves artists, musicians or poets, people Rudy and Jojo had accumulated as friends, and some who had just latched onto them. The house was run as a commune though it was paid for through The Strikes. Rudy had been attracted to Joan during her pregnancy, so whilst Nigel was excited and inspired by becoming a new father, his young wife was working to regain her figure – not for him, but to rekindle the interest Rudy had shown. Their first LSD trip together sealed the union before Cherry was a year old.

Nigel had always been keen that the circle of self-destruction of her mother and grandmother would not be closed by Daisy; the nannies he employed for Daisy's day-to-day care were very thoroughly vetted. They were in constant contact with California and their employer. They would send photos and videos of the growing Daisy. She had seen his collection on most visits to him; he would get them out at any opportunity.

Daisy was sixteen years old when Cherry died and she was still ashamed of how little she felt and how little she had grieved for her mother. It was as though an acquaintance had passed from her life. The sadness she had felt and the tears she had shed were more about regret, not the strong feelings of the loss of a mother.

She remembered the house they shared and she knew the house had been paid for by her grandfather. She had seen the grief behind his glistening eyes whenever they talked of her mother, his daughter.

She had begun to quiz her grandfather more and more during visits to California. Her own father was another mystery to her; her birth certificate showed no father's name and up until now her grandfather had told her nothing. Perhaps he didn't know. He would say little and her questions always brought a brooding silence. They would finish with a hug that would tell her that Nigel could say no more. On one occasion he had alluded to his guilt, asking if his money had allowed Cherry to indulge in the too-easy lifestyle that had ultimately killed her. She was gone before her daughter's success, and had contributed little to Daisy's character, which was so different from her own. Daisy felt confident that the time was nearing when she would get answers about her mother, her grandmother, and maybe her father.

Chapter Sixteen

The sky was a cloudless blue, the temperature around twenty-five degrees. Nigel had had a restless night and was pouring another cup of coffee at his kitchen counter, stirring absent-mindedly. He gazed out of the window across his backyard, beyond his pool and beyond the scrub to the hills of Agoura that appeared to be blue from this distance. He put the spoon down on the counter; a soft clink of metal in the silence. He was thinking about Daisy's repeated requests for him to visit the United Kingdom, requests that were lately becoming entreaties. How could he explain to his beloved granddaughter? Well aware that he owed her more honesty, and that he should visit the country he no longer knew, the country he had chosen to leave and never return to.

"My house will never be warm till I know you've slept in it, Grandfather," she had said a few nights ago on the telephone, a phrase she had repeated in two emails since. He allowed himself a smile at the calculated pressure of this latest tactic she was using. The clear February sky of California from his window was broken only by the vapour trails from jets that were already out of sight. A similar jet might soon take him back to the cloudy skies of England and his family, his only family. His coffee was nearly cold.

Tears filled Nigel Glover's eyes as he watched his father drive away. The Ford Zodiac turned at the end of the road and was lost from view. The empty feeling in the pit of his stomach was overwhelming. His chest ached as if it might cave in and his whole body trembled as though in shock. His eyes burned. He sniffed into a cotton handkerchief his father had handed him only minutes before. It smelt of his stepmother, and the tears flowed faster. Ronald Glover had driven his only son Nigel across the Downs on that bright September afternoon. His school trunk had been unloaded and two older boys had been called to the headmaster's study to take Nigel and his trunk full of new clothing, new games kit and the few reminders of home up to the dormitory. The boys joked and laughed between themselves about things Nigel knew nothing of. "This way," they occasionally turned to say as he tried to keep up with them. They led him through gloomy corridors and up a small, creaking, wooden staircase; the dark-brown, varnished staircase that he would soon learn to dread.

The dormitory was in an eaves room. Black iron bedsteads with striped mattresses stood either side; eight one side, eight the other, Nigel counted. A corner was sectioned off at the far end and one bed was just visible behind the partition. This was the prefect's own separate bedroom, he would learn: another place to dread. On each bed there was a neat pile of sheets, a pillow of striped ticking, several rough, grey woollen blankets with red over-stitching on their edges, and a single blue cover.

The boys put his trunk under the farthest bed. One of them, a pale lad with freckles and ginger hair, beckoned Nigel nearer.

"This is your bed," he said.

They then left him standing there. He stared at his surroundings. A shaft of autumn sunlight from a high dormer window highlighted dust motes in the air and illuminated a small area of scrubbed, bare wooden floorboards. Nigel heard the boys thunder back down the stairs, then silence. He stood beside his bed and looked around, confused and desolate. The room was gloomy as the late sun dropped away from the high windows and it seemed to become colder despite that it was still a fine, warm autumn day outside. He pictured his bedroom at home and the view from his window there, and emptiness engulfed him.

Then his father had appeared at the door down the other end of the dormitory; he looked uneasy as he called Nigel to him. They went down another larger set of stairs, passing other boys in the corridors as they returned to the headmaster's study. The Reverend Eric Hales held his hand out towards Nigel, and Nigel's dad motioned with his head to indicate to his son to take the offered hand. Nigel shook the man's hand. It felt large and fleshy and soft, a bit like a beef joint he had put into a baking tin whilst helping in the kitchen one Sunday. His stomach fluttered and saliva filled his throat.

"Welcome to King Harold's School." The Reverend Hales smiled weakly as he spoke, the small, dark eyes in his pink, fleshy face darting between Nigel and his father.

"Your father tells me you have been looking forward to being a boarder at our school," he said, looking at Nigel's father, not at Nigel. Nigel noticed this. His father and the Reverend Hales held each other's gaze for a moment and then they both looked down at Nigel at the same time.

"What do you say, Nigel, my boy?"

Nigel had never heard his father say 'my boy' before and wondered why he was saying it now. For a few seconds his mind spun on the words.

"Thank you," Nigel finally whispered. "Thank you, sir."

He didn't know what he was supposed to say. For a few moments the teacher and his father said nothing and the silence stretched. Nigel looked from one to the other, his look resting on his father in the end. The headmaster broke the silence.

"I understand you like music, Nigel." He said it like a statement so Nigel didn't speak. He then went on about how the school tried to encourage boys in their likes whether it was academic, sports, arts or music.

Outside again, by a gateway, his father shuffled on the spot. Finally he put a hand on Nigel's shoulder and with the other shook his son's hand.

"Goodbye, Nigel. Work hard," he said. Then he got into his car and drove away. Nigel watched the car till it went out of sight.

Nigel poured fresh coffee into his cup and remembered the awkward, silent moments with his father as they were driving to the school, and recalled how uneasy his father had seemed at the meeting with the headmaster, and he felt a brief reminder of that bleak sensation in the gut.

Other boys were getting out of cars and taxis, their mothers dabbing eyes. Boys carrying cabin trunks and tuck boxes; boys and men shaking hands. Nigel stood and watched the activity, the pain in his chest and bewilderment almost overwhelming. He was still rooted to the same spot in the school car park when the commotion seemed to finally cease and he found himself on his own, unsure of what to do next. That was when Anthony Smith made him jump.

"You're new, eh?" he said. Nigel nodded. Tony Smith was a year older and about to embark on his second year at King Harold's. He asked his name and told him his.

"Don't worry," Tony reassured him. "I know how you feel."

Nigel didn't believe that the other boy could possibly understand the misery and sense of abandonment that he was feeling at that moment. He was yet to find out how much reassurance this other boy, Tony Smith, would be offering in the following twelve months and for many years beyond those first school terms.

"I'll show you the way. We have a meal first and then we will have to go to the dormitory to sort our clothes out and make our beds," Tony said. "Then when the term gets going it will be 'prep' in the evening."

'Prep' turned out to be short for 'preparation'. Day-boys called it homework, but it couldn't be 'homework' to boarders.

Thousands of miles away from King Harold's and so many years later, as he nursed a fresh coffee in his beautiful house, Nigel could still recall the misery of that first year at school. He would watch the day-boys going off after school, and always the same empty feeling as they went out of sight; home to a safe house and a dinner prepared by a loving mother.

Then there was the fagging. Fagging usually means being the servant of an older boy, always at his beck and call. At King Harold's it consisted of cleaning three locations: the library and the corridor leading to it, the locker room – a room with sixty or more lockers, one for each boarder, a place where even muddy football boots were cleaned – and the prefects' study and the corridor to that room. The first-year boys would keep all these immaculately clean on a three-week rota. Keeping the library tidy was manageable, but the other two were an absolute nightmare: the smallest missed piece of paper or mud would nearly always bring a beating. It was humiliating to be standing later in the evening in pyjamas outside the prefects' study waiting for a beating. Sometimes, in colder months when they were allowed an open coal fire in their room, they would roast your backside first in front of the fire and then whack you several times. It hurt more.

This was life at King Harold's: constant fear of attack by older boys, of prefects and their gym shoe, of teachers and their canes – terror twenty-four hours a day and constant humiliation.

But then there was Tony Smith. This other boy, who was good at sports and popular with most, had no need to stand up for Nigel, but Smudger, as most of other boys called him, came to his rescue many, many times. Their friendship grew throughout the following years but that first year of hell might not have been survived without Tony. Nigel had been slightly smaller than most other boys of his age so was an easy target for bullying. There had been times when he had contemplated ending his own life.

His mother had died giving birth to him. He kept a few black-and-white photos of her. Even he could see as he reached adulthood that he had got his looks from his mother and not his father; the slightly olive skin and the flat dark curls tight to his head. He had always considered that his mother looked quite exotic and beautiful in these photos. He had shown them to Daisy and they both assumed it was her eye colour they both shared.

Nigel had sensed some years ago that his father, who had soon remarried, had always, maybe subconsciously, blamed him for his wife's death, and so was distant towards him; as if he resented the baby who lived. He could have loved and respected him more if they had both known and understood this before his father died. They didn't fight or row, they just treated each other with indifference, Nigel receiving neither praise nor encouragement from his father for the music that was so natural in him. His father had died just before his stepmother some years ago, after he had moved to America and after a lot of his successes. Neither ever visited him, though he had asked them many times, and neither did he attend their funerals. His English lawyers sorted everything out and the proceeds of the sale of the family house in Bournemouth went to his children's charity anonymously.

Nigel's father had inherited a small insurance brokering business that his own father had started. He was quite handsome in a way but to his chief clerk Elizabeth he was a very good catch. The sympathy and help she offered when his young wife had died in childbirth were rewarded with a wedding ring and a large house in a nice district of town. The baby boy to look after was the only condition, but Nigel proved easy to deal with. His love of learning to play various musical instruments kept him happy and money for tuition or to buy instruments was not a problem. Ronald had agreed readily that a minor boarding school would suit him when the time came. Elizabeth had suggested it, saying it would 'toughen him up'. She arranged for extra tuition to make sure he passed the eleven-plus examination and could get into King Harold's, a school she had decided was 'affordable'; he did pass. His father was genuinely proud of him for this and looked forward to him getting a good education in readiness to take over the brokerage in due course. So King Harold's was arranged.

The phone rang and interrupted Nigel's memories. It was an associate of his, a fellow musician he had been working on a project with. They discussed the next session, which was set for a few days' time, and said goodbye.

Money was no real problem; royalties flowed to Nigel in a constant stream. He composed at least one film score per year and still played as a session man whenever he was asked. The years of accumulated work only brought him more and more money. His accountants and lawyers looked after him well. He had so much more than enough for his modest way of life and he knew that there was plenty invested on his behalf; he always paid his taxes on time. Daisy had been self-sufficient for a while. He was probably worth hundreds of millions of dollars.

Nigel enjoyed playing acoustic guitar in the background in the Cantina Rosa when asked and he often sat in with bands jamming at the Wood Ranch BBQ. He sometimes played one or two old Strikes hits. He supported Agoura festivals in any way he could and some local charities had benefited from his donations. He encouraged local bands by allowing them to use his studio and he would enjoy lending his expertise in mixing or just giving general advice on recording techniques.

Agoura Hills suited him well; it had around twenty thousand residents, low unemployment and a relatively low crime rate. The music scene had become really varied and interesting, with Battle of The Bands competitions the highlights. Nigel had become very involved with this effort to help kids through music. The Canyon Club put on live music, and national performers appeared there. Linkin Park would probably be the best-known band from Agoura but it had produced some other exciting bands too.

Before Nigel was born, never mind lived in Agoura Hills, it had been known as Picture City. Back in the 1920s most of the area was used by Paramount Pictures for westerns. Nigel absolutely loved this part of its history. It had been perfect country for filming around the Simi Hills and the Santa Monica Mountains. He would often spend time at the library researching this history or chatting about it with his buddy WT Allen – Tom to his friends – down at the library.

However, recently he had spent hours and hours engrossed in his studio using his ability to play a variety of instruments to record what had become a very lengthy piece of music. Last year he had released four instrumental tracks from it, just to 'test the water', and they had proved hugely popular worldwide; much to his surprise and pleasure. He had even mastered the tracks himself; just to keep the whole project 'in-house'. At one time he considered asking Daisy to add some vocals but had now decided not to use her. They had talked about it on her recent visit. Nigel had thought she might be offended if he didn't ask but Daisy hadn't wanted to do it anyway.

He recently believed that he might have found exactly what he was looking for. Could Ashley sing? He now hoped she could. He liked the tone of her spoken voice; it had a husky, smoky, lilting timbre to it that might come through in her singing voice, and in any case some spoken-word parts were needed even if it turned out she couldn't sing. It would also suit his idea that new voices, unknown voices would be better. She might bring a new, naive freshness, untainted by any show-business past. He knew she liked country music too and some of his 'opus', as he began to think of it, had country-music influences. He had brought the 'Twenty-First Century Project', his opus, about as far as he could on his own now, and was anxious to introduce the other elements of his plan. Up until now very few others had contributed, and those that had were all friends of his from the past, some of whom were very glad that the four tracks already released would be bringing them cash. Nigel was very generous with his terms.

He had thoroughly enjoyed the creative process of this project and only now had begun to explain more to close friends or even Daisy. She had been trying to get him to send her more of the opus. She told him that she had played the four tracks to Lisa, Dave, and Tony Smith and that they had all liked them a lot. So far he had refused to send more. A few extra sessions, and his parts would be complete, apart from mixing. He had promised Daisy that she would be first to hear it in its entirety. At present it was ten hours long. He had done a great deal of editing – working and reworking whole sections in an attempt to reduce it to two-and-a-half hours maximum, but it had proved harder than he had expected.

It came to him now though. Why reduce it? It could be 'Beginning, Middle and End'. Nigel decided there and then. "Beginning. Middle. End," he repeated to himself as he made yet more coffee, still repeating the three words. He thought of the old acronym in most endeavours of life: KISS (keep it simple stupid).

Nigel's fame cut no ice with his neighbours when he first moved to the area. For quite a while they were suspicious, fearing him and the reputation that Pete Davis had brought to the band, but they soon came to like him, in spite of his fame, not because of it; the quiet, unassuming Englishman was now a popular member of the community. His fame as a rock musician seemed brief compared with many who still performed but it still brought him civic invitations despite The Strikes not having existed for over thirty years. He rarely turned down a request for musical help from a school or a young band, and had noticed in recent months that these requests had increased. He guessed that this was because an article in *The Acorn*, the local newspaper, had mentioned the fact that Daisy Belle Bliss was his granddaughter.

He was very content in Agoura.

Chapter Seventeen

We were now busy working on a restaurant in town, having all but finished at Daisy's. There were still a couple of rooms she had not made up her mind about, but we would be back when she was ready. I was finishing an early-morning cup of tea and gazing down my garden towards the studio; I was beginning to naturally think of and refer to it as 'the studio'. I hadn't seen Charlotte coming or going for a while and I hadn't seen any lights on during recent evenings. I didn't think she had been there at all during the day when I was at work either. I knew she had a commission in Oxfordshire, near Henley-on-Thames, and another booked for somewhere in north London; perhaps she was doing one of those. I was not enjoying the work at the restaurant. As usual with that sort of job it was rush, rush, rush and all different trades in each other's way.

In a trough of gloom I closed the front door. I trudged up to the corner of my road for Lisa to collect me. It was drizzling, and dark clouds scudded overhead as I saw the van coming. My mood was just as dark. For this job she would have picked Dave up first, so he would be chirping away about his sex life, or, if we were lucky, Arsenal, or some other football story. Lisa looked across him and our eyes met as I climbed into the van next to Dave. He talked all the way across town. It didn't lift my mood.

"Come on, you miserable ol' bugger! Get out of the van and let's have a smoke."

I got out and Dave slid out after me.

"You've got the miseries this morning," he said with a grin. "Get your fags out. I ran out of tobacco last night."

I didn't have the strength to comment or argue; I just offered him the open packet. He looked at it as if it might have been poisoned.

"Bloody not as good as roll-ups." He blew the smoke from his first drag in my face, a habit of his that amused him more than it did me. There were vans and cars everywhere. A plumber's van had pulled in behind us, and it was now too tight for us to open the back doors of our van, so Dave had gone off to find the plumber so that we could get our kit out.

Lisa raised her eyebrows in resignation and I had lit another cigarette, as if that might magically help my humour. It didn't.

"You OK, Tony?" Lisa had asked me, but she hadn't waited for an answer. She'd gone in the back door of the restaurant, emerging a few minutes later with Dave and the plumber in tow. The plumber got in his van with no word of apology and pulled back a couple of feet. I tried the doors and could open them, so I gave the driver a thumbs-up, whereupon he scowled at me as if I was the one at fault. He had reversed into an old Peugeot 206, denting the driver's door.

"You fucking idiot!" he screamed. "Now see what you've made me do!"

I stood a few inches from his young face and asked him to repeat what he had just said. His face was colouring red from the neck up and he made an unintelligible noise.

"I suggest you go in and find the owner of the car," I said. "And be very careful not to speak to me like that again." At this point Dave appeared beside me and fixed the plumber with a stare. The plumber clenched and unclenched his fists, made another incoherent sound, then turned and went back into the building. Dave looked at me and smiled.

"You wouldn't have backed down, would you?"

He grinned and landed a hand on my shoulder. "Fair play," he said, in a tone of voice I took to denote respect. I didn't answer Dave, but no, I would not have. I now had to have another smoke. We went in then.

It was pandemonium in there with drilling, banging, sawing, shouting, bantering, and Radio One pulsing at high volume from an unseen corner. My head span. The cacophony filled my ears, my body felt heavy and sluggish, my shoulders slumped. I went through into the seating area. I had wallpaper to hang behind and around the bar area that particular morning and my mood would not help. There were enough distractions as it was, and I like to hang wallpaper in peace and quiet. I rubbed my temples with my fingertips and willed myself to ignore, to shut out, as much as possible. The day went slowly. I found myself slipping out of the building more often than I usually would to gulp fresh, cold air and have a cigarette. My clouds didn't lift, however.

The long rear wall was to have a mural of a skyscraper cityscape. Each unique section of it was numbered so that the mural could be assembled in the right order, and there could be no second chance if you made a bad cut or trim. I finished the other wall-covering and found Lisa. I told her I wanted to put off doing the mural until nearer the handover date, so that I could put it up in peace when most of the other blokes had gone.

"If we do it now it might get damaged before the handover," I added. I think she knew I was not myself even before the incident with the plumber. She listened to me burble away. I could feel some of the tension leave my body as she spoke.

"Tony, it's none of my business, but what is wrong with you today? My guess is that it's personal. It's Friday, so why don't you finish early. Better than that, I'll find Dave and we'll all finish now, then I can drive you home, OK?"

I nodded. I could feel tears prick my eyes as she said this. It was sheer relief. I was so grateful to this young woman that I wanted to step forward and hug her, employer or not. *I wanted to hug her, as I should be able to hug my daughters.* She smiled and put a hand gently on my arm, and then helped me pack up my tools. She put away the paint she'd been using and we went out to the van.

I stood beside the van and Lisa told me not to worry.

"It will still be there next week." She put a hand on my arm again, a small gesture that expressed so much reassurance. I felt a bit silly. The urge to hug her simply for understanding welled in me again but I just touched her shoulder and thanked her.

She dropped Dave off first. I could feel her glance every so often as we drove across town. Even Dave couldn't resist a comment when he got out of the van. He stood on the pavement at the open van door and told me to cheer up. "It's Friday. We're going home early and Arsenal are playing Spurs tomorrow." He slammed the door and waved as he walked away. I smiled thinly as we pulled away from the kerb and exchanged a warmer smile with Lisa. I scolded myself for my lack of control as she changed up through the gears.

"I don't know what's eating you, Tony, but I'll listen if you want me to."

This was such a nice thing to say but I didn't know how to answer. That's how it came about that Lisa followed me into my kitchen.

Lisa and I rarely chatted about personal stuff. Whenever her mother was ill she would tell me, and she occasionally asked me about my daughters. She had told me about a miserable holiday she took a couple of years ago with a boyfriend she dumped as soon as they got home, bits and pieces about Emma and her wealthy parents, and a few stories about her own family. It was surprising how little I knew about her. Equally, I assumed, she wouldn't know much about me. We would chat about television or news items or exchange anecdotes about jobs, or people we had worked with, but we never revealed much about ourselves.

I liked the young woman a lot, though. I liked her contained and composed ways. I liked her ambition within her chosen business. I enjoyed the fact that a young woman could thrive in what is still the very male-dominated world of building trades. I admired the way she would put down cheeky blokes, and how, if the language became too crude around her, she would approach the culprit and calmly say: I don't wish to listen to that sort of language. In future show some respect.

I told her to sit down whilst I made some tea. She asked for coffee instead. She had been in my house before but not very often, so she was looking around.

I put a coffee mug in front of her on the table along with the sugar bowl I had started using. I sat down heavily opposite her and sighed. I apologised again and she dismissed my mutterings with a wave of her hand. The kitchen went quiet. I wasn't sure what to say and she was just sipping coffee, peering over her mug at me. I felt a bit self-conscious, as I had done at times with Charlotte. She broke our silence.

"Tony, if you don't want to tell me what's the matter, it's no problem. As I said before, it's none of my business and I don't wish to pry, but we've known each other for quite a while now and I know something is bothering you." She put a hand across the table on mine. "And if I can help, I will."

It seemed a kind and genuine offer. I cleared my throat and began. She listened without interrupting. It helped to tell someone. I admitted I was lonely. She looked pained when I related my history with my ex-wife and my daughters. I told her some of my older history: being sent away to boarding school; about my mother's illness – but not the final chapter of that story. *I would probably never tell anybody that part.* I could see her wanting to reach out but fearing it might stop my flow. I explained how working at Daisy's house had seemed to trigger dark memories for me. I even promised to tell her the full story one day of my history with Daisy's grandfather; *though I doubted I would.* Her eyebrows raised somewhat when I told her about the hut in my garden and how it had become Charlotte's studio. She was probably surprised that I was only telling her now when it had happened some weeks ago.

"Ah, that was when she asked me for your address…" she began, but trailed off.

Finally I looked at my watch and stopped talking. Over another drink I apologised for keeping her so long and thanked her for listening to my ramblings. I only just contained my urge to hug her. I think she could tell.

She told me that she and Dave could handle everything left to do at the restaurant except the mural and that there was still time to put that up the following week before the handover date. This time I did take her hand. She jumped slightly but left her hand in mine.

"Thank you," I said.

When she'd gone the kitchen seemed emptier than ever. I was hungry but didn't want to eat. I smoked two cigarettes one after the other at my back door. The shed was a just a black rectangle down the garden. I realised it had helped to talk and I really wanted to tell more, either to Lisa or to somebody else.

I did feel better in the morning, and far better still after a shave and a long shower, but I was still going over what seemed now to have been a very strange evening of revelations to Lisa. I had an unopened pack of bacon in my fridge and I put it all in my frying pan. The smell of it made my mouth water in anticipation as I drank tea and smoked to stay patient. The morning was dreary and grey; I guessed the temperature outside was not much above freezing. The prospect of days off made me realise how tired I had become lately, and the thought of doing nothing felt luxurious. I turned the bacon and reached for two eggs from the rack. As I took them it occurred to me that Jenny, my ex-wife, had bought the rack, and this made my spirits fall once more. I snapped the radio on to derail this train of thought. I soon sat up and took notice when the announcer mentioned Daisy Belle Bliss and Nigel

Glover, and I listened attentively as I watched the eggs cook in the bacon fat. It seemed that Daisy's grandfather was planning to visit England for the first time since the mid-1970s. They told how he had lived in the Los Angeles area of California for so many years and how he hadn't even returned for his second wife's funeral. The report ended and I wondered what I might have missed before I put the radio on. The eggs were done. I sat down to eat, my mind racing. Why was he coming to the UK now? After all these years, why now? What would he look like? Would I get to meet him? At Daisy's party – of course! Would he recognise me? Would I recognise him? Would we get on? We had nothing in common now. The last day I saw him in 1975 he swore he would never return. We shook hands with a last forced joke of 'Goodbye, Smudger' and 'Goodbye, Smiffy'. I watched him go through to Departures at Heathrow with a one-way ticket to Los Angeles in his hand. He turned and waved; I waved back, not believing that I would never see him again. I remembered the heavy sadness I felt as he disappeared. I had stood for some minutes with an ache in my throat and my eyes burning, watching the place where he had gone out of sight. Parts of our history were swirling though my head.

We had been friends since the age of eleven or twelve. He'd married his pregnant teenage bride in a register-office wedding at only nineteen and I was his best man. I was almost the only man, in fact. Joan had three girlfriends with her, but neither set of parents turned up for the ceremony, so it wasn't much of an occasion. We all went to a Berni Inn called The Duke of York on the edge of town. The bride's parents turned up there.

I thought that was going to start trouble, but not a bit of it; her dad drank a few pints of bitter and her mum downed a few port and lemons, then cried and apologised for not having been there. It was very strange. 1968, and the sixties were in full swing... somewhere! I managed to get Nigel and Joan out of the Berni and across the road to the railway station and we all waved them off to Torquay. Nigel told me a few weeks later what utter misery it had been in a dull bed-and-breakfast with a shared bathroom and toilet along a landing. Joan had moaned about everything from the bed to the breakfast. He loved her just the same, he assured me. I believed him, but even as a youth myself I sensed that theirs was a doomed relationship. I knew he would try his utmost to make it work though; believing it to be the beginning of a happy family.

The trouble was she couldn't see beyond him on stage with a guitar in a group. He just saw an attractive girl paying him attention. How easily they fooled one another!

It didn't surprise me later, when The Strikes had begun to make it, that she left him.

By then they had had two big hit singles from their first best-selling album, and the second album was selling very fast. They supported Led Zeppelin, Ten Years After, Fleetwood Mac and others at the last jazz and blues festival in Bath, and had stolen the show on the Saturday night at the first Reading Festival in 1971.

They toured much of Europe, followed by Australia, Japan and the USA. Their second US tour had smashed even some Beatles concert-attendance records. Nigel's wife was with the band's singer on some of these earlier tours, though not all the time. Sometimes she would have been at Pete's 'commune' near Ringwood with baby Cherry to look after, although she had already handed most of Cherry's care to whoever happened to be at the house at any given moment, and there were always plenty of them. I would read about the band's exploits in the press or catch something on the television or radio news and I would wonder about the shy boy I knew from King Harold's School; my friend, whom others had tormented. How was he coping with it all?

The *News of the World* had had a field day with Joan, or Jojo, as she had started to style herself since leaving Smudger Smiff. But I knew he could cope. He would switch off. His purpose was to make music. When a female interviewer asked him about his relations with Rudy and Jojo she could not believe the indifference with which Nigel answered her. She repeated her questions as provocatively as she dared but still he refused to be drawn. "I make music. If my wife chooses to love another what have I lost? I don't own her."

Sometimes he would ring me out of the blue to arrange to meet when he had managed to find time to visit his home town. We still got on well; it was always easy to pick up where we'd left off. He dressed more flamboyantly, though, and we sometimes had to be careful where we went for a drink or a meal. People would approach all the time – girls mostly, but just as often it would be boys and men; The Strikes' music was a bit more sophisticated than a lot of pop music. Of course the reflected glory I basked in did me no harm at all in the eyes of the local girls. In fact Jenny had come up to me in a pub to ask me how I knew Smudger Smiff of The Strikes; that was how we met.

The downside of these meetings with Nigel would be me sometimes questioning why I was a painter and decorator. Then Nigel would say: 'I make things sound better – you make things *look* better!' I was still ambitious then and was earning quite well, so I would agree with him. We would laugh and then the conversation would move on.

I had a couple of office jobs after school but really could not settle. I needed a change in my life. One day in the spring after I had lost my parents I walked onto a building site and asked for the foreman. That was how I met Bill Bowes. He was a friendly bloke in his forties, and I liked his Yorkshire accent. He told me I could start as a 'brush hand' the following Monday.

The money was more than I earned in the office and I loved the job immediately: the feeling of freedom, the jokes, and the easy-going characters I met. Like Billy Murphy, the short, plump digger-driver who knew more jokes than I knew people, and Samuel and Benjamin, two West Indians who were terrible painters but lovely, generous-natured people who sparked my love of bluebeat, ska, and then reggae. I loved Ben's tea made with CDM, condensed milk. I still couldn't say 'CDM' without trying in his accent. I could still hear his chuckle. *He's probably passed away by now*.

In our teenage years when Nigel was in and out of different local groups *(they were called 'groups' in the sixties; 'bands' played in dance halls)*, I would hire church or village halls and book local groups to play. It was a way of making sure Nigel or whichever group he was with at the time got bookings. It allowed him to rehearse, and if I made any profit I would share it with him. He would sometimes say that I had helped him through the horror of King Harold's and now I was trying to help him launch his music career, but really I played no part in his success. He had real talent, a fact I recognised when he was just twelve years old.

Chapter Eighteen

One September, at the beginning of the school year, we were told that every boarder would have to perform 'something' at an end-of-term concert before we broke up for the Christmas holidays. It was my fourth year and Nigel's third, I think, so I was fifteen and he would have been fourteen. He was dabbling with the school orchestra by that time and was beginning to get a name for himself for his musical ability. Some of his erstwhile tormentors left him alone because of it but others, perhaps jealous of his talent, increased the intimidation and harassment. I still fought his corner when it happened, and won more often than not.

I had no particular talent and was at a loss as to what I would be able to do, but we were told later that term that the winner's prize would be to go home three days early for the holidays, so we thought a bit harder and decided that I would recite 'If' and Nigel would compose and play some atmospheric background music to accompany me. He was already quite proficient on a few instruments at that time but we decided he would play the cello.

On the big day we had asked for the curtains to be drawn and the lights to be off as we set up. In case I forgot the words I had the poem on a lectern, illuminated by a torch. In the darkness it created a soft glow around the stand and on my face, and Nigel had another torch positioned to shine up at the cello: one down, one up. We had tested the effect, and it was simple but effective, we believed. Nigel began the introduction; the chattering stopped and the school hall hushed. I recited the opening lines: "*If you can keep your head when all about you/ Are losing theirs and blaming it on you*", and the cello wove a bare, mournful sound between my words until the final "*you'll be a Man, my son!*" I knew we would win as soon as we finished. The hall was silent for some seconds before it erupted into cheers and foot-stamping. We travelled home together. Nigel's dad picked us up from the station and moaned all the way till he dropped me off at my house. I had to wait for hours in my next-door neighbour's house till my dad got home from work.

I still love the melancholy sound of a cello.

My father was a nice man – everybody said so. He was a quiet man too, but perhaps, in hindsight, weak. He worked in a local department store. My mother, however, couldn't cope with life. It started with what we thought were tantrums. She would argue or be difficult with my dad. Why was he late home from work? (He was home at his usual time.) Why did he get brown bread when he knew she liked white? (She had asked him for wholemeal.) Sometimes he would look at me to back him up but I was maybe only seven or eight. I learned to stay out of her way as much as possible.

One day I had been round a friend's house watching their new television set. When I got home, blood was pouring from a tea cloth wrapped around Mum's arm; she had smashed her hand through a frosted glass panel in our back door and the kitchen floor was awash with blood. I ran next door to get help. Mrs Cuthbert, the neighbour, tried to calm her down. Mum was screaming, laughing and making gurgling noises. Mrs Cuthbert ran down the road to the call-box and phoned for an ambulance, then rang his work for my dad.

It would take more than half an hour to get home on the bus so he told Mrs Cuthbert that he would go straight to the hospital. I thought it was an accident or maybe my dad told me that it was – I don't remember. But I do remember her laughing and I knew by then that people didn't laugh if they had injured themselves in an accident. Mrs Cuthbert had fetched a towel as the tea cloth filled with blood. I was crying in the back garden when the ambulance arrived. Sometimes, still, I recall that day if I hear somebody laughing in a certain way, or even when I smell fish, because Mrs Cuthbert's house always smelt of the fish she boiled up for her cats. She told me to wait in their house and gave me some orange squash.

My mother came home from hospital about a week later. Then the incidents started to become more frequent. There was no telling what I might come home to from school. Sometimes she would be fine; she had made a sponge cake or rock cakes or scones and would be happy and normal. Another day she would shriek at me or Dad that she hated us and wanted us to die. We never knew what to expect. The neighbours tried to keep out of the way; they too had suffered from her words or deeds. My dad used to go round and apologise. He seemed to shrivel. He would go to work whatever happened. Glad to be out of the house for a while, I assume. She was banned from the shop on the corner of our road and so were me and my dad but we never did find out why. Then she became more dangerous.

I would cry at school occasionally and the teacher would ask me why. I couldn't help it. That was how the school came to know about us and why I ended up going to a boarding school. The headmaster talked to my dad and then they knew I was telling the truth.

I'm not sure if I was eight, nine or ten when it was getting much worse. I was hanging around outside the school gates when everybody had gone home. I didn't want to go home. Mrs Hawkins, a teacher at the school, came out and asked me what I was doing. I couldn't speak. I burst into tears. She softened immediately and asked me what the matter was.

"My mum is mad," I sobbed.

Chapter Nineteen

Lisa and Dave had battled through the painting at the restaurant. Most other trades had finished. The wall tiler on his own in the kitchen, grouting, seemed to be the only other person there that Monday morning when the three of us pulled up. I had had the whole of the previous week off, and had been half expecting a call asking me to go in at the end of the week to hang the mural, but it didn't come until the Saturday morning. Lisa told me what they had done during the week and said it would be good if I came back on the Monday.

I was beginning to feel Charlotte might have abandoned my garden. I had been down there having a good look round it on my own. Several canvasses were leaning against the wall but the two easels stood empty. They seemed to spell AA, and I hoped it was not a sign, and that drink or drugs were not the reason for her absence. I had mixed feelings as I gazed around at her things. Had she abandoned it? Had I done the right thing? What would I do if she didn't come back? It was cold in the hut... so I put the electric radiators on. I went back up to the house and returned with a cup of coffee and another packet of cigarettes and sat on the chaise longue she had brought in. I leant back and closed my eyes. I could smell her. I could smell her on the seat over the mixed aroma of thinners, white spirit and paints as I leant back. I had noticed how she smelt of soap and flowers and thinners – a funny mix – not unpleasant at all, but distinctly her. I smoked a cigarette and finished the coffee, glanced round again then turned the radiators off, switched the lights off and padlocked the door. Sunday was nearly over, my week off was nearly over and it was back to work tomorrow. I put the television on and managed to watch a whole episode of a period drama before going to bed.

Monday morning and the restaurant was quiet, thank goodness. The tiler in the kitchen had BBC Radio 2 on and the only other sound was Dave whistling tunelessly along. Lisa was busily checking her snag list, making sure they hadn't missed anything. She asked me if I wanted a hand. I was about to say no but when I looked over at her I sensed that it was not a question.

"I'd like to help or at least watch you," she said. "I'd really like to learn."

I was very happy with this. It always gave me pleasure to see how interested she was. "OK, you watch; I'll describe what I'm doing and why."

I got her to measure bits for me and I showed her how to trim neatly around obstacles as we encountered them: switches, power points, and an extractor fan. It was a long wall with one step in it towards the front window of the restaurant. This allowed me to show her how to go round an external and an internal corner.

"You OK?" Lisa whispered as we stopped just before our lunch break.

"I am. And thank you for listening to an old man last week – it really helped."

She smiled and stepped back a couple of paces to inspect the effect of the mural so far.

"Wow, it looks great." She tipped her head slightly sideways as she spoke.

I went and stood beside her. "Yes it does, doesn't it? Good effect."

I asked her where we were working for the rest of the week. We would be completely finished by the end of the day. Dave was touching up marks people had made on things we had finished. The three of us had some lunch and the tiler joined us. He had finished his last few 'bits and pieces', he told us. A chef turned up during the afternoon inspecting his brand new kitchen. Lisa and I finished the last few lengths of the mural by mid-afternoon. She'd told me that we were back at Daisy's house for the couple of rooms that we hadn't touched and that she might change one or two other areas. I hoped not.

We had a chat to the chef; the grand opening was on the coming Friday evening. He told us it was a sell-out. He gave Lisa a complimentary invitation for two. She seemed very pleased with that. I had noticed the chef taking an interest in her all afternoon. I also thought I detected that the interest was mutual.

It was time to go. I was tired but my first day back had been good. I teased Lisa about the chef and she coloured a bit, two pink spots appearing on her cheeks. Dave had been unaware of the situation and I began to be sorry I had said anything before he got out of the van. Lisa took his questions and teasing well, though. It was not until Dave had shut the door when we dropped him off that she told me she had made a date with the chef for the following week. The time was not fixed, though, for Glen, the young chef, did not know the new roster for the restaurant yet. The pink spots were still on her cheeks and she raised her eyebrows.

"We exchanged mobile numbers," she said, "and I'll see him on Friday if he can get out of the kitchen. I've never dated a chef before."

She told me that she was going with her mum and that she hoped that wouldn't frighten Glen off. She didn't often talk about her personal life and I couldn't recall whether I had ever met her mother. I knew her dad had cleared off some years ago and that she lived with her mum and that both her brothers had left home but beyond these basic facts I knew very little about her. I resolved to ask sometime but now I would meet her mother at the opening night of The City Canteen, as they had named the new restaurant. Whatever happened to exotic names like The White Elephant Restaurant or French names like *l'Oeuf d'Or*? I suppose it's just that 'canteen' conjures up images of filthy building-site establishments that I have survived in the past. On big sites there was nearly always a canteen where you could get a mug of strong tea and a fry-up.

"See you in the morning," she said with a grin.

I had been very lazy during my week off, and had eaten badly. I had enjoyed it, but knew I needed to eat something green and healthy. The steak pie I had bought for tonight was not a good start to my resolution, but I would begin in earnest tomorrow. The pie could go in shortly after the roast potatoes had got a head start. I was lighting-up at the back door when I was startled by the sound of the side gate, and Charlotte popped into view.

"Sorry, did I make you jump?" she said, laughing. "I'm always doing that to you!" I could see her better as she came under my so-called veranda and into the light from the back door.

"Have you got time for a drink?" I asked. A look flashed behind her eyes and her smile weakened. I realised how my question might have sounded. I told her that I thought she looked good. I was sure she had put a bit more weight on and her face had filled out a little more. She was looking so much healthier than when I first saw her although it was only a matter of a few weeks. I put the external light on. I hoped it wasn't too evident that I wanted a better look, but I think she knew what I was doing.

"You are looking so well," I mumbled. Really I wanted to say 'gorgeous' or 'beautiful'. I asked her where she had been lately, trying very hard for this to sound like casual curiosity and not like a sulky comment. I didn't even let her answer before I was asking her if she would like some dinner. She said she would. She glanced down the garden towards the hut, her studio. So I then told her I would come down and call her when the dinner was ready.

"I'll tell you all about where I've been over dinner. I'll bet you were beginning to wonder where I'd got to."

I hung around and watched her walk down the path to the studio. She fiddled to get the key in the padlock and then I saw the lights go on.

I was making gravy and putting two plates to warm in the oven as she came in the back door. In the full, bright light of my kitchen she really did look better than I had ever seen her look. She had colour in her cheeks, she had make-up on and her eyes were definitely clearer. Her whole demeanour was confident and comfortable. She sat down at the kitchen table.

"How have you been?" she asked me.

"OK. I've had a week off work since I last saw you. And I stuck a mural on a wall today. What about you?"

"I've been working in London, in Hampstead. I've been doing a mural too, but painting mine, not sticking it on," she said.

She went on to tell me about the job. It was for Arabs from Kuwait. She told me how charming and polite they had been, and how they had insisted on giving her a one-thousand-pound bonus.

"I hope that's not too big?" I asked apologetically with a nod in the direction of her plate. I would have made this dinner do for two days and warmed it up again tomorrow if Charlotte hadn't turned up.

"It looks all right to me," she said as she poured the gravy. "I might come again."

"Bon appétit," I said as I chased a bit of hot roast potato round my mouth. My eyes watered. I got up from the table and returned with two glasses of water. Charlotte was tucking in. I ate and waited to see what she might have to say. She had lots to say. She told me how frustrating it was to have to decide whether to accept commissions or work on her own paintings in the studio. This dilemma troubled her, and she talked so much about it that when I had finished my dinner she still had plenty on her plate.

"Have you missed me?" she said at last, looking up from her plate and watching me for my reaction. I felt a bit silly, as if she had read my mind. I considered how to answer. She took the delay for indifference and said so. Then I completely overdid my rebuttal of that. I could see her amusement at my burbling.

"You are so sweet." She put her hand over mine. I felt a shock go through me and hoped she didn't notice.

"Well," I said, "I did miss you." I had a horrible feeling I might even have coloured up a little when I said it. I had over-emphasised my words again. I stood up and began clearing my own plate and the table generally. I caught the fragrance of thinners, flowers and soap as I passed near her. I would wash up and then have a shower. I asked her if she would like some milk to take down with her.

"Thanks, but I'd sooner come back here and have coffee with you – unless you're trying to get rid of me, that is." She was smiling but I was not sure if she taking the mickey out of me. "That was gorgeous, thank you, Chef." She put a hand on my shoulder.

"Oh, I forgot to tell you about Lisa," I said. "She has a date with a chef called Glen from the restaurant we finished today."

Charlotte raised her eyebrows and rolled her eyes approvingly. "Woo hoo! Are you jealous?"

I told her I was very pleased for Lisa and that I hoped it would go well. I waffled on about the difficult hours that chefs worked. Again she asked if I was jealous and again she was watching me. I laughed. I told her that I thought the world of Lisa and wished my daughters were like her. "I'm really pleased for her," I repeated. "He seems like a nice young bloke."

"Not jealous, then," she said. She was still watching me when I said I was off upstairs for a shower. She went out of the back door as I left the kitchen. I showered in record time. It was still early when I was back down in the kitchen, looking out of the window at the lights from the studio.

Chapter Twenty

Nigel had begun to think back to the early days of his marriage and fatherhood in England, though he had hardly been involved when Joan had left with their baby. His band had been taking off then – at least it seemed they were playing more and more – but how they could afford to live or how they got to gigs he couldn't remember.

It was still a mystery how Mike Appleton from the BBC had first heard of the band. Probably something Tony had arranged! The Strikes would never look back after their first appearance on the BBC's *The Old Grey Whistle Test*. Although Rudy was already becoming a prat by this time, and he and Lou Lewis, the lead guitarist, behaved badly during the recording, the show brought them a new audience to add to the growing army of fans accumulated from their never-ending live tour of the country. University students' union bookings began to flood in the following day. It wasn't long after this that they made the first of many appearances on *Top of the Pops*, and numerous other television appearances followed. The best money was in touring then; their fee went from three figures to four. Festivals and European TV shows pleaded with The Strikes to appear.

Nigel had often bumped into Pete Davis through other local bands; Pete would be singing Cliff Richard songs and his band would be copying The Shadows behind him. Pete had a very high opinion of himself but he could actually sing, Nigel had recognised. Pete and The Planets had asked Nigel to come to a rehearsal at Pete's house one evening. Pete had heard about Nigel and his ability to write songs and how he was able to find original sounds through his versatility on many instruments. Nigel in turn was aware that Pete Davis knew lots of people in the local music scene and had connections in London. They'd even played on *Saturday Club* with Brian Matthew a couple of times.

The upshot of the evening was that they asked him to become their bass player. He agreed to join them on condition that they change the band's name, which was important to Nigel. He sensed from the start that he couldn't really trust them, but was sure he could stay one step ahead of them, and did mostly. They had contacts, but he had songs. That was the main message he left with that evening. He would always make sure that songs he had written were credited to him, and he would always thoroughly vet any managers, agents, lawyers and accountants. The other members were careless, but he made sure he protected himself. They underestimated him and thought him malleable, which was their mistake.

Nigel saw the arrangement with the other three purely as business; if it advanced his career then it was to be done. The drive to make new, exciting music was surging within him, but he couldn't do it alone. He had considered going up to London on his own in hopes of meeting like-minded musicians, so when Pete and the others got in touch with him it had seemed fortuitous. He left the first meeting excited with the prospect. They were all a few years older than Nigel and they had been patronising him, he knew, with compliments about the recordings of his songs that he had taken along to that first meeting. Musically, however, they were able to very quickly pick the songs up from the tapes. Nigel noticed a look of recognition they exchanged that evening. He knew almost immediately himself that he could work creatively with them. He also knew he must try to protect himself from some of their personal habits.

Making music meant more to Nigel than anything. As they began to seriously rehearse a set that was now entirely made up of his songs he could feel his excitement build. He had talked endlessly to Joan about making his own music. She would listen but without much comment. He dismissed her apparent lack of enthusiasm; she was pregnant, but after Cherry was born he became more driven than ever. He persuaded Joan to come and listen to them play at a small local church hall, and a babysitter was booked.

Pete and the others had argued that this small hall was not for them, but Nigel had booked the hall with Tony's usual enthusiastic help, done some advertising, and they contacted anyone they could think of in the local music scene to invite along. It was booked for two weeks' time. This was the historic first gig for The Strikes. It would be their first indication of what people thought of their music – of Nigel's music.

Pete Davis aka Rudy: vocals, harmonica, maracas, tambourine and acoustic guitar; Robert Lewis aka Lou Lewis: lead guitar, guitar treatments and vocals; Brian Updike aka Zip: drums, percussion and backing vocals; Nigel Glover aka Smudger Smiff: bass guitar, steel guitar, keyboards, violin, flute, cello, saxophone, harmonica and other assorted instruments. This was The Strikes.

Nigel would one day look back at that evening for another reason: he had seen Joan smoking for the first time. He had noticed her talking to the others halfway through the evening as the band took a break. It had puzzled him that she was smoking, but he almost forgot it with everything that was going on. The thrill and sheer energy had begun on about the third number. There had been an eerie silence from the crowd at first and he had felt fear wrench his stomach, but after the third number they had gone wild. 'Unbelievable' was a word many used to describe the opening of the set; hence the silence. It was awe.

He was still seeing Tony quite a lot, and would discuss most things with him. Tony's opinions were important to him; he was altruistic and protective, and it gave Nigel confidence. He also mentioned seeing Joan smoking, but when Nigel asked Joan about it she just brushed it aside.

"I thought I was being sociable with your new band. I thought that was what you wanted."

She began turning up to more and more gigs. Nigel suspected nothing at first; he was pleased that at last she was taking an interest in his music. She would often bring Cherry along, so this allowed him to see his baby daughter. It was Tony who had tried gently to draw his friend's attention to Joan's increasing interest in Pete and the possibility that she was sharing more than just the odd spliff with him.

He had dismissed Tony's concerns. The express train of The Strikes was racing so fast along the tracks that it seemed nothing would stop it or even slow it down.

The band's bookings increased; they were playing further and further away and more often. Their following was growing. Festivals, tours, television, filming, and recording – the pace became frantic. Nigel was still somehow finding the time to write new material at a tremendous rate. He'd thought it was positive that Joan wanted to come on tour with them. When serious money began to reach them after a year or so Nigel had asked Joan to look for a house for the three of them. He hadn't read anything into it whenever she told him that she hadn't found anything suitable.

Then Joan left him. There was nothing he could do about it. The situation very nearly unhinged him, but his inner strength and his ability to mentally insulate himself then prevailed; the band came first. Somehow he must ignore the humiliation. He would phone Tony if he was away or go and see him whenever he got the chance, and his support helped him stay sane. The need to keep the band together became his focus. The humiliation increased for a while as the affair reached the papers. Photos began to appear of 'Rudy' and 'Jojo' together. They were even printing details he'd been unaware of. At first Nigel was coldly curious of such reports. How could she? How was it that he had not seen it coming? It was under his nose, after all. In the end, the cruel pleasure that the newspapers seemed to derive from the situation only steeled Nigel all the more. He only had to share the stage or recording studios with Pete Davis.

"If you love somebody, let them go. If they love you, they'll return; if not, you've lost nothing," Tony would say.

Their lives had changed so much and so quickly at that time. Nigel had more money than he knew what to do with now that the stream of royalties from the band's record sales and appearances had really begun. Tony still appeared to be the same strong, kind and supportive friend he had always been, but even Nigel had begun to notice a change in him about this time. He rarely talked about his own business ideas, and seemed to be settling for working in the building trade. He was becoming more conventional, even boring. His curiosity and interest in everything was fading. He was less fun, his manner more hesitant generally. He hoped it wasn't some form of jealous reaction at The Strikes' success.

He filled his coffee mug and looked from his window to the clear blue Californian sky beyond the hills. He wondered about Tony's life. What had changed? He had had so much promise, but if he was painting houses still... The boy he remembered had been so good at sports, so popular, so full of life and fun and so full of interests. He pictured them shaking hands for the last time at the airport. A shard of guilt pierced his heart. He should have made contact. It should have been him; after all, he was the one who had left his home town and country. Tony wouldn't have had a clue where he ended up. Tony had never asked for anything. The only things he had ever shared had been problems: his, never Tony's. He should have stayed in touch; helped Tony in business, even if it was only with money.

He remembered his promise of help.

Chapter Twenty-one

When Joan had moved in with Pete Davis, Nigel had tried to warn her for her own sake that it wouldn't last. She laughed in his face and sneered at his 'boring innocence'. He watched her beg to be allowed to go on their US tour, but Pete was tired of her by then. It had lasted about a year and that was longer than everybody had predicted. As far as Pete was concerned, their time was up.

It was on this last tour, as it proved to be, that Nigel began to think about moving to somewhere in America – probably California. This was when he'd visited Malibu and driven up into Agoura by mistake. The tour was over, they had a couple of rest days, and Nigel had no wish to spend more time with the others than necessary. He could handle being in the recording studio with them and could even overlook their excesses, just because it occasionally made them more creative, but in general he had no desire to be part of their destructive and self-centred lives.

When Nigel returned to England after this tour he phoned Tony and made plans to go down to Dorset and talk to his friend about the future; they were to meet in a few weeks. There was some business in London first, some studio time booked and a couple of television dates. This time produced 'Beyond the Pale Horizon', which was their last album (apart from several compilations of 'Greatest Strikes Tracks' on CD issued later in the nineties) and the second-biggest seller after 'If Only'.

It was then that Joan phoned him. Screaming hysterically and sobbing, she had begged for his help.

Nigel could not have known that that phone call would determine not only the course of his own life, but also that of Tony's.

As he thought back, he felt guilty once more about the way he had abandoned his friend. His life had become very comfortable and fulfilled in California; he had virtually no reminders of those last few weeks in England. Tony was not so fortunate; financially he was tied to England with his new wife. Nigel's own financial security was established. The English lawyers and accountants would sort out the details and the future for him. Nigel could sit back with few or no worries. His part in the mess could now be forgotten. His lawyers would set up trust funds for Cherry and later for Daisy. The accountants could do the rest.

He made a few contacts in Los Angeles and having chosen Agoura it soon proved to be a lovely area to put down his roots. Subsequent years of writing scores for film and television fulfilled his creative needs and he could sit in with a band sometimes at The Ranch or other local bars. He could write and record for pleasure these days in his own home. His social life recovered post-Sarah Hambledon.

Smudger Smiff would be asked in to a television studio occasionally to talk about the music scene of the seventies. MTV had recently found him for some nostalgia documentaries they were producing. His music project was coming along nicely, just waiting for some vocals to be added. Ashley was becoming very interesting too.

Life in California was pretty good for Nigel Glover.

Chapter Twenty-two

It was a Saturday morning at the end of February, and my kitchen felt warm and cosy. I got up, shaved and showered, and was feeling relaxed because it was Saturday and I had little to do. I had some cereal and a slice of toast and marmalade then I clicked the kettle back on for another cup of tea and went to the back door for a first cigarette. The lawn was white with frost and I shuddered as cold air enveloped me. As I gazed down the garden towards Charlotte's studio a tear came to my eye. It arrived unannounced. Nothing was on my mind that would have encouraged it to come; maybe it was just the freezing air. I wiped my cheek with the back of my hand and lit up. Yes, it was just the initial shock of the cold, I told myself, and was almost convinced, until more followed. I shook my head in an attempt to dispel the overwhelming feeling of misery that by then engulfed me. I wanted to go back in and get warm but I also wanted to smoke there on my veranda. I went indoors, still overcome with feelings of sadness. Where had they come from? Seemingly out of nowhere. I had never, or so I thought, been prone to self-pity but right now that seemed the only explanation. But why? Why now? There was no obvious trigger. Then it occurred to me: Burley!

The New Forest National Park has many beautiful parts and Burley is one of them. It is an attractive village at the meeting-point of three roads, with its war-memorial cross on a small green in the centre. It has tea rooms, gift shops, art galleries, several good pubs, and a cider farm. It oozes old-world charm and often has cattle or ponies wandering the roads. Bicycles can be hired on which to explore the forest. There is something for everyone. But for me, Burley holds dark memories.

Lisa had been telling me on our way home the previous evening that we had two jobs in the Burley area. One, she said, was a beautiful, extended thatched cottage in nearby Burley Street, the other a hotel at Clayhill. I hadn't been near Burley since 1975. It crept into my thoughts at times, triggering dark and depressive moods; it had filled my being with regret and remorse. It had, I fairly recently concluded, ruined my life. Burley was like a dark crow, just on the periphery of my vision, watching me with a knowing eye. I had tried to forget it and managed to avoid it for so long, but the black, beady, shuttered eye still watched me.

When we were teenagers, Nigel and I, along with other friends, spent many happy times driving over the cattle-grids and through the forest to Burley, or more specifically to The White Buck Inn. We liked other pubs in the village and in the surrounding villages but The White Buck had live music. Since the sixties it had been a mecca for music in the New Forest, and for miles around, and had hosted many well-known bands and singers. It was here that The Strikes broke attendance records even before they became nationally well known. I was with them the first time the village was brought to a complete standstill; cars, motorbikes and scooters were abandoned all around the pub, throughout the village, and on up the hill towards Bisterne. The parish council was outraged, and persuaded The White Buck not to book the band again, so the last time they played there went into local legend; an 'I was there' moment for fans. They still visited the village, not for the fudge or the witches' shop but to see the scene of The Strikes' origins. Beatles fans go to The Cavern site or the Abbey Road zebra crossing; Strikes fans go to Burley village and The White Buck.

What happened in Burley affected me in ways I could not have imagined. It squatted in my brain, somehow imperceptibly eroding me. I could see that my personality began to alter. I understood how Jenny gradually changed towards me, unable to conceal her disappointment in me. I assume now that the guilt and my conscience undermined my confidence just enough. I didn't spend all my waking hours thinking about what we had done but the knowledge just sat there: that watching crow. I remember hoping Jenny's attitude towards me would go back to how it had once been. I hoped that our first, then our second daughter's arrival would give us back the love of the early years; it was not to be.

It was September 1975. I had a call from Nigel to say he was coming down to his home town on a break from touring. The Strikes had been on a tour of some southern states of America finishing in California. He told me that they had a few dates in London and some television appearances and a bit of recording time booked and that he hoped to catch up soon, 'in a week or two'. It was good to hear from him, we gossiped a bit and he had a bit of a moan about some of the others' behaviour on tour but he sounded quite happy in himself.

I gleaned what I could from the newspapers, radio and television to keep up with them, or at least with Nigel. I would wonder what it was like for him, the constant travel. New cities we once only dreamed of seeing, places we talked about: Kansas City, Memphis, St Louis, and of course Chicago and New York. Just names to me, but images to Nigel, or so I thought. When I talked to him some while back he told me they didn't see much of anywhere because they were either on stage, in a hotel, or travelling, and fans would make going out sightseeing impossible. The local radio stations they called in on all looked the same.

He told me once how on that tour Rudy and Zip had nearly been arrested in Jacksonville just for wearing make-up. Their American tour manager had done some fast talking on their behalf and had dumped all their drugs before the deputies got to their hotel rooms. It was a mystery how none of them were arrested on this tour. "They came the closest yet!" he told me. Nigel would often criticise the other three band members, and to be honest, I used to look forward to hearing his tales about The Strikes' tours and the wild parties. I wondered how he stayed above it all.

I was busy at that time trying to do as much work as I could. I worked long days and most weekends too. If I worked a whole weekend I would still go out with Jenny on the Saturday night at least; it might only be to a pub or for dinner with friends but we always did something. I still had ambition and I had that hope that Nigel's promise of his financial help might be sorted out on his next visit home.

When he was last home he mentioned he would be happy to invest some cash. I was excited by that prospect but also desperate to save some of my own money; it wouldn't have felt right to just be using his. I was really formulating my ideas to give him as clear a picture as possible of what I was planning. I wanted a furnishings, furniture and decorating shop. Rattan furniture, basketware, designer fabrics and wallpapers; upholstered furniture too, but not traditional stuff; modern – for modern, seventies interiors; perhaps even clothing too; I wasn't completely clear because I was permanently busy with little time to think.

Jenny moaned about the hours I was doing and when I told her some of my ideas she would tell me not to be 'silly'. If I asked her what was silly about ambition we would end up arguing and she would just tell me I was stupid to think I could afford a shop premises. I'd had a very busy summer, lots of exterior work (*when it was not raining*) and many new contacts made, so I had to think about employing some help. Mostly the work was local but I also had jobs at Winchester, Southampton, Weymouth, Shaftesbury and Brockenhurst. I had begun to look at what shops were available and what they might cost in rent and business rates. I'd asked Jenny to check insurance costs and any other legal costs I might incur. Staff: what sort of wages to pay? There were so many new things to find out about.

'Plan, or plan to fail', as the saying goes.

I was raring to get started.

Chapter Twenty-three

It was a Thursday evening towards the end of September that year, and I was watching television at home while Jenny was out at her cookery class. She had been going on Thursdays for some weeks, and I enjoyed the end results on the following evening; Friday's dinners were more interesting than usual. The previous week we had had one of my favourites so far; something we had never had before: it was called pizza. I'd never even heard of it. I had had spaghetti bolognese a couple of times in a new restaurant in town but nothing else 'Italian'. I really liked it. *This was exotic.*

Nigel had rung a few days before. He'd told me a few things about The Strikes' latest tour and I looked forward to hearing more. I knew he was sometimes reluctant to talk about such things; he was sometimes self-conscious about telling me of places we used to imagine we would one day visit together. Like New Orleans: we both liked Fats Domino singing 'Walking to New Orleans'. Nigel told me how the Mississippi was a muddy orange colour; he played everything down.

He was doing more. I was doing less. It didn't really bother me; I was interested in where he had been and excited for him. I wanted to know more.

I'd been having some hard days at work and was dozing in front of the television when the phone rang, making me jump. I hadn't expected to hear from him for a week or so yet; I understood he was staying in London for a while, recording. When he spoke his voice was breathless and my brain was foggy from sleep so I didn't grasp what he was saying immediately.

"Tony, Rudy is dead," he repeated, his voice ragged and strained. I told him to calm down and tell me again. "Rudy is dead... The Strikes' singer Rudy Davis... Pete," he said. I knew who their singer was. I asked him if he was really telling me he had died. I was already thinking 'drug overdose' from stories Nigel had told me of his band's habits, especially Rudy's. *A self-inflicted disaster of some sort no doubt.*

It was sinking in now. I was awake. I asked if it was a heart attack. He made a strange noise down the phone in response to this question; a sort of strangled laugh. I asked him several more times to slow down. This was so unlike Nigel. I heard him take a deep breath, then he started again more slowly.

"Joan has stabbed Pete to death."

Nigel's ex-wife had found a naked Pete Davis with a young girl in a stable-type wooden outbuilding in the grounds of the house they shared. The girl had fled the scene. I knew about the large country house Joan and Pete had bought and how they called it a commune. Others, with and without children, all lived alongside each other at Rudy's expense. This amused Nigel, I knew. The 'hangers-on', Nigel always called them. He wrote a song once called 'Weekend Hippies' and he told me it was about them.

Joan had rung Nigel and asked for his help. It seems she was hysterical: shrieking, crying and begging him for help. He said he had at first told her to call the police and an ambulance. She had screamed that it was too late for an ambulance, and became even more hysterical, asking who would look after Cherry if she went to prison. This seemed ironic, he told me as an aside now he was becoming more coherent. He had agreed to go to the house and help her, and now he was asking me for my help.

"We'll need your van, Tony."

I gathered that he was ringing me from the phone at the house. He'd taken a black cab all the way to Hampshire from the West End hotel Joan had tracked him down to. He'd got the taxi driver to drop him well down the road in the village centre and even given him an autograph. It was important to appear calm and normal to the driver even though his fear of what he was about to find was growing, he pointed out.

He found the house unlocked and was puzzled as to where all the hangers-on were; the whole place apparently deserted. Nigel had called out from the hallway when he got to the house. He'd listened carefully for a while. *Nothing!* Having passed a wooden outbuilding on the way up the drive he then wondered if that was what Joan had meant by 'wooden shed'; she had repeated it several times. He started back down the drive. He called out again. Not a sound. As he began to walk down the shrub-lined gravel drive, Joan had appeared. Her pale face was streaked with mascara, strands of hair were stuck flat to her forehead and her eyes stared wide at him. She was wearing a thin cotton floral dress that was stained and dirty, and was gripping a large torch. When she saw Nigel she had begun to whimper. Her appearance disgusted him but he knew he must contain any personal feelings, and forced his revulsion away. He took the torch from her hand and shone it into her face. He could now see that she was covered in blood. Her eyes pleaded with him. She threw her arms around his neck. He wanted to shrug her off but had instead gently levered her arms away.

"What have you done?" he whispered, looking into eyes he had once known.

"Help me, please, Nigel. Help me." She tried to put her arms around his neck once more. "You must help me."

She had then gone into convulsions of sobs, her arms wrapped around herself.

Bending forwards, she dropped to the gravel. Nigel's patience was evaporating, he told me.

"Show me what you have done," he insisted. "Get up." He helped her to her feet.

She made a huge gulping noise and pointed to the half-open wooden door of the nearby outbuilding. He shone the torch in the direction she was pointing.

"In there?"

She nodded, eyes screwed closed, and whispered a 'yes'. Nigel had cautiously pulled the door further open and then stopped abruptly as the pool of torchlight highlighted the white, motionless male body lying sprawled on straw towards the back of the building. He could see dark patches and rivulets across the body from congealed blood. He recognised his band's singer.

I could hear the disgust in his voice as he related this.

When he had finished his tale I felt like asking him 'why is it your problem?', but he was begging for my help because he had already agreed to help Joan. He muttered that it was for Cherry's sake that he must help.

I was to help get rid of the naked, blood-soaked body Nigel had described: Pete Davis's body.

Why naked?

It seemed that Joan and Pete liked to make love in as many places as possible around the house and its several acres of gardens. They had had fresh hay delivered recently and scattered in the former stable buildings for precisely this purpose. It seems it was to be the first time to try their game in the hay. Pete, addled with alcohol and chemicals, had failed to resist the urge to have a trial run of the 'roll-in-the-hay' with Lucy, a seventeen-year-old from the village. Lucy liked to visit the commune and help with the children. The girl had grabbed her clothes and run at the first sight of Jojo.

The wooden outhouse had a few rusty old tools hanging from cobwebbed walls. Joan had grabbed some sort of knife from the wall and plunged it into Pete's chest as he lay back with his eyes closed. In a frenzied fit of rage she had gone completely berserk and stabbed him many more times. The first blow had killed him, going right where she had aimed: straight through his cheating heart.

I had managed to ask where all the other people were. I learned later that Pete had returned to the house from the recent tour while on a 'bad trip', and in a paranoid fury had frightened everyone away, chasing one last reluctant couple along the drive almost to the village wearing only underpants, screaming obscenities and waving a sword from a display in one of the downstairs rooms. Earlier, Joan had been to the village to collect Lucy to look after Cherry whilst she attempted to calm Pete down. The house was a total mess when she returned: furniture upended, people's clothing and children's toys scattered everywhere and Pete sleeping like a baby on the couch.

She had watched him sleep the sleep of the innocent for hours, and darkness had fallen. In the morning he was in exactly the same position. He had wet himself; she had shaken him awake. As he became aware of how wet he was he simply pulled himself up, glanced at her and told her he was 'off for a shower'. She told Nigel how he seemed unaware of how he had behaved less than twenty-four hours previously. He had slept for about eighteen hours. He had also asked where Lucy was as he left the room that morning. She had thought this a strange question. As far as Joan knew he took no notice of her babysitter. Lucy had helped with several of the other children in the house for some months. Everybody thought she was beautiful in looks and spirit.

She lived with her parents in the village and was in the sixth form at her school in the local town. Lucy got excitement from the house; the freedom was so different from school and her parents and the village. To actually know famous rock stars made life interesting, and the money she earned was really good too.

When Rudy had first tried to seduce her, she had been terrified. She had trembled until her jaw ached as he felt her. Her heart almost stopped when he put her hand on him. She had looked up into his face, her body rigid. When he began she did not speak or protest. She couldn't. She felt faint and her breathing seemed to stop.

This had happened in Jojo and Rudy's bedroom. She had wandered in assuming the room was empty.

It was midday and she had no reason to think Pete was in there on his own. He had patted the bed as if to say 'sit here'. Lucy had moved nearer but stood beside the bed. That was when he got out of bed. She had explained that she was looking for clothes for Cherry. He had just smiled and told her how pretty he thought she was.

Pete gave no more thought to the incident in his bedroom until Lucy had found a moment to ask him if he meant it when he had said. He would find her looking at him and she would blush if he caught her eye. He became aware of how tense she became when he entered a room she was in. It amused him.

On the day, he asked her if she had seen the old barn down the drive and would she like to give him a hand with some hay there.

He slipped quickly through the doors and pulled them closed. A single streak of sunlight shone between the doors onto the dirt floor. Dust motes flew in its light. The smell of hay pervaded the place. He cupped Lucy's face in his hands and kissed her lips. He opened his hand, held an oval white pill to her lips and nodded, then held one to his own lips, and after showing it on his tongue, swallowed it and nodded to her to do the same. She complied, but then started to run towards the doors. He caught her and reassured her. Her body trembled from head to foot.

"The pill will relax you," he told her in a whisper. His eyes glittered and a tiny drop of saliva appeared at the corner of his mouth. Rudy tugged her towards the hay strewn at the rear of the building. He pulled her down beside him. It was still bright daylight outside but the only light inside was from cracks in boards or joints that had shrunk open with age and a narrow line of light between the front doors. Pete was on a high and would not be deterred now the pill had topped him up. He took a tiny bottle from his pocket, sipped it, and held it to Lucy's lips. She sipped. Nirvana beckoned.

Chapter Twenty-four

Nigel had told me again how he'd already agreed. I was wide awake by now and told him I would help. I heard a sigh from his end of the line. I had assured him once more that I was on my way and would be there as quickly as I could. He whispered his thanks.

I began to have second thoughts as I wrote a note to Jenny. She would be home soon and I didn't want to be there when she arrived. Telling her lies about why I wouldn't be there when she got home was not easy, but I hoped I would have time to think of a plausible story. I hadn't washed after work; I intended to wash when I went up for bed, and I still had work clothes on. I rushed upstairs, splashed cold water on my face and grabbed a pullover. I scribbled: 'Jenny, somebody has died and I have to go to help Nigel. Back soon. Don't worry xx'.

As if she wouldn't worry or wonder who had died... or get angry. I went out to the garage where I kept my tools and my work kit, grabbed a few things I thought we might need and threw everything into the back of the van. At a filling station I topped up with fuel; the last thing I wanted was to run out. My wing mirrors reflected the final shades of a beautiful pink-and-grey sunset. Darkness was already over the New Forest ahead as I began my journey out of Bournemouth.

I lit the first of many cigarettes and settled in for the drive. It had been a lovely early-autumn day with sun and clear blue sky but now as darkness closed in I had a thousand thoughts of what I had agreed to and what the night would bring. I felt tired, with gritty eyes and aching neck muscles; I should have been getting ready for bed, not going out. The nearer I got, the more I worried about what I might find.

As I approached Rookery House, the huge black iron gates were open and I drove slowly through them onto a gravel drive with evergreen bushes on either side, as Nigel had described. I looked at the petrol gauge; loads still. I could smell smoke.

Nigel appeared from a wooden building on the left that stood just beyond what looked like a pair of semi-detached houses; obviously the converted stables he had mentioned. I could make out the silhouette of the large main house further down the drive, its outline visible against a clear, moonlit sky. He sort of grimaced and we shook hands as I got out of the van.

"Thanks for coming," he said, patting me on the shoulder and meeting my eye. I guessed he was checking out my demeanour.

"What's burning?" I asked.

"The hay. The blood in the hay."

I didn't know what he meant.

He looked away. His face was drawn. We stood in silence by my van, neither of us knowing what to say or how to begin our grisly task. In the end it was me who spoke first.

"So where is he? In the wooden building there?"

His body stiffened. He drew breath noisily and stared at me.

"Joan is up in the house, that's the light in the window you can see upstairs."

"But where is...?"

He nodded in the direction of the wooden doors nearby.

"In there still. I've been burning straw from in there... blood everywhere... there was blood everywhere. Are you sure you want to help me?"

I didn't answer him.

He switched on the torch he was carrying; I reached into the van and grabbed one of mine. I took a deep breath and pulled one of the doors open, raking my torch-beam across the floor, front to back.

What on earth was Joan thinking to have done such a thing? Nigel had followed me in and was shining his beam on a red, brown and white shape nearer the back of the building. I could smell the hay, I thought I could smell the metallic aroma of blood and I could also smell that his bowels had gone. I put a hand to my nose. Nigel glanced at me and put a hand on my shoulder once more.

That smell of blood. I had an involuntary flashback.

"Let's get him out of here, get rid of the rest of the hay and get moving."

Nigel nodded and we went nearer. Gravity had begun to move blood down to Rudy's back. His eyes were open; so was his mouth. I could see smudged rivulets of the mascara he wore. I began to mutter again, asking what on earth Joan was thinking.

"I gave her some Mogadon I found in a drawer upstairs and I put her to bed. She won't wake for hours," said Nigel. "Then I came down here to start getting rid of the bloodstained hay. I tried to move him once but almost threw up. That was just before you arrived. I'd just come out for air as I saw your headlights by the gates. I'm so, so sorry to drag you into this, Tony. I'm just so sorry. But so grateful."

I'm not sure how convincing I sounded as I tried to reassure him.

I shone my torch onto Pete Davis. "Shall we?"

Nigel exhaled; I did too, and we bent to pick up the body.

"Mind where you tread," said Nigel. It turned out that he had actually vomited, but it didn't seem quite the worst thing to stand in at that precise moment. I put my torch down close by, from where it cast eerie light-patterns across the hay-strewn earth floor and onto the rigid body of the famous singer; but it was enough to see what we were doing.

"Sorry, Tony," Nigel whispered.

"You get his legs and I'll get under his shoulders," I replied. "Lift."

We couldn't seem to get hold of him or get a good enough grip. We tried several times; he would slip from our hands. I asked Nigel to wait a moment and went to my van for a twill dust sheet. I laid it folded lengthwise beside the body and suggested we roll him onto it. The sheet would be easier to grip and therefore would make it easier to lift him. *And keep unwanted excretions from our clothing.* Nigel was nodding to my suggestions; he shuddered and looked at me rather than at the body.

This was the second time I had touched a dead person. I had seen my dad that Boxing Day and that image now haunted me. I saw him in his coffin, after the morticians had tidied him up so much that he just looked peacefully asleep, the cut hidden by a scarf. *I still regret not kissing him goodbye.*

Blood had run over the side of Pete Davis' body into his armpits and was still sticky. I prepared myself.

"Ready?"

Nigel let out a sort of gurgling noise which I took as an affirmative. I was on my knees behind a cold, naked man with my hands under his armpits. I swallowed and shuddered, then heaved. Nigel grunted and we rolled him onto the sheet.

He may have considered himself a giant when strutting on a stage but Pete Davis, although over six foot tall, weighed less than eleven stone. Nigel backed towards the doors, and I stood and moved slowly forward at Nigel's pace. My eyes were closed, not because of the exertion of lifting but to avoid seeing what I was gripping. Nigel backed out onto the drive, glancing over his shoulder, and as I followed I realised I had forgotten to open the back doors of the van. I cursed.

"What's up?" Nigel asked anxiously.

"I've left the van doors shut. I should have left them open... ready. We'll have to put him down."

As we did so, his penis moved, and we both looked up at each other. I wanted to laugh. I opened the rear doors wide, leaned in and put the little interior light on and jumped up into the van. I moved some cans of paint, roller trays, kettles and a pot of brushes tight against the back of the passenger seat. Then I pushed the pile of dust sheets up to the back of the driver's seat but took another two off. I laid one over the floor of the van and kept the other to cover the body up with. I jumped down. Nigel was retching into a bush nearby. I went over and put my hand on his back. He turned and stepped forward again and bent to take Pete's legs.

"Sorry, mate," he said quietly. "One-two-three…"
We bundled him in, I covered him up, switched off the
interior light and slammed the doors shut.

I heard Nigel spit and I leaned against the back doors
and lit a longed-for cigarette, inhaling deeply. A fox
flew out of the laurels just down from Nigel, and I
heard a strangled scream. It ran past me, glancing back
as if to say 'I know what you're doing'. I picked up a
stone from the gravel drive, threw it, and the fox
vanished. I lit a second cigarette from the first and
thought about what we still needed to do. Nigel
wandered back over.

"Don't say sorry again," I challenged him. He almost
smiled. "We will have to make as sure as we can that no
blood or anything else is left in the hay."

He just nodded, switched on his torch and we
returned to the outbuilding. I found a rusty rake hanging
on a nail and raked the rest of the hay into a pile. We
quickly grabbed as much as we could at a time and relit
it where Nigel had previously been doing the same. I
raked the whole floor over then trod it back down in
hope that no blood would still be visible. I cast the light
all around the floor thinking that if there were any
liquids they would reflect my torchlight. It showed
nothing. We shut the doors, one each, and I put a stick
through the metal hasp to hold the doors shut. I checked
my watch. Time seemed to be flying.

Nigel took my hand.

"I'll be able to do something for you soon, I hope."

I thought of my business plan despite the situation.

His eyes glistened with tears.

"Are you sure there is nothing in there that might
incriminate?" I shone my torch at the wooden doors.

"No," Nigel replied but not confidently. "Well, I can't be certain. I just hope not."

"Where's the knife she used?"

For a moment Nigel looked shocked and angry. "I put it in the back of the van."

I didn't say so but although I hoped he hadn't, I was not about to check.

"We have to get a move on, Nigel," was all I said.

I went to the bushes to pee, and Nigel then did the same. Nigel got into the van and exhaled loudly.

"Are you sure you're OK about leaving Joan?"

I barely heard his 'yes'.

"Let's get going, then!"

Chapter Twenty-five

I started the engine; checking my watch again. I couldn't wait to get away from there. We exchanged a look and I put the van into gear and pulled away. The tyres crunched on the gravel till we reached the road proper. We crept past the Fox and Hounds pub and some cottages. The lights were off downstairs in the pub but there was one still on upstairs. The moonlight glowed through the windscreen onto Nigel's drawn face. I glanced at him as we went slowly through the village. Nigel stared ahead. We passed the football pitch on our left and headed out of the village past the doctor's surgery towards the main road. I had full-beam headlights by now and no other vehicles passed us. It was just twelve-thirty but it felt like I had been hours and hours at the house. That was good news and a surprise.

"You OK, mate?" I asked him. He nodded.

He began to tell me more details of what had happened. He told me how he was worried about leaving Joan and relieved that Cherry happened to be staying with Lucy's parents, as she sometimes did. I had forgotten her initially, but at least she was safe, poor mite, though what would become of her in the future I couldn't imagine. I was puzzled at his concern for Joan though. Had she not humiliated him and left him, taking their child? Nigel had gone very quiet. I smoked, and he appeared to sleep. He looked up every so often and across at me each time but said nothing. My eyes were becoming gritty with tiredness and the muscles in my shoulders and the back of my neck ached. I rubbed knuckles in my eyes and stared ahead. It would not be long before we reached the part of the New Forest I was heading for, a part I had thought of on the way over to the house.

Nigel woke. "Where are we going exactly? Where are we heading?" He hadn't spoken for most of the journey.

I wound the window down to get some fresh air. My mouth tasted dry and foul. We had discussed that it might be safe to bury the body within the New Forest. I told him that I had spades and a fork in the back of the van, if he hadn't seen them already. He said he had seen them but hadn't realised what they were for. I looked at him when he said this to see if he was kidding. Did he think I might need them in my day-to-day work? I didn't question him further. I told him I would turn off at Picket Post and then decide exactly where to stop, either before Burley or beyond the village, up Bisterne way. He nodded at this. He had similar memories to mine of good times in New Forest pubs and especially The White Buck Inn. Somehow it seemed right. They began here. I was trying to see my watch in the moonlight through the windscreen; we would be there in a short while.

"I couldn't cope with this without your help, Tony." He was staring at me now in the gloom of the van. "As usual it's your support that gets me through."

Then he told me how he had found many different drugs in the house and that when he recognised

Mogadon in their bedroom he had known to give Joan several. It had worked. He described undressing her to put her to bed. Laying her on towels he had washed the blood from her body as she slept. He had burned her dress and underwear with the hay from the scene.

"Not too far now," I told him.

I wondered what Jenny had made of my note. I told Nigel what I had put in it and how I was wondering what she would think.

"I think Jenny has a low enough opinion of me already," Nigel replied.

We both knew that but I still had to think of a plausible scenario to satisfy her.

I tried to glance over my shoulder at our cargo, but couldn't see anything more than a dark lump. We exchanged a look.

"I put the rake from outbuilding at the house on board too. I don't think they'll miss it."

I wondered what would happen with the house and its contents, including Joan. I assumed it was all owned by Pete Davis.

"Not far now," I said once more. I lit up again with the window wide open.

It really was not much further to the turn-off for Burley at Picket Post. The filling station and The Copper Kettle were in darkness but a lorry was parked up there. I supposed the driver needed sleep and could wait till morning for fuel, both for himself and for his truck.

I desperately wanted a drink but we had work to do. My neck was stiffer than ever, and I had the beginnings of a headache. I turned off the main road and we rumbled across a cattle-grid. The forest was very still on either side of us. You had to be careful through here even in daylight; cattle and ponies, even deer, would be wandering in the road or grazing on the verge without a care in the world; this was their space. Most houses have their own cattle-grid across the driveway.

As we crossed this stretch towards Burley Street, there were a couple of houses set back on our left in darkness, too near for us to consider stopping in this area. To the right the ground sloped away from the road and so it might be disastrous to try that side. Then came the houses of Burley Street. Two ponies were in the road, but weren't interested in us and wandered out of our way. I steered slowly by, fearing we might even brush the chestnut-coloured one. Two more looked up at us from the grass bordering the roadside perhaps to see the action, their eyes glowing in the van's lights.

We passed a few cottages shrouded in early-hours' darkness, nestled down for the night beneath their thatches, wide eaves like old men's eyebrows overhanging small windows. We passed the little fire station. Nigel fidgeted. Burley village was silent and dark. My headlights picked out the stone war-memorial cross on its little patch of grass in the centre of the village. The parish council would never know that The Strikes' singer and bassist had been there once again. We both knew this area well. We started up the hill out of the village, passing the turn for the inn and continuing to the top beyond the school. I told Nigel that I was now looking for somewhere to pull in off the road. My heart beat faster and my mouth was dry. Nigel stared ahead in silence.

It was now getting on for two o'clock. The road at this point was just about level with the verge so I pulled over. I drove cautiously across the grass, aware that the forest had many streams, some not very visible and with boggy areas and rabbit burrows we could get stuck in. I switched off the headlights, leaving just the side lights to illuminate the way. I just wanted to be out of sight of the road. I pulled onto what looked like a flat, open grassy area beyond some gorse bushes and shrubs that I thought would hide the van. I turned the side lights and engine off. We stood at the back of the van and looked each other in the eye. I opened the doors. Clouds slid across the moon.

The smell that greeted us was not my paint pots as I pulled the sheet from Pete Davis' stiffened body. I could see a clawed hand still with many rings on. I reached in, ignoring the passenger as best I could, and grabbed a spade. I handed it to Nigel then took the fork and the other spade.

"Let's not go too far from the rear of the van," I whispered. "Then we won't have to carry him... it... him... too far. We're on an open, flat piece of grass here that's big enough for us." I shone the torch around then propped it in a bush at an angle to shine down on the grass. I dug two marks about eighteen inches or so apart then paced out what I estimated was a little longer than the body, digging two more markers to form the four corners of our intended trench.

It would not be 'six-foot-under': this was not Boot Hill.

I then scratched the spade sideways, joining the marks with my cuts. I put the spade down and grabbed the fork. Nigel watched me but was continually looking about nervously. I trod the fork in on my lines; the ground was extremely soft. I looked up at Nigel.

"This is going to be easy," I hissed. "Get digging, my friend." Almost immediately a distant sound made me stop. I listened to the darkness. *Nothing*. Nigel began to dig at the other end, straightening his back and rubbing it after almost every spadeful. Then a rustle in a nearby bush made us both freeze. My heart thudded in my chest. My mouth went dry. The clouds opened and the moon lit a pony's eyes. We had obviously disturbed him and he had come to investigate. He gawped at us blankly. Nigel went over to him and patted his neck. The pony turned and vanished back into the gloom. I had stepped into the bushes to hide and gorse tore at my jeans when I turned to go back to our trench. I inhaled deeply. Nigel was digging already. He stopped as the pony appeared again but this time with two more. They stood and stared. It was as though the first had told the others to come and see what was happening. Nigel came round the shallow trench to where I was standing and tugged my sleeve.

"Let's go and find somewhere else. If one of these horses falls in we are in trouble."

I agreed.

We quickly refilled the trench and trod it down. I went to the edge of the grassy clearing, gathered up some longer grass and twigs and scattered them over where we had begun digging. I couldn't see very well but hoped that made it look more natural. We chucked the tools into the back of the van and I shut the doors as quietly as I could. All this activity was still being watched by the ponies, one of which had stepped nearer to the ground we had disturbed and seemed to be sniffing it.

The clouds parted and the moon defined the way I had driven off the road. I backed up slowly and we set off again. I now had to put dipped headlights on to see the road ahead in case of ponies or deer, or at least to see where we were going. We needed to find somewhere else, and quickly; we had wasted a lot of time. My shoulders hurt now; I tried to roll them gently to ease the stiffening and tired muscles. Stars winked through gaps in the clouds as I drove. A short distance up the hill we forked off the road down a narrower lane. Again it was scrub and gorse with some small trees of ash and alder, but only low cover.

I steered the van up the track to a dead end. Nigel got out with his torch to test the ground for softness or boggy areas and to guide me into the scrub as far from the road as possible. He stumbled ahead, glancing back and beckoning me on. At one point he caught his foot in a rabbit hole or a tussock and went sprawling. He got up and again waved me forward. We must have been only about fifty yards from solid track or road so I motioned to Nigel but he waved me on. I could now see what he had in mind; there appeared to be a small clearing between some large clumps of gorse. He raised his hand. I stopped the van and switched off the engine.

I jumped out into gorse and it tore through my jeans into my leg. I got the tools from the rear of the van, swallowing sour bile as I reached over the body to get them. We began marking out an area similar in size to the one we had done before. Nigel was breathing deeply. We dug and we dug. The soil, soft and loamy – peat almost, I guessed – yielded easily to our spades but I was soon nearing exhaustion; I certainly hurt. Nigel had some blisters, one or two of them bleeding. We nodded to each other as the moon reappeared and shone into our grave. Black water was oozing upwards by the time we agreed it was deep enough. We pulled the body to the back lip of the van with the sheet and manoeuvred it till we could get a grip.

"We'll have to take a side each," I said, and Nigel nodded. I held my breath so as not to smell anything but also to gird myself for the effort. The corpse seemed to glow in the moonlight. Nigel was swallowing hard. Our hole was only a few feet from the back of the van, so, grunting and heaving, we dragged Pete out and into the gaping ground in one continuous movement. As we did so his head hit the back lip of the van and we winced in unison. With the body safely in the hole, Nigel turned away and retched, bent over with his hands on his knees. I closed my eyes, gulping air. I wished I had thought to bring some water to drink to wash the sour taste from my throat. I was hot despite the pre-dawn temperature. Nigel was down to a tee shirt.

Pete's body lay on its side; it seemed to glisten with a grotesque whiteness down there in what light it caught. A squelching noise issued from the grave, caused by the weight settling in the marshy soil or by air escaping from the singer's body for the last time. I turned and gagged, my eyes streaming. Nigel put a hand on my shoulder and nodded. We immediately shovelled and scraped soil over the body. Nigel dropped something in as we began but I was too breathless to ask what it was; I would ask later. The knife? I raked dry twigs, leaves and grass across the fresh grave. Forty-five minutes had passed since I last checked my watch; it was after three o'clock. I didn't want to hear birdsong yet. My jeans were wet with black mud almost to my knees from the spongy ground and Nigel saw me looking and pointed to his own. Again he put a hand on my shoulder. "Thanks."

"Let's go," I replied.

Back in the van, I started it up and slowly reversed, hoping I was near enough tracking our way in. Nigel was spitting on his hands and squirming to get a pullover over his head as the van bucked and rocked. When we reached the road I put the lights on and relaxed a little as we drove away back in the direction of Burley village. When we passed our aborted grave I realised with horror that it was very near, if not on, the golf course. Relief flooded Nigel's face; his eyes were closed and his head was back as we went down the hill and through the centre of the village again. The only light anywhere was a dim security light in the back of a shop, just a slight orange glow.

"Sorry," Nigel whispered.

I just looked at him. We continued back through the village, bound for the A31. I turned the van's heater up as we crossed the cattle-grid and reached the main road at last, heading for Bournemouth, a mug of tea and bed... and Jenny.

Chapter Twenty-six

I unlocked the front door, stood back and motioned Nigel in. He carried on through to the kitchen. We blinked at each other in the bright fluorescent light, the glare hurting our eyes for a moment. We were both filthy. Our bell-bottom jeans were black with peaty mud from the knee down, and our shoes were beyond help. I had several rips in my jeans and my shins stung with gorse scratches. I put the kettle on and lit a cigarette while Nigel ran cold water over his blistered hands, wincing. My kitchen clock said four-forty. The dawn chorus had begun some while ago; close by the back door a blackbird was singing beautifully for his breakfast. The sky was taking on streaks of yellow, pink and red, gradually dispelling the dark blues and greys; a watercolourist's dream, if he or she were up. It would soon be light.

I handed Nigel a towel and he gingerly patted his hands dry. I had just made two mugs of tea when we heard movement upstairs and the landing light lit the bottom of the stairs in the hallway. We listened. Then came the sound of the toilet flushing and the light went off. I was very relieved that Jenny hadn't come down. Then I began to tremble; my whole body shook. Nigel was silently sipping the tea I'd handed him. He had sat down at the kitchen table and was staring at the contents of his mug.

He looked up. "Go to bed, mate," he said. "I'll stay here until it's light then take a taxi to my parents' house. I've still got some clothes there but I don't want to wake them up now. Go to bed yourself."

I glanced at the clock again. Jenny didn't normally get up until about seven. I had already decided I wouldn't make any attempt to get to work. I was only painting the external of a friend's grandparents' bungalow over near Poole. I would ring them later just to reassure them that I would be back on Monday. It wouldn't do any harm missing a day.

Nigel pressed me again. "Go on – bed! I'll come back and see you on Saturday." He hesitated. "If that's OK – if Jenny won't mind?"

"You can't get in a taxi looking like that. I'll get you some clean clothes and a towel and you can clean up a bit at the sink."

He looked down at himself. I had never understood why Jenny had taken such a dislike to Nigel right from the start; it was not rational. I went upstairs and came back down with a long-sleeved tee shirt, some clean jeans and a pair of dry socks.

"Sorry I haven't got any spare shoes. Perhaps wash yours off?"

Then we shook hands without another word and I left him in the kitchen.

I heard the downstairs WC flush then I heard him use the phone. It was not very long till I heard a car pull up outside. He wasted no time; I guessed he was happy to avoid bumping in to Jenny. I cleaned up and checked the scratches on my legs. The jeans were ruined.

As I crept into bed, Jenny murmured and turned towards me, asking if it was Nigel downstairs, but she said nothing more; she didn't even ask me who had died, or where I had been all night. I lay staring at the ceiling, head swimming. The events of the past few hours began whirling through my giddy mind. The top of my head felt like it was floating, my eyes were gritty and sore from lack of sleep and my shoulders and neck ached. I lay listening to Jenny's breathing, the image of Pete's body in a dark hole in the New Forest clear in my mind's eye. I could feel the cold flesh and smell it in my nostrils. I drifted in and out of a hazy sleep. I heard the town waking outside. I was vaguely aware of Jenny getting up but pretended to be asleep to give myself time to rest before her inevitable questions.

But Jenny didn't ask me where I had been when I saw her later that day, and on the Saturday I even brought the subject up myself, and from time to time long afterwards, but she would always repeat the same thing: "I'm not interested."

Sometimes nowadays I thought that her chilly indifference did seem to date back to that night. Not that I could ever tell her the truth, of course. I had worked out a story that I thought sounded plausible but I never did have to use it. I often wondered how come she didn't put together that night with the subsequent stories of the disappearance of Pete Davis that began soon after that day. And Joan's death – Jenny would never discuss that with me either. I think I might have drawn conclusions or at least had suspicions from the connections. Or did she choose not to say? Did she think I was involved? Had she made any connections? *Not something I ever chose to press.*

I stayed in bed until midday or thereabouts and then had a very long, very hot bath. I had cleaned myself quickly before getting into bed but the hot soak was bliss. My sleep had been a confusion of lurid dreams mixed with recurring images of the night's events. I ate a slice of toast, washed the dirty clothes and put the jeans in the dustbin. Jenny would comment on this, I felt sure.

She was late in from work but seemed relaxed and I waited for the questions that never came. I had burbled about Nigel and his recent tour. I skirted near the story I had scripted about Nigel having been called to Ringwood to help Joan clear up a mess she had made in the house there and how he had begged me to help with my van to fix the place up before Pete returned from London after the American tour. At this she made her only comment, saying what an idiot Nigel was to help Joan. Her face showed her distaste as she added that Joan was a self-centred prima donna. *So, she didn't like either of them.*

On Saturday morning Nigel turned up at the front door just after ten o'clock. Jenny let him in and was polite with him. She made three coffees and managed to ask him some questions about American cities he had visited. She left us to it when she went out for an eleven-thirty appointment with a hairdresser.

I told Nigel how she had not wanted to know where I had been on Thursday night/Friday morning. He too thought that was odd. It was then that he revealed that he had intended to move to the USA when the band broke up; whenever that might be. He'd told me on many occasions of the antics and habits of the other three and how he didn't like it, but I also understood his explanations of why he hung on to further establish himself and the music. He said he was going to stay in town for a few days with his parents and make some arrangements for a flight from there.

We spent an awkward morning after that, not knowing quite what to talk about. It was difficult to imagine at that point where Friday's events might lead; I certainly couldn't guess as I stood in my garden when he had gone. Jenny didn't return till about five in the afternoon. She just replied "Shopping" when I asked her where she had been. I told her that her hair looked nice.

We had arranged to go out with Debbie and her husband that evening. Debbie and Jenny worked together in the same solicitors' office, both secretaries to different partners but friends for some while. Graham the husband was a junior solicitor – a nice enough bloke but we had little in common. We were going to the local steak house, so that was all right by me. My stomach had been rumbling since mid-morning and though I couldn't eat any more than that single slice of toast during the day I was now hungry. I went upstairs and changed. Jenny was wearing a new dress that she had bought that day and was busy putting make-up on. I told her she looked nice and she just shrugged with one of those watery smiles that don't reach a person's eyes.

We had a row when we got in that night because I had apparently yawned throughout the evening and offended her friends. I didn't think they had noticed. I said that maybe Graham had noticed her dress and had made it a bit too obvious and was that not offensive to his wife? I quickly regretted saying this; I was only trying to attack in my defence. She slept in the spare bedroom and I slept like an innocent baby in ours. That

Sunday was spent almost entirely in silence. She tidied the house and I tidied the garden. We had beans on toast for dinner and slept back to back that night.

On Monday morning the newspaper I bought mentioned how Rudy Davis, The Strikes' singer, had gone AWOL, as they put it, when he had failed to turn up for a television interview. The newspaper dredged up previous faux pas of The Strikes in general and Rudy Davis in particular, and retold some of the more lurid incidents from their recent past. They weren't very complimentary about Joan either.

I did a day's painting; it was distracting enough to gloss some windows. When I got in from work and picked the local paper out of the letter box my scalp prickled as I noticed the headlines. VANDALS ATTACK GOLF COURSE. The report described mindless damage on the seventh green of Burley Golf Club's course. A photo on the front page told the story. There was a long rectangular pile of dirt and grass, its straight edges screaming 'man-made', and off to one side was the green with its flag. The article also said that a vehicle had driven onto the green; its tracks from the road could be clearly seen. The police were quoted as being 'as puzzled as the Burley Golf Club staff' when they were called later on Friday morning. Until Ted Nobbs, the head green-keeper, deemed the seventh playable, golfers would play on a seventeen-hole course. Ted took some of his own photos and showed them to his wife when they were developed. "Shaped just like a grave," he said.

When I looked up from reading this in the paper, Jenny seemed to be looking at me very closely. She sensed something, I felt sure. Later, when we had finished dinner, I saw her reading the story, and as she read it she kept glancing up at me. She still didn't say anything about it, but did ask if I had seen Nigel during the day. I had recalled this particular moment many times over the years. I always concluded the reason she didn't press me was because she had already lost interest in me. In other words she wasn't bothered what I did or why. Had she already begun her affair with Graham by then? I didn't want to believe she could have; we were together for four more years after that weekend and had two children together during that time. They were mine... weren't they?

Chapter Twenty-seven

Nigel rang as he said he would. He asked if I would drive him to Heathrow airport when he had booked his flight. He said he planned to go to the Los Angeles area where the music scene was 'vibrant'. He asked if I had read any national newspapers or seen the early-evening television news and I told him about the local newspaper's front-page story; he hadn't seen that. He told me speculation had begun already about The Strikes. It seemed that all four had been due to give a television interview the previous Friday and only Zip and Brian had turned up for it. Why it caught the media's interest is not recorded, since the members of The Strikes were known to be unreliable, particularly Rudy. Several speculated that he might be in rehab somewhere.

Somehow it had been discovered that Nigel was visiting his parents in his home town of Bournemouth, and reporters from three daily papers, one Sunday, and the *New Musical Express* had already rung.

One reporter, Chalky White of *The Globe*, was not to be deterred and had turned up at Nigel's parents' front door that afternoon saying how he had tried unsuccessfully to contact Rudy and Jojo. He knew of the house near Ringwood and had already visited it the day before, the Sunday. Nigel told me that he hadn't been aware that Chalky was friendly with Zip, and that Chalky had a lot of information that seemed very private. None of this sounded significant to me, but Nigel was anxious, I could tell.

"If Joan wasn't there, where was she?" Nigel asked me now. "I have to know where she is and what she's doing." He sounded stressed and breathless.

What if Cherry was still with the family in the village? Joan would be very fragile, I was sure. In the end we decided that we must go to the house ourselves, and quickly. We had to find her, and that was the place to start; whatever her state of mind, we had to know. She had committed murder, but under the influence of God-knows-what chemicals and she might not know what she had done, whereas we had consciously contrived to hide her crime, stone-cold sober and compos mentis. We were complicit. Worse still, people might conclude we had more to do with it than Joan did. Nigel, after all, had the strongest motive for wanting Pete Davis to disappear. Would anyone believe that we buried a body just to help out a frail woman who was high on drugs? A woman who had left my friend, taken his only child, and gone to live with somebody else he worked with!

I pulled up outside his parents' house the following morning. I left home before Jenny was up. I didn't want to have to explain myself to her that early in the morning. I did leave early for work sometimes anyway, so it wouldn't seem unusual. I had had no reason to call at his house for some years now since Nigel had left. It looked the same to me from the outside, but as I waited for him a chill ran through me that I couldn't explain. Nigel half raised a hand in greeting, but his attempt at a smile was even less successful. He pulled the door shut and stepped off the front porch into the morning.

When we got to Rookery House we both must have registered the same thing.

What we had seen... what we had found in the outbuilding... the body...

He looked at me as we stood in front of my van and I looked at him. A rook cawed in a nearby poplar and we both glanced up at it. We approached the front door of the large Georgian house. We had passed the wooden stable building. The piece of wood I had jammed in the hasp-and-staple was still in place. Nigel had a key. He hesitated as he put it in the large, panelled wooden door, but the door was not locked. He turned to me and shrugged. I motioned him in first. He pushed the door open, causing the huge brass lion-head door-knocker to rattle. The house smelt – a sweet, musky concoction with sour and unpleasant notes of stale body odour and marijuana. Most houses have their own smell, and once you are inside you get used to it, but this one did not leave my nostrils.

Nigel called out 'hello' as he wandered around in the large hallway. The flagged floor echoed his calls but otherwise silence reigned. Scattered toys and items of clothing – signs of a hurried departure – adorned the untidy rooms.

"Her bedroom," he whispered now as we found ourselves at the bottom of the stairs. I led. They creaked, loud in the silence, as we went up. The polished mahogany handrail gleamed. Dust motes floated in the light from a beautiful stained glass window halfway up. I glanced back at Nigel, close behind me, as I reached the landing.

"Down the end, last door on the left," he said, pointing.

I turned the china handle. I could smell the problem before I had fully opened the door.

"You don't have to come in here," I told him. I stood in the doorway blocking his view.

Joan looked beautiful in death, if that isn't a weird thing to say. She was lying on the bed in the centre of the room, on her back, wearing a simple cotton dress. Her slim arms and legs were suntanned, their fine hairs glistening in a shaft of pale sunlight which fell across her. That she was dead was obvious; she lay so still, and it wasn't sleep – no rising and falling of her chest in gentle breathing – just stillness. Pill-bottles and boxes surrounded her; paracetamol I recognised, but God knows what else she'd taken. Her bodily fluids had flowed; I retched at the smell as I leant over her and took her wrist in vain hopes of a pulse. I touched her face – it was cold. Her eyes stared unseeing and her mouth was open, a dry trail from one corner of still blueish-pink lips. I turned. Nigel stood behind me staring at his former wife, his eyes wet. He shivered and turned away with his face in his hands, shoulders hunched.

"Come on," I said. "Downstairs. There's nothing we can do."

I took his elbow and guided him towards the door. He looked back, and so did I. We stood on the drive in front of the house and didn't speak. Nigel put one hand on the trunk of a chestnut tree and stared up into the branches as if it might provide him with some answers. I leant on the bonnet of the van and smoked. I had many thoughts racing through my mind but for now I stayed silent so that Nigel could absorb what we had just witnessed. Could we tell the authorities? What could we tell them? They would need to know why we were here. Could we just drive away?

It was broad daylight but we hadn't passed a soul coming through the village to the house. As far as we knew no one had seen us anyway. The shop was open, the little garage workshop was open, the pub was not. On the far side of the village square the church stood watching over everything. What reason could we give to the police for being here and finding Joan's body? I could not imagine.

Nigel came over to me. He seemed reasonably composed.

"Let's go," he said quietly, climbing into the passenger seat. "Let's get out of here while the village is quiet. When we get further away, perhaps in Ringwood, I'll phone the police from a call-box and suggest they check the house out."

"I'm so, so sorry, mate," was all I managed to say as I started the engine. He blew out his cheeks and stared straight ahead through the windscreen, features rigid and eyes glistening.

"My life is about to change forever," he whispered, more to himself than to me.

As we headed back towards Bournemouth I had a thousand questions for Nigel – for both of us, I supposed – but it was he who spoke first, and I was relieved when he did.

"I hope we weren't seen going to the house... going through the village. It's a good job your van is not sign-written." This had crossed my mind a few times that day... and the previous Thursday.

"We were never there," I agreed.

We stopped at a phone-box on the outskirts of Ringwood and Nigel rang the local police to tell them to investigate Rookery House. He described roughly where it was and what it looked like, declining to leave a name when asked. Neither of us could remember if we had shut the wrought-iron gates or not.

We agreed that when the police reached Joan they would know soon enough from an autopsy that drugs were the cause of her death. They might well take an interest in whether it was suicide. Ultimately the most popular of police theories would prove to be that Pete Davis had vanished after his girlfriend had died of an overdose. They would pin their hopes on finding the singer; then all questions would surely be answered.

I dropped Nigel off at his parents' house that day. We spent the rest of the week together, drinking at pubs we had visited growing up, with the exception of The White Buck Inn. We went into town, we walked along the promenade, and we climbed Hengistbury Head and looked over Christchurch Bay towards The Priory. We walked the length of Bournemouth pier and sat on a bench halfway down and talked about the time I had booked the Pier Theatre for The Strikes to play in. I hadn't lost money but it had been close, and later on they had sold out the whole pier for a Strikes concert.

All over town people came up to us for Nigel's autograph or to have a photo with him. He obliged with patience. Most asked where Pete was hiding. The local paper had revelled in the fact that they were a local band – 'Our very own Strikes'. Joan was a 'local beauty' too, they declared. School friends, teachers and neighbours were sought, Lou's Mum and Dad were quoted, and Zip's brothers. The questions were being asked nationwide too. 'Where is Rudy Davis?' 'Where is The Strikes' singer?' 'Did he kill his lover Jojo?' 'What will happen to their child?' 'Was it suicide or murder?'

As we sat on the bench the sky darkened and rain began to fall. It increased quickly and we ran for the car park and my van. This would be one of Nigel's last memories of his home town. A rainy pier!

Jenny's mood definitely lightened when I told her Nigel was going to live in California; she was pleased but she didn't actually say so. She did wonder what would become of The Strikes, though – as did the whole country and some of the world, I guessed. The anonymous call to the police at Ringwood was now public knowledge, and the mysterious disappearance of the 'outrageous' singer of The Strikes was discussed ad nauseam, including every aspect of Joan's life. Her parents were sought out; her sister in Aylesbury. Lou Lewis and Brian 'Zip' Updike were followed almost permanently by a pack of photographers. All four of the band's faces appeared everywhere one looked, it seemed. Sales of their whole catalogue of albums nearly took over the charts.

On the Monday we had been drinking quietly in the bar of The Crescent Hotel, then suddenly flashbulbs were going off in our faces. This was when I knew I had had enough – I told Nigel I had to get back to doing some work, and he apologised for about the hundredth time for getting me involved. I had given up trying to talk about my own long-term plans, but more immediately I had to earn some money – I had to pay the mortgage. It had been two weeks of mayhem for me: the weather had turned rainy and I still had external painting work outstanding; Jenny only spoke to me if she had to, and she still turned her back to me in bed. I tried to remain patient – keep my mouth shut and not start arguments. *Things would get back to normal when Nigel had gone.*

I parked in the short-stay car park at Heathrow, took Nigel's luggage out of the back of the van and we made our way over to the terminal. After he'd checked in we went to a bar and found a seat, but I didn't want to drink. Neither of us said much. I asked him what time his flight was.

"Still over an hour yet," he told me. I looked at my watch.

"You can go if you like," he said quietly. "You've got a long journey home."

"Not as long as yours," I said. He smiled weakly at this.

"I'm so sorry to have got you enmeshed, Tony."

He turned towards me. I couldn't answer; my throat was constricted. I patted him on the shoulder. I've no idea what that conveyed to him.

"When I'm settled in with somewhere to live I hope you'll come and visit me."

"Of course I will… try keeping me away," I told him. "Do you really mean it that you'll never come home?"

He assured me very gravely and concisely once more that he would not. He said again how happy he was just being in the airport knowing he was on his way to leaving behind such terrible memories. As he stood ready to go through to departures it crossed my mind that I wouldn't be leaving behind those 'terrible memories'; I would be living just a few miles away from them. I also felt certain the police would want to talk to him some more yet. I walked to the departure gate with him and we shook hands. We let go then shook hands again.

"Please stay in touch," I croaked. My throat ached. He walked a few paces; half turned, and raised a hand. I lifted a hand and smiled and he was out of sight. Feeling foolish because I had tears in my eyes, I looked around, but no one was taking any notice of me. I stood there staring at the closed doors.

Chapter Twenty-eight

For the first few weeks and then months I expected to hear from Nigel, but then as each year passed and I still had not heard from him I became less and less disappointed. Sometimes, still, I hoped that I would find a letter on my mat when I got home from work. *If only.*

After Jenny left me it did cross my mind that maybe he had written and she had destroyed the letters before I saw them; I did think that she was capable of such a spiteful act. I would probably never know the truth of it.

When Lisa had told me that we had jobs in the Burley area it hadn't helped my frame of mind. The urge to tell somebody was becoming stronger. I found myself thinking back more and more.

One morning, I heard the side gate and my spirits immediately lifted. Charlotte, I assumed. I listened. It went quiet. I got up and went to the back door. There she was opening the studio door. She had bright pink jeans on and her usual black quilted jacket and a funny woollen hat with sort of ears and tassels. She didn't turn round. I watched her go in. The lights came on. I wanted to go down there but restrained myself. It would be wrong, I knew. I lit a cigarette and smoked it, hardly taking my eyes from where I knew she was. I returned to my kitchen; I was cold. I stood at the window staring down at the closed door. I had to get a grip.

I was upstairs later in the afternoon cleaning my bathroom when I heard a call from downstairs. It was Charlotte. I went to the top of the stairs and shouted hello. She just wanted to use the downstairs toilet, she told me, but added, "How are you?" I heard the door closing before I could answer her. I busied myself all afternoon. I listened to the football results. In the end at about six o'clock I couldn't stop myself. I knocked on the studio door. Charlotte opened it with a smile.

"Come in, quick. It's only just started to feel warm in here; you'll let the heat out."

I didn't know what to say now. I wished I hadn't disturbed her. On an easel was a canvas she had obviously been working on. She glanced over at it. It was a portrait, I could see – just head and shoulders of an elderly lady with pure white hair, fine bone structure and smooth skin.

"You can smoke if you want to, Tony, and can I have one, please? I forgot to buy any."

I held my lighter up towards her and she cupped the hand that held it nearer to her mouth; I almost sighed audibly. I was so pleased to see her and talk to her again.

"How are you?" I asked. She smiled, eyes sparkling.

"I'm good. How are you?"

"I'm not so good." I had answered without thinking, and I even noticed the light in her eyes dull a little.

"You look beautiful," I told her.

She chuckled, and small pink spots rose in her cheeks. "I am feeling so well lately. I hope it lasts."

I wished I had not said what I had just said. I felt awkward now, and uncomfortable.

"Sorry," I mumbled.

"Why are you sorry?" She looked genuinely puzzled.

"What I said then... about you looking beautiful." I was mumbling again. She came up to me and put her face just inches from mine. My breathing stopped. She put both hands on my shoulders and looked me straight in the eye.

"Are you trying to tell me you didn't mean it?" I caught a twinkle in her eyes at that moment. She was teasing me. She laughed and leant forward and kissed me on the cheek.

I started to speak but she put a finger over my lips to stop me. Perhaps she knew I was about to say something stupid. She let go. I put my cigarette out and lit another.

I went and stood looking at the canvas. "Who is she? She's beautiful." Charlotte softened visibly and came and stood beside me. "My grandmother."

I wanted to ask if she was alive but couldn't find words. She told me anyway; the girl was a mind-reader.

"She died a few weeks ago. That's why I haven't been here much lately. I was with her as she died. At the very last second, her hand released mine. It was a lovely moment – so poignant." Charlotte studied her painting as she spoke.

"I've been coming during the night lately to do it. I had to do it without talking to anybody first." She glanced at me. "Not even you," she added. She took my hand and squeezed it quickly.

"I can see the likeness now: the eyes... the mouth... the bone structure."

I was still looking at the portrait. Meanwhile Charlotte sat down and was watching me.

"Is it finished?" I asked. I wasn't sure because the paint was applied so thinly, almost translucent. There was something ethereal about the face floating on the canvas.

"Do you think it is?" she replied.

"I do."

"Then it is," she said quietly. "It's how she looked to me at her last breath – I tried to catch her very last moment alive. That's why she appears to be fading." Her voice dropped to a mere whisper. "You could see that, couldn't you?"

I nodded and turned to face her. "Yes, I could." I looked back to the work on the easel. "I want to say goodbye – it makes me want to say goodbye. I didn't know you, but... goodbye."

I turned to look at the artist. A tear rolled down her right cheek.

"Can I have another of your cigarettes, please, Tony?"

"Of course," I muttered. "Of course," I repeated more clearly, and held them out.

"Why haven't you married again?" she asked as I gave her a light.

I was a bit taken aback, though I was getting used to the fact that she would usually say whatever was on her mind. I told her that I didn't know. I mumbled something about not having met anybody daft enough to have me. She didn't reply, and this unnerved me. I said the first thing that came to mind.

"Well, maybe a person can be excused one mistake, but two is foolish and entirely your own fault for not learning your lesson." It was a glib answer, I know, but I sort of meant it. I like female company but whenever it had come close to a serious relationship I brought it to an end, either deliberately or accidentally. "If I had met someone like you when I was young enough I might well have wanted to risk it again," I found myself saying.

Charlotte stood and then came up behind me. She put her hands on my shoulders, and I could sense her very close.

"I wish," she breathed.

I turned to face her.

"Do you mean that?" she asked. I didn't have to think about my answer.

"Of course. You've lit up my life since I first met you."

She had a small, strained smile on her lips. I watched it twitch there.

"That's a lovely thing to say, Tony," she sighed, then continued. "I haven't told you this before but it was for you that I was able to get clean."

"But you were trying when we met," I interrupted.

"I know, but it was for you I could maintain my resolve and my conviction. And you choose to call me Charlotte even though I told you most people call me Charlie."

She said this straight-faced and serious.

I was holding my breath at her proximity. Then my stomach gurgled loud enough for us both to hear and the moment evaporated instantly. She squeezed my shoulders as she let go, and asked if by any chance I was hungry. We decided that we would go over to a local Harvester pub together. I left her in the studio and went back to the house to put on a clean shirt and pullover, and a little Calvin Klein 'Eternity'.

She said she would drive. I hadn't ever been in her little van. She had said I could have a beer or two if I didn't drive.

I ended up having three drinks before we got a table and I was beginning to feel them on my empty stomach. I asked about her grandmother. It seemed Charlotte had been mostly brought up in Camden, north London. Her parents' marriage had disintegrated when she was quite young. Her father was a lawyer and her mother a journalist; in fact I recognised her name. I had even seen her on television several times. She was the sort of intellectual they wheeled out on all sorts of serious discussion programmes. I thought I could see some likeness now I knew. She was probably in her sixties, but still a good-looking woman, with the kind of striking violet eyes that defy age; she would still be attractive in her nineties. Charlotte's eyes, however, were chestnut brown. It seemed, though, that her parents had some unconventional ideas about their relationship; 'open marriage'.

We had never really talked much about her family – or mine, come to that. This seemed to be the theme tonight, though. Amelia, her grandmother, did sound rather wonderful. She had nurtured Charlotte's talent, encouraging her to paint and create, to study, and to 'explore herself' and the limits of her capabilities. Charlotte explained that this was maybe because she had once wished to pursue a career in art for herself but had been thwarted by her own parents. She had then doted on her granddaughter. "We were friends of different ages, just like you and me. That's how I think of you and me, Tony."

At this point we were told that a table was available for us. I was thinking about that comment as we looked at the menu. "Friends of different ages."

I had a mixed grill that was a challenge even though I was hungry and Charlotte had a pasta dish. She asked about my ex-wife and my daughters as we ate. I began to think there might be a connection between her father and the man Jenny left me for. Both lawyers, and both in north London. Perhaps they did know each other, we decided, but we couldn't connect them.

I saw a plumber mate of mine on the other side of the restaurant, and he waved in acknowledgement. I guessed he was out with his wife and another couple. He was coming over our way. I was just finishing my dinner – I have always been a fast eater – but Charlotte was still only halfway through hers. I leant back in my chair as Dennis came up. He stood behind Charlotte. He was more interested in her than me, I could tell. He made her jump when he spoke.

"Hello, Tony. Out enjoying yourself?"

I agreed I was. "This is Charlotte," I said, nodding across the table. "That is Dennis, a mate of mine, hovering behind you," I told her as she turned. "It was Dennis who did the plumbing in your studio."

"So is this one your daughters, Tony?" he asked with a straight face. He knew very well it wasn't.

My brain was stumbling over a selection of possible answers, but Charlotte beat me to it.

"We're friends," she said. "I'm not his daughter."

Dennis was leaning out of her sight line and pulling silly faces; grinning like an idiot. I tried to distract him by asking who he was with. His wife and next-door neighbours, he told us. "This is a big night out these days, a Harvester meal. We're going back to the Soldier's Rest now, though, for a few more drinks, if you fancy joining us."

I didn't want to say yes and I didn't want to say no. I said, "Maybe." That would at least allow me to see what Charlotte might want to do without Dennis leering at her. I could see his wife and neighbours looking our way, ready to go, waiting for him. He noticed them and said goodbye.

"Might see you later," he added with a wink at Charlotte.

I thought this would annoy her but it made her laugh her head off.

"Fancy winking at me," she chuckled. "It's only old blokes and Simon Cowell who wink these days." She went into a fit of giggles. "I guess that was a good chat-up method once upon a time." She shook her head. "Dear me," she concluded. "Do you want to go to the pub? I'm happy to, if you want to go to the…"

"The Soldier's Rest," I finished for her. "It's a little hole-in-the-wall-type old fashioned pub just a few streets from my house. I used to go there a lot at one time. I'm surprised it's still in business with so many pubs closing down these days."

"I *would* like to see, then," she said. "I'd like to see where you used to go."

"You don't have to," I said, but I knew she had made up her mind. I was just concerned about her and alcohol.

"I'll park my van by your house and we'll walk round there together." She said it so positively; she meant it, I could tell.

I asked for and paid the bill. It was only about twenty past ten. We dropped the van off outside my house. She slipped her arm through mine; it felt comfortable, and we walked round to the pub. It turned out to be a really enjoyable couple of hours till we said our 'goodnights' at about twelve-thirty and parted company.

"I'm normally in bed by ten-thirsty," I said to Charlotte as I attempted to put the key in my front door.

"Thirsty?" she repeated.

"No, not now," I replied. "I've had more than enough."

She asked if she could make some coffee and went through to the kitchen. I attempted to follow.

"Go and sit down comfortably, Mr Smith," she ordered, pushing me back into the lounge. After considering the sofa I slumped into my armchair.

I could just make out the clock on my mantelpiece: five to five. I was cold. I managed to get upright. I used the downstairs WC. No sign of Charlotte, I noted, as a vague memory returned. I climbed the stairs slowly. My bedroom door was open but the other two doors were shut. I realised that Charlotte could be in one of the spare bedrooms; they both had beds in, though neither would have been made up. Or would she have gone down the garden to her studio? She did have a divan there. I couldn't resist – I peered into the most likely. Sure enough, there was a lump in the bed there. It stirred slightly and murmured. I quickly shut the door, went to my own room, and got undressed and climbed into bed.

The next thing I was aware of was the phone ringing downstairs. I was confused for a few moments. My bedside alarm said ten-fifteen. The phone still rang. I put my dressing gown on and hurried to answer it. It was Lisa, asking if I would like to have Sunday lunch with her and her mum. I was confused.

"This is Tony here," I said, thinking perhaps she had rung my number by mistake, and thought she was talking to somebody else. She assured me that she knew it was me.

"You OK?" she said. She had never invited me round like this. We'd had the odd drink in the evening and a few meals in cafés after work, but that was all.

"Two o'clock," she said, and hung up. I had said 'yes', though.

I went back upstairs and found three empty bedrooms. I had a long shower, shaved and got dressed. My head ached, so I searched my cupboards for paracetamol.

I put the radio on at low volume and went to the back door to smoke. The studio lights were on. The kettle boiled and I made two drinks, then knocked the door as best I could with a hot mug in each hand.

"Good afternoon, sir. Do come in." She stood back from the door, smiling.

"How're you feeling?" she asked with a knowing look on her face. "You had a good time last night."

"Did I?" We both laughed.

"I enjoyed last night too," she told me and sipped the tea I'd made.

She offered me a cigarette.

She was so natural, so comfortable with herself this morning. All my little fears evaporated; it just felt normal to have a joke and a cup of tea and a smoke with her. I told her about Lisa's phone call and invitation.

"Oh, that will be nice," she said, uncharacteristically uninquisitive. "You are going, aren't you?"

I felt like apologising because I was going and she wasn't.

"I suppose I should," I muttered. I explained that it was unprecedented; that I'd been to the door before but had never even been inside the house. I added that I didn't know Lisa's mum either. I agreed that perhaps it was strange since I'd worked for Lisa so long, but she always did the driving and picked me up or I just drove myself to a job, so maybe it wasn't so odd after all. Charlotte explained that she just wanted to make a few tiny additions to Amelia's portrait and I took the hint and left her to it. I told her that I hoped we could do something similar again, but as I walked back into the house this felt like a silly thing to have said and I wished I hadn't. Charlotte hadn't replied and I hoped I'd not caused embarrassment between us. We were friends of different ages. That was all.

Chapter Twenty-nine

I popped to an out-of-town supermarket and bought some flowers to turn up to Lisa's mum's house with. As I pulled up Lisa was standing at the front door already. It was spot-on two o'clock. Had she been looking out for me from the front window?

Her mum's house was a neat semi on an estate; I had worked on these houses when they were being built in the seventies. Lisa looked very nice and I told her so as I reached the front door. She called me an 'old smoothie' and stood back and ushered me in. She was wearing tight red jeans and a simple light-grey cardigan with red buttons. I was still clutching the bunch of flowers in cellophane as she introduced me to Diane, her mum.

Diane had the same natural, relaxed and uncomplicated manner as her daughter. She was in her fifties, but at which end of them I couldn't say for sure. I knew Lisa was now in her early thirties and I was trying to work it out. She still had a nice figure, again the same as her daughter only a bit more rounded. Her hair was going quite grey but it suited her. I was older than Lisa's mum but I think had more colour left in my hair than her. She was weighing me up as I was her. Her face was nicely made up; she had black jeans on.

Lisa asked if I would like a drink. The room was really nicely furnished with a big flat-screen television opposite quality beige tweed sofas. I handed Diane the flowers and she smiled and sniffed them. She held her hand out to me and I took it. I think I held it just a few seconds too long for politeness. It felt nice in mine. I met her eyes and something did pass between us. Lisa was watching me in that way that she had. Her eyebrows did 'that' arch, I noticed.

Lisa left the room then reappeared carrying a bottle of lager complete with a wedge of lime in the neck, took the flowers from her mum and handed the misted, wet bottle to me. I took a sip. From the kitchen came the smell of the roast, a warm and homely aroma that brought back memories for me. I must have shown something; Lisa took my arm.

"Sit down." She led me to a sofa.

I glanced around the room – it's impossible not to in our line of work. Hairdressers look at haircuts, gardeners at gardens and decorators check out rooms: colours, styles, and quality of workmanship. Over the years, I'd picked up some good ideas from this habit: colour combinations, new wallpaper patterns.

"Are you checking my work?" Lisa asked with a grin.

She went back to the kitchen and Diane came and sat beside me, a glass of white wine in her hand.

"I hope you like beef, Tony, because that's what we're having today," she said. I told her it had been many years since I'd had a home-cooked roast-beef dinner. She said that she and Lisa still tried to have a 'proper' Sunday lunch, as she put it, but how it had been a long time since she had cooked one for a man. She had a teasing twinkle in her eye that I liked already; she was very easy company, and I felt very comfortable talking to her, so I was a little bit sorry when Lisa announced that lunch was ready.

I peered into the warm kitchen; it was much bigger than I assumed it would be. A huge square room with skylights, it had been extended into the garden. Downlighters were scattered in the ceiling and there were huge, folding patio doors and plenty of maple units with black granite worktops. In one corner was a table laid for three with bright multicoloured mats and shiny cutlery, in the centre of which stood a small glass bowl containing a single, orange daisy-type flower that may have been real or artificial.

"Well, this is very nice," I said.

"You like?" Lisa spread her arms expansively.

"It's lovely," I told her genuinely.

"Mum had this extension done to cheer herself up."

Diane was now filling three plates on a worktop near the cooker. Beef, Yorkshire pudding that looked home-made, carrots, parsnips, peas, cabbage, roast potatoes and even a small baked onion. My mouth watered. Lisa topped up her own and her mum's glasses and handed me another beer from the fridge. She asked her mum if she wanted a hand. Diane said that she would serve it as Lisa had done most of the work.

Lisa had never talked much at work about her family circumstances. I knew her dad had left her mother and I knew her mother was a schoolteacher, but that was pretty much it. She would have told me more if she wanted me to know, I always concluded. I now learned that she was head teacher of a large comprehensive school in Southampton. She was witty and funny and I quickly found myself really enjoying her company; the only thing that made me uncomfortable was a feeling that I wasn't as well educated.

The roast was delicious. I told Lisa that she was a good cook and would not need her new boyfriend. We had some ice cream and a tin of fruit cocktail. I then shamed myself by going to sleep on a sofa for at least an hour.

Lisa wasn't around when I woke. She had gone to see Gary. I told Diane how I wished I had a daughter like Lisa. We seemed to get on quite well but I had gathered she was following a period drama series on television that started at nine o'clock so I had made up my mind to leave before it started. She offered a cheek at the front door and I obliged.

As I drove home the gloom began to return. I had had a completely different weekend to normal and was returning to the reality of my narrow, solitary life. I realised I hadn't smoked at their house but I smoked two on the way home. It crossed my mind again that I must try to give up.

As I put the key in the front door emptiness engulfed me. I sat at my kitchen table for a long while not sure what to do with myself. I had had the best weekend for years and I was feeling miserable. The hut was in darkness; Charlotte had gone. I realised just how lonely I was. I realised that life had almost passed me by. I had talked with Lisa's mum about retirement. She found her job stressful; government changes and pressures were becoming harder to take, she had told me, and the daily drive to Southampton was not enjoyable. She was contemplating early retirement, and asked if I had any plans to retire. I'd told her that I wouldn't know what to do with myself if I did and would probably never see a soul. She asked me where I liked to go on holiday.

I must have sounded like a real misery when I told her I had not been on holiday for years. It seemed she went away every summer with a friend of hers, another teacher, a spinster in her sixties. She told me that each year before the Christmas term ended they would decide where they were going the following summer; they would then spend months investigating their intended destinations before they went. They would study the language and places to visit. She had asked me over dinner if I had learned to use a PC, and Lisa, when she had stopped laughing, had told her of my computer-lesson exploits. Diane had been greatly amused but she had also offered to teach me.

My thoughts jumped randomly from one aspect of my life to another here in my kitchen: I thought of Jenny and my daughters; I thought of Nigel. I pictured the grave in the dawn gloom of the New Forest all those years ago. I thought of Charlotte. I had begun to think I was in love with her. I admonished myself for that thought. The futility! The age difference! *Bloody silly old fool!*

My mind was swimming, then I felt tears arrive. I wiped my sleeve across my face and lit another cigarette. We were going to be working in Burley tomorrow. I went to bed but couldn't sleep; I tossed and I turned.

I was driving my Transit van in the 1970s; I was sitting on Diane's sofa; I was stealing a sideways look at Charlotte; I was up a stepladder hanging wallpaper in Daisy's beautiful house; I was talking to Lisa at the back of her van. I checked the glowing LED numerals on my bedside clock-radio; it blinked two forty-seven. I was hot and uncomfortable. I slid from the bed, went to the bathroom, found my dressing gown and went downstairs.

At the back of a kitchen cupboard I discovered a jar of drinking chocolate I had no recollection of buying. I thought it would be better than the caffeine of tea or coffee. As if I could sleep anyway! I smoked at the back door in the cold night air, staring at the shadowed outline of the hut a short way off. I pictured Amelia on canvas. I marvelled once more at Charlotte's skills. I pictured the fantastic magic she had created on Daisy's walls. I thought of her beautiful face and her elegant long fingers dirty with paints. I pictured her standing back to assess her own efforts, her head tilted sideways, and I recalled her new habit, since he had had her hair cropped short, of rubbing the top of her head when in thought, and I fancied I could smell soap, white spirit and flowers.

Eventually I climbed back into bed. I pulled the duvet under my chin and tried to dispel the alternating pictures in my head. I guess I drifted off because the alarm of Radio Four had begun at six o'clock and I was hearing the six-thirty summaries. I forced myself to get out of bed. I didn't want to go to Burley; I didn't want to leave my house. I went to the bathroom then put on my work clothes. When I saw myself in the mirror I looked how I felt: washed out and old.

The thatched cottage in Burley Street was beautiful. The people who had recently bought it as a holiday home had yet to move in. It was surrounded by camellias of many colours; some in flower, some past flowering and some with promise.

Lisa and Dave had both commented on how bad I looked when I got in the van that Monday morning. I tried to find an opportunity to thank Lisa for the previous day's invitation, and finally got the chance at about one o'clock when Dave popped out to the garden to smoke. I thanked her and I told her how much I enjoyed her mum's company. She pouted jokingly at this and I quickly added, "Yours too."

"My mum liked you too. Charlie and I had discussed how we both thought you two would get on well."

This jolted me. "Charlotte?"

"Yes, I was telling her that I thought you and Mum would get on OK. She knows my mum."

"Well I didn't know that. How?"

"Charlie used to take after-school art classes at Mum's school in Southampton some years ago, before…" Lisa trailed off but I knew what she meant.

"Before drugs and drink?" I finished her sentence.

"Yes," Lisa sighed. "When we met for Daisy's job I was telling Mum one day about Charlie's lovely work, and she realised it must be the same Charlotte. They're quite good friends again. Mum even went to her gran's funeral recently."

"Well, well, you just never know. So it was a joint conspiracy between the three of you?"

She didn't answer at first but then a grin spread across her face. "You could say that."

I hadn't expected any joy from this day but I had some women who did care about me!

"I wish I had a daughter like you," I told Lisa. "And one like Charlotte too," I added before going out to the garden for a smoke. Birds were singing in the trees that surrounded the cottage and I could hear, but not see, a busy woodpecker somewhere nearby.

"What did you do this weekend, ol' man?" asked Dave when I found him, sandwich in one hand, roll-up in the other and mug of tea at his feet.

"Not much," I replied. I wasn't about to let him spoil my memories of the two days by telling him and having to listen to his inevitable crude comments.

"You looking forward to the party at Daisy Belle's?"

"Yes, I suppose I am."

I knew I sounded less than enthusiastic. In truth it was getting to me as it got nearer. The thought of seeing Nigel now gave me mixed feelings. Working in the Burley area was not helping me but the next job was nearer still. It was the other side of Burley village centre up the hill towards the grave.

The job at the cottage was going to take a couple of weeks; this one was mostly emulsions with wallpaper in the main bedroom. The house-owners were staying at the hotel we had to work on next, but they popped in sometimes to see our progress. They would move in when we had finished.

Each night when we turned back onto the A31 a tension seemed to leave me, but it would return the following morning as we rumbled over the cattle-grid on the way to Burley. However, I was quite enjoying the job, despite everything. It was a nice place to work, and the husband-and-wife owners were friendly people – not always 'on our case' as some can be who can afford a near million-pound holiday home.

On Thursday that week, after Lisa had dropped Dave off on the way home, she asked me what I was doing on the coming weekend.

"Mum said would you like to pop round on Saturday sometime. I'm out with Gary; I'm going to the restaurant and then back to his flat when he's finished work."

I was a bit flustered at this. I thought of Charlotte. Was this the week she brought Chinese food? I couldn't think. I felt guilty when I said 'yes' to Lisa. I asked her what time. It seems Lisa and Diane had already had a discussion and they had decided I would make the decision. I was flustered again. I was under pressure.

"How about six o'clock and I'll take her out for something to eat? I'll think of somewhere before then – a surprise."

"Great," said Lisa. "I'll tell her tonight. Six. See you tomorrow morning. Bye, Tony." I watched the van's tail lights until she turned the corner and went out of sight. *I had a date.*

Chapter Thirty

I hadn't noticed if Charlotte was there or not when I'd arrived home and gone to the kitchen, so she made me jump when she knocked at the back door.

"Have you lost your key? You don't have to knock, you know."

She explained that she knocked because she saw the kitchen light come on and therefore knew I was 'in residence'.

"I wouldn't just waltz through when you're here!" she said with a smile.

"I didn't know you knew Lisa's mum," I said.

"I do indeed," she replied. She was studying me in the way I had become used to.

"I'm seeing Diane on Saturday evening."

I seemed to blurt it out rather than mentioning it casually. She came over and stood very close in front of me and did her 'watching' for what seemed like minutes but in truth was probably only seconds. She put her hands on my shoulders, leaned in, and kissed me fully on the mouth.

"I'm so pleased for you. We both – that is, Lisa and I – hoped you would get on with each other. Diane's been on her own a long time too you know, but it was you I worried about. So when I asked Lisa about how you were at work we soon hatched our plan."

She still stood close to me; I eased forward and hugged her. I had longed to hold her and now I could – and for the right reasons. I clung on. She wriggled and made exaggerated puffing noises. I let her go.

"Sorry."

"Don't be sorry. I enjoyed the hug." We hugged again.

We clung to each other for some minutes.

"Thank God we're friends," she said at last and stood back whilst still holding my hands.

"Yes, I know what you mean," I agreed. For different reasons, I'm sure. I had begun to fantasise about having a relationship with her. I'd told myself that sometimes older men marry beautiful young women. I had come very close on several occasions to saying the wrong thing. I was brought back down to earth by her remark. She was another 'daughter', but one I loved... like Lisa.

I kissed her on the forehead and told her I loved her. I didn't feel uncomfortable this time and I knew she understood how I meant it. She put a finger to my mouth as she had done once before to stop me talking. I said no more.

She walked over and opened the back door, then turned. "I love you too, Tony," she said, then shut the back door behind her and left me standing there, slightly bewildered. A feeling of peace entered me.

I lit a cigarette and stared at the lighted window down the garden. I thought of the unusual young woman there. It began to rain. I had a frozen dinner of hotpot or whatever it was and was in bed by nine-thirty, drifting off to sleep to the sound of voices on the radio.

About halfway through the next morning I caught Dave and Lisa standing in the doorway of the room I was painting, looking at me. When I looked round they both had soppy grins on their faces.

"Lot of whistling going on in this room this morning," Dave said. They looked at each other like naughty children and ran off giggling. I smiled to myself as I cut in the window reveals and gazed across the back lawn to where it met the forest.

I was up early on Saturday. I laughed at myself when I became aware that I was whistling. It was one of those tuneless whistles. I did a bit of shopping at the supermarket for the following week, I put some clothes in the washing machine, I had some cheese on toast with ketchup on it at lunchtime and I tidied up my bedroom and changed the sheets and pillowcases. I only use one pillow but I had always changed both pillow cases ever since Jenny left.

I showered and got ready. I changed my mind several times about what shirt and trousers to wear and finally decided on the white polo-shirt and new black chinos I had bought after Christmas in the sale. I put on my new black, quilted Barbour jacket with the corduroy collar, splashed on 'Eternity' and went out into the rain to my van. I had bought some chocolates from the supermarket that morning and I grabbed them from the passenger seat as I pulled up on Diane's front drive. The front door opened; it framed her in the light. I put a hand on her shoulder and pecked her on the cheek. It felt silky smooth and soft. She smelt of something expensive and musky. *Not thinners, flowers and soap*. I handed her the chocolates. She playfully smacked my hand and told me never to buy her chocolate again. I was about to apologise when I realised she was joking.

"I'll get my coat," she said.

I held the door for her to get in my van.

"Where shall we go then? Where are you taking me?"

I hadn't been out with a woman for a meal for many years; well, not on a date. I had checked the local paper's adverts for restaurants, eventually deciding on a hotel on the East Cliff; the advert for their newly refurbished art deco-style restaurant made it sound worth a try. She told me she had never been there and that seemed like a good start to me. I had at one point thought of the restaurant where Gary worked, where Lisa, Dave and I had decorated, but of course Lisa was there tonight, so that was hardly an option.

We pulled into the car park at the rear of the hotel; I had seen the lighted entrance to the restaurant at the side. It was raining quite hard now. I hadn't noticed before but Diane had brought an umbrella with her. She stood at the front of the van under it and waited for me to lock it up.

We went in and were shown to a table straight away. It was very quiet in the dining room. The lighting was subdued blue LED and the décor had used plenty of chrome accessories against a deep purple wall-covering. Aubrey Beardsley prints in black frames with grey mounts adorned the walls. I really liked the look they had achieved. We ordered some drinks and I looked around at the décor. There were a few other couples dotted about and one table of about ten which we guessed was a family celebration of some sort. I had a beer and Diane had a gin and tonic. We had asked the waiter to give us about half an hour before we ordered.

"Cheers," said Diane and we clinked glasses.

She looked really nice, so I told her so.

We ordered starters.

Diane wanted wine; I had to ask her to choose it, as I had no idea, though I felt a bit stupid admitting it. I found I quite liked what she had ordered and soon we were on our second bottle. The starter I had was really nice – a salmon gateau – and Diane had a salad with orange segments and a ginger dressing. It looked good and she cooed at the first mouthful. We both had the same main course: 'chargrilled rib-eye steak and garlic-scented sautéed potatoes with grilled mushroom and tomato' – which was delicious. When the waiter returned for our plates I ordered a third bottle of wine; I was definitely beginning to feel the effects of the alcohol but had got a taste for it. We were getting on really well too. She was very intelligent and good fun as well. I found myself more and more at ease – an unaccustomed feeling. By the time we ordered a sweet I was beginning to slur my words. When I popped out to use the gents' I also went out to the terrace and inhaled some cold air. I really wanted to smoke but I didn't want to go back in smelling of cigarettes. I tried to gather the senses that the unaccustomed wine-drinking was dissolving. When I got back to the table I apologised for being so long and told her that I had been gulping air.

She thought it funny rather than annoying and asked if I'd had a cigarette. I confessed I wanted one but didn't want to smell of it. She told me she wouldn't have minded. I described the little canopy for smokers the hotel had outside. I also told her that I could feel the wine. Again this amused her and she even topped up my glass as I was telling her this.

We exchanged anecdotes about work. We even talked of our failed marriages. I told her how I often wished I had a daughter like hers, like Lisa. She didn't comment but listened carefully as I described my own daughters. She told me how she had met her husband at university and how they used to go to The White Buck Inn... my world was shrinking! Immediately a flashback came of a cold, damp grave that seemed to be summoned by any mention of Burley. The wine I had drunk hadn't kept the image at bay.

I reached across the table and took Diane's hand. She didn't resist. It felt soft and smooth and comfortable. I looked up; she was just watching me.

"Do you mind?" I asked her.

She made no attempt to pull away.

"Why should I mind?" She said it quietly and with the mischievous twinkle in her eye that I was already enjoying and which was beginning to beguile me. I didn't let go.

She told me then that she had known she would enjoy my company. I was puzzled. What was she telling me? I certainly wasn't used to compliments. She continued by telling me how Lisa had always talked about me and how fond she was of me.

"She had said for a very long time how she would introduce us. She told me that I would like you."

I paid the bill when we'd finished our coffee. Diane wanted to pay half but I wouldn't let her. We went through to a bar and she excused herself and vanished for some minutes; long enough for me to start to think she had called a taxi and gone home. She reappeared though and sat down beside me on a sofa. I asked what she would like to drink. She hesitated. I was feeling really tired though it was not much past ten o'clock yet. I blamed the wine.

"I'm going to ask for one of those cocktails I've just seen someone with but I'll go to the bar. Would you like another lager?" She had stood up again. "And you can go and have a cigarette – I know you want one."

I did, so I took her cue. In fact I smoked two in their shelter before I returned.

"Better?" she asked as I sat down in an armchair opposite her. She made an exaggerated pout and patted the sofa cushion beside her. I accepted the invitation.

"I'll have to call a taxi to get us home," I told her. "I've drunk too much. I'll come back down tomorrow to retrieve the van."

"Well, thank you for a lovely meal," she said. "Are you tired?"

She had noticed me glance at the clock over the bar. It was a simple, straightforward question, I could tell – no sarcasm or criticism in her tone of voice.

"I'm usually in bed by ten-thirty," I said, before thinking what a bore I must have sounded. But she smiled.

"I'm sorry to keep you up. If you hurry you won't be late." She had that glint in her eye that I was starting to recognise when she was teasing.

"I'd better get somebody to call a taxi for us. Let's go to reception and ask."

She picked up her clutch bag and followed me through from the bar to reception. She stood in front of me as we waited for the young woman there to finish a phone call. We were looking into each other's eyes as the receptionist put the phone down and looked up.

"Hello, how can I help?"

"Key for room thirty-nine, please," Diane answered. "Well, you're in no fit state to drive home," she declared, before I could say a word. She put the key card into my hand, watching my reactions closely with a half-smile on her face. We reached the landing and stood for a moment outside room thirty-nine.

"I booked the room earlier," she whispered.

She put her bag under her arm, took the key card from me and swiped the door lock, held my hand and led me into the darkened room. She stood in front of me and I stroked her face and kissed her on the lips.

She sat on the side of the bed and asked if I intended standing in the same position all night. I went to the bathroom. I looked tired in the mirror as I washed my hands. I splashed cold water on my face and went back into the room, having gargled with toothpaste.

Diane had hung her dress on a hanger and was now sitting cross-legged on one of the armchairs by the window. She was watching me. I smiled. I didn't know what else to do.

I could see attractive freckles on her shoulders and her chest now as she sat in white bra and pants.

"Are there any toothbrushes in the bathroom?" she asked. "I won't be a moment."

I got into bed; the sheets felt as good as they looked. I had jumped out of my trousers and hung them up in the wardrobe next to my jacket and Diane's dress. I draped my shirt over a chair and put my socks in my shoes. My head was swimming with pleasure, drinks, anticipation and tiredness. I listened to the tap running in the bathroom. The enveloping warmth of the duvet was bliss. I thought of the lovely woman I could hear nearby. The image of her in her white bra and white silk knickers was in my eyes. My brain swam. My thoughts swirled.

I tried to see my watch when I woke. The only light came through the curtains from a lamp of some sort somewhere outside. For a few seconds I wondered where I was. Then it registered. I could feel the heat from a body beside me. I felt her there and wondered if I was dreaming. The bed gently rose and fell to the soft, even breathing of Diane. I slid from the bed and went to the bathroom as quietly and carefully as possible, fearing that the flush would wake her. I checked my watch in the bathroom light: four-twenty. I washed my face with cold water, rubbed toothpaste across my teeth and gargled water around.

Putting the light off and allowing a few seconds for my eyes to adjust to the dark once again, I crept back into bed, finding my way by the dim glow of light from outside. I was looking at Diane lying on her side facing me. I could make out her face and her hair. The feeling of having somebody beside me sent a wave of melancholy through me at first as I realised that such a simple sharing had been so long absent, then one of sheer bliss at the sense of peace and comfort it brought. It was astonishing; I hadn't realised how much I had missed. I could feel her breath. The melancholic feelings evaporated. I moved forward fractionally and kissed her. She smelt warm and perfumed. I could smell the cocktail on her breath: fruity and alcoholic, mixed with toothpaste-mint. I kissed her again, feeling the urge to hold her, to hug her to me, but I didn't want to wake her so I just watched her sleeping, and soon drifted off to sleep myself.

The next I knew was hearing birdsong and seeing the lightening sky behind the curtains. I went back to the bathroom once more. I quietly gargled some cold water and again splashed my face. It felt good. I could have dressed and made tea but instead slid back in between the sheets. Diane was disturbed this time. She turned over onto her back, sighed, and then turned on her side facing away from me. Serves me right, I thought. I smelt her.

Her hair was a dark auburn, mixed with some white. It was soft and well cut; fairly short. I could see the white nape of her neck so I blew lightly at the small fluffy hairs there. She squirmed and I retreated. I stroked an exposed shoulder with a finger and looked at the freckles. I brushed her neck with my lips, wanting to kiss it. She moved again and I stopped quickly and closed my eyes.

I opened one to peep and found my face inches from a wide-eyed Diane watching me. I smiled. She smiled and puckered her lips and closed one eye. I obliged.

"Good morning," I said.

"Good morning," she whispered.

We made love.

Later, as I watched her return with more coffee from the hotel's breakfast buffet and stir sugar into her coffee, I began to have hopes for the future.

Chapter Thirty-one

The rest of that Sunday at home went quickly. I had dropped Diane off at her house and we'd agreed that I would phone her during the coming week. I watched her close her front door after she turned and waved goodbye. I wanted to blow a kiss and only just stopped myself from doing it.

Sunday nights are nearly always depressing: dark, uncomfortable thoughts would descend as the afternoon became evening. That Sunday, however, brought mixed feelings. I was still wide awake at one-thirty. I'd been in bed before eleven but sleep wouldn't come. Burley and its connections floated through my mind accompanied by sombre feelings of foreboding. I forced myself to think about Saturday night and Sunday morning, and peace came, with warm feelings as I recalled the pleasure of Diane's company and of making love in the dawn light. I could feel the warmth of her body and I imagined her breath on my face.

The alarm went. My clock-radio burst into life with the usual reports of wars and atrocities in far-off places.

I had three women in my life again. Three I liked. Three I loved. Diane had seemed shocked when I'd described my relationship with my daughters... well, lack of relationship. She couldn't comprehend it; after all, she and Lisa were so close.

When Lisa picked me up for work I could tell she was dying to talk about the weekend... mine, not hers. Dave was already in between us. She glanced behind his head and looked at me meaningfully.

"Did you have a nice weekend, Tony?" she asked nonchalantly as we pulled away from the kerb.

"Yes, thank you," I said. "Very nice indeed."

"Me too," said Dave, and for the next few miles he proceeded to give us too much information about his sexual exploits with his new girlfriend. Leanne was obviously quite athletic, it seemed. Not quite 'Olympian', but 'club level', was Dave's assessment. I had no recollection of him playing any sports at all, to be able to judge others' abilities in that way.

Lisa smiled to herself and glanced knowingly at me as Dave chuntered on and on.

I jumped from the van, grateful to light up, hoping to ignore Dave. He lit a roll-up and leered in my face.

"What did *you* get up to this weekend, Tony?"

"Oh, a bit of cleaning and shopping, watching telly – the usual exciting stuff I do most weekends."

And since this is what I told him truthfully most Monday mornings he just shrugged.

"You wanna get a life, mate," he advised me.

Lisa then told us which rooms we were going to do. It seemed today we would all three do the enormous kitchen, followed by the snug-room and then the lounge at the other end of the house. It had once been three workers' cottages but had been knocked through to become one house.

Eamon Friel, a poetic singer/songwriter was on the radio and all was well with the world. His soft, lilting Irish voice fitted my mood this Monday morning; his backing musicians perfect. The song, 'Here Is the River', was a positive message – a love song of hope in spite of the flags and anthems that divide his city.

We spent almost two hours sheeting-up and masking everything, remembering to rescue the kettle, milk, and mugs before we covered them up, and then made tea in the utility room. It was a fresh morning with a clear blue sky of the type that makes you breathe in as deeply as you possibly can when you first step outside. Dave and I had a quick smoke in the garden and Lisa ate a banana. She was looking at me and I was deliberately avoiding her gaze but was doing so for fun, not to be awkward. I knew she was dying to quiz me and it amused me to make her wait.

Later I popped out for a cigarette when Dave was busily rolling-in the ceiling so couldn't stop; I thought Lisa was helping him but she came out with a mug of tea and a plate of biscuits.

"Bribery," I said nodding towards the biscuits.

She didn't beat about the bush. "Fancy keeping my mother out all night on your first date! I didn't know you were such a…" She trailed off, trying to find the appropriate word for me, but it never came.

"I enjoyed your mother's company very much, thank you," I said, just as the top half of the stable door flew open and Dave peered out at us.

"Is anybody gonna help me or not?"

At the end of the day we dropped Dave off first, but when we got to my place, Lisa asked if she could pop in for a moment.

"There's something I need to ask you."

"Sounds ominous," I laughed. "Come on in and I'll make you a coffee."

One date with her mum, and she's going to lecture me!

I filled the kettle, clicked it on and gestured Lisa to sit down while I got the drinks sorted out. I went to the back door and lit up. Lisa had watched my every move without a word so far.

"What?" I said to her.

"You know very well what," she replied.

"What?" I asked again.

She got up, poured boiling water into the mugs and stirred, still not quite taking her eyes from me.

"I will look after your mum."

"It's not that, Tony. I know you will. I like you, you know that, and besides, Mum is no fool. It's not that I'm referring to." She looked away, searching for words.

"What, then?"

"Come on. I've known you for long enough, Tony. I may be young and you may be... not so young." She grinned at her own clumsy words, then continued. "There's something eating you. I know. And if you're going to see my mother shouldn't I know what it is?"

"There's nothing, honestly," I said. "I don't know what you mean."

She came over to where I was standing and put a mug of tea in front of me without taking her eyes from me.

"Tony, please tell me so that I can help. *We* can help."

I wanted to hug this beautiful young woman. A tear came to my eye and I turned away.

"Tony?" she whispered, "is it something you could perhaps tell my mum easier than you could tell me?

Mum detected something and Charlotte has too. We're women... we know."

"No," was all I muttered.

"Is it something to do with Charlie herself?"

I thought I heard something in Lisa's tone of voice as she said this.

"What on earth do you mean?" I glanced down the garden at the hut... the studio.

Lisa looked uncomfortable now. She sipped her coffee then peered at me over the mug for a long time. Finally she sighed, drew a deep breath, looked at the ceiling, and began.

"When you asked Charlie if she would like to use your hut did you think it would lead somewhere?"

"Of course not."

I lit another cigarette and turned away. I realised that the two young women in my life had been talking about me and I was feeling uncomfortable. I had let my feelings for Charlotte show, then. My scalp prickled with embarrassment. I knew that I had been so near on many occasions to making a complete fool of myself. I would have lost a friend, a good friend whose company I cherished. It would probably have caused a problem with Lisa too. *What a bloody fool.*

"So your mum agreed to be a distraction?" I tried very hard not to sound acrimonious. "What a fool I am."

"No, Tony, you're not a fool. Never will be or have been."

I did hug her then. *This was my employer I was hugging.*

"Have you got half an hour or so?" I asked her.

Her look was quizzical but she said that she had.

"I can make you something to eat." I put the kettle back on and peered in my fridge and then my store cupboard.

"Beans on toast? Sorry," I said.

She laughed. "I do have a chef as a boyfriend, you know," she replied.

"Sit down, Lisa. Please."

She acquiesced. She sat looking up at me, her eyes following me around.

I made two more hot drinks and sat down at my kitchen table with her. I put my hand over hers now.

"It's Burley," I began. "I've never told anybody any of this, but in 1975…" She frowned, clearly puzzled, but stayed silent, watching me.

I told her the whole story. Her mouth fell open a few times and she closed her eyes tightly on a number of occasions. A few tears appeared at one time but she silently thumbed them away. I told of my friendship with Nigel, which she knew something of from the time at Daisy Belle's house when Daisy was acknowledging her grandfather knowing me. Lisa was aware of this much of a connection but it now took on far more significance for her. As I was finishing, Lisa leaned back in her chair and studied the ceiling. She blew air through pursed lips.

"That's why I've not been back to the Burley area in over thirty years," I concluded. I had told her about the flashbacks, how they had increased recently, of being tearful and confused, or depressed.

I stood up and put some bread in the toaster and poured a can of baked beans into a saucepan.

"I can't eat, Tony," she said.

I turned the gas off and stopped the toaster. I could see her questions forming and queuing up. They were tripping over each other behind those pretty brown eyes.

Then quietly she said, "Tony, you poor man." She stopped for some moments and it was my turn to keep quiet and allow this young woman to absorb what I had just confessed to her.

"Tony." She breathed the word. She sighed and rubbed a hand across her forehead and into her hair, and then continued to run her fingers through her hair, all the while never taking her eyes from my face.

I felt relief; I had finally told someone, even though I was already having doubts about the wisdom of it. Would Lisa inform the police? Tell her boyfriend and he would want to? Tell her mum? Would Lisa hate me, lose respect? That I could not bear. I loved this girl like a daughter, yet I wouldn't have told my own daughters. What had possessed me to tell her? Would I lose Lisa, Charlotte and Diane? All three? It was foolish to tell after all these years. But I did feel relief.

"Please, please don't think less of me," I finally said.

"I don't, Tony. I don't. I do not. I don't know how you've lived with that knowledge of helping your friend with such a thing. Then he abandons you completely..." She trailed off. "He didn't look after you as I'm sure you expected. It was probably what corroded your marriage and your relationship with your daughters. You must have been so angry at times. Bloody hell!" Lisa shook her head. She came over and hugged me hard. "You haven't got to come to Burley tomorrow if you don't want to. Me and Dave can handle it."

I thought about that.

"No, I'll help. I'll stay to help finish the cottage. But I'd very much like to get out of the hotel job the other side of the village – it's nearer the scene."

Lisa shivered at the reminder of my story.

"That'll be fine, Tony. I'll have to hang any wallpaper there, though. It'll do me good not to stand back like I do. I might even try to get another person to help with the job, because each room needs to be handed back as quickly as possible. I've asked for two rooms at a time and it's not a very big hotel." Then she added, "And it'll be half-term that week and my mum'll have time off, so perhaps you two could get to know each other then. You know… go away for a few days. I don't know."

I handed Lisa her coffee.

"That would be nice," I said. "I would like that a lot. And perhaps I could tell her the same as I have just told you myself?"

She kissed me on the cheek at the front door.

"I really must stop kissing my employees," she said. "It's becoming a habit." I laughed and shut the door. It was getting on for eight o'clock. I was tired… but somehow elated.

I showered and went to bed early but had a disturbed night, woken frequently by lurid nightmares about open graves. I was up very early the following morning. The first thing on my mind was Lisa's reaction to my confession. I felt close to her. *Another reason to risk telling Diane.* I had over an hour before Lisa would pick me up for work. I wondered how she would feel now about my crime. After breakfast I went down the garden and pushed a small piece of notepaper under the studio door. It said 'I love you. T xx'.

I rang Diane on Wednesday evening and arranged to see her on the Saturday. She would come to my house at lunchtime. I knew Charlotte would be at the studio on Saturday and I hoped she would find the note before Diane arrived.

We finished the rooms in the cottage by Friday and the owners came round. They handed me and Dave a twenty-pound note each 'for a drink'. This doesn't happen very often these days not even at Christmas. It was a nice little gesture of thanks though. Lisa was very pleased with herself too; they had recommended us to some friends of theirs.

Somehow or other, despite neither Lisa nor I saying anything, Dave had cottoned on that Lisa's mum was coming to my house on the Saturday. He must have overheard something. He had joked relentlessly about it.

"Say good night to your dad," he said to Lisa as I slid from the van at the corner of my road.

"Bugger off, Dave," I said.

Daisy had finished her Spring Tour. The O2 Arena had pulsated to Daisy Belle Bliss and her band, she had done several television interviews and chat shows and now she looked forward to making final plans for her house-warming party. She had wanted to take time off from her work because she also feared becoming over-exposed, as well as to allow time for her grandfather to visit her; if he agreed. He had agreed; he would at last be back in the United Kingdom in three weeks' time.

She phoned Emma and Lisa as soon as she arrived in Dorset and they met for drinks at The Haven Hotel. Some stared at them but the hotel was used to discretion when celebrities needed it. They had lunch together. Lisa told Daisy of Tony's date with her mother. Daisy was intrigued.

"Will he bring your mum to my party?"

"I'll sack him if he doesn't," Lisa assured her.

Daisy needed Emma and Lisa's help to set up her house for the party. She had selected the caterers and booked some of her friends to provide music, while the lighting company from Nootronic had promised a light-show and effects in the house and garden.

Emma and Lisa exchanged many sideways glances, intrigued by what Daisy had in mind as she explained her plans. When she told them of her grandfather's excitement and apprehension at the prospect of seeing his old friend Tony Smith, she caught Lisa's change of expression and asked with concern if it was a problem. Lisa was unsure how to explain herself.

"What's wrong, Lisa?" prompted Emma, now as curious as Daisy.

Lisa excused herself from the table and went to the ladies' room with the intention of giving herself a moment to think and compose herself. She didn't want to cause unnecessary concern or curiosity, for Tony's sake. She leant on the basin and looked at herself. After a short while she took a deep breath and went back to the table.

"Are you all right, Lisa?" Daisy asked. "You looked a bit odd just then."

"I'm fine, thanks. I just felt a bit faint. Must be all the food and wine. So, is your grandfather coming on his own?"

Daisy chuckled and looked around the room, as if checking that no one else was listening.

"I believe he's bringing a new-found friend. This friend was born the same year grandfather left England – 1975." Emma and Lisa were both doing the maths.

"Still in her thirties, then," said Emma, getting there first.

They discussed the age difference, but all concluded they didn't really see anything wrong with age differences in a relationship, and quoted a few well-known examples to each other.

"Are you seeing anybody, Emma?" Daisy asked.

Emma shifted in her seat, not comfortable to be the subject of conversation.

"Well, perhaps I can invite someone for you and me, Emma..."

"That would be nice," Emma said quietly.

Chapter Thirty-two

Nigel phoned Ashley and invited her over, and an hour-and-a-half later she was dropped off at his gate in Agoura. He stood in the open front door and watched her approach. The sun was on her. Nigel thought she glowed.

"Hello, darlin'," she drawled, and they kissed several times at the door.

"You look…" Nigel sought for a compliment he hadn't used before. "You glow," he finally said after standing back a pace to look at her.

"Thanks, honey," she replied with a modest grin, stroking him under the chin with a long, suntanned finger. She poked a bright-red fingernail at the centre of his chest.

"You're pretty cute yourself."

"Would you like coffee or wine?" Nigel asked as they reached the kitchen area. Ashley stood close to him and he slipped his arm round her waist.

"I don't want to affect your voice," he added more seriously.

Ashley had been recording at Nigel's place. He was already intrigued by her voice. She would giggle when he complimented it. Her singing voice was higher than her talking voice. It was a complete surprise when he first heard it. He had expected, perhaps even hoped, in truth, that she would have a husky, smoky 'country' voice, but what he heard was as beautiful as crystal. Initially, he thought she was deliberately distorting her voice. It was unique – and very sexy, Nigel had concluded.

Ashley asked whose CD was playing over Nigel's house sound-system.

"Junior Wells, a fine old bluesman."

"OK, honey," Ashley said. "I like him. You know him?"

"No, I don't know him but I did meet him in the seventies. He died back in the late nineties though. Oh, before we go into the studio today I have something to ask you."

Ashley raised her eyebrows and waggled them suggestively. "Ooh, nice," she cooed playfully. "Yes, please."

He put two coffees on the table and patted the sofa beside him.

She sat down. "I like you," she said and put a hand on his knee.

Nigel laughed at her childlike warmth.

"What you want to ask me, honey?" She smiled at him and sipped her coffee cupped in both hands.

"Would you come on a trip with me?"

"Sure, honey," she said.

"Hang on, Ashley… before you decide…"

"What's to decide? I like you and I'll go on a trip with you."

"I would like you to come on a trip with me to England." Nigel said it quietly.

"OK, honey. That sounds nice. I've never been there," she replied, a serious look on her face.

"But don't you need to think about it?" He took her hands as she put the coffee down.

"I have, honey." Here she seemed to hesitate, but then continued, "I don't have to think about it any more. I would go anywhere with you. Anywhere you asked me to go. Where you go, I go. That's how it's gonna be. When we goin'?"

Nigel exhaled; he hadn't been aware that he'd been holding his breath.

"In only a couple of weeks' time. We'll stay with Daisy."

Ashley jumped to her feet. "We'll stay with Daisy Belle Bliss? Really? Wait till I tell my mom!" She danced around the kitchen – 'Queen of the Rodeo'.

Eventually she sat back down next to Nigel. Solemn-faced, she took Nigel's hand. "But honey, it's cold there and it rains all the time. I'll have to get some different clothes."

Nigel often watched the BBC World Service on cable; he kept up with most news and politics; it didn't always mean much to him but he followed it regularly. He followed the UK music scene to some degree and if he heard of a British or Irish band playing nearby he would go to hear them, but most names in the British chart were a mystery to him if he looked on the net now, with the exception of his granddaughter.

He had watched some royal events, had seen the dark, heavy skies overhead during TV interviews, and via a webcam he had observed grey clouds forming over Bournemouth Bay, the dark green-grey sea ruffled with white-frilled waves. He would see the pier too.

He had now spent more of his life in California than in England. A memory of his parents' house crossed his mind. The gloomy hallway. The patterned carpet.

Coloured glass in the front door. The panels of knobbly, obscure glass each side of the door, through which he would make faces at the postman. He was on the pavement by the road outside the hedged front garden. Shiny-leaved hedges that you couldn't see over from the downstairs front windows. Tony was standing there, bell-bottom trousers and shoulder-length hair. It was almost dark and the images evaporated. Tony was gone.

"Honey, honey!" Ashley was kneeling on the sofa with a hand on his cheek.

"Where you gone?"

"I was thinking about England and my old home there. Yes, you're right, it's cold there. And it rains a lot." He kissed her nose.

Nigel held her. They were some minutes hugging till he broke away.

"I'm so happy you're coming with me."

She kissed him. "OK, buster, me too.

Nigel had added Ashley's voice to parts of his recordings. She had been learning more of what he wanted her to sing. She was patient and composed when she sang. She would stop and start again if he asked her to; she didn't make any fuss or complain. He was captivated by her voice and he now knew what other voice he would need to finish this work, a work that had already taken close on three years to complete. If he remembered Tony's voice correctly – its timbre, the slight rolling Dorset accent – it would be just perfect. He hoped that years of cigarettes had not brought too much change. Daisy had told him that Tony still smoked cigarettes. He knew very few people who smoked cigarettes regularly. It would be complete when... *if*... Tony read Rudyard Kipling's poem 'If'.

He could easily do the few introductory parts Nigel had scripted with him in mind. He now knew for sure it had to be an English voice.

Nigel asked Ashley if she wished to stay with him before they left for England, and she had readily agreed. "OK, honey."

He had even promised to go clothes shopping with her in LA, but they agreed it might be hard to find suitable clothes.

During the next few days Nigel's increasing apprehension was relieved by Ashley's enthusiasm for the trip, and by her endless questions about the UK and Daisy and 'the *real* Smudger', as she now often referred to Tony, after seeing how much it amused Nigel.

He found that the planned visit stirred memories long buried: the boy Nigel, the teenage Nigel, the young Nigel, the rock musician... Smudger Smiff.

He searched the web obsessively: Bournemouth; Dorset; London; The Strikes. Pete Davis' face would appear. A litany of conspiracy theories about Pete's disappearance. Endless material. His own young face. Zip's and Lou's too and sometimes Joan's. More and more. He went on Google Earth for some parts. The New Forest, his parents' old house, the pier. Sometimes Ashley would look over his shoulder and ask more questions.

There were only days left to go. First-class tickets had been booked; new suitcases lay open in a spare bedroom, thermal clothing hung nearby, sweaters sat folded in neat piles, shirts in packets, shoes in a row – everything was ready.

She had noticed how tense he was becoming.

"Don't you want to go, honey... to England?"

He had been watching a live webcam view of Bournemouth pier for hours and hours. A hazy grey sky, sometimes a person walking a dog on the beach, a couple shuffling up the pier or sitting huddled in layers of clothing on a bench. Those greenish-grey waves flopping listlessly on the sand. No surfers. No surf. He had seen two couples, younger than normal. They had stopped halfway down the pier where the little theatre was. He recalled how Tony had booked The Strikes to play there, and the day they'd played on the whole of the pier to thousands on the sand below and the TV film made of that day. Tony had helped launch the band; Tony who was always helping him; Tony who he had let down and ignored for well over thirty years. For some reason he now recalled a conversation about Tony's plans to open an 'emporium'. He had called it an emporium rather than a shop – Tony always had 'concepts' not 'ideas'. Now it occurred to him that his old friend's ideas... 'concepts'... had not come to fruition. Why else would he be painting his granddaughter's house? A dull pain throbbed in his temple; an overwhelming heaviness engulfed his body. His shoulders ached as he sat in front of the screen remembering Bournemouth... and Tony... and his promises.

Ashley kneaded the back of his neck, where the muscles were taut and tense.

"What is it, honey? What's the matter?"

He switched his PC off and turned. "My friend... I let him down."

She led him away from the office and sat him on a big couch overlooking the garden, the pool and a clear blue sky.

"Sit there, Mister Nigel. I'll take care of you." He made to get up but she pushed him back down and pointed a manicured finger at him. "Sit!" There was always coffee on the go; she poured him a mug full and sat down beside him.

"Now, you want to tell Mamma?" she said in a soft teasing voice.

He took her hand.

"You're a breath of fresh air in my life." He kissed the hand; Ashley snatched it away. "Don't you try to sweet talk me, Mister Smudger!" She smiled at him and then remained silent; an uncommon state for Ashley.

Nigel turned to face her. "You are beautiful," he said and leaned and kissed her gently on the lips.

"There's something bugging you, honey, and I don't know what it is, but it's about going to England, that's for sure."

He was surprised at her insight and touched by her concern. He was realising that this young woman was more sensible and astute than she made out; it was what he was falling for. Her concern was genuine. He had been apprehensive about their age difference; worried that she might be an opportunist ready to part an old fool from his money, but he had gradually come to realise that this was not the case. He drew in his breath, trying to decide what to tell her. He didn't want to lose her now – he felt very comfortable with her. Whenever she returned to LA he missed her. She had openly told him how staying at his place would save her money.

"I'm a working girl, honey," she had said. "I have some savings, but… "

That was where he had stopped her, aware of the parallels with Tony. 'I have money,' he thought. 'They don't, but they help me – Ashley and Tony.' He had found a way to help Ashley by pretending he had to pay her for her singing so that her pride was left intact, and he had treated her to clothes for their forthcoming trip, enjoying her excitement and enthusiasm as she emerged from changing-rooms to show him and ask his opinion. His pleasure was intense. It was the pleasure of giving – something he knew he had almost denied himself until Ashley. His guilt over choosing to forget Tony Smith was now equally intense.

"Come on, Nigel honey, you can tell me." She leaned over and stroked the side of his face.

He turned and looked at her directly. He drew breath.

"When I came to California... the USA... in 1975, I swore I would never ever return to England... to the UK."

He hesitated.

"I fear losing you... by telling you this... I couldn't bear that now..."

"We all have a past, Nigel. You're a beautiful man now. You won't lose me... I will not let you go. Ever."

Nigel smiled, reassured enough to continue.

"Do you know the mystery of Pete Davis... Rudy Davis, The Strikes' singer?"

"I know he vanished. My mom told me when I first told her I had met you. She was a fan and Rudy was special to her." She laughed at this. "I don't mean she knew him but she said she had posters of him and idolised him when she was young."

"The mysterious circumstances of his disappearance." Nigel went on, "I know where he is." He watched for her reaction to this. She remained straight-faced. He could not guess her thoughts. Then her look changed to concern. She took his hand and told him to continue.

"My ex-wife killed him in a fit of jealous rage over a young girl… and my friend Tony and I hid his body… buried it."

Ashley's eyes widened as Nigel related the whole story and the circumstances that led up to it, but she remained absolutely still and silent throughout.

About an hour later Ashley was quietly eating a bowl of strawberries and Nigel was drinking yet more coffee from a fresh pot he'd made. They hadn't spoken since he finished the revelation. She had glanced at him once in a while but had remained silent.

He was watching a jet's vapour trail overhead, white in the pale-blue springtime sky, but his thoughts were on a dark forest sky of a September morning many years ago. He stood at the patio windows overlooking the pool. Ashley came up behind him and put her arms around his waist and pressed her face on his back.

"It was a beautiful, sympathetic thing you did for your wife… your ex-wife… who didn't deserve someone as nice as you, honey. I can understand why you did it."

He turned to face her. "Can you?"

"Yes, honey," she said, in a matter-of-fact tone.

"I've agonised about it so many times over the years. I had to leave Cherry but I did it for her. I couldn't bear to think that if we got caught, my daughter would find out so much about her mother, let alone about what I'd done. I paid for her care but it didn't help till Daisy."

"But what about your buddy – Tony? Why did he help? Was it money? Did you pay him?"

Nigel was shocked at the question.

"No! No, of course I didn't pay him."

"OK, honey. Then he did it for *you*."

Nigel considered Ashley's succinct summing-up... and agreed.

The flight attendant offered Nigel a drink. Ashley was sipping champagne already and chatting with the attendant, admiring her bright red suit. Nigel chose orange juice, and touched glasses with Ashley.

"I never thought I'd be travelling first-class, honey." She chinked glasses once more, her eyes shining. "Or going to England," she added.

The captain introduced himself and informed the passengers that the weather was fine over the Atlantic and that he expected a very smooth flight.

Nigel glanced at Ashley; her excitement would help him get through this, he knew. The 747 roared down the runway and with a slight lurch was airborne. It climbed and climbed. Ashley had not stopped smiling.

She learned that one of the flight attendants, Sophie, lived in Bournemouth, and was excited to tell her that was where they were heading. They had a drink at the bar before returning to their seats. Sophie showed them how to drop the seats to form a bed and they slept until two hours before the aircraft began its descent. Sophie woke them with a hot towel and then fetched them some orange juice and coffee before they had breakfast of a bacon roll and more coffee.

The giant jet gently descended into the grey clouds over England. Nigel leaned over and pointed out the Thames, Big Ben and the Houses of Parliament, but was not familiar with the London Eye, The Shard, and several others buildings. Once more he was comforted by Ashley's obvious excitement.

"We're here, honey!" she said, and kissed him.

"Have a good holiday," Sophie said to them as they left the cabin. "See you in Bournemouth!" she added playfully.

Chapter Thirty-three

I had rung Diane on Wednesday night and we'd chatted for over an hour. Now, Saturday, she was coming over and I had determined to tell her what I'd told Lisa. She arrived clutching a holdall that, she informed me, held her wash bag, her make-up, her 'nightie' and some fresh clothes.

I must try to keep up! It hadn't occurred to me she would stay the night, and I could so easily have said the wrong thing.

I showed her round my house. I'd been cleaning and tidying all morning; you could still smell the polish. She liked my bathroom, she said. I'd had it done up less than two years before with a separate shower cubicle and a new bath. I must be getting old or something because I felt embarrassed showing her my bedroom, especially when she asked if she could go downstairs and bring her overnight bag back up to leave it in the bedroom. The other two bedrooms looked tired and in need of some new paint and wallpaper. They were untidy with things I'd left in them for years.

We sat at my kitchen table. Diane had made some tea. She seemed at home. I liked that. She had a comfortable way of taking charge of situations. It was a nice spring day, so I opened the back door to let some air in. The sun was out and the sky was blue, with a few white clouds casting passing shadows; April was looking very vibrant in my garden.

I lit a cigarette at the back door and apologised. "You don't mind?" She shook her head and handed me my tea.

"Can I see your garden?" She followed me out. She looked up and around and down towards the hut; taking it all in. She was wearing a pink cardigan, gold-coloured pumps, and beige linen trousers. I watched her walk up the garden towards Charlotte's studio. She looked back once or twice, and again as she tried the door.

"No one in," she said.

She came back down to where I was standing and sat in one of the wicker chairs.

"I like your shoes," I said, more for the sake of saying something.

"Ballet pumps," she answered.

I wasn't sure if she was joking or not. Both my daughters did ballet for a while; pink satin was more usual.

"So, is that Charlotte's famous studio?" Diane nodded in the direction of the former hut. "Can we look?" she asked. I told her that although I did have a key I didn't like letting myself in when she wasn't there. I suggested she look through the window instead. She went back up the garden and peered in, hands cupped against the glass. She turned back to where I was sitting and called out, leaving a steamy patch from her breath fading on the pane.

"Wow, from what I can see it's very nice. It's as good as she told me."

She came back and sat down. I lit another cigarette and she told me that I smoked too much. I agreed and said that I ought to try to give it up before it gave me up.

"You're a very nice man, Tony," Diane said. "That was such a wonderful thing to do, to allow her the use of your hut, or whatever you call it. I thought she was exaggerating when she first described it to me, but it's perfect for her to work in."

I said that I thought it could do with more natural light.

"Well, from what I can see through the window it seems perfect for her. And quite the little home-from-home, too – I didn't expect that. The facilities you've added... and a bed. Fantastic."

"I confess there was perhaps a selfish reason behind my offer of the hut," I said. She looked puzzled at this and asked me what I meant. I explained that when I had asked Charlotte if she would like it, I'd very much hoped she would. I enjoyed her company and knew I would get more of it if she took it, I said.

Diane laughed. "Do you fancy her?"

I tried to avoid answering but she asked me the same question again. It obviously amused her for some reason.

"I know you think I'm a silly old man who fancied a young woman."

She stopped me expanding on this and told me that she understood. I was feeling silly now. I thought she was taking the mickey out of me. Then I got it; she really did understand.

"Yes, I was lonely. I hadn't thought about it much in the past but I am feeling it more and more the older I get. I turned sixty some while back and the thought of having to stop working is depressing. I love working for Lisa but each week seems longer. Work seems harder. So continuing to work is becoming hard and depressing too. Work or no work? My life is very narrow: work, sleep, work. The only conversation I have is with your daughter or Dave or maybe a neighbour sometimes. But when Charlotte appeared at Daisy's house I admit I was instantly taken with her. She didn't patronise me as 'old', we just got on well right from the start. We became friends. And I haven't got many of those. I hoped to help her stop doing drugs... in a fatherly way. But..." I stopped. I was saying too much.

"Go on," she prompted.

"So I was just feeling more and more..." I searched for the right word. "Desperate? My life had flown by. I had done nothing. Achieved nothing... and Charlotte..." I fizzled out and took another cigarette from the pack on the table in front of me. Diane sat back in the chair and watched me. Then she took my hand before I lit up. My throat constricted.

"I know, I know. I do understand," she said quietly. "I have always had Lisa living at home. She goes away on holidays with friends... we have separate holidays these days but not all the time, we still go away together sometimes like we always did. So I've always had a companion; she's my daughter but we're friends too. I see so many people in a day at school that to be on my own is bliss... when it happens. I have lots of friends and activities through the school... and always Lisa too."

I told her yet again how much I thought of Lisa.

Diane squeezed my hand. A silence followed. I smoked my cigarette. Then I went back in the kitchen and made more tea. I made two rounds of cheese sandwiches and took them out with a dish of cherry tomatoes.

"Are you warm enough?" I asked.

Before she could answer, I heard a noise at the side of the house and Charlotte came round. She seemed surprised to see us. She kissed us both. "Look at you two." She was grinning from ear to ear. She looked healthy. Diane commented on this before I could. They chatted for a while. They seemed very comfortable with each other. Diane then stood, didn't say anything but followed Charlotte down the garden. I watched them both. I felt a bit ashamed of the feelings I had been developing for Charlotte. I realised Diane somehow knew.

Charlotte's weight gain had given her a lovely figure and I compared them as they headed for the studio – Diane wider and shorter, but still attractive. She turned and looked over her shoulder and I had a flash of guilt: she had read my mind! She just smiled, though.

They were gone for over half an hour and I began to get cold as the temperature dropped so I went back into the kitchen. After an hour or so I went through to my lounge and put the television on. I don't know why, because I didn't really want to watch it. A programme about antiques lulled me to sleep, and when I awoke, the clock said ten to six. I was cold and stiff and for a few seconds I wondered where I was. I then remembered that I had a guest – or rather, two guests.

Charlotte and Diane were chatting happily in my kitchen.

Diane grinned. "Feel better?" she asked.

"Sorry," I said. They had stopped talking as soon as they saw me.

Diane stood and clicked the kettle. "Tea?"

Charlotte was scrutinizing me the way she did with people.

"Where are you two going tonight?" She looked at me then Diane.

Diane shrugged. It sounded quite odd to me, but nice, though: 'you two'.

Diane went on through to use the toilet, putting a mug of tea in front of me on her way.

"She's lovely, isn't she?" Charlotte nodded in the direction Diane had gone.

"Yes," I replied.

She chuckled. "Come on, Tony, try to sound more enthusiastic!" She took my hand across the kitchen table. "I really hope..." She didn't finish whatever she was going to say.

Diane came back in.

"What are you two looking so shifty about?" She stood between us looking from one to the other. Charlotte got to her feet and said she'd come to paint and not to drink tea. She turned and opened the back door, hesitating in the doorway. "Have fun, you two!" She raised her eyebrows, smiled, and the door closed behind her. I looked at Diane. "What would you like to do?" I asked.

She told me she didn't mind. I suggested a meal then a pub.

"I'll just go and check my make-up in your bathroom mirror," she told me.

I took this to be a 'yes' to my suggestion. There was a small, family-run Italian restaurant up on the main road nearby; I had never eaten there despite the fact that it had been there for many years, but I had a vague memory that Jenny tried it not long after it had opened.

"Do you like Italian food?" I asked when Diane came back downstairs. I got a waft of perfume as she returned to the kitchen.

I went upstairs, washed my face and hands, gave my teeth a quick brush and yes, squirted a spray of my familiar aftershave on my neck and chin. I took a jacket from my wardrobe and put it on. It smelt a bit musty, having been in there rather too long, but it looked OK in the wardrobe mirror so I sprayed some aftershave on the lapels and hoped. Diane was waiting in the hallway. She fanned her hand in front of her face as I reached the bottom step.

"Have you spilt your aftershave?" she deadpanned.

"Very funny," I said. "I was just freshening the old jacket up – it doesn't get out much."

She looped an arm through mine and said, "Then it's high time you and your jacket got out more."

At the busy restaurant, Nello managed to squeeze us in, seating us in a tiny alcove under some stairs. It was cosy enough, though, and it left us out of the flightpath of the waitresses who bustled up and down the narrow gaps between rows of tables. The lighting was from olivewood wall-lights the likes of which one would expect to see on *The Antiques Roadshow* rather than on the wall of a working restaurant. Little tasselled shades cast light down the rough-plastered walls that had been colour washed in Tuscan hues. The décor was definitely from another era. I looked around at the framed pictures of lakes and mountains that I took to be in northern Italy. It was all very old-fashioned but cosy; I liked it. Diane was watching me.

"Checking out the décor?" she asked. "Lisa does the same wherever we go."

"Occupational hazard," I replied.

She was looking at the wine list. I was still deciding from the menu.

Nello, the owner, returned for our order. Diane asked for a bottle of something I didn't catch the name of and I ordered a Peroni.

"I think I'll stick to beer tonight." I nibbled on a bread stick.

"I used to come in here with Lisa's dad – my ex," said Diane.

"Is it a problem? I'm sorry – I wouldn't have suggested it if I'd known."

"How could you possibly have known? No, it's not a problem at all, I was just saying, because it looks the same now as when I was last here and that must have been more than ten years ago."

She told me a little bit about her husband. Their history was not dissimilar to mine and Jenny's: apparently happy at first but destined not to last long. She talked of what it had been like when he left – how the teenage Lisa had been hurt by it all and how he had been indifferent to her ever since. The drinks arrived. She told me that she didn't know where he was now.

"He found someone at work more attractive than me. And that was that."

Her only regret was wasting tears, and months of feeling sorry for herself, she told me.

I had finished my tagliatelle, whilst Diane still had plenty of food on her plate. I nibbled more bread sticks, poured her more wine and ordered another beer for myself. It turned out she had met her husband at The White Buck Inn at Burley and we discussed bands we had seen there. We both finished up with Neapolitan ice cream, and as I was paying, Nello held Diane's jacket out for her to put on. "*Ciao, bella signora*," he called as we reached the door. Diane looped her arm in mine again. We walked down the road and turned off to The Soldier's Rest. "It's not the height of sophistication in here," I told her as we neared the pub.

"Do you want to smoke before we go in? I know you do," she said. I felt guilty but I quickly lit up anyway.

"I don't mind," she added. "I used to once. But you should give up if you can."

Diane found a seat and we sat down with our drinks. She asked me more about Jenny and my daughters; about how Jaime had come to emigrate; and had I been to Australia – she'd always wanted to. We talked about where she'd been on her 'adventure holidays', as she referred to the trips with her teacher friend. I learned that she'd had a few men friends – mostly teachers – since her husband; how they hadn't divorced until six years after he'd gone. She laughed a lot at the story of my chatting up the computer teacher, and told me again how she felt she knew me from Lisa talking about me. I told her how Lisa and I had hardly ever talked about personal things until very recently and how I knew so little about her.

Back home, we had coffee to round off our night out. Then it felt quite natural to be following her up the stairs to my bedroom.

Chapter Thirty-four

We left late on Sunday morning, Diane driving her car. It was much more comfortable than my van; newer and cleaner too. I could smell plastic and newness as I got in. We had decided to just head along the coast, perhaps into Devon, and stop if we liked the look of somewhere, but our first stop was still well inside Dorset, at Bridport, a lovely little town. We walked about, stretching our legs and exploring parts of the town centre. We had a really tasty carvery lunch of roast beef in a little old hotel we had noticed, and we booked a room for the night. We hadn't come very far but I readily agreed when Diane suggested staying, because it felt so welcoming.

It was easy to talk to Diane but it was just as easy to be quiet with her. I had already decided she was a lovely person but now I began to find out more about her. She could be fun and she could be serious; she was intelligent but with no ego. I never expected to find another person I thought so much of in my life. I had mentioned some of my past, even back to my schooldays with Nigel and I found myself wanting to tell her the whole truth. I had told her daughter more than anyone else so maybe Lisa had told her some of it – I didn't know. I supposed she would tell me, if that were the case. I had some of the most enjoyable days of my life on this short excursion. We only ever reached Seaton; not Devon's prettiest spot, but the company was good so who cared? We walked along the seafront and ate fish and chips sitting on a concrete wall and they were as tasty as Lucky's.

As we drove home on the Thursday I told her how much I had enjoyed the last few days. "Me too," she said simply, glancing at me fleetingly before returning her eyes to the road ahead.

I asked her to stop so that I could smoke, and she pulled into a lay-by about a mile further on, saying she would enjoy stretching her legs. As we strolled around the rest-stop area, I found myself telling her the whole truth of the last few days I spent with Nigel. It was very hard to gauge her reactions as I told her; she remained inscrutable throughout. She quietly asked a few questions to clarify some parts of the story, saying each time, "Hold on, please – let me get this clear in my mind."

At last I finished, and she said, "So, is this correct? You and Nigel go to a house out near Ringwood and collect Peter Davis' body in your work van, take it into the New Forest and bury it there during the night back in 1975?"

I nodded. Diane thought for a moment, then continued her summing-up.

"He then clears off to California stating that he will never return?"

"Yes," I said.

"Didn't the police ever speak to you?"

I was waiting for that question.

"They were already convinced that Pete had caused Joan's overdose – whether deliberately or accidentally – and run. They told me they were only interviewing me for background after talking to Nigel because we are... were... friends. When asked where he was and why he wasn't in London with the other band members he told them he was visiting me. I'd got rid of the clothing I was wearing that night and cleaned my tools and my van by then. There was nothing to link me to Joan's death or Peter's apparent disappearance. There was no connection to me or indeed to Nigel being anywhere near Ringwood."

She nodded throughout my answer.

"And you've never heard anything since?"

"No. Except on a few occasions when various journalists have found me. Not the police, though."

She seemed to consider my reply for some moments.

"You, I think, then lost your way in life. You became distracted from your plans… your hopes and ambitions. You lost your drive. The result was that your wife lost respect for you… and I assume, began to fall out of love with you, and despite subsequently having two daughters, the marriage didn't survive. The whole episode seemed to undermine your self-respect, and changed you from who you were…"

A small tear formed in the corner of her right eye at this point and she thumbed it away.

"I think it had a profound effect without you realising. It seems to me that you sacrificed yourself many times… consciously or unconsciously… your life… your whole life… somehow." She faded away, shaking her head, and didn't finish whatever it might have been she had intended to say.

After a few moments she started the engine and pulled out onto the road. She was tutting and clicking her tongue and shaking her head as she drove.

As we pulled in to a café at a farm shop for something to eat she turned to me. She switched off the ignition, removed her seat belt and we sat in the parked car facing each other.

"You bloody fool. You bloody lovely fool. How on earth are you going to feel when you see him? It'll be soon now. I still can't understand why he never contacted you. After everything you did for him all your life... his life. His so good... and yours so bad." She dried up again, shaking her head.

"If," I said to her.

She looked at me strangely. "What did you say?"

"If," I repeated without any explanation at first. I suppose I was thinking aloud.

"Nigel says that! All the way through his latest CD he's whispering 'If'."

I was very impressed that Diane had Nigel's latest CD. I knew she liked rock music, and had been to the Rolling Stones' Hyde Park concert way back in '69 (mainly to see King Crimson, who were from the Bournemouth area originally), but she'd already told me that she hadn't liked much of The Strikes' music back in the seventies. She was full of surprises!

"Why would he do that?" she said. "You know why, I can tell. There is some significance."

We were still sitting there forty minutes later as I explained how Nigel and I had loved Kipling's poem. I stumbled around trying to explain how at eleven, twelve, thirteen years old I knew of the poem and how it became a symbol that helped Nigel to withstand the bullying. Diane knew the poem well; in fact she could recite most of it. She nodded with understanding of the inspirational qualities of the poem. She took my hand in hers at one point and watched me as I tried to explain the significance of 'If' in the past. She had played me the

CD on the second day of our travels. I had of course been intrigued to hear Nigel's repeated use of the word, but hadn't had an opportunity to explain it.

"Well, now you know everything about me, can we go and get something to eat?" I said at last.

Diane smiled. "Come on, then. I think that was worth at least one coffee and a cheese sandwich."

Outside my house, I took Diane's hand and kissed it. I liked the smell of her but as I leaned further to kiss her I nearly jumped out of my skin. Charlotte, standing on the pavement, was tapping on the car window, beaming all over her face and wiggling her eyebrows in an exaggerated, mock-suggestive way. We both laughed. I kissed Diane goodbye, grabbed my holdall from the back seat, and got out. With my arm round Charlotte's shoulder we waved Diane off.

"Thank you," I said to Charlotte. She tried to look puzzled and innocent.

"I know you were in on the conspiracy to introduce me to Diane."

She just laughed. She followed me in the front door telling me how I was lucky that she had some fresh milk.

We had some tea and a smoke together outside. I told her she looked good and she stroked my hand but now it felt like a natural, normal thing to do. We looked at each other and we acknowledged this without a word.

"I thought you would like Diane," she said as she got up and returned to the back door.

"I do," I told the back door as it shut.

Chapter Thirty-five

A week later the spring weather had continued to improve and I was sitting outside with a coffee when Charlotte came round the corner of the house. She smiled and waved. I pointed to my mug and she nodded. I pointed to my cigarette and she nodded again. We just sat not talking.

"I need some more coffee," she said, and went through to the kitchen. When she returned with a refilled mug she seemed to want to talk – and talk she did. She told me stories of her childhood, and of her hopes and plans. She talked so long that in the end I had to excuse myself to use the toilet and get another pack of cigarettes. Then she told me she thought she was in love with Emma, Lisa's work partner. This was a revelation. I told her I had no idea.

"Neither has she," she replied. I stood and went round to her side of the wicker table and hugged her.

Daisy had finally decided that her party would be the third weekend in May; the date was now set, and the time was to start at 6pm on Saturday.

Diane and I saw more of each other as the month wore on. One evening, when we were at the restaurant where Gary, Lisa's boyfriend, worked, she told Lisa and me that she had decided that the school summer term would be her last; she had handed in her notice, and would be finishing in July. Whenever I'd seen her lately, she had suggested that I retire; I now knew why. I usually dismissed the idea by saying that her daughter's business would collapse without me, but she had pointed out that Lisa and Emma had taken on four more decorators recently, having acquired a lot more business. I had even worked with a couple of the new blokes and knew they were quite good decorators, but I still couldn't help instinctively trying to protect Lisa and Emma. I wanted to see the new blokes' work and to see what they were like as people; *it pays to look after a good reputation*. However, of the two I knew, Jason was a very good paperhanger, and Emma and Lisa needed that. He had done a rare, proper, apprenticeship at a west London company with impeccable standards, was half my age, and knew more than I did. He was perfect for the firm, and was happy not to be working in London all the time, and happy to kite-surf at weekends and evenings.

A lot of Emma's connections were in London, but I didn't want to work there; those days were over for me. Diane knew this. I was beginning to allow myself to see a future with Lisa's mother instead of Lisa. It was my guess that if I stayed with Diane, as I now hoped I would, her pension would be better than mine. I hoped that wouldn't cause any problems.

So I had agreed to give some serious thought to stopping work. The idea of it was like a fluffy white cloud floating blissfully in my brain but then the prospect of not doing anything and not earning money swiftly turned the cloud grey.

That evening at the restaurant I was tired, and I was going back to Diane's house. Gary was chatting, teasing about mothers in general and his and Lisa's in particular, but when he innocently asked me about my mother I couldn't control my emotions. The smell of fish abruptly filled my nostrils and the image of my father that Boxing Day morning flooded my mind. This had never happened before. It overwhelmed me in an instant. I told them I was going outside for a smoke, and Diane followed soon after. It had been Lisa who noticed me go pale; she knew something was wrong.

"Can we just go? I will tell you what's wrong. I think I can," I said.

I had to smoke in her back garden when we got home. Diane was clearly very concerned. She called from her side door that she had made some coffee and to come in from the cold. "Go and sit in the lounge," she said.

I was shaking; I couldn't disguise it no matter how I tried. I had to put the coffee mug back down for fear of spilling it. She just watched me and held my hand.

"Was it that bad?" she asked gently. "What on earth…? Is this something to do with Pete Davis and Nigel?"

She was crying before I had even described the bedroom, sensing the horror before I got to that point. I had described hearing the laughter, the hysterical, cackling laughter, and my mum singing 'She Loves You'. Diane already knew something of the years leading up to this final act of my mother's breakdown, but when I finally managed to tell her what I had found that morning she just stared at me.

"You carried that around on your own since you were a teenager? Oh my God, my love… How? How could you stay sane? Nobody… then to visit her for so long afterwards."

Jenny had been incapable of showing any sympathy on the only occasion I had tried to tell her this. She had stopped me halfway through and consequently never knew what my mother had done to my father, or understood why Christmas was a difficult time for me. I never again attempted to tell her.

I had to smoke again. Diane put her coat on and came out with me, holding my hand and squeezing it whenever our eyes met. I would never let this woman go. I had three girls again.

Chapter Thirty-six

In a few days Nigel would be arriving back in England. The feelings this thought stirred were astonishing; my whole being seemed to reel from excitement to black despair via everything in between. I was trying to banish certain thoughts and memories that kept surfacing. My confusion was overwhelming at times; times when I was not with Diane, I guess. She was holding me together. Lisa seemed to understand that I could not work, but I was irritated with myself for many things: tears surfacing too easily, sleeping badly, smoking too much. *And having so much attention.*

'An old friend I haven't seen for well over thirty years, that's all!' I thought. We would be strangers.

I learned of Daisy's arrangements through Lisa. The plan was that Nigel and I would meet before the party, but they wanted me to decide where this would take place. I suggested a restaurant that had a balcony terrace overlooking the pier, the last place where we had talked at any length all those years ago. I asked if Diane could be with me, and it was then I learned that Nigel was bringing someone too. I wasn't sure if this would make it easier or not, but I just felt much better about meeting him with Diane there for support.

I now knew he had arrived in England and was staying at Daisy's. I could sense him there. The weather was grey and cold and I wondered what his first thoughts were on his return, as it had been drizzling when they touched down, just as it had when he went. Bob the driver had collected them and brought them down the M3 and across the New Forest.

What would he look like? I wished I'd asked Daisy to show me a recent photograph of him and I cursed myself for not thinking of this till now. I was pacing my kitchen. We were due to meet at six o'clock. Apparently jet lag would not be a problem, I was told, when the time was discussed. Diane was going to pick me up from my house at around five o'clock. I really wanted to be there first. I hoped this would give me a chance to see him before he saw me and to compose myself. Diane knew the bar quite well; she and her girlfriends had been here often. I had also been on two occasions with her.

We both went to the central bar together then took a table by the windows overlooking the almost empty beach. Two young mothers watched, bored and chilly, as three little boys dug in the sand. They stood and chatted unheard by us. We didn't speak until Diane asked if I wanted her to sit next to me or opposite as we took a four-seater table as far from the entrance as possible. We had told a waitress we would like to wait for some friends to arrive before we ordered anything to eat. I didn't think I would be able to eat anyway; my throat had almost completely constricted. I let Diane in against the window and sat next to her. She had a tall glass of diet cola and I had a lager. No words came out as I stood and returned to the bar. I don't like spirits but I quickly downed two brandies, one after the other at the bar. I looked back at Diane; she just smiled. I returned to the table with another lager and cola, all the while checking the doorway nearly opposite.

"It doesn't matter if it helps," she said.

I must have looked puzzled.

"The brandy," she explained.

"I'm sorry. I know I'm pathetic," I said.

"Go onto the outside terrace here quickly whilst you have time for a cigarette. I've just seen somebody smoking out there, so it must be OK. Be quick while you have a chance."

By the time I came back in Diane had got me another brandy and a beer. She had a cup of coffee in front of her.

A tall blonde woman over by the entrance caught my eye. She was wearing very tight denim jeans that she must have been poured into. Her tanned skin was accentuated by the crisp white shirt that hung to the blue jeans. She was striking in a slightly brash way. Diane was looking too now.

"Someone looking for you I guess," she joked.

"I hope so." I returned the joke.

The woman was scanning all around the restaurant. We were now both intrigued. I had swallowed the brandy, its warmth burning down to my knees. I sipped my lager without taking my eyes from the doorway as a slim, tanned man with pure white hair took the hand of the blonde woman and gazed around too. I gulped air in. I felt slightly faint, blood seemed to rush in my ears, but I stood and began walking over towards my old friend Nigel. I looked back at Diane and inhaled deeply. She nodded almost imperceptibly in encouragement, eyes shining.

He stood still and watched me cross the room. A smile of recognition crept across his face, and those once-familiar amber eyes glistened. He had changed so much, yet so little. His companion gripped his hand without ever taking her eyes from me. She stood back half a pace to allow us to shake hands then we both stepped back and weighed each other up, both of us still without words. Nigel spoke first, in his quiet way, but now with a trace of an American accent.

"Hello, my friend. I'm so sorry it's been so long." He choked over the last of these few words and I knew they were sincere.

"You look well," I managed to say, despite the tightness in my throat.

I turned to Nigel's friend and held out my hand.

"Hello, my name's Tony…" I tried to let my introduction linger like a question.

"This is Ashley." Nigel glowed as he said her name.

I leant forward, took her soft hand and kissed her cheek.

"Very pleased to meet you, Ashley. Welcome to Bournemouth… and England. I'm sorry about our weather," I added.

"I knew you were Tony," Ashley drawled. "I'm very pleased to meet you at last."

'At last' – what did that mean?

Nigel was now looking past me to the table I had come from.

"Come and meet my friend," I said.

I led the way and stood by the table. I introduced Diane to Nigel and then to Ashley, noticing for some reason that she was the same height as Nigel. Then they sat down either side of the table, Ashley next to Diane. A waitress came and took our order. Nigel asked for a beer, I pointed to my lager, and Ashley asked for a Chardonnay. I asked the waitress if it was a Californian wine. "That's where these two live," I burbled by way of explanation, and then wished I hadn't said it.

Ashley was now sitting opposite me. She gave me a beautiful, dazzling white smile, shrugged her shoulders and wrinkled her freckled nose.

I turned to Nigel and asked obvious questions about what time they got into London, what time they got to Daisy's house. Ashley and Diane, meanwhile, seemed to hit it off. I heard Ashley saying 'Diane, honey' this, 'Diane, honey' that, and telling her how excited she was to come to England for the first time. Somehow Nigel and I did not have so much to say. We had both mentioned the last time we had walked up the pier. We agreed we could not believe where the years had gone. He rubbed his wiry white hair and asked how I still had natural colour in mine. It felt a bit awkward – not terribly so, but it was not comfortable. We would try or both would start to say something at the same time. However, when Nigel joined Diane and Ashley's conversation it did go better. Maybe it was my fault.

I caught Diane's eye. She asked Ashley and then Nigel if they smoked. She mentioned that it was permissible on the boarded balcony the other side of the windows.

They both said no but Nigel looked to me.

"You still smoke," he said. It wasn't a question, though. I thought, 'Here we go'. It's common knowledge that hardly anyone smokes in California.

"Thank goodness some things never change. Thank goodness you still can if you choose to. Not many still do in our part of the world." He leant back in his chair and laughed.

I wasn't sure if he was being patronising or not.

"Come on, buddy, let's go outside so you can smoke," he said. Ashley shrugged. Diane smiled.

"Go on," she encouraged.

Nigel was already on his way to the balcony and held the door open for me. I lit up. Nigel had never smoked, I recalled; no cigarettes, no drugs.

"It's great to see you, Tony. And I am so, so sorry we didn't stay in touch. I let you down. It was selfish in the extreme. For so many years. So, so many years."

"Please don't apologise. There's no need to be sorry. Life takes over." I didn't really know what to say. The past flew away. Forty years passed us by. We talked about Daisy. That led to my work. He looked uncomfortable.

"I often wondered what business you went into. I mean, what about the shop business you talked about? What happened to that idea? You were so full of ideas."

After forty years these questions seemed ridiculous. I couldn't believe he could have become so crass. I changed the subject by asking about Ashley – when and how they met.

I was starting to tell Nigel how much I thought of Diane. I told him the connection with her daughter and I told him a little about Charlotte.

He gave me a brief description of Agoura, his adopted home town. I smoked another cigarette. I could feel the brandies; they had certainly settled me. My head swam slightly, though. I noticed him shrug his shoulders and guessed it was the temperature. Not what he was used to, I supposed.

"Let's go back in and see the ladies," I said.

I soon learnt to enjoy the daft questions that poured from Ashley. She was like an excited child but charming too. Diane was obviously enjoying her company; she hardly looked away from the younger woman as we sat back down.

"Would you all like to order something to eat now?" I tried to butt in.

Nigel asked Diane if she had ever been to America. She said she had spent a 'touristy few days' in New York, had been to Naples in Florida and to some sort of teaching convention in New Orleans, all of which was news to me.

"Never to California?" he asked.

She hadn't, but had very much wanted to when she was young, she informed him. I didn't know this either.

After we'd ordered some food and more drinks I visited the toilet, or 'bathroom', as Ashley had called it earlier. I was puzzled at how easily all this seemed to be going. I still had all sorts of silly little strange feelings ricocheting around my brain. I was rinsing my hands when Nigel appeared over my shoulder in the mirror.

"It's so great to see you, buddy." He hugged me. I suddenly had this dread that someone, another bloke, would come in and see us hugging. I pulled away a bit too abruptly, I suppose. A fleeting look of disappointment crossed his tanned face.

When I told him why I'd done it we both went into fits of laughter. At that moment, two young men, jeans hanging halfway down their backsides, came in. They looked at us, which started us off again. As we left, and they were stood at the urinals, I heard one say: "I want what they're having."

When we got back to the table there was another woman there. Nigel glanced at me and I shrugged. Ashley was beaming at Nigel. Diane met my puzzled look. The woman turned as we crossed the restaurant. She was probably in her sixties but dressed a bit too young for her age and she had a modern, asymmetric haircut which was dyed in a red that was one shade too shocking.

"I'm sorry to be so rude but I couldn't help coming over," she gushed. Nigel looked at me as if I could explain. "You *are* Smudger Smiff, aren't you?" she said to Nigel. I wanted to laugh.

"No, *he* is," he said, nodding in my direction. The woman looked baffled.

This started us both laughing again. He then apologised to the woman.

She asked for an autograph after explaining that she had been in the crowd on the beach all those years ago when The Strikes played on the pier. Nigel graciously signed his best wishes to her name and they posed for her phone camera. He shook her hand and thanked her for remembering him and she went off happily to another table of people who all stared our way as she sat back down. Nigel explained to Diane and Ashley that it had been me who organised the gig on the pier. He looked out of the window at the view down the pier and wistfully pictured that day.

"The sun was shining. The crowds were huge." He stopped, and then added in a whisper: "It was a lifetime ago."

The meal was fine; the ice was broken. Nigel waved to the lady with red hair as we left the restaurant. Then we walked to the pier entrance.

"This sight was my enduring memory of our last meeting." Nigel swept a hand towards the pier. "I have to walk it."

Ashley said she had looked forward to seeing the real thing, and it was my turn to be confused. She explained that Nigel had shown her the pier on a webcam. We walked the length of the pier to the little theatre where The Strikes had played.

Ashley and Diane walked ahead of us arm-in-arm. Ashley was taller and slimmer than Diane, but they could have been mother and daughter. I idly watched Ashley's long, slim, denim-clad legs as the two women talked easily and animatedly. I marvelled at them both. So many differences but so instantly at ease. Nigel stopped at the theatre as we began to walk back, and turned to me.

"Do you remember 'If'? The Kipling poem?" he asked. This seemed to come out of the blue. He fidgeted almost nervously. He was standing directly in front of me staring into my face.

"Do you?" he asked again, a trace of anxiety in his tone. "Do you remember the bond it seemed to give us? You wrote it on a piece of paper and gave it to me at school. You saved my life. You helped me get through. You were always helping me out. With my bands then with The Strikes, even, at the beginning. 'If', you would say... you helped me." He swallowed and looked across the horizon towards the silhouette outline of the Isle of Wight. It seemed he was searching for some words or a memory, what to say. I just waited for him.

"You helped me with Peter Davis... Rudy... for Joan's sake... for Cherry's sake... no complaining, no questioning... you even took me to Heathrow when I

295

left the UK... England." He swallowed again, staring hard at me now, and took my hand in both of his. "And I walked away and forgot you." He blew air and the grip of his hands tightened on mine.

"I know I promised to stay in touch. I know you were hoping for help to get your business going." He shook his head, eyes closed, and blew air again at the twilight sky. Clouds scudded across the skyline as night thought about arriving; hints of purple on the horizon.

I didn't know what to say when he finally seemed to have stopped. He had let go of my hand but was still standing in front of me watching my face, waiting for some sort of answer.

"My life hasn't been so bad," I reassured him.

When you talk about your life after you've turned sixty it seems to have vanished as if by magic, without your being conscious of where it has gone. I suppose the feeling only intensifies from this age onwards, with so much more behind you than in front.

So, for me the time had gone, and I tried to explain this to Nigel. It had gone. The time had gone. I hadn't started my emporium. I told him how when my wife and daughters – my 'three girls' – had gone my life had changed.

I said of course I remembered the poem and that I reread it sometimes, also that Diane could almost recite the whole thing. He chuckled at this, appearing relieved. Ashley and Diane had stopped walking and were looking back at us.

"I have a favour to ask you whilst I'm here. I'll tell you about it tomorrow, if I may." I was intrigued. We caught the ladies up. When we came off the pier we walked up through the gardens to the taxi rank. People stared. I don't know whether they recognised Nigel or it was the attraction of his companion. Diane squeezed my hand as we waved them off in the taxi.

"OK?" she asked.

"Yes," I told her. "I think so."

That night, when we were back at my place, Diane came into my bedroom after visiting the bathroom. I lay looking at the ceiling, a million thoughts, memories and feelings zigzagging in my brain; Nigel had even mentioned Pete Davis! Diane lay down on the bed and leaned over me, propped up on one elbow.

"I'm glad I know you, Mr Smith, 'friend-of-the-stars'."

I had been teasing her about being 'celebrity obsessed' because she was so excited about going to Daisy's house the next day.

"You know what?" she said. "Perhaps we should go to California for a holiday."

I thought about images I had of California from films and television. I thought about the sixties and seventies exalting California as the place to be. If we go to San Francisco I'll have to see if I've still got some flared jeans and some hippy flowers for my hair.

Diane leant down and kissed me on the lips.

"What do you think?" she prompted.

"I guess it would be nice. How long does it take to fly there? I've never been on a long-haul flight."

"Oh, just over eleven hours, I think." I knew she was trying to distract me from darker thoughts by keeping the conversation light, but the image of the grave in the New Forest loomed in my head. The tune of Scott McKenzie's 'San Francisco' meandered through, and a Strikes anthem called 'Blessed' vied for space, Pete

Davis' voice as he extolled the virtue of 'being blessed by you' echoing across the image of that September morning in 1975.

I opened my eyes; Diane was still leaning over me, her sweet breath slightly minty. She stroked my forehead. I felt like a child. Dad used to do that sometimes if I couldn't sleep, and he had a little song he would sing that had no proper words. A tear slipped down the side of my face.

"I know... I'm a silly old bugger," I managed to say with a smile.

"Why don't you get up and make yourself a cup of tea? Have a cigarette... if you can't sleep. Don't just lie there tormenting yourself."

I raised my head and kissed her.

"Do you mind?"

I went downstairs in my ancient dressing gown. I filled the kettle and opened the back door to smoke. There was a light on in the studio. It lifted me to know Charlotte was down there. I didn't understand why, when I had been feeling so miserable just moments before in bed. Diane was being her compassionate and caring self to me but she had not moved my mood. Just the sight of that light did, though – just knowing Charlotte was there, whether she was awake, asleep, or working. I shuddered from the chill night air. My kitchen clock said nearly two o'clock; we had been in bed since around eleven or eleven-thirty and I was wide awake drinking tea and smoking cigarettes.

I thought about Nigel. I pictured Ashley, his young partner. The image of his pure white hair, his tanned face. His American accent. He looked very fit and seemed relaxed to be here. I thought about his declaration back in 1975 that he would never return. I pictured him walking through to departures at Heathrow and then going out of sight. Where had those years gone? I wondered if he had shed any tears. I could recall the drive back home. It had felt like I had a hole in my chest. It was definitely a physical sensation in my body as I drove across the New Forest.

A young man raised his hand in one last wave that day and an old man remembered now.

Chapter Thirty-seven

Diane was looking apprehensive. We had pulled up in front of the high wooden gates to Daisy's house; I had pressed the intercom and announced our arrival. She glanced slightly anxiously at me as the gates opened to reveal the drive down to the house. Now it was my turn to encourage. It was unlike her not to have an intelligent, rational explanation for her apprehension, as she did for most things.

"Wow," she murmured as she saw the house. The sun had made an appearance that morning and the house glowed white against a blue sky broken only by a few wisps of springtime cloud. The drive, a short avenue of mature Chusan palms, led to an open parking area in front of the garaging. The sun flashed off the front windows at this time of morning making the house look even more dramatic with its black glass, white stucco, sharp angles and stainless steel balconies.

Not that I had seen the house in sunshine very much when we were working on it only weeks before.

It looked spectacular to me too, seeing it again without contemplating a working day in prospect.

"I don't think I've ever..." Diane didn't finish her thought. Ashley was at the door, looking good in tight white jeans and an equally tight white vest. Her smile greeted us as we got out of Diane's car.

"What a lovely little car, honey," she enthused, taking Diane's hand before she was even fully out of her seat and kissing her on both cheeks. They were like old friends already, it seemed to me. Nigel was now standing in the doorway. He stepped down and kissed Diane on the cheek.

"Good morning," he said. "How are you this morning? Hi, how are you?"

He shook my hand. "Hi, Tony. Sleep well?"

I knew he didn't expect an answer but I gave him one.

"Not very well at first but then really well."

He was already ushering Diane into the hallway

"What a lovely house!" she said, thereby excusing herself to have a better look around. She had noticed the glass wall of windows overlooking Poole Bay and Brownsea Island, and she walked confidently on through and stood admiring the view. Ashley joined her. She linked her arm through Diane's in the cosy way the two of them had begun yesterday on their first meeting. I went up beside them. A seagull screeched by and several more wheeled over the garden towards the water's edge. There were a few small pleasure-boats about. I asked Ashley if she had seen any ferries heading for France. She giggled as if I was teasing her and waggled an elegant, well-manicured finger at me in admonishment. She took some convincing that France was only two-and-a-half hours away by ferry.

A voice behind us asked, "Who would like a coffee?" It was Daisy.

She came over and said hello to me. I introduced Diane to her. She talked about Lisa and asked how she was. She mentioned that she wanted to meet Lisa's new boyfriend. Diane was quieter than normal for a while; a bit awestruck, just as I had been when I'd first worked for Daisy. We all went and sat over on the other side of the room near the kitchen, where we could still see the view. Daisy stood at the end of the table and handed out two jugs of coffee which she placed next to the white mugs, one jug of milk and one cream and a bowl of sugar. She made an aside to Diane – something about 'American-style… but no doughnuts' – and chuckled.

She stayed standing and coughed for attention.

"I would like to officially welcome my grandfather, Nigel, back to England. I would also like to welcome Ashley to England for her first-ever visit and I also welcome to my house Diane, the mother of my friend Lisa." She drew breath and I even thought I heard a catch in her voice as she spoke.

"But most of all I would like thank Tony for being here because if he wasn't, my grandfather might not have returned to the town of his birth. I would also like to thank Tony – the *real* Smudger, as you know – for being my grandfather's friend when they were young. I have heard Tony Smith stories all my life, and thank goodness he came to my house in January as if by magic." She did push away a tear from her eye now. She leant over and kissed me on the cheek. "Thank you," she whispered.

Ashley had a tissue to her eyes. Diane was watching me and her eyes glistened. Nigel was also watching me. I was embarrassed. I poured myself some coffee, added some sugar, and concentrated on stirring it in, not wanting to catch anyone's eye. It was Diane who broke the silence, announcing that she had not received an answer from me to her suggestion of a holiday in California. This started a conversation, and Daisy then left the four of us to it, explaining that she had lots to do in preparation for the party.

The mood changed when Nigel asked if The White Buck Inn still had live music. I told him that I hadn't been there since the seventies. Initially he looked baffled by what I was saying, and there was an awkward pause. When Ashley realised what I meant she explained that Nigel had told her what had happened in 1975, adding that it was her 'birth year'. We all looked at each other. Then Nigel asked Diane if she knew what we were alluding to.

"I do," she said, adding that although we hadn't known each other very long, it was some years since I had begun working with her daughter, and so she felt she almost knew me before we met. Ashley perked up at this and agreed she also felt she 'knew Tony before'. It seemed Nigel had begun telling her more and more of his past. He too, I gathered, had been looking back a lot recently. Ashley quite obviously cared about him. She had a natural intelligence that was becoming obvious too.

I became the subject again. Diane told Nigel about my flashbacks and my recent disturbed thoughts and memories. I was willing her not to mention my dad or my mum; that memory was too painful to relate. Nigel looked uncomfortable when Diane spoke of how he had escaped constant reminders of the past; she had not accused him directly but it was not hard to work out what she was saying. Ashley took her hand after she had finished talking.

"Nigel is aware," she said simply, looking carefully at me.

"Have you really not been to Burley since?" said Nigel after another awkward lull in the conversation. I told him I had not until very recently, and described the job with Lisa and Dave at the cottage. He seemed stunned. I explained how Burley had come to personify everything negative about my past, but since meeting Diane I had begun to feel better. Diane began to say something and checked herself. I think she was going to ask Nigel if he knew of my parents. We were very good friends in those teenage years but he knew only that my father had died that Christmas. And somehow teenagers don't quite react to an older person dying unless it is a close relative of their own. He did not question my stories of how my father died of a heart attack and my mother was overcome with grief. That was what I told anyone who asked. Only the Cuthberts and I knew the whole truth.

The conversation turned to Pete Davis. It went quiet whenever Daisy came into the room. Nigel had told us that she knew nothing of this slice of the past, her grandmother's deed or our part in covering it up.

I had promised to take Nigel and Ashley to Burley. We were going to go to the jazz night. I knew from lots of people about The Chicago Jazz Aces playing there every Thursday for many years. I'd heard good reports of the food there too.

It would be as much a walk down memory lane for me as for Nigel. I had also promised to show Ashley some typically English pubs, of which there are many really good examples in the New Forest.

I asked if Nigel had brought a guitar because sometimes The Aces let others sit in and jam or feature themselves. I'm sure they would be honoured if he did. I asked if Daisy might like to come too. I knew most of the Thursday-nighters at The White Buck were over a certain age and therefore not very likely to bother her. There might even be a few who had not heard of her. But I said this as a joke. Everybody, it seemed, knew Daisy Belle Bliss. I thought it might be a distraction for Daisy, with her party taking place that weekend, but I also thought it would be a distraction for me too. Diane told me later she realised that was why I had suggested it. Diane had promised to go shopping with Ashley, and I had agreed to visit 'a few old haunts', at Nigel's request.

In truth I didn't feel completely comfortable with him yet; his accent was distracting, for a start. We had so little in common, and after around forty years, this was unsurprising. He was rich and living in another country and had probably had a varied and exciting life, and here was I, Mr Average, having led a narrow life in one town with one occupation, few friends and even fewer experiences. His job was creative, mine humdrum and manual. He had a laid-back coolness now, whereas I had become more introspective with each year that passed.

I was to pick him up in my van the following day, and Diane would drive Ashley.

The next day Diane and I set off from my house together. She was excited and intrigued; I was apprehensive and intrigued! We had a cup of coffee at Daisy's house; the sun was trying to come out just enough to allow us to sit out on a patio.

People had arrived at the house to set up lighting and speakers in the garden and in the large canvas gazebos. Daisy had hired tents and a long row of camper vans for overnight guests, and the grounds resembled a ramshackle campsite, albeit one bedecked with colourful bunting. She was so uncomplicated and natural, it seemed to me. If anybody had reasons to be neurotic she did, but she wasn't. She kissed everybody goodbye with a peck on the cheek. Ashley got into Diane's car, Nigel climbed into my van, and we all left together. Daisy had recruited Lisa and Emma to help with the last few days of preparation, and as we left, they arrived, waving excitedly from their van.

Diane was soon out of sight; she knew where she was going. I asked Nigel if he would like to go anywhere in particular. To my surprise he wanted to go to Weymouth. I didn't remember him having significant connections with Weymouth. He explained when I put this to him that he both wanted to see some Dorset countryside on the way and to see an archetypical British seaside town. We left Poole and headed west. It would take about an hour.

He was quiet and I tried to make conversation. I wanted to ask about his life. I was annoying myself with these sorts of thoughts when he came right out and asked.

"Have you ever been to the place we buried Pete?" He was waiting for my reactions as well as for my answer. I glanced away from the road and met his eyes briefly.

"No," I told him. "I've avoided Burley and that part of the forest since that day." I heard him suck in air and he stared ahead at the road.

"I know I let you down, my friend."

I didn't know what to say. He continued quietly, watching me as he spoke.

"I went off to a privileged life... in the main." He added 'in the main' in an even quieter voice, and I assumed he was remembering Cherry and Sarah. "I've had a very good life apart from some upsets along the way."

'Upsets' seemed like a monumental understatement to me and I nearly said so.

"California and Agoura are not difficult places to live if you have money." He went on to tell me more of his life there and it certainly sounded easier than mine. *A lot easier.* I listened without comment, though. It wouldn't be difficult for him to completely guess my day-to-day life, but his was very different from mine, and most people's, come to that. He would have huge amounts of money for a start. If he was ever miserable he could at least be miserable in comfort. Sitting by a pool under clear blue Californian skies would not be too bad for most of us. Add to that the fact that he could satisfy his creative urges with the best recording equipment money could buy, pop to one of his favourite restaurants for company, or sit in and jam with a band. He got lots of pleasure too, he'd already told me, from helping the local colleges and youngsters with their music.

"I would have liked to have seen where you live," I said. I rather blurted this out, and I think it might have sounded a bit petulant and sour. I didn't mean it to... *or did I?*

I noticed him stiffen slightly in his seat and look at me.

"I'm so, so sorry, buddy." He almost whispered this.

I was beginning to feel uptight; the 'buddy' annoyed me. I know that sounds petty, but 'buddy'! I told him not to keep apologising. "We went different ways in life, that's all."

We had turned off the main road and were heading for Weymouth through rolling green fields that would dip to the distant sea: a lovely sight.

"When we parted at Heathrow all those years ago you said to me to stay in touch. I didn't. I knew you had ambitions. You helped me out for so many years, you held me together so many times. I could have helped you… should have helped you. And now I have another favour to ask of you while I'm here in the UK."

'Oh? Now what?' I thought, but didn't say.

"I want to record you reciting 'If'. Just like in the school competition all those years ago. You remember that?"

"Yes, of course."

"Do you?"

He seemed surprised. *I don't forget everything.*

I must have looked completely baffled, however, because he was still explaining what he had in mind as we drove along the promenade at Weymouth; the beach to our left and small hotels and guesthouses painted in bright colours to our right. We passed the painted statue of George III towards the end of the esplanade and pulled into the car park by the theatre and the dock area. I knew something of his recordings and had of course heard the CD Diane had but I didn't know the full extent till now. He told me about Ashley's singing voice and then he told me my part. He put a hand on my arm. I still had my hands on the steering wheel and was idly watching a gull on a railing as he spoke. I could feel tears welling.

I said, "Wait here. I'll go and get a parking ticket from the machine."

In truth this was just to gather myself, to give myself a breath of air. I was going to have to start getting a grip on my feelings. I lit a welcome cigarette and walked over to the pay-and-display machine, my head whirling with images old and new: of Nigel as a boy, as a youth, and as the tanned and white-haired man in the front of my van. I glanced back and saw him watching me. I paid, the machine whirred, and I triumphantly displayed the ticket in a raised fist.

"Shall we go and get a coffee?" I said. We stood silently at the railings for a while and looked across the bay to the far side of the almost deserted beach.

"What happened to your emporium idea?" he asked again.

I looked at him closely. Where did that come from? How on earth did he remember that? Yes, it was an idea I had had for a retail business back in the early seventies. He'd offered to invest in it. I remembered how excited I'd been, working all the hours under the sun to save some capital to get started, and how Jenny was indifferent to the idea but Nigel had appeared interested.

"Come on, let's get that coffee," I replied. We found a little place overlooking the seafront and sat outside so I could smoke. A few pensioners were shuffling along the promenade taking the sea air and enjoying cheap early-season hotel rates. One couple stopped and hesitated on the pavement near us. I knew they'd recognised Nigel. I was getting used to people coming up to him. The wife seemed to be unsure, the husband convincing her.

"Are you Smudger Smiff?" the man finally asked.

Nigel put down his coffee and smiled weakly. "We both are," he said.

The man looked puzzled and his wife tugged his arm.

"Leave it, Ron," she begged him.

"You are, I know you are," the man persisted, addressing Nigel. Then he turned to me. "Are you one of The Strikes too? You were fantastic back then. I've got every album you made." He was getting very excited. "What on earth are you doing in bloody Weymouth?"

His wife had relaxed her grip on his arm. "Do you mind if we join you? Come on, Doll," he said, beckoning to her.

What could we say? He sat down beside me, opposite Nigel, and gesticulated for his wife to sit down. He stuck out a hand. "Ron Fudge – and this is my wife Doris. I call her Doll, though – always have; Dolly Daydream, it started as," he said with a diffident chuckle.

"We're from Stafford but the first time I saw you and your band was in Birmingham. We were courting then. Weren't we, Doll?"

Nigel looked from me to Ron and his wife. I tried to make out what he was really thinking; maybe he was used to this sort of thing. Ron Fudge called the waitress over.

"Did you know you had a famous rock star in your cafe?" he asked her. She looked blank and stared at me. It was entirely possible that her mother had not yet been born, let alone her, when The Strikes were at their peak.

"Not him," said Ron. He pointed at Nigel's chest. "Him!"

She shrugged without a word and blushed slightly.

"When I first heard you on *The Old Grey Whistle Test* with Whispering Bob, I knew you would be huge."

Ron helpfully listed every album The Strikes had made, hardly pausing for breath. This meeting had 'made his holiday'; he could 'hardly wait' to get home to tell his mates and his sons and daughters. He produced a small camera from his anorak pocket and held it up. "Could we?" I took the camera and Ron sat next to Nigel, then he stood with Nigel between him and Doll. I marvelled at Nigel's patience but remembered the boy and the youth unfazed by most circumstances. He politely smiled for the camera. Ron was finally persuaded to leave by the promise of a signed copy of Nigel's as-yet-unreleased boxed set. Satisfied and ecstatic, he gave Nigel his address, he and Doll then shuffled off along the promenade, Ron turning every few yards to wave until they were finally out of view.

Nigel and I laughed.

"You will do me that favour? Record 'If' for me," he said.

"I was afraid Ron might ask about Pete Davis," I said, and the laughter stopped. "I was waiting for it."

Nigel slid a ten-pound note under his saucer. "Let's walk," he said, getting to his feet.

We talked about what happened that day in 1975. We talked about the whole industry of conspiracy theories that had grown since then. I told him of some of the newspaper and magazine stories I had seen over the years that he was unaware of. Nigel said he'd seen a German documentary that purported to show Pete Davis locked up in a Thai prison for paedophilia. A bribed prison officer had taken photos using a hidden camera. Nigel said whoever it was did look somewhat like Pete; he was white, lank-haired and skinny like Davis, at any rate. The programme apparently spent about fifty minutes leading up to the final pictures of 'Rudy Davis' with clips of The Strikes at a Nuremberg concert and other documentary clips taken on German soil in the early seventies. They even interviewed Lou's sister who still lived in Dorset and even more remarkably showed Pete Davis' old family home in Boscombe.

I told him that recently it came back to me more and more. I explained the flashbacks. He shook his head at this and a sad expression clouded his eyes.

I asked him if he ever thought of it. He told me that for the first couple of years living in California it had crossed his mind a few times, but only rarely since. He sounded apologetic, and touched my arm as we walked. I asked if he had ever wondered what we would say to the police if we were questioned now. He told me that he had not.

We turned and walked back towards the car park, stopping at a fish-and-chip shop on the way. We sat on a bench overlooking the harbour and ate. Then to the van to drive back to Bournemouth. It seemed a long way to drive for a coffee and fish and chips but for some reason I now felt more relaxed with Nigel. I was still curious as to why he wanted to visit Weymouth, and he told me on the way home: he had spent happy times there with Joan, and how he wished could have taken Daisy there as a child.

"I just needed to see it now and remember how it was. It's very much as I remembered it, I'm glad to say."

We chatted away, so much more relaxed on the return journey.

Chapter Thirty-eight

I had agreed with Diane that she would go back to my house when they'd finished shopping. I told Nigel that was what we were doing. He hadn't been to my house since that September morning in 1975, and had been surprised to learn that I still lived there. We pulled up outside; Diane's car was there. I told Nigel how I'd looked forward to introducing him to Charlotte. Nigel marvelled at her skills at Daisy's house and already expressed his admiration. I had asked her to be there if she could that afternoon; I'd even joked that she might get some work in California.

I stood back and motioned Nigel in my front door. He hesitated. I could hear the women chatting in the kitchen as we went through. Nigel kissed Ashley on the cheek. Charlotte looked relaxed and happy. I could tell her moods now. I introduced Nigel to Charlotte. They seemed to consider each other for longer than most would on a first introduction, but I guessed it was because I had told both of them so much about the other. Diane got up and put the kettle on. "Tea?" she asked, but she had two mugs out already. She smiled at me. "Where did you two go, then? Old haunts?"

I only had four chairs around my kitchen table so I brought in one of the old wicker ones from the garden, sneaking a crafty smoke in the process. I was starting to feel ashamed of the habit now I was in the minority.

The ladies seemed very relaxed with each other. Nobody could sound as enthusiastic as Ashley in full Texan flow about Charlotte's work in Daisy's house.

"Would you show Ashley and Nigel the portrait?" I asked Charlotte.

"Which one?"

"You know – the portrait of your grandmother."

"Oh, OK. Sure. Perhaps you'd all better come down."

Nigel shrugged at Ashley's quizzical glance.

"My studio is in Tony's garden," said Charlotte by way of explanation.

She led the way out of the kitchen, fishing in her jeans pocket for the padlock key. I caught a hint of that fragrance as I followed.

She undid the padlock and ushered us all in. There were two easels set up side by side. On one was a canvas covered with a cloth, while on the other rested a portrait of a man. I recognised his face: it was me. I looked older, somehow, but it was a beautiful portrait. That was my first impression… 'beautiful'…even though it was me.

Diane stood in front of it and tears started down her cheeks. Ashley looked from me to it and back and Nigel patted me silently on the shoulder. I guess we were all a bit spellbound, not least me. This was not expected. I just stared. Charlotte was standing back watching all the reactions with a half-smile of curiosity playing on her lips.

"I don't know what to say," I said.

"Then don't say anything!" Charlotte replied with a grin.

Diane was transfixed in front of it still. Then she turned to Charlotte.

"It's wonderful. You have such a talent." And she hugged and kissed her.

"You sure have," added Nigel. And Ashley smiled.

"Where's the other?" I managed to ask.

Charlotte pulled the cloth off the other easel to reveal the portrait of her grandmother. Ashley gasped and Nigel muttered something. Diane moved to stand square in front of the lovely head-and-shoulders portrait of the old woman with the beautiful violet eyes; sympathetic and intelligent eyes framed by soft waves of pure white hair; lips full and red, despite her obvious age, and the whole face seeming to float just off the canvas. Nigel took a step back. He looked shaken. I noticed his reaction and so did Charlotte.

"What's up, Nigel?" she asked. "What is it? What can you see? What's wrong?"

But Nigel went outside. I followed. He had gone back up the garden and was breathing heavily. He looked pale, his skin grey and pallid beneath the suntan.

"What on earth...?"

"That is Lucy's mother. She is older, much older but I would recognise her anywhere." Nigel looked at me as if I had some sort of answer but I had no idea what he was talking about.

"Who is Lucy? Who's Lucy's mother?" I stood in front of him half expecting that I might have to catch him at any moment, that he might pass out or something. He sat down heavily in one of the wicker chairs under the veranda and held his face in his hands, elbows on his knees.

"You're not making sense, Nigel," I said.

He looked up at me standing over him. The women were still in the studio but Charlotte was watching us from the doorway. Nigel had what I can only describe as a scared or haunted look in his eyes as he stared into mine. "Lucy was the young girl from the village who helped with the children in Pete and Joan's commune."

I still wasn't getting it. He continued.

"Lucy was the young girl who Pete had been with when Joan stabbed him. He had been having sex with her."

I was getting it now. Fast.

Nigel explained how after a visit to the commune he had given Lucy a lift back to her house in the village. He had met her mother on that occasion. She was a strikingly good-looking woman with violet eyes. Lucy had inherited her looks. She had quizzed Nigel about the commune and expressed her concern for Lucy. He had conveyed his distaste for the place too. She had been even more alarmed after this conversation and had tried to stop Lucy from going up there, but this had proved futile. Her daughter was beguiled by then and nothing apart from keeping her under lock and key would stop her. Her mother had conceded, warning Lucy of the dangers and hoping that her daughter's assurances that she knew what she was doing were to be trusted. When Pete Davis chased all the occupants from the house, the village knew about it and were not surprised at his antics.

They did not, however, predict that he would suddenly vanish forever or that Jojo would kill herself with an overdose or indeed that Lucy from the village would announce some months later that she was pregnant.

It had begun to dawn on me what Nigel was telling me. I quickly told him that Charlotte knew and sympathised with what had happened on that day back in 1975. He looked concerned. So would I have done it if I'd known what would follow? Charlotte was astute. She had sensed Nigel's reaction was significant. Now she stood over Nigel, ignoring me.

"What could you see?" she demanded.

Nigel shook his head. Ashley and Diane were also under the veranda by now. Ashley looked puzzled and asked Nigel what had happened. Diane looked at me and her look asked the same questions.

Charlotte did not take her eyes from Nigel.

"Please tell me what you saw in my grandmother's portrait, Nigel."

All four of us were looking down to where Nigel was sitting, still looking distressed and shaken.

"Did you know Charlotte's grandmother, Nigel?" Diane asked.

Nigel threw his head back, exhaling a long breath. He gulped an equally large lungful as he stared at Charlotte.

"Is your mother's name Lucy?" He watched her closely.

"Yes," she breathed, "it is."

Nigel looked from one to another; Ashley and Diane were still bewildered. Nigel explained about his one meeting with Lucy's mother and how he recognised her nonetheless.

"Her hair was darker then... not white," he said, "but those eyes and those features... it had to be; I knew instantly."

Diane and Ashley had somehow managed to find each other's hand without taking their eyes from first Nigel and then Charlotte with an occasional glance at me. Nobody spoke.

I couldn't remember his looks exactly but found myself trying to think if I could find any resemblances between Charlotte and Pete Davis. Would his remains now be recovered at Charlotte's insistence? Would I spend the rest of my days in prison? Would Nigel too? Would Diane stay with me? Did it change our relationship? Of course it would if I was in prison. Would Charlotte hate me? These thoughts tumbled in.

I lit a cigarette; the answer to all my problems, except how to give up smoking. Still nobody spoke a word. I got two beers from my fridge and handed an open one to Nigel. My mouth had gone very dry. Everybody seemed to be looking at the others and each seemed to want somebody else to say something but the silence lingered on. Finally it was Ashley who spoke. She gently took Charlotte's wine from her and put it on the table and held both her hands.

"Well, honey, I guess that was quite a shock for you."

Charlotte shook her head silently. She then began to relate how, when she was about thirteen, she had commented to her mother one day that she didn't look much like her younger siblings (two brothers and one sister), and was told that she had been born before her mother had married her father. That her father was not her father. Charlotte had often wondered about his indifference to her; how he seemed to treat her with much less affection than he did the others. That was why she spent so much time with her grandmother: to avoid her parents. It was instinctive when younger but out of choice from that day on. Her parents didn't seem to have much respect for each other either; they seemed to live separate lives under the same roof, and employed a nanny to help with the children. Her father was a busy barrister and Lucy, as Charlotte now referred to her, had been, and still was, a well-known journalist. It was her grandmother who had encouraged her art. Charlotte related all this.

Ashley's question still hung in the air. Charlotte continued, though haltingly.

"Whenever, after that day, I asked about my real father – my natural father – my mother would tell me that he was the love of her life and that he was a famous singer but couldn't cope with the pressures of fame and had run away... and that nobody knew where he'd gone. 'His spirit is free', she would always add."

Chapter Thirty-nine

When I woke in the morning after yet another patchy night's sleep, I began going over last night's revelation. It was Thursday, the day we had decided to go to the The White Buck Inn for dinner – all of us, Daisy included. Diane had phoned the pub to ask if that was OK; Daisy usually caused quite a stir wherever she went. They were delighted if a bit overwhelmed. They promised as quiet a corner as possible. Diane had assured them no special treatment was necessary.

I was still going over and over the events of the previous night as I shaved and showered. Charlotte and I had had a long conversation till the early hours; we had both smoked too much, and she'd slept on the bed in her studio. Our conversation had been mainly about our families, a topic we hadn't exhausted even before this new part of her family had become known to her. I couldn't imagine how she was going to react about her real father's burial place or especially who put him there. Perhaps she would say that everything should stay the same, *even though nothing ever stays the same*, certainly not when you find out that your friend buried your father in a wood many years ago. She was an intelligent woman; she wouldn't do or say anything without considering all the options and possible repercussions of her decision. We would have to wait. I now felt that I was in her hands. We always knew we had committed an offence. I accepted Nigel's reasoning, and I did it for him, not for his ex-wife or his daughter. At the time it seemed the right thing to do. *We are all responsible for our own actions.*

As I went downstairs, the image of Nigel dropping something into the grave after the body floated into my mind's eye. After all these years the image returned as clear as if it was yesterday. I could see him doing it, and, bizarrely after so long, I clearly remembered thinking at that moment that I must ask him later what it was. How peculiar of the brain to allow that back in so clearly after nearly forty years. I couldn't wait to ask. I hoped he could remember.

I filled the kettle and washed up the previous night's glasses and mugs while I waited for it to boil. I stared down my garden to the hut and pictured the young woman there. What would she do with the new knowledge? Would she want the past dug up – literally? Would she still come to the New Forest with us? Would she still want to come to The White Buck Inn with us? I idly wondered whether to take her some tea or coffee but decided it was best not to disturb her. I switched the radio on, popped one slice in the toaster and clicked the kettle for a second cup of tea. I could see the door and I waited for some signs that Charlotte might be up. She would sooner or later need to use the bathroom in the house.

As I watched from my back door she appeared, bleary-eyed, her short hair spiked in all directions. She scratched her head, looked at the sky then noticed me there. A weak smile flickered across her lips. She came down the path clutching a bundle of clothes and a wash bag. I wanted to hug her as she reached me but I just stood aside. I asked if she would like some tea or coffee first and I told her where fresh towels were. When she smiled at me it didn't reach her eyes. She put her clothes down on a chair and threw her arms round my neck and wailed. Her shoulders heaved as she sobbed noisily. I just held her; I held her tight; it felt like any father comforting a daughter. Her head was in my neck, and I could feel warm tears wetting me. She leaned back, and a red-eyed, runny-nosed face kissed me. "Thanks, I needed that," she sniffled. I moved from her grip and grabbed a box of tissues from the shelf. "Thanks," she whispered again.

"Now then, young lady, what would you like first? Tea, coffee, orange juice – a cigarette?"

"I'll take one of each, please. Well, maybe just coffee, not tea as well," she said, smiling. Then she added that she was sorry for crying. She used the bathroom while I boiled the kettle.

When she returned I took her hand. She had two cigarettes, two coffees and even a slice of toast and marmalade, then went back upstairs for a shower. No mention had been made of the previous night at that point. I had resolved to get to the subject when she came back downstairs. I washed up the breakfast things and thought about how to ask.

She smiled at me.

I tried to sound relaxed.

"Feel better?" I asked, and she agreed that a nice long shower can make you feel better about most things. I fleetingly thought, '*Most* things'.

"How do you feel about what you learned... what we all learned last night?"

She sat down then stood up again and went to the back door and out. I followed. She was sitting on a wicker chair staring down the garden. I put a clean ashtray on the table along with a new pack of B&H and a lighter.

"Help yourself," I said.

She glanced at me and studied me as she did with people. She looked me directly in the eyes. She was reading my mind.

"I don't want to go to the police, Tony, if that is worrying you. How could I do that to you? Or Nigel," she added. She continued staring directly at me. I lit a cigarette as much for distraction as anything else. She shook her head when I offered her the pack. "But..." she said, and I felt my heart-rate increase. "...I wouldn't like to think of him spending eternity in a hole in the ground in a forest. I think I'd like him to have a decent burial." She hesitated, then added, "I know I didn't know him, but don't you think that's the right thing to do?"

I didn't think so. In fact, I thought I'd like nothing to change.

Documentary-makers and journalists would eventually tire of questioning where he went; ponies and foxes would continue to wander through the forest oblivious of a once-famous rock singer beneath their feet; Nigel would go back to California with his beautiful friend Ashley, and I would probably ask Diane to marry me. This was the first time I had thought that. Lisa would probably live with Gary and have children; Charlotte would no doubt become very famous for her art. *Surely?* Let sleeping dogs lie. The 'right thing to do', as far I was concerned, was nothing.

I took her hand across the table.

"I... we... have to respect whatever you think now, Charlotte. We thought we were doing what was right back then. Nigel's main motive was to protect Cherry from the knowledge of what her mother had done; I merely did my bit to help him. Then it became Nigel's need to protect Daisy from the truth."

She looked away.

"That truly was altruistic of you, Tony. To do something like that... something that was against the law, even... then to find it altered your life forever. That's my understanding; it seeped into your personality, the knowledge of what you'd done – it sapped your self-confidence. It distorted your life."

I went to say something but she raised a hand to stop me.

"And then he left you. He ended the friendship which you so honoured."

"What exactly do you want to happen, then, Charlotte?"

"I have sympathy for what you both did and why, but I think I would like him... my father... to be given a proper burial."

I thought about the implications. Court. Prison. Shame. I even briefly thought of Ron Fudge from Stafford: what he would think of somebody burying his hero, the singer of his favourite band of all time, in a swampy black hole in a forest? The image of that grave came to me again as I contemplated the consequences of what Charlotte wanted. He, or his bones at least, would have to be exhumed. The publicity would be huge, possibly even worldwide. People would demand retribution. They might not even believe that Joan had stabbed him. They might think I, or Nigel, more likely, had killed him... and perhaps even killed Joan too. I was feeling faint, and sick in my stomach; cold sweat prickled on my forehead.

"I'd be sent to prison, I'm sure, Charlotte," I managed to say.

She looked into my eyes again. She took my hand this time. "I've no wish to see that, Tony – you're my best friend." She looked up at nothing. "I don't know exactly what to do."

I was about to speak when the doorbell went. Diane, I assumed.

Nigel followed Ashley in. Both looked serious.

I was just shutting the front door when I saw Diane's car coming around the corner so I waited for her. She looked serious too. She pecked me on the cheek as she went through towards the back of the house. Ashley and Nigel were already outside with Charlotte.

"Charlotte and I have just been talking about last night's revelations." All eyes were on me. "Charlotte wishes for his body to be exhumed to put an end to years of speculation and so that his financial affairs can be tidied up, but most of all so that her father has a proper and decent burial."

I let that sink in with Nigel. I noticed Ashley shudder but it could just have been the cool English May-morning air. Nigel's expression hadn't changed. No one knew like I did how he was able to contain himself so well.

Ashley spoke. She put her hand over Charlotte's.

"But, honey, that might send Nigel and Tony to jail. A jury might not believe that they didn't kill Rudy. Nigel had plenty of reasons to." She looked at Nigel.

"You did," she told him. This was no dumb blonde from Texas, I thought.

"Surely, honey, you wouldn't like to send Nigel and Tony to jail?" She glanced around the table for support and confirmation.

A tear rolled down Charlotte's cheek. We all saw it. Diane inhaled noisily. Nigel adjusted his sitting position. Ashley put her head on one side and stroked Charlotte's hand. I watched. Diane remained impassive. We all watched Charlotte.

"I realise all the implications… the consequences. I didn't know him, but…" She trailed off and took her hand from Ashley's. "He was my father." She said this so quietly. A blackbird chattered somewhere in the garden and a pigeon landed on the lawn only to flap noisily off when it saw movement from us.

"He was my father," she repeated.

"What would your mom say?" Ashley asked. "She thinks he's still alive somewhere, doesn't she? Surely she'd be happier to carry on thinking that, honey?"

I don't think any of us had thought of that aspect. I certainly hadn't. I was intrigued. I waited for Charlotte's thought on that. I could see Diane perk up at the question too. Nigel leaned forward a little.

"Are we all still going to the New Forest today?" said Charlotte, looking at me for her answer. I checked around the table for any comments.

"I guess so," I confirmed.

"Can you take me to where he… where you… can we go to the New Forest? Can you remember where? Could you take me there?"

Nigel was looking at me, inscrutable still.

Diane took my hand. "I'm sure Tony will find it very difficult to return to the spot, but he will do it if that is your wish, Charlotte. Won't you, Tony?"

What could I say? All eyes were on me. I wasn't sure how much anybody might have told Ashley but the others all knew I had avoided Burley since 1975. I had already agreed to take them there and up the road just a little further to The White Buck Inn for dinner that evening, but that had all been arranged before this new dilemma. Life had become complicated since Nigel's return.

"Do you mean you'd like us to take you to where Pete's buried?" I managed to ask, just to make sure.

"Yes, that is what I'd like. I feel that would help me to make a decision about what to do for the best... for all of us. If I could just see..."

Chapter Forty

Charlotte slid across the rear bench-seat of my van, Ashley followed, and Nigel got in beside her and pulled the sliding door shut. Diane joined me in the front, and I started up and pulled away. I was feeling very nervous and slightly nauseous. I could see Ashley in my rear-view mirror but not quite the other two. She caught my eye and a little smile of encouragement crossed her pretty mouth and reached her cornflower-blue eyes.

A while later we left the main road, slipping off at the junction that took us under the dual carriageway and towards Burley. No one had spoken since leaving Bournemouth; no sound past Ringwood, no chat as we passed the filling station and crossed the cattle-grid to enter the quieter forest area. My stomach was knotting. Ashley, I could see in the mirror, was interested in all she could see from either side-window. It was all new to her and she would normally have been full of questions but even she had remained quiet and kept her natural exuberant curiosity in check.

"I have to ask," I said, "but do you wish to go straight to Clayhill or stop in the village itself?"

"If Clayhill is where he is…" Charlotte said quietly.

Nigel and Ashley glanced at her and Diane turned to look. "It is," I told her. As we reached the village outskirts three cows came plodding up the road towards us.

"Is this normal?" Ashley asked, sitting forward to get a better view through the windscreen. She chuckled. "Wow," she said, and looked at Nigel for an explanation.

"Not all over the country, only in a few places like the New Forest. Ponies too, New Forest ponies, and deer in parts," he said.

The cows meandered to the side of the narrow road. I steered the van slowly by. Two went one side and one my side, she gawped in my window with those gormless big brown eyes, saliva dribbling from her mouth. What did she know? Did she know where we going? Or why?

I turned up the hill beside the pub. It looked the same as I remembered it. We went on up towards Bisterne, reaching the brow of the hill where you turn for the White Buck, but we went on, past the school and the open grassed area on the left. The golf club seemed unchanged, and I guessed that the seventh green had long since recovered. The giant oak that had witnessed our crime would have grown bigger over the years but kept our secret. I was desperately trying to remember exactly where we had turned off the road the second time, after the abortive attempt at the seventh green.

I knew it had been on the left, I could remember that, but it had been dark then and so many years had passed. I recalled how the sky had been tinged with pinks and yellows and purples some of the time; the colours of bruising. My head felt light. I drove very slowly. The others sensed my growing anxiety, I knew. I wanted to ask Nigel if he recognised anything. A car overtook us and I could see the driver's irritation at my low speed. He had flashed his headlights at me a short way back.

A sign for parking directed us off to the left. The track led to a gravel car park with neat signage. It was, I supposed, for hikers and dog-walkers. There was only one other vehicle parked there. I pulled in and stopped. I jumped out and stretched my legs and arched my back. I fished for my cigarette pack and lighter. Diane had come round and linked her arm in mine.

"Is this where…?" she asked, but not finishing the question

I told her that I wasn't quite sure but that I thought so, that the car parking area had not been here back then and how we had driven straight off an unmade road into brush.

"Are you OK?" she asked me quietly. I nodded, but I didn't feel it.

Ashley had followed Nigel out but Charlotte was still in the van. Ashley was kissing Nigel and gripping his hands.

I walked back towards where I thought the road had been forty years ago, attempting to reorientate myself. It seemed impossible. It had changed and yet it all looked the same: small trees, gorse bushes, tussocks of grass. How could you tell after nearly forty years – forty years of rain, sun, snow, hail and whatever else the weather had wrought on scrub bush? Some plants would be bigger; some would have long since died, to be replaced by similar bushes, trees and shrubs. *This was a bad idea.*

Charlotte was watching me from the van window. I knew she was willing me to find something. I walked all around the edge of the gravelled parking area. Nothing was familiar. At the entrance to the car park another track led towards a locked gate. It was a tarmacked road of sorts. I wondered. Was that the original road? Did it once lead somewhere? Diane was still following me around. I beckoned Nigel over. He leaned in the van and now Charlotte followed him and Ashley towards us.

"I think I may have found roughly where we drove that night... that morning."

Nigel gazed out over the view. He nodded slowly as if a memory was forming, then began to walk down the track. The rest of us looked at each other. Diane had now linked arms with Charlotte. I thought I could see Charlotte trembling. Ashley shrugged to me but we followed Nigel who was already some twenty paces ahead. I glanced at my watch; it was two o'clock – where had the morning gone? I had a hollow feeling in my guts but it wasn't hunger. Nigel had stopped and was looking back towards us. We reached him.

"I wouldn't swear to it, but those two trees that form a shape over there seem vaguely familiar. I remember lots of bushes, and how we tried to get your van behind them. Well, those familiar trees may be bigger now, but..." He stopped and was watching me for my reaction.

I said, "How on earth can you remember the shape of small trees from forty years ago?"

"Look again and you'll see," he replied. He left the road and began walking towards them. I called him back. He stopped briefly but didn't come back. We all caught him up; it was mainly grass tussocks and gorse here. The grass was wet but not difficult to walk on.

"You seem convinced we've found the place, and maybe we have – your memory was always so much better than mine – but there's something I've been meaning to ask you." Nigel looked puzzled. "Go on, then," he said. I took a deep breath. "I recalled recently – very clearly – that after we'd..." I turned to look at

Charlotte, unsure of how to phrase my long-delayed question for her sake. "Well, after we'd laid Pete in, you threw something in on top of him. What was it?"

Nigel continued to look puzzled for a few moments and then he obviously remembered, because it was as though a light had gone on. "Yes," he said to himself as if in confirmation, "it was the knife that Joan used." I told him I knew that, but there had been something else with it. He thought for a moment.

"It was his passport! I found it in their bedroom. I wanted… needed it to look like he had run off and taken his passport with him."

It had been reported at the time that Pete's passport was missing and that this was significant since the band had only just returned from America. It lent credence to the theory that Pete had left the country.

Removing the passport and disposing of it in the grave was a very clever thing for Nigel to have done, I thought. *Wow.*

Nigel moved off. He stopped, almost obscured by some bushes. We caught up.

"It's here," he said confidently. I knew Nigel's way: when he was right about something he just knew. He never elaborated or made any sort of fuss about things. So my inclination, despite not recognising anything myself, was to believe him. There was nothing to confirm it, of course: no grave-shaped mound of grass; no sign of the twigs with which I had attempted to disguise the disturbed ground all those years ago. No headstone with 'RIP' on it.

"How come you're so sure?" I asked him.

"I'll show you when we're back at the van," he replied. I was puzzled, but even more convinced that he was right. The others were just watching and listening. The two of us had almost ignored Charlotte till now.

"Are you OK?" I asked, taking her arm. Diane had the other one. She looked composed. I was surprised to see this, but she was.

"I'm fine," she said, staring down at the grass.

"What now?" asked Ashley.

We all looked at Charlotte. She continued to look down at her feet, occasionally looking up at Nigel, then at me, without saying a word. Then she went down on one knee and gently touched the grass with her hand. She gazed all around, then once more at her feet.

"We can go now," she said.

"Would you like us to give you a moment?" I asked her.

She hesitated, but then shook her head. I took the lead and we returned to the van. Charlotte stood aside from the rest of us.

"Why were you so sure, Nigel?"

"If," he said. *What the hell was he talking about?*

"Look back from the road at the two trees beside where we just were."

We all looked. The tree on the left had only a few wispy branches growing from its trunk and was basically a pole, while the other one had just two main branches, but they stuck straight out on either side at almost ninety degrees, making the tree appear to form the letter 'F'. When you ignored the leafy canopy of each tree from this distance and this point on the road the pair spelt out 'If'. *With a bit of imagination!*

"You *are* clever, honey." Ashley was clinging to his arm as she said it. "Is that why you named your house 'If'?"

Nigel looked at me. He appeared uneasy as he caught my eye.

"Shall we go?" Diane asked.

When everyone was settled I started the engine. Lunchtime had come and gone, but it seemed no one felt like eating, and if we were going to have dinner at the White Buck then it was far too late to eat anyway. We headed back down the hill towards Burley, everyone apparently lost in thought. I was waiting for Charlotte to say something; I really wanted to know if she was still set on the exhumation. She had said so little. She hadn't looked distressed when we were at the grave; she had neither shed tears nor thrown herself to the ground; she had remained perfectly composed. I hoped she was not hiding anything. I knew what that could do, after all.

I drove slowly through the forest, eventually turning off the road onto a gravel track. Diane looked baffled and mouthed 'Where are we going?' at me. The High Corner Inn was somewhere we could sit and reflect – a lovely, quiet pub in the 'middle of nowhere'. Ashley at least appeared excited.

"I wondered why you were going down tracks into the woods." She got her phone out and began taking photos. Events had almost completely distracted us all from the fact that she'd never left America before and 'just loved' our 'little green place', as she kept saying. I was grateful to her for reminding us of normality.

At the pub we went around to the rear patio; we were the only ones there, though a few guests were inside finishing a late lunch. I went to the bar to order some drinks. The young man behind the bar was very obliging and soon a smiley young waitress looked after us. We all noticed that she was very taken with Ashley, lingering near her. The mood became more serious when the girl left us. I had to ask.

"Charlotte, how did that make you feel? Do you still feel the same about dig... exhuming the remains?" Diane winced at my directness. Everyone waited. Charlotte looked at us each in turn.

"I'm sorry, Nigel, and I'm sorry, Tony, especially, but I still think yes, he should have a decent burial. Plus it'll put a stop to the endless speculation and conspiracy theories."

The blood seemed to drain from Nigel's face and my stomach knotted at this news. Ashley took Nigel's hand. He stopped eating his sandwich, putting it half eaten back on the plate, then he got up and walked down the pub garden to the forest's edge. Ashley joined him and took his arm. They stood there for some ten or fifteen minutes. Diane was silent. Charlotte picked at a sandwich. Nigel returned.

"We must honour Charlotte's wish, then, Tony," he announced.

When we were young I had always been the decisive or positive of the two of us; now the roles were reversed, it seemed. He was right, of course, but fear consumed me.

"I suggest we have our dinner at The White Buck as planned. My granddaughter is about to find out that her grandmother was a murderer and that her grandfather was an accomplice in concealing her crime and has kept the truth from her all her life. He also abandoned her for others to bring up. I would still ask that we try to enjoy tonight and then Tony and I will go to the police in the morning."

He looked at Charlotte. The implications of Daisy finding out the truth had crossed my mind, and I had even imagined how the mighty media-machine would go into overdrive when this story broke. It would be bad enough for Nigel but infinitely worse for Daisy. The media enjoy building up celebrities but not half as much as they seem to enjoy knocking them down.

Charlotte kept repeating 'I'm sorry' to all of us in turn. When she got to me I told her that I had survived worse.

"I know, because you've told me about your flashbacks and your increasing anxiety caused by what happened in 1975. Perhaps this might help in the long run."

I couldn't think how.

I saw Diane look at me. She'd realised that Charlotte had no idea what I'd really meant when I said I'd 'survived worse'. I shook my head to say, 'No, I haven't told her'.

She mouthed a 'thank you'.

Our English tea had not gone well. Nigel had been into the bar and paid for the drinks.

"I hope you'll have room for dinner later on," he said as he returned, trying hard to sound upbeat. I spent the next couple of hours giving everyone a guided tour around some of the prettier sights of the New Forest: quiet glades, drifts of bluebells, little streams cutting through hummocky greensward. We watched birds, ponies, deer, old men with dogs, children climbing trees. Thatched cottages delighted Ashley, and even Charlotte eventually lightened up and joined in, pointing things out. By the time I pulled into The White Buck Inn's car park the atmosphere in the van was almost as it should have been; it would have been impossible for a watching stranger to have guessed the secret of its occupants.

Chapter Forty-one

Diane introduced herself to the receptionist, explaining that it was she who had phoned to ask on behalf of Daisy Belle Bliss. The man could hardly contain himself at the news. It seemed Dave was not the only one she had that effect on. He came rushing out from behind his counter, looking everywhere for Daisy, no doubt. Diane said that we were early and that Daisy would be half an hour or so yet. He ushered us past the bar and around a corner to a large table situated in a recess, nicely hidden from most areas of the pub and restaurant. It faced a small dance floor surrounded by tables and chairs, and an equally small stage against the far end of the room. I tried to remember how it was back in the sixties when Nigel and I were here so often. My memory was of a haze of cigarette smoke and a floor sticky with spilt beer.

I went to the bar and fetched drinks for us all. I was determined to drink whatever I wanted, and asked Diane to discreetly go back to reception and book as many rooms as they might have vacant for tonight. I'd decided to try my best to ignore what was going to happen tomorrow. Nigel admitted that he too couldn't remember the layout. We agreed that this was because it had always been dark in there. Other couples were taking their seats and looking at the menu. Diane was making sure Charlotte had company; they usually enjoyed each other's conversation anyway. Nigel had gone to have a look at the double bass that was on the stage along with other band paraphernalia such as mics and stands and a drum kit. Diane and Charlotte went back to the bar for more drinks, while I explained to a puzzled Ashley the traditional English pub way of fetching your own drinks at the bar: no waitresses.

While they were gone I noticed people looking along towards the far end of the bar, but whatever was causing the commotion was obscured from us, so I got up to see. It was Daisy, Lisa and Gary; they'd stopped to talk to Diane and Charlotte. Daisy was used to this sort of reaction and ignored it all as though it were nothing to do with her. When they all came over with their drinks, Daisy sat next me. I caught the eye of a middle-aged bloke ogling her from across the other side of the dance floor, and he looked away instantly. I was enjoying the reflected attention. Ashley had been getting plenty of attention herself and Charlotte her share. The place was filling. People would sometimes peer around the corner at our table. By about seven-thirty we had ordered our meal.

Lisa had commented when she arrived that we all seemed to be enjoying ourselves, and Daisy agreed. *If only they knew.*

For some obscure reason The Doors performing 'Riders on the Storm' kept going round and round in my brain.

The food was very good. I whispered to Diane up at the bar once more that I hoped we had a room booked. I'd had too much to drink already to drive home. She assured me that we had but only after joking that they were fully booked.

The Chicago Jazz Aces arrived on stage at eight-thirty to plenty of applause and launched into 'Little Brown Jug' and then a bluesy tune I didn't recognise. After a great rendition of 'St Louis Blues', the singer took a bow and seemed to look our way a little more obviously. Then she asked the audience if they remembered a band called The Strikes. There were some cheers of acknowledgement and a whistle from somewhere nearby. She invited Nigel up on stage. He protested weakly but soon she was handing him a guitar. He took the plectrum lodged in its strings and tentatively strummed a few jazzy chords, then sat on a chair on the stage, bent over the instrument, and let rip with a virtuoso performance of some jazz standard that I didn't know, but which the band clearly did. It drew wild applause and even foot stomping from the crowd. He then beckoned Ashley onto the stage. She too protested initially, but then stood beside him with one hand on his shoulder and the microphone in the other and they both captivated the audience with Hank Williams' 'Honky Tonk Blues' followed by 'Cold Cold Heart' as an encore. Nigel was still beaming and Ashley shone for a long time after they returned to our table to tumultuous applause for their joint effort. She waved to some people across the room. The Aces applauded from the stage and told them to come back any time they wished, "Ashley especially!"

Although the evening continued well I noticed Charlotte staring off into space sometimes, and my alcohol intake was unable entirely to blot out thoughts of what was going to happen in the next few days and weeks. *'Into this world we're thrown…'*

I hadn't been so drunk for years. When I woke for the toilet as the dawn chorus began outside our bedroom window I couldn't remember coming upstairs. I had a vague recollection of saying goodnight to Lisa and Gary, and when I looked around the hotel room I did slowly realise where I was. I knew that I would suffer from a hangover though it hadn't begun yet. My clothes were neatly piled on a chair by the window. I couldn't remember getting undressed. I looked at Diane sleeping and wanted to wake her to apologise. I went to the bathroom and drank as much water as I could manage. I felt slightly sick and the bed seemed to whirl again as I got back in. I guess I did go back to sleep though because the next thing I was aware of was Diane sitting fully dressed at the dressing-table mirror applying eye-shadow and lipstick. I watched her reflection. She noticed me awake and came and sat on the edge of the bed beside me.

"How are you feeling?" she asked.

"Not too good."

She told me that we had danced last night, and said how well the evening had gone despite the afternoon's events. She took my hand as she said this and I knew that this time I would at least have support through whatever was going to happen to me. I kissed her hand. "Thanks for…" She stopped me.

We met Nigel and Ashley and Charlotte for a coffee downstairs. My head was hurting and my eyes felt sore. It seemed Charlotte had now decided not to go to the police until after Daisy's party. They told me this and Nigel asked if I agreed with the decision. Anything that delayed it was fine by me. Diane said that it made sense.

She met Charlotte's gaze for confirmation. Charlotte nodded.

Lisa and Gary had taken Daisy back home the night before, all three still unaware of the situation with the rest of us. Charlotte had stayed the night, as had Ashley and Nigel. Ashley had been enthralled by the sight of so many stars in the sky, and mentioned how much she'd enjoyed hearing the birdsong from her room earlier that morning. She agreed with Diane and Charlotte that it would have been nice to have had fresh clothes to put on, though. Nigel and I were unshaven.

I dropped Nigel and Ashley off at Daisy's house after leaving Charlotte beside her little van on the way to Sandbanks. We went back to Diane's, I dropped her off and she told me she would ring me later. On my own for the first time in a while, the full realisation of what was about to happen engulfed me. A lawyer would need to be found. Long interviews in a police station. Would we be locked up on remand straight away? I assumed we would. I didn't know. A feeling of foreboding flooded through me, and I regretted the beers now; I was unable to think clearly. I sat in the kitchen and drank tea to wash down a few paracetamol. I took my tea into the lounge and fell asleep in an armchair despite my headache.

My mother was sitting in her hospital chair. I asked her if she loved me. She made no reply, just looked at me with blank amusement. Then I was in a dormitory bed at school. I looked across at the row of black-enamelled iron bedsteads against the opposite wall. Each empty except one. My dad stared at me from the bed, wide-eyed. His head lolled to one side and his throat gaped open, red, like a slice of watermelon. He got out of bed and came towards me, his eyes now mournful and with a look of deep entreaty. Appealing. Begging for help. Pitiful. He held out one hand in front of himself. He was wearing old grey trousers, and the greyish-green sleeveless pullover he often wore over a white shirt. Parts of it were bright red, the pullover darker green down the front, splashes of wetness darkening his trousers. He stumbled across the wooden floor; I could hear the squeak of his bare feet on the boards as he came towards me in slow motion.

I awoke with a start and Charlotte was there. It took me a few moments to realise she was real and that I wasn't dreaming. She was leaning down with a hand on my shoulder.

"You were shouting. I heard you as I came down the side of the house. You were shouting something as I came through your kitchen. You frightened me. You were having a nightmare, Tony. I woke you. I shook you. You were thrashing about in your armchair as if you were trying to escape something. What was it, Tony? Was it the grave in the forest? Then you were shouting 'She Loves You'."

I began to come to. My mind was clearing. Charlotte looked down at me.

"Was it the grave yesterday? Were you having more flashbacks? Worse flashbacks? Oh, Tony." She sighed.

The nightmare began to evaporate. I felt cold. My forehead was clammy. My head ached and I remembered my hangover. I recalled last night at the pub. I remembered the afternoon in the forest. Charlotte held my hand. I squeezed her hand and tried to smile.

"I was only dreaming," I tried to reassure her.

She went to the kitchen and I heard her filling the kettle. I tried to sit up a bit straighter. The memory of the nightmare had almost gone but I knew it hadn't been Peter Davis in the dream. I stood stiffly and went through to the downstairs toilet. I rinsed my hands and splashed cold water on my face.

"I'm out here," Charlotte called from the veranda. I peered out the back door. She had two steaming mugs on the table.

"Do you want to talk about it?" she asked as I sat and lit a cigarette. "Tony, if you're having nightmares in the daytime, I... I could choose to leave the grave undisturbed. God knows it's done enough damage to your life. I know you'd have a difficult time with the police, and the last thing I want is to see you locked up. I wouldn't like you to suffer any more for your friend. You could have easily not become involved. You wouldn't be having these flashbacks and nightmares now forty years later. You might even have fulfilled some of the hopes and dreams you've told me that you once had. Those plans that Nigel once offered help with."

She watched my reactions.

"I'm sorry if I'm being too personal." She put a hand over mine again. "He did you no favours and he could have done so very easily. And should have done."

I didn't want to tell her what the nightmare had really been about; it was best that people didn't know. I had told Diane, and now wished I hadn't. Did she think differently of me as a result? I didn't want pity.

The phone rang. It was Diane. She asked me with a chuckle how my head was, and told me to come over when I was ready. I said that Charlotte was with me.

She asked how Charlotte seemed, then she went silent for so long that I had to ask if she was still there.

"Just come when you're ready," she said, and put the phone down. I told Charlotte that it was Diane even though she hadn't asked. She'd made some fresh tea while I'd been on the phone.

"Are you OK now, Tony?" she said.

I told her that if she felt strongly that Peter Davis should have a proper burial then she shouldn't change her mind, and she should not put all the blame for my mistakes on Nigel. Again she told me that the thought of me being locked up might trouble her more than the thought of Pete in his grave.

"Anyway," she concluded, "I've got a painting I'd like to finish and Diane is waiting for you and we all have a party to go to tomorrow." She stood. "Don't do anything hasty," she added, looking back at me as she went up the garden. I lifted a hand and waved to her in acknowledgement, then went upstairs, got ready, and drove over to Diane's.

Chapter Forty-two

Nigel and Ashley were already there when I arrived. Nigel asked if I had a hangover, and the conversation stayed on what might be called 'normal'. Ashley answered Diane's questions about Texas and Los Angeles, and Diane answered questions about school and her life in general. There was an easy friendship developing between them despite the difference in age and background. I told Nigel that Charlotte had hinted that she might not insist on exhuming Pete's body after all.

"How come?" he said.

I could see that Diane had overheard and was also waiting for my answer. But I couldn't fully explain, because I knew the dream involved my mum and dad, and I certainly didn't want that as a topic of conversation.

"She hasn't made up her mind yet," I said lamely. "We'll need legal representation, won't we, if she goes ahead?"

Nigel then talked about the London lawyers that he'd used for so many years and said he was happy they would give him the best advice. I hoped he might share that advice with me. We joked grimly about the fact that it was not the sort of thing one could ask a lawyer hypothetically: 'Say I disposed of a body in a forest forty years ago – what punishment might I expect?'

Nigel had booked a local recording studio that Daisy recommended; 'their equipment and expertise was pretty good'. He had been over there already to check it out. This was for me to 'do my bit', but it still seemed rather ridiculous to me; plenty of people could do a better job than I could of something like that, I felt sure. *Me recording?* But Nigel was insistent: he wanted my voice and no other. I had reread the poem a few times with this in mind. The booking was for early the following week but was now probably not going to happen, certainly not if bail was refused. I shuddered at the thought of our prospects.

At ten o'clock a taxi-driver rang the doorbell and we watched Nigel and Ashley climb into the cab. Diane made a cup of coffee and sat down beside me. She quizzed me about my conversation with Nigel that she'd overheard: the part about Charlotte maybe changing her mind. I told her about my dream, or at least its subject, if not the detail. I said it was the first time I had dreamt of my dad for some while. I described what I could as bits and pieces came back to me. I asked if I should call it a 'daymare', but she still looked concerned, ignoring my weak joke.

Later, in bed, she asked me again to confirm that Charlotte did not know about what my mum did to my dad. I was able to reassure her that I had only confided in her.

"Thank you," she whispered.

I held her. I told her that I loved her, and fell asleep in her arms.

I had a shave and shower and then breakfast with Diane. I rarely had cereal but ate my offered bowl like an obedient child. I asked for tea not coffee. I stood behind her and hugged her as we waited for the kettle to boil. I generally had Radio Four on, preferring talk rather than music, but Diane had tuned to an oldies station, and we discussed what each of us was doing at the time of some of the records they played. It was so nice to share; it was why I intended asking her to marry me. I had resolved not to ask until we knew exactly what Charlotte would decide though. We were so comfortable together; no jittering heart of youthful new love, but love nonetheless. The Beatles came on with 'She Loves You'. Diane took my hand in hers. "Now, was this one nineteen-sixty-three or four?"

At once I felt the blood drain from my head. I must have looked pretty awful, because I was aware of Diane saying, "Tony, what on earth is the matter?" before slipping from my chair to the floor.

I came to with Diane kneeling over me, fanning me with a place-mat.

"You fainted," she informed me gently.

"Sorry," was all I could think to say.

I lay there feeling stupid and a bit bewildered. The Beatles' song 'She Loves You' and its chorus rang in my brain. It was what my mother had sung on the stairs that Boxing Day morning in 1963. I recalled how she cackled with laughter, then started the song all over again. At the time, half the country was chanting 'Yeah, yeah, yeah' wherever you went; milkmen would be whistling the tune... everyone temporarily caught up in the magic of the song, but it seemed I could never escape it. I could never escape it or the images it conjured up.

Diane cradled my head for a while until I felt able to sit again. Then I told her the part I had omitted from my previous account of the events of that morning: I told her about my mother singing that song on the stairs. She looked shocked, shook her head and came back around the table and held me silently. There were tears in her eyes. Eventually I reassured her that I was OK and told her to go and get changed for the party. I would wait, and when she was ready we would go to my house for me to change. When she came back downstairs she looked fantastic in a black dress and dangly blue earrings with a matching chunky necklace and similar-coloured shoes. I told her she looked lovely.

We set off for my house. The old van had never smelt so nice: Diane's perfume was one she had bought in Russia on one of her trips. I had a quick shower, dressed, and splashed on some 'Eternity' bought in Bournemouth. We got back into the van. We would be staying at Daisy's so we had a small bag between us for fresh clothes and a wash bag each. I put the van into gear and we set off. When we reached the end of my road I looked over at Diane, and she glanced back and smiled.

"Would you marry me, please?" I asked, despite my earlier decision to wait. As I'd hoped, it caught her completely unawares. I hadn't wanted to be corny, to ask in a restaurant with candles, soft music and too much to drink. She was grinning. She stared straight ahead at the road for some moments; I kept glancing away from the road at her, waiting.

"Yes, I would," she said finally.

I pulled into Daisy's a happy man. If I were sent to prison I doubted it would be for the rest of my life, despite my age. We held hands till the front door opened.

It was only about eight-fifteen and there were not many people there. A uniformed young woman had let us in; another brought us a tray of champagne and said good evening. I recognised a television presenter. He was with a younger man who appeared to be uncomfortable. He would continually cast his eyes about as if in fear of somebody approaching him, as if ready to run if they did. I took Diane through to see the beautiful silver and gold threads wall covering. She was amazed. More people were arriving. We just stood and watched. Diane recognised another girl singer but I had no idea who she was. I saw Ashley chatting to a semicircle of attentive men, most of whom were probably in their twenties, most of them with beards; I wondered where Nigel was. Ashley was wearing a white dress with a big silver star on it that she was trying to persuade her audience was the Texas Lone Star. Whenever she threw her head back and laughed her silver-star earrings sparkled from the small diamond at the tip of each point. She saw us and waved. Nigel appeared and he waved over to us too. Ashley's audience began to saunter off one at a time. Lisa and Emma joined Ashley and Nigel.

I heard guitars being tuned outside and wandered off to have a look. Under a canvas gazebo, a pair of tall, upright pole-stands of coloured spotlights stood at either side of a low stage where a band played a relaxed reggae beat. A microphone stood at the front, middle but there was no singer as yet. Still more guests arrived. Diane recognised someone else that I had never seen or heard of. I could hear Dave's laugh somewhere nearby. I couldn't see him but it was him without a doubt. Then I spotted him and Leanne talking to Charlotte. I had wondered where she was. I tried to see if she had brought anyone with her. I turned and Diane was kissing Daisy on the cheek. Daisy turned to me and gave me a hug. I looked round when she'd moved off, hoping that Dave had noticed this affection. Pathetic, I know, but I did. And he had; he was making crude signs to me behind Charlotte's back until he saw Diane turn his way, whereupon he continued innocently chatting to Charlotte and Leanne.

The band were still playing a subdued repertoire of reggae and jazz versions of classic hits, some old and some more recent. A male singer with ringlets was now quietly crooning words I couldn't distinguish but which added well to the sound. He had on a white suit, white tee shirt and bright red shoes. Diane liked what she saw she told me.

"If only he wasn't half my age," she informed me with a grin.

Nigel then appeared as if from nowhere at my side.

"How're you feeling, my friend?" he asked, after kissing Diane on both cheeks and complimenting her on her looks.

Before I could answer the question he added, "I'm still hoping Charlotte will change her mind." I had been feeling quite good until he said this.

"We really like this young band," I told him, motioning to the group nearby. The singer had been joined by a young woman. She was a blue-eyed blonde, young enough to be Ashley's offspring, very slim and pale, wearing old-fashioned black-and-white basketball boots which looked very cute on the end of the slim legs exposed beneath a shimmering, sequinned pink mini-dress, her long thin arms waving behind her as she leaned in to the shared microphone.

I was captivated by her. She seemed to wave like a reed in a breeze beside a stream. Her make-up reminded me of the sixties: lots of mascara and bright red lipstick on a pale face. And she could sing. She had a breathy but full voice that belied her size; it was rich and round and she moulded words around the microphone in a liquid jazz style.

Nigel interrupted my trance. "Her stage name is Trixie Smith, so she could be related to you, Tony."

I had to ask what her real name was.

"Patricia Smith," came Nigel's reply.

Diane commented that it was an old-fashioned Christian name for a young woman. Trixie finished her song and stood back from the centre of the stage as the male singer came to the microphone to start another. I recognised the introduction instantly. The blood drained from my head, and as Diane told me later I just crashed sideways, bowling Nigel and several other people over. The heap of bodies scrambled to their feet but I stayed there. Apparently a young man was straddling me as he got up, shouting obscenities, assuming alcohol was the culprit.

When I fully came round I was upstairs in one of the bedrooms. Nigel and Diane were there. Charlotte and Lisa stood at the bottom of the bed looking anxious. I began realising where I was and what had happened but how I got to the room I had no idea.

"I must leave the champagne alone," I tried to joke. Nobody laughed.

Diane had hold of my hand. She knew the significance of the tune but she didn't know that my mum's name was Patricia! Patricia Smith.

I tried to urge them to go back to the party. I reassured them all that I was OK. And I was, really, apart from a jittery feeling in my stomach. I hadn't hurt myself; others had inadvertently cushioned my fall. Lisa gave me a glass of water and I sat up with Diane's help. I drank with all eyes watching me. It dawned on me that these few people in the room were the people I loved the most; not many, to be sure, but all – for different but related reasons – my friends.

"What was that about, Tony?" Lisa asked. My head swam slightly but was almost clear again. She had tears in her eyes.

"Is it the worry of going to the police? Of reporting my father's burial? " Charlotte said this in such a quiet voice but we all heard it clearly enough.

Lisa looked puzzled. She stared at Charlotte.

"I told you that I could change my mind. I would..." She hesitated. "I won't insist. What would be the point? What would be the point of watching somebody I love go to jail? Peter Davis is in a beautiful place already."

I noticed Nigel's jaw relax. I absorbed this. I knew that Charlotte would consider every aspect and implication. I met her eyes. They were shining, the second time I'd seen Charlotte cry. We recognised our understanding in that exchanged look but for me that raised another question: did she think that the possibility of the exhumation was the cause of my distress? Diane realised what I was thinking. The room was silent apart from the muffled sounds of laughter and music from below.

I knew Diane was anxious; I could see. She took Charlotte's hand. Charlotte reassured Diane that she was sure of her decision not to insist on an exhumation.

"Do you think you could tell Charlotte... and all of us?" Diane said.

I saw Lisa and Nigel both stiffen. But it was Charlotte who should know. I couldn't let her make her decision based on a false supposition. Whatever the outcome, I couldn't allow her to do that.

I began. I explained to Charlotte that what I was about to relate was the real reason I had collapsed: that it had not been the anxiety of whether or not she insisted on an exhumation. I said I would understand if she reversed her decision; that I would not wish her to have made it based on wrongly reasoned sympathy for me. I expressed how much she meant to me; how much everyone in the room meant to me. The room was still and silent apart from some muffled music from the band outside. Then I told them what had happened on that Boxing Day morning.

Diane's grip on my hand was getting tighter and tighter as I told my story. When I'd finished, there was total silence. Everyone was in tears. Nigel was the first to speak, his voice cracking.

"I cannot believe you carried that around with you for so many years. You never told me. I had no idea. I knew your mum was in a hospital but... God knows, I've had some extreme events in my life but..." He trailed off, shaking his head. "You think you know somebody. You think you know all about friends..." Nigel was whispering this as if thinking aloud," shaking his head as he wiped a tear away with a knuckle.

Lisa bent and kissed me. "You poor man," she said. I felt strangely exhilarated.

Charlotte met my eyes once more. "I think you have been through enough." They were all staring at me.

"I have one more thing to tell you all," I said. The room froze. There was a collective intake of breath. Eyes widened. Diane's grip on my hand intensified; her nails now dug in. I waited a moment.

Then I told them.

"I asked Diane to marry me earlier tonight and she said yes."

Chapter Forty-three

They all left me to collect my thoughts; everyone went back to the party except Diane. She waited with me while I gathered my wits. After about twenty minutes or so we kissed, then went back down to join in. We even danced and we lasted till gone two o'clock in the morning in the end. The party was still going when we went up to bed but mostly indoors by that time and much quieter, certainly not loud enough to keep me awake. We said our goodbyes to most people we knew, including a very drunk Dave and a smiling Leanne. I wondered to myself what Emma and Charlotte might be talking about so earnestly when I noticed them sitting in a corner as we headed for the lift.

In the morning Diane and I were first up. We were enjoying the fantastic view with our breakfast. The assorted accommodation in the grounds seemed still and quiet. The bunting in the trees and shrubs looked forlorn and untidy now in the morning breeze. A young man came out of one of the temporary toilet cubicles down towards the water's edge. He didn't see us looking from the house and went back into one of the rented Airstreams. We had promised to wait for Ashley and Nigel and not to go home. Ashley looked as fresh as any rose of Texas but Nigel was wearing dark glasses. It was getting on for eleven o'clock.

Diane made some fresh coffee and I found an unopened pack of croissants. Ashley picked one apart and ate it, Diane had another but Nigel refused the offer and stuck to nursing his coffee mug and staring at me.

"Are you OK, buddy?" he asked with a hand on my shoulder and coffee in the other. Diane and Ashley also waited for my answer. I assured them truthfully that I was, now that they all knew everything. Nigel was very quiet, which was not unusual, but Diane and Ashley were soon talking over the events of the party. Ashley had found Dave amusing although she hadn't understood much of what he said. I wanted to tell her that not many people did, but I didn't bother. We all agreed how much we'd liked the band. The four of us decided we would meet up the following day, then Diane and I excused ourselves just as Daisy appeared. We both thanked her and she thanked me again. The catering van up by the top garages was busy serving bacon-and-egg rolls as we left, and several people there waved to us.

We drove back to Diane's and she went upstairs to change clothes. Then we sat quietly on her sofa. I enjoyed the peace after the excitement of the party. We held hands while the television softly talked to itself across the room. Diane turned it off later and made me read 'If' aloud to her several times, giving me a few tips about emphasis and timing. She seemed to know what she was talking about. The following day was to be the recording of my recitation of Rudyard Kipling's most famous poem. Later she told me Lisa was staying over at Gary's flat so I suggested an early night.

The recording studio was a nice-looking, new, oak-framed, oak-clad building built in the style of a single-storey barn. There was no shortage of modern finish inside, however: the white walls of the reception area were covered with Wassily Kandinsky prints, glossy black-and-white photos of old chrome microphones, and various 78 and 45rpm records. Rod and Andy, the two owners, talked to Nigel, and their receptionist Louise led Ashley and Diane to some comfortable-looking couches. I could feel my nerves rising and my mouth already drying, and I tried to recall Diane's tutoring from the day before. They showed me into to the 'live room', as they referred to it, then went into the control room. Behind the glass, they sat with Nigel on big, black leather swivel chairs facing consoles and computer screens. I could see Diane looking very comfortable with a coffee mug in her hand and a magazine on the table in front of her. They asked me to move in front of a microphone that hung from the ceiling. I was clutching a printout of the poem. I had the earphones on that Andy had handed me. They asked me to begin several times to get the 'levels'. They were checking equipment to make sure all was responding correctly. Andy came out again and made some sort of adjustment to the microphone in front of my face.

"Just start reading once more," he asked. Rod gave him a thumbs-up. Nigel looked relaxed. *I doubted I did.* I then got a thumbs-up from Andy and I began. I had to read it six times in all, after which Nigel told me he had chosen my third effort. I really couldn't tell how it was any different to the others but he seemed very sure, and Rod and Andy agreed. I then read several other unrelated short pieces which Nigel assured me would make sense once I heard how they had been mixed.

A little later, as we were driving away, Nigel explained that the recording would be sent to him to mix into his work. I didn't understand much of what he said about the processes involved, though.

I had asked Nigel earlier if he was up for laying yet another ghost. The recording studio was in Ringwood not far from the house that Peter Davis and Jojo and their entourage once lived in; yet another scene of bad memories. He'd agreed.

In the end, however, when we found the house, we were disappointed: the large, ornate, wrought-iron gates were closed and we could barely see the house in the distance. I could see the wooden building. I didn't remember the drive being quite so long. Rust was showing through flaking paint on the gates and what we could see of the drive was full of weeds: the shrubs beside it overgrown. Could it really be empty and abandoned all these years later? It hadn't occurred to me that the house would still be uninhabited and that it would be derelict. We left to go home.

I dropped Nigel and Ashley at Daisy's house, where they would be staying for only two more days, after which we would be seeing them for the last time.

We would all be going back to where Peter Davis lay and where Charlotte now planned to say goodbye to the father she never knew. She would definitely not go to the police. She would definitely not insist on exhuming his remains, but she wanted to mark where he was; that was her only request.

The day arrived. Charlotte came round to my house. Diane had stayed with me. The three of us waited in silence for Nigel and Ashley's taxi to bring them. They would be going home soon, so this would be another 'last' look at Dorset, Hampshire and England for them. I was to do the driving again. Soon we were turning off the A31, clattering over the cattle-grid and heading on through Burley, past the pubs and up the hill. I knew exactly where to go this time. We pulled up in the gravel car park. I was tense. This would almost certainly be Nigel's last view of the New Forest and I wished it was mine too right at that moment.

Charlotte hadn't said a word on the drive here and now stood staring across the scrub and the gorse and the trees and grasses before us. She often wore black clothes so I was unsure if there was any significance in her all-black attire that day. Across from us, I could see the two trees almost forming the short word. Nigel was looking in the same direction. I wondered if Charlotte wanted to go alone but she answered my question before I had asked it.

"Would just you and Nigel come with me, please?"

She looked apologetically at Diane and Ashley. We set off. I glanced back once; they stood watching our progress across the coarse grass, around bushes and small trees towards the larger cluster of trees. It was mid-morning and the May sunshine was drying the dew-wet grass we walked on. Charlotte followed Nigel and I walked behind her. She looked round at me once or twice. She was clutching something wrapped in white cloth; it appeared to be quite heavy from the way she held it. We reached the place where Pete Davis rested. As I looked more closely in this bright sunlight I seemed to be able to make out an oblong shape where the soil had sunk slightly. *It could have been my imagination.* There were no signs of animals having dug for his bones, it was just the way the grass had re-established on soil disturbed all those years ago. Nigel's jaw was tightening; he didn't speak. His eyes were cast down to the place in the grass.

Charlotte looked from one of us to the other and back. She didn't speak as she unwrapped what looked like a piece of new Portland stone from the cloth. She held it up. It was about the size of a man's fist. Then I could see that it was a perfect sculpture of an old-style microphone. She laid it gently in the grass without a word. Then after looking first at Nigel and then me very deliberately, she turned and began walking back to the van. Nigel watched her go. I bent to inspect the sculptured piece of rock; in small, neatly engraved letters it read: 'His spirit is free'.

Diane had her arm around Charlotte's shoulder when Nigel and I got back to the van. The three women were sitting in a row on the bench seat in the back with Charlotte in the middle. Nigel climbed into the front passenger seat and stared ahead through the windscreen. I stayed outside and smoked a cigarette.

In my rear-view mirror I saw Charlotte dab her eyes as I pulled off the gravel.

"Thank you, Tony, and thank you, Nigel. It's over. He can sing to the birds and the trees. His spirit is free."

She turned and looked over her shoulder as we drove away.

I dropped her off at her home and hugged her before I let her go indoors. Then I took Nigel and a subdued Ashley back to Daisy's house and left them by the gate. Nobody had said much since we left the New Forest. Finally Diane and I were back in my kitchen. I felt exhausted but at peace. I described the sculptured microphone and told Diane what the inscription said. Perhaps somebody would find it one day...

I made two cups of tea but they went cold as I held the woman I loved, the one I was going to marry in July in a small Californian city called Agoura.

I pulled up at Daisy's house two days later and Diane and I put Nigel and Ashley's suitcases into the rear of my van as they kissed and hugged the young singing star. Lisa had brought Charlotte to say goodbye. Diane hugged Daisy as I slid the door shut on Nigel and his friend and we set off for Heathrow airport. As the gates closed behind us I looked in my mirror and glimpsed three small figures: three young women – Charlotte, Lisa and Daisy – standing in a line, arms linked, lives linked, waving madly.

THE END

EPILOGUE

I was reading the booklet that came with Nigel's musical story and was thrilled to see my name in the credits. Royalties that came my way some time later seemed disproportionally good. The sleeve notes told how some experiences at school shaped the music of 'The Beginning' on CD 1; they described his life's influences on CDs 2, 3 and 4, 'The Middle', and CD 5 included me reciting the complete poem. I was on all the others too, quoting parts of it, particularly on part 1. At the end of the notes it said: "You may think you know all about your friends but you may not. Try harder."

I left the three women in my life at Nigel's house and went down to the post office in Agoura City with my best man of a few days' time and posted off a copy of his five-CD boxed set "Beginning, Middle and End" to an address in Brunswick Terrace, Stafford, West Midlands, UK.

Lightning Source UK Ltd.
Milton Keynes UK
UKHW011835270320
360990UK00001B/45

9 781839 750328